ENCHANTINGLY YOURS

BOOK TWO IN THE MAIDENS OF FAIRHAVEN TRILOGY

DANA GRICKEN

Cover art by Dar Albert at Wicked Smart Designs

Published by Oliver-Heber Books

0 9 8 7 6 5 4 3 2 1

CHAPTER 1

Gemma Solace really hated nightmares.

They haunted her in every dream, reminding her of her mother—and what she had lost. Senator Remus' manipulation of her, her mother fleeing to the surface to avoid punishment for allying with him, the fear of not knowing if she was alive and well. Her mother's face would appear out of nowhere, screaming and calling out to her.

"My precious little Gem, save me!" she would cry before fading into darkness. "Please find me, before it's too late!"

It kept her up most nights.

Groggy and exhausted, Gemma woke up that morning, hating something else.

Weddings. Too many people, too loud, too fancy. It just wasn't her cup of specially brewed, magical tea.

But there had never been a wedding like this one in Fairhaven's history—with the bride and groom as heroes, saviors of Fairhaven and the surface world above.

Gemma recalled the story in her head, the juiciest gossip in Fairhaven. It had been a year since Princess Esme had been cast to the surface by her father, King Tedros, after a streak of mischievous behavior. There, she had learned how to survive on her own, help people, improve herself, and even found love along the way. In the process, they had stopped an evil plot by a Fairhaven senator named Remus to get magic to fully work on the surface, something that had never been possible before, save for a few non-dangerous potions.

After a lengthy investigation by Princess Esme, some betrayals, and a lot of dead humans, Senator Remus and his family were behind bars in the dungeons. Their evil Fairy Godmother Zamira, an elixir expert who had made magic on the surface possible, had been killed in the final battle where the senator had tried to enslave humanity but failed. Luckily, Fairhaven's fairy godmothers had erased the minds of all humans who were involved in the battle, and life went back to normal on the surface. No one suspected a thing.

As for Fairhaven, everything was peaceful again—much to everyone's relief. Gemma's too, as it gave her more time to read and relax.

King Tedros allowed his daughter to return. And today, after many challenges to get to their happily ever after, she and her fiancé were finally getting married. Gemma wished more than anything that it could be her instead. But the men she liked were fictional, and none of the real ones had caught her eye.

Not yet, anyway.

Gemma watched from the library window as Princess Esme stood at the altar outside, wearing a glowing pink dress, her blonde hair in soft waves. Her soon-to-be husband, Noah Crawford, a human from the surface, stood across from her with a big grin. He looked handsome in a tux. All their family and friends had come out to see the big day, and the few people from the surface who were invited promised to keep it all a secret, their memories spared from being wiped.

The kingdom itself, hidden beneath the storm drains of

Toronto, was usually dark and quiet, but today, glittering lanterns glowed around the perimeter of the city. Magical fireflies inside burst with color and gave everything an otherworldly glow. All the citizens gathered near the castle to celebrate the nuptials as the river nearby floated along with ethereal colors. Streaks of light from the human world above trickled through the storm drains, illuminating the golden, brick-covered streets and its well-dressed citizens.

"Do you, Princess Esme Fairhaven, take Noah Crawford to be your lawfully wedded husband, in our world and on the surface?" Fairy Godmother Odelia asked, beaming in a purple gown with her wand attached to her hip. She was a kind old lady with white hair, a green gown, and soft wrinkles around her shimmering blue eyes. Gemma was jealous that Princess Esme had ended up with a fairy godmother like that.

She wanted one that reminded her of a sweet old grandma, baking magical cookies. Instead, she'd ended up with a loud drunk.

Princess Esme nodded, smiling at Noah as she squeezed his hand. Gemma watched their lovers' caress from the window with an envious sigh. "I do. I really, really do."

"And do you, Noah Crawford," Fairy Godmother Odelia said, turning to Noah, "take Princess Esme to be your lawfully wedded wife in our world and yours?"

"I do," he said with a grin. "There's no one else I'd rather save the world with."

That made Esme laugh. "Me either."

"Oh, I'm so happy for you two," Fairy Godmother Odelia said, wiping away a few tears. "I now pronounce you husband and wife. Let the festivities begin!"

With one eye on her book, Gemma watched as someone in the crowd set off a magical sentient firework, causing it to fly around and explode in beautiful colors. It played the bridal chorus long after it had vanished. The people watching clapped and cheered as Princess Esme and Noah kissed. Then King Tedros welcomed him to the kingdom, crowning him as an honorary prince.

As the kingdom put on a parade to celebrate their princess' big day—complete with the couple fly around on a dragon—she was the one person who wasn't interested in parties at all. Why would she, when her mother—the one she used to attend parties with—wasn't there anymore?

Gemma was tucked inside the castle's library, sitting on the floor near the back wall. Her head ached from having her red hair tied in a messy bun, her green eyes tired from staying up late to read another book—a fantasy romance from the human world, her favorite. Her ruffled lilac dress bunched around her waist, allowing her to sit comfortably on the floor next to a large bookshelf.

It was her job to sort through the books on spellcasting and magical elixirs and help people find which book they were after. They even had books about the technologies and inventions of the surface world. But most of the time, Gemma preferred to read fiction, finding some interesting authors from the surface that had ended up on their shelves. She much preferred the company of books; they didn't expect her to socialize or ask questions she didn't want to think about.

Plus, she could see the whole wedding from her spot in the library, with no uncomfortable conversations to navigate. When a phoenix roared outside the window, engulfing the married couple in a fiery heart—to many oohs and ahhs in the crowd—Gemma only shrugged.

"Eh, I'm not missing much," she said to the quiet library, flipping another page of her book.

The chamber doors opened, then footsteps echoed inside. Gemma set her book down to rise to her feet and see who needed help. Just as she prepared to ask them what they were doing in here instead of at the wedding, she noticed it was her father, Caspian Solace. He was a musician for the kingdom of Fairhaven and often used magic instruments in his performances.

His green eyes—identical to her own—scanned the library, then settled on Gemma before he walked toward her. While he usually dressed casually, he had on a blue suit with a matching cape in honor of the big day. He noticed the book in her hands and snorted.

"Oh, Gem," he began. "Some things never change, hmm? Whether you're three or twenty-three, you've always been in this library."

She looked down at the book. "Well, yeah. The library is awesome. And I just got to a good part in my novel. Big fantasy battle to protect Earth. I couldn't put it down for anything."

"I bet. Where's your fairy godmother?"

Gemma shrugged, sinking to her knees again as she flipped through another page. "Somewhere, I guess. Probably dancing and getting up to no good."

"Yes, that sounds like her."

"You know, I don't get it." Gemma rested her book on her lap. "Fairy Godmothers are supposed to be just like their families. But Blanche ... well, she's not like us at all. And that's putting it mildly. Why is that?"

Her father shrugged. "I don't know, kiddo. Maybe the fairy godmother council thought we needed her and she needed us. Anyway, I'm going to play a song for the married couple any minute now, and I'd like you to be there. Will you come out? For me, please?"

Gemma sighed. "Oh, I don't know, Papa ..."

He reached for her hand. "Seeing your beautiful face eases my performance anxiety. I know you don't like big crowds. And if I can be honest for a moment ... I haven't felt like playing since your mother left. Having you there might give me the encouragement I need."

Since her mother had vanished to the surface, Gemma's father was deeply depressed. He spent his nights struggling to come up with new songs while eating magical, floating chips on the couch. The bags under his eyes suggested he hadn't slept in a while. Watching her father lose his sense of identity and wander aimlessly through life caused both resentment and sadness toward her mother.

If she could do something to ease his pain, she would. Even something as small as being there in the crowd for him.

"All right, Papa. Lead the way."

But he hesitated. Gemma caught it, raising her eyebrows.

"Papa ... is something wrong?"

When he broke down in tears, Gemma feared he was hurt. She looked him over for injuries, but she didn't see any. She was just about to yell for a fairy godmother's help before he dried his eyes.

"It's just ... I miss your mother so much," he said, sniffling. "This is my first big performance without her. Even playing music doesn't feel the same without her around. I just ... I wish we had answers. Why she betrayed Fairhaven, where she is now, what she's planning to do. For both of us."

"I know, Papa." Gemma swallowed the lump in her throat. "I wish we did too. She isn't here anymore, but I am. And I know you're going to do great out there."

He smiled and thanked her, drying his eyes one last time before holding out an arm for Gemma to take. She linked her arm with his and followed him out of the library. After they walked through the empty castle, they stepped out into the streets.

Gemma took deep breaths, feeling nervous in crowds herself, as they walked toward the altar. It looked like Princess Esme and Noah were playing some sort of magical wedding game while the crowd cheered. After Noah won, Gemma's father nudged her.

"My time to shine," he said with a smile that didn't quite reach his eyes. "Wait for me here, okay?"

She nodded, staying on the edge of the crowd as he pushed through the people. Fairy Godmother Odelia magically set up a small stage for Gemma's father to perform. As he reached for his flute—one infused with magic inside it to sound more heavenly—Princess Esme and Noah shared their first dance while everyone gazed on.

"Aren't they so cute?" Esme's best friend, Alva, asked the crowd. "Relationship goals!"

They really were adorable, Gemma had to admit. She would've killed to find a love like that—like those romance novels. But she was too shy and into her books for that to ever happen.

She took another deep breath, trying to melt her anxiety away. All these people were making Gemma's head spin. Her fairy godmother, Blanche, had given her some anxiety-calming elixirs, but Gemma wanted to beat this on her own. She kept them in her pocket but never took them.

When she felt a tap on her shoulder, she spun around, coming face-to-face with her fairy godmother. She was different from the other godmothers—a little younger and a lot more mischievous. But Fairy Godmother Odelia had seen something in Blanche and her strong elixir abilities and had granted her the power of becoming a fairy godmother.

And much to Gemma's disappointment, Blanche had been the one assigned to watch over her and make her feel magical. To cheer her up, to design her dresses, to be her official spellcaster since only fairy godmothers could cast magic in Fairhaven. And the older woman had done anything but.

She was a partier, consuming magical elixirs constantly and trying to get Gemma to go out and "live a little." Gemma refused every time, preferring to stay inside with a good book. It annoyed her fairy godmother to no end.

"Gemma, I'm surprised to see you here," Fairy Godmother Blanche said, hiccupping. She carried a chalice in her hand with some strong-smelling magical drink overflowing and oozing down the side. "Usually that butt of yours is in that damn library."

Gemma sighed. "Coming out here wasn't my choice—believe me. But my father was playing for the bride and groom and asked me to come. He's amazing, isn't he?"

Gemma turned, watching her father play. The melody was mesmerizing. Even though Gemma could tell his heart really wasn't in it.

"He ain't bad," Fairy Godmother Blanche said, taking another swig of her drink. "Maybe we should dance. What do you think?"

Gemma turned back to her, shaking her head. "No, thanks. I'm not a good dancer, and I hate people staring at me—"

"Oh, stuff it!" Fairy Godmother Blanche set her drink down, tugging on Gemma's arm. "Come on, we're dancing. Make way, people!"

Blushing in embarrassment, Gemma was dragged by her fairy godmother toward the stage. Princess Esme and Noah looked on with laughter as Fairy Godmother Blanche began swaying to the beat. Gemma's cheeks burned, longing to escape the spotlight. She glanced around the underground city as people stared at her. Some even laughed at her fairy godmother's dance moves.

She was *never* going to live this down. Her breaths sped up, her hands going clammy. She had to get out of here.

As her fairy godmother continued to dance around her, drunk and singing badly out of tune, Gemma locked eyes with Princess Esme. The last thing Gemma needed was for the beautiful, capable, perfect Princess Esme to see her have a panic attack.

She averted her gaze, glancing toward the ground. How could Fairy Godmother Blanche do this to her? She knew how much Gemma hated attention and crowds. "Sorry, Princess. I'll just be going now."

Gemma felt Princess Esme's eyes on her back as she scurried inside the castle. After Gemma closed the chamber doors, the room seemed to grow smaller and smaller with each panicked breath. Sweaty hands, a fast heartbeat, swirling thoughts—she had struggled with those since she was young. After ten minutes of deep breaths and solitude, she began to calm down.

For now, there were no more crowds or judging eyes. That was torture.

She ran back to the library at the end of the hall, her heels clicking on the ceramic tiles. Once she was inside and sitting in her favorite spot near the private back corner, Gemma felt much better. The anxiety slowly eased from her body.

"Home sweet home," she murmured, then opened her book.

A few moments later, the door to the library opened. Gemma lifted her head, thinking it would be her father again after his solo, but it was her only friend—Callister "Cal" Glynn.

He was the castle's chef, having overseen the preparation of all the food for the wedding. Magical potions he ordered from the fairy godmothers had made it all possible in such a short amount of time. Everything from the main course to the desserts were doused with magical potions to taste even more delicious. She watched through the bookshelves as he tiptoed through the library, carrying a big plate of cake.

"Gem?" he whispered. "You in here?"

"Back here, Cal." Gemma rose to her feet, setting her book aside. For the second time. "What's going on?"

When he stepped around the corner, finally laying his blue eyes on her, he smiled. He was quite handsome, Gemma had to admit, and only a few years older than her. He had dark, curly hair, freckles, and was always wearing a stylish, purple chef's outfit. They had met when Gemma first started her job as a librarian and hit it off. After some awkward advances on Gemma's part, she had learned Cal was gay. After the initial awkwardness had dissipated, they became fast friends. Since then, he had been in a couple relationships with men from around the kingdom.

And once again, Gemma felt like everyone found love except for her. Fairytales were all she had to fill the romantic void in her life.

"Just wanted to bring you a slice of wedding cake. Made it myself." Cal handed the plate to her. "I know you don't like parties and crowds, so I wanted to make sure you got something to eat."

Gemma smiled, taking the plate. "Thanks, Cal. Wow—this looks amazing."

She picked up her fork, then took a bit of the cake. Her eyes closed in pleasure as Cal laughed. "Glad you're enjoying it. The food is my favorite part of a celebration, and I really wanted you to try my latest creation."

"I appreciate it. You really are the best."

He nodded. "No problem. I should get back to the party before they wonder where I went off to. Enjoy your book."

She smiled at him as he left, then slunk down again and finished the slice of cake. She savored every bite of the creamy strawberries and lavender icing. When she finished, she set the plate aside, then picked up her book. The fact that Cal respected her enough to not ask her to return to the party was why they had become such good friends.

A few hours later, the boisterous sounds of talking and music outside the window began to die down. Gemma yawned, growing tired as she stood and looked outside. The tables and chairs were being magically cleaned up and Princess Esme and Noah were entering the castle to spend their first night together as husband and wife. King Tedros shook hands with Gemma's father, thanking him for the performance. Gemma could hear what they were saying outside the window if she strained.

"... and I'm still so sorry about your wife, Mr. Solace," King Tedros was telling him. "Senator Remus destroyed a lot of lives, both here and on the surface. We'll make sure he never gets out again."

Her father sighed. "Thank you, your Majesty. It's been hard —especially for my daughter. But I guess this is the way it has to be."

Gemma didn't want to hear anymore. It hurt too much to think about her mother, almost like she had died. She swallowed the lump in her throat and walked out of the library.

She waited until the crowd of people had passed— including Princess Esme and Noah and all the servants—before walking down the hall. Her father came in a minute later, gushing to her about the performance before they walked back home together. They lived in a row of townhouses a few blocks behind the castle.

"And I really do appreciate you coming out to watch my performance," her father said as they walked the streets, heading home with the rest of the civilians. Noah's family and friends were being escorted back up through the storm drains by the guards. "I know you don't like crowds so it means a lot."

"Of course, Papa. I just can't believe Fairy Godmother Blanche would embarrass me like that. Did you see her dancing?"

He laughed. "Yes, I did. That's just her way. Don't worry—no one was talking about you, kiddo. After she threw up … whatever that strong drink was, she decided to go home and rest. She looked pretty out of it."

Gemma shook her head. Out of all the fairy godmothers in Fairhaven, she ended up with that one? A drunk party woman? Blanche and Gemma couldn't have been more different. Gemma questioned the wisdom of the fairy godmother council for pairing them together, but she knew better than to voice her concerns. The deal had already been made.

When they arrived home at their little Tudor house, one with a magical garden out front made of all kinds of colorful plants, they both yawned and went inside. The house was small, a tiny bungalow with only two rooms, but Gemma and her father made it work.

"I should get to bed," her father began. "I'm performing at a child's birthday party in the morning. Hopefully I can pull it together. I can't wait for Princess Esme and Noah to have kids. A royal baby? Now that's going to be the talk of Fairhaven."

Her father's mood seemed to have improved from their conversation before his performance. Music seemed to have a healing effect on him. Gemma removed her shoes, leaving them by the front door. They magically organized themselves on the rack. "As long as people aren't talking about me, I'm happy. Goodnight, Papa. I have an early shift at the library tomorrow so I should get to bed soon."

He nodded, kissing her cheek. "All right. Goodnight, dear. Try to sleep tonight, okay? Hopefully you won't have more nightmares. If it gets bad, you could always ask Blanche for a sleeping potion."

Gemma faked a smile, watching her father head down the hall to his room, but she had no intention of getting a potion from that woman. If anything, the nightmares about her mother made her feel closer to her. That was the only place she could see her now.

She could go to the surface to see her again, but Gemma had no intention of doing that. She heard the population of Toronto was larger than Fairhaven—and more dangerous—and there was nothing she hated more than a crowd. Besides, she had no idea where to start to look.

After heading into her room, then removing her dress, she looked at the picture of her family that stood on her dresser. Their faces moved with glittering magical particles inside the frame as they smiled. They had been so happy in Fairhaven—until Senator Remus poisoned her mother's thoughts. She hated that man. The day he and his family were sentenced to prison, Gemma cheered.

With a sigh, she set the photograph down, then got into bed and tried to fall asleep. The nightmares came as usual—with her mother begging for help on the surface—and kept Gemma awake. She needed to find her mother.

As scary as the surface world was, she'd never be able to rest again until she did. And her father's sadness might improve if Gemma found her. But how? Right now, she didn't know. But in the morning, she needed to form a plan.

She turned over in bed, forcing herself to drift off again as anxiety pressed in on her hard-fought calm, as she knew those same nightmares would come for her again.

They always did.

CHAPTER 2

A soft knock on the front door woke Gemma, and she yawned and stretched before rising, her bed magically making itself behind her. As her slippers flew across the floor, attaching themselves to her feet, she left her bedroom and walked down the hallway. She poked her head into her father's room and found it empty. He must've already left for work.

No one ever came to visit their family—especially not this early. Who could it be?

Gemma walked toward the door, then opened it. Princess Esme's smiling face greeted her. She looked as graceful as ever in a yellow, pastel dress. Gemma immediately bowed.

"Your Majesty," she murmured. "What an honor it is to see you."

"Please, call me Esme," she replied, gesturing at her stance. "And you don't have to bow. Unlike my father, I don't really care for all that posturing."

Gemma nodded, looking up. Making eye contact made her even more nervous, but she forced herself to do it. She was in the presence of a princess—she needed to show proper respect.

"Of course, your Majesty—I apologize. What are you doing here, if you don't mind me asking? Not that I object, of course."

Gemma cleared her throat, her cheeks burning. She hoped the princess wouldn't call attention to her nervousness.

"As I said, it's just Esme. And there's no need to be sorry." Esme gestured inside the home. "What a cute little place you have! Reminds me of all those homes on the surface. Would it be all right if I came inside?"

Gemma stepped aside. "Of course—make yourself at home. Would you like some tea?"

"Oh, that would be wonderful, thank you. Fairhaven can get so cold, something I realized on the surface. Living underground is freezing."

Gemma nodded, letting Esme enter. The princess glanced around before taking a seat at the table. Gemma headed into the kitchen where she boiled a pot of tea. Her hands shook as she took two cups to the table.

Esme took the tea with a smile, sipping it slowly. "Ah— that's lovely. Since going to the surface, I actually prefer their coffee, but Fairhaven tea is still amazing. You've never been to the surface, have you, Gemma?"

The princess knew her name? Gemma was surprised. She was practically a nobody in Fairhaven, overlooked and forgotten. And she had no problem with that.

Gemma sat across from Princess Esme, shaking her head. She was too nervous to even reach for her cup of tea. "No, your —um, Esme. Never."

"I see. It can be scary at first, yes, but it's really a lovely place when you get used to it. It's where I met my amazing husband, of course. Noah Crawford. He's still sleeping, I'm afraid. But I got really lucky."

"Yes, I know—I could see the wedding from the window. Uh, no offense for not coming out, of course, but crowds freak me out. I came for my dad's performance and then headed back to the library."

"Where you work as a librarian. Yes, I chatted with your father at the wedding. He's a very nice man. I know about your mother as well. I'm so sorry she was poisoned by Senator Remus' beliefs."

Esme reached across the table, placing a hand over Gemma's. It was comforting—and reminded Gemma of her mother. She would've given anything to have her back.

"Yeah, well ..." Gemma looked down. "It's too late now, I guess."

"Don't give up hope. I never did—and look where it got me. With the man of my dreams and back home in Fairhaven." Esme took another long sip of tea. "Sometimes, things work out."

Not for me, Gemma wanted to say. She didn't think of herself as lucky.

"I guess so. It was really cool how you saved Fairhaven, by the way. And got everyone to see that Senator Remus was evil. I mean, making magic work on the surface?" Gemma shook her head. "That's crazy. And planning to use it as a weapon just isn't right."

Gemma was rambling, something she did when she was nervous, and Esme nodded along. "You're right. It was a group effort, though—Noah helped a lot. We're planning to split our time between Fairhaven and the surface world. Fortunately, we've managed to keep Fairhaven's existence a secret. There have been no more problems since Senator Remus and his family were captured."

"That's good." Gemma shifted nervously in her seat. "Um, I'd still really like to know why you're here. If that's okay."

"Of course, of course. I didn't answer before. Sorry—got caught up." Esme finished her tea, then set the cup down with a quiet clink. "The reason I'm here is, well … you caught my attention. When I spoke to your father, I realized how similar we are. Feeling like outsiders, struggling with the loss of our mothers. Yours is still alive, of course, but it's mostly the same. Don't you think we're a lot alike?"

"I'm not royalty, though—"

"True," the princess agreed, "but in other ways. Think about it."

Gemma paused, considering her words. "When you put it that way, yeah. But I still don't understand why you're here. Did you want to be friends?"

Gemma hadn't had much luck with friends—most of hers lived in books. She hoped she wouldn't have to attend balls or give speeches. That sounded like torture, and she didn't envy Esme's life.

Esme smiled. "I already consider us friends, of course. And everyone in Fairhaven. As long as they remain civil and don't support Senator Remus. But no, it's not just about that. I have something to give you."

Esme reached into her pocket, pulling out some human cash. Gemma knew all about it from surface books she had read. She watched closely as Esme leaned across the table and handed her a few hundred-dollar bills.

"Once upon a time, after some bad behavior on my end, my father banished me to the surface world. To mature, mostly," Esme explained. "It helped me a lot. And I want the same for you."

"Am I … am I being banished?" Gemma asked, looking up. "Did I do something wrong?"

"Oh, no—of course not. I'd never banish anyone, especially someone as sweet as you. I know how scary that feels." Esme shook her head, looking like she was reliving some bad memories. "If anything, I just wanted to help you live a little more. To get out and explore the world. That's what the money is for. We don't live forever, you know, not even with all our magic. I know what it's like to want to stay hidden away, in the safety of your library, but that's not living. There's so much more waiting out there for you."

Gemma remained quiet for a moment, wondering if it was true. She had never even considered a life outside of the library. Could Princess Esme be right? Her mother lived up there, after all. Maybe this was the encouragement Gemma needed to get out and find her.

It was almost like one of those fantasy books Gemma had read—where a hero visits a new land for adventure and curiosity. It was beginning to sound more and more appealing to her.

"If you do agree to head to the surface, you won't be banished," Esme continued. "So, no worries about that. You can return at any time. And I already spoke to my husband—he's willing to lend you his apartment while we honeymoon here. As a safe place to enjoy the surface world. If you wouldn't mind, of course."

"Wow ... really? That's awfully generous of him. Tell him I said thanks."

Esme smiled. "I will. He's going to make Fairhaven proud as its new prince. Anyway, no need to give me an answer right now. Just think about it—think about visiting the surface. You'll have some spending money to start out with if you do. I won't be mad no matter what you decide. But just know that I've been in your position. Getting away from home was the best thing that happened to me. I met my husband, helped save Fairhaven, and made friends with some lovely people and changed their lives. It really was worth it."

Princess Esme made the surface world sound so fun and glamorous, but deep down, Gemma knew it wasn't. There were many dangers up there—more dangers than Fairhaven. Everything was so different, so unpredictable, yet Esme seemed to love it.

Still, going up there *would* get her closer to her mother. To finding out what had happened to her. Maybe with that knowledge, her father's mood would improve and her family could reunite. And Gemma would have an apartment at least, something that helped her make a decision.

And maybe the nightmares would leave her alone up there. A girl could try.

"Okay, I'll think about it," Gemma stammered. "I'll have to speak to my father first."

"Oh, no need—I already spoke to him this morning. He approves of my plan. He wants you to get the most out of your life. And he wants you to be careful, of course, which I promised him you would be. We'll check up on you. I want to stress that you won't be alone—not like I was. I'll make sure of it."

A promise of safety *did* make her feel better. Gemma still felt overwhelmed, wondering what she should do.

"Thank you," Gemma began, "but please, next time, don't go over my head. Let *me* speak to my father."

"You're right—I'm sorry. I just wanted to be thorough and make you feel better. Anyway, I'll be on my way now. I have some royal duties to tend to, plus I want to spend time with my husband," Esme said, walking toward the door. Her yellow dress flowed behind her like a colorful shadow. "Thank you for the tea. I hope to see you around some more, Gemma. You know ... life is hard sometimes. Cruel and unfair. But it can also be beautiful and inspiring. But to see it, you'll have to come out of that library. Just for a little while. Goodbye, Gemma."

As she left the house, Gemma waved goodbye and shut the door. While she was curious to see the surface—the very place Princess Esme had met her husband and saved the world—she was anxious. That familiar knot of nervousness balled in her stomach.

She looked down at the money, thinking it over, and decided she needed a friend to lean on. A confidant. Someone to listen to her, to bounce ideas off of. Didn't everyone need that sometimes?

She got dressed, then stuffed the money deep into the pocket of her ballgown; she enjoyed wearing them as they made her feel like a princess from one of her beloved fantasy novels. After leaving home, she crossed the bridge over the magical river, heading toward the castle. Noah had awakened and greeted dukes outside the castle with Princess Esme.

Gemma just smiled as she walked by, heading inside the castle. But instead of going to the library, her favorite place in the world, she followed the winding corridors to the kitchen. She found a bunch of chefs inside, including Cal, cooking magical foods for the royal families.

He stood over a stove, garlic adding itself to the pan. Cal stood there and observed to make sure it all came together. Once it finished, Cal checked the internal temperature, then left the plate on the counter. A servant delivered it to the dining hall as Gemma entered and cleared her throat.

Cal turned around, wiping some kind of blue food onto the side of his chef's outfit. Then he smiled at Gemma. "Hey, Gem. What are you doing here?"

"I needed some advice. Do you have a second to chat? I know you're working and pretty busy, but—"

"Nonsense. I always have time for you." Cal glanced toward another chef. "Hey, Percy? Cover for me. I'll be back in five."

The other chef nodded, then took over cooking Cal's meals. Cal gestured for Gemma to follow as he led her out of the kitchen through a side door and down a quiet hallway. Everything was secluded, the perfect place to talk as the aroma of delicious-smelling food wafted through the air.

"So, what's up?" Cal asked. "You doing okay? How are your nightmares?"

Gemma nodded. "Oh, yeah—I'm fine. The nightmares are still there. Always about my mother."

"Sheesh, Gem." Cal frowned. "I'm sorry. I wish I could stop it somehow."

"It's all right—I can handle it. Mostly. But that's not why I'm here to talk to you. Princess Esme came to see me this morning. She wants me to go to the surface. Apparently, my father agreed. They both want me to live a bit more—see all that I can see."

"Hmm. Interesting." Cal paused to think for a moment. "You *do* spend a lot of time in that library, reading the day away. But that's what I like about you. You always have your head in the clouds. And trust me, the perfect guy will find that adorable one day."

"Here's hoping. So, what do you think? Should I go up to the surface?"

Cal shrugged. "I can't make that decision for you. What do *you* think? Do you want to? It's your life, Gemma."

Cal had a point. She had to set aside the princess' and her father's wishes to focus on what she wanted. This was Gemma's life—and so far, it had been the same old every day. Maybe going to the surface would be a good thing, a change of pace. And it wasn't like she couldn't return.

"I think ... I think I will. I'm free to come back anytime in case it doesn't work out," Gemma said, then smiled. "Gosh, I'm nervous. But also excited. Like ... my anxiety has butterflies."

Cal laughed, placing a hand on her shoulder. "Don't worry, Gem—you're smart enough to figure everything out. I'd come with you, but they need me here at the castle. I've got a lot of work coming up."

"Yeah, I bet. For years, being sent to the surface was a punishment—just like it was for Esme. And people like my mother. But now, it feels like an adventure. I guess I should feel lucky I get to go and be able to come back. Besides Esme, I can't think of anyone else who has."

"That should show you how special you are. Be careful, all right? I worry about you. Anyway, I have to get back to work. But when you get back, I want to hear every detail."

"Sounds like a plan. Maybe I can even find my mother this way. My father and I would sleep a lot better if I could. Anyway, see you later, Cal."

When Gemma went to turn away, Cal pulled her into a hug, much to her surprise. He had never shown her that kind of affection before. After hugging for a few seconds, Gemma smiled at him before leaving the castle.

She went to see her father next, quickly telling him the news as he performed at a birthday party. He stepped aside with a nod as kids played and screamed behind them.

"I know—Princess Esme told me she was going to ask you to head to the surface. She sees something in you, you know. Something similar to her. It seems she's made it her personal mission to help you."

"That's nice of her. Unnecessary, but nice. But how do you feel about it? Really, without the princess around?"

He paused for a moment. "I want you to be happy, Gem. If that means heading to the surface for some adventure, then so be it. Just promise me you'll be careful. I already lost your mother. I can't bear to lose you as well."

Gemma pulled him into a big hug. "Oh, Papa. You'll *never* lose me. Not now, not ever."

That made him smile.

After heading home, she packed a few things, taking only one magical suitcase with her. Each item shrank as she put it in, making room for enough dresses to last Gemma a month. She packed mostly clothes and books—the fantasy romance kind. The suitcase was heavy as she lugged it toward the castle where she found Princess Esme and Noah in the dining hall. They were eating breakfast and chatting with some royal advisors. King Tedros was busy on the other end of the hall, speaking with dignitaries. Royal life seemed stressful.

"... and I want more guards sent to the surface. For patrol and protection," Princess Esme told them. "My father's put me in charge of this, since I was the one who uncovered Senator Remus' plot. With my darling husband, of course."

When she caressed Noah's face, he smiled. "We did it together, babe. But my wife is right—more guards are always good. Just in case someone decides to follow in that senator's footsteps. Those sympathizers haven't done anything on the surface, but we need to be ready in the event they do. We'll have to find them first, of course. There's only, what? A dozen who escaped? I hope they won't be too difficult to find."

Gemma's ears perked up. She listened carefully, wondering if she'd learn any information about her mother's whereabouts.

"Me either. And we need some fairy godmothers to head to the surface and find those pockets of magic that Zamira unleashed," Esme added as the advisors took notes. "There are some parts of the city that are still able to use magic. We need to stop it—to make magic possible only in Fairhaven as it once was. Or we could have more trouble on our hands."

As the advisor nodded, Gemma cleared her throat. "Um, Princess Esme? I'm heading to the surface after all. I just made up my mind."

Princess Esme's head shot up, then she rose to her feet with a smile. "Oh, I'm so happy! You're all packed and everything—

good. Here, my husband will give you the key to our apartment in the city. Feel free to stay there as long as you'd like."

Noah nodded, reaching into his pocket and pulling out a silver key with a piece of paper. "Here—you insert this into the doorknob and twist to unlock it. Much different from magically opening doors around here. The information on how to find it is on this note. And maybe you should consider getting some new clothes. Either buying them or having the fairy godmothers magically sew you some jeans. Because people don't really wear ballgowns where I come from. Just saying."

"Got it. And thanks, but I like wearing dresses. They remind me of home. Anyway, I appreciate this so much." Gemma tucked the key and note into her pocket, then reached down to grab her suitcase. "I have to ask, though. What if I run into the sympathizers on the surface?"

"Stay hidden," Princess Esme replied, "and let us know where they are. They all vanished to the surface before we could punish them. Sadly, your mother was one of them."

Gemma swallowed hard. "Right. And got it. What if they, I don't know, want to attack or something? Humans *or* Fairhaven?"

Princess Esme shared a look with the advisors. "That's a possibility, yes. One we're trying to avoid. We've done enough to the human world already. Anyway, if a situation arises, the guards I'm sending out will stop them and bring them back here for punishment. Which is what would've happened in the first place if they hadn't fled like cowards. No offense, of course, considering your mother's involved."

"No, you're right," Gemma said with a sigh. "My mother *was* a coward. And I want her to explain herself."

"Then we hope you can find her and the others. We've got a nice cell waiting for them already," Noah added. "One right next to their beloved senator."

Gemma nodded, though she wasn't sure she could turn her mother over so easily. Not without speaking to her first.

She nodded. "Okay, I understand. I was just curious. Well, I should get going. Not sure how long I'll stay up there. If I get stressed out, I might come right back down."

"Of course, Gemma. I'll get a guard to stand watch near the storm drain in case there's trouble. Someone will come to the surface every so often to check on you should you decide to stay." Princess Esme gestured at the doors. "And, of course, please don't use any magical potions from your fairy godmother on the surface. It's not exactly a crime, but we just don't want any trouble up there. Earth isn't meant to have magic, and we want it restored to those days. My father and I are in agreement on that. Anyway, we'll walk you to the ladder, at least."

"Oh, that's nice of you, but you don't have to. Sit and enjoy your breakfast." Gemma smiled at them all. "See you again soon."

Princess Esme nodded, sitting with Noah and resuming her talks with the advisors. They wished her well as she zipped through the dining hall of royals and dignitaries. As she left the castle, she had no intention of heading up to the surface just yet.

There was one thing she needed to do first—something she was sure Princess Esme and everyone else wouldn't approve of.

CHAPTER 3

The dungeons were on the far side of Fairhaven, tucked away and quiet. Several prison guards did their rounds on patrol as Gemma entered the dark building. There had been little crime in Fairhaven, so the dungeons were mostly empty—except for Senator Remus and his family.

He had once petitioned King Tedros to make magic compatible on the surface, and his wife, magical scientist Dr. Breya, had found a way with the help of their fairy godmother. When King Tedros disapproved and asked them to drop it, they hatched an evil plan that was foiled by Princess Esme.

Gemma shuddered to think what would've happened if Esme hadn't gone to the surface.

A nearby prison guard looked her up and down. "What are you doing in here? We don't normally get visitors."

"I know," Gemma said, setting her suitcase down. "I'm sorry—I didn't mean to cause any problems. I just wanted to speak with Senator Remus."

"You do? Why?"

More than anything, Fairhaven was concerned that more might follow in Senator Remus' footsteps. He already had sympathizers who had fled to their surface because of their involvement in his scheme.

"I'm heading to the surface. My mother escaped there to avoid punishment for being a sympathizer," Gemma explained, hoping she didn't make herself sound guilty. "I want to track her down—have her explain how she could follow a man like that. And I'd like to speak with the former senator to see what he has to say. I'm sure Princess Esme would let me through. She's my friend." That might have been a little bit of a stretch, but the ends justified the means. "I can go get her if you'd like?"

"No, it's all right. I'm sure she's very busy." The prison guard started walking down the hall. "Just make it quick. There's a reason we don't allow many to see Remus."

Gemma promised she would be, then chased after the prison guard. She hauled her suitcase behind her before they stopped at a cell at the end of the row. Fairy godmothers had used their potions on the lock, ensuring Senator Remus could never escape. Little particles of pink magic floated in the air.

The former senator looked awful in his gray prison uniform; his beard grown out. He sat on the bench in his cell with a dejected look on his face. In cells around him, his wife, daughter, and Duke Cullen—all traitors that Princess Esme had exposed—looked just as miserable.

"Hey, Remus?" the guard asked. "You got a visitor here to see you."

"I do?" Senator Remus rose to his feet, a smile forming on his face. Then it faded when he noticed Gemma. "Oh. I don't know you. What the hell are you doing here?"

Not a very warm welcome. Not that she expected good manners from a man who wanted to enslave humanity.

Gemma cleared her throat, determined to not look afraid in front of the traitor. But Remus *did* intimidate her. How had

Princess Esme ever found the courage to stand up to him? Gemma didn't know.

"Um, hi," Gemma began shyly as the guard stood behind her. "My name is Gemma Solace. I believe my mother was a sympathizer of yours. You know, before she fled to the surface with the others."

"Good for her. I only wish I had followed." Senator Remus shook his head. "Fairhaven could be so much more—more powerful, more fearsome. We could rule over the puny human realm now that I ensured magic was compatible up there. But King Tedros and his daughter are fools who stopped our progress. Our natural evolution."

Gemma didn't believe a word of it, but she needed something from the senator. So, she forced herself to play along.

"Right. Now, I'm looking for my mother, Katherine Solace. Do you know where she is? And why she agreed with you?"

Senator Remus stepped toward the bars. He placed his hands on the magical steel. "I don't remember her, no. You and your family are a bunch of nobodies. As to why she sided with me? That's simple. She sounds like a wise woman. I wish I could meet her. If I ever get out of here—and trust me, I will—she'll be the first one I'll thank for supporting me."

Bile churned in her stomach. How could her mother support such a vile man? So much for playing along.

"Well, you're never getting out. Your plan was dangerous. And you paid the price," Gemma said, growing more confident. "I'm glad you're behind bars. And to be honest, I hope you and your family never get out."

The senator's wife, daughter, and the duke all glared at Gemma from their cells.

Senator Remus shook his head. "I can see you're just as stubborn and foolish as the others. Too bad you didn't follow in the footsteps of your mother. It's been nearly a year since I was put in here, you know. And I have something planned for my anniversary. It's going to be spectacular. I only wish my fairy godmother was here to see it."

When he started laughing, everyone else in his family joined in. Their evil chuckles echoed around the prison. Senator Remus wasn't going to give her any information about her mother, so she sighed, turning to the guard.

"I'm ready to leave now," she said. "Sorry to impose."

The guard shook his head. "No worries, miss. Come on. I'll escort you out of here."

Gemma nodded, walking behind the guard. She took one last look over her shoulder at Remus and his family. They had an air about them that was so evil—so cold. She wondered how they got away with it for so long.

As she neared the doors, the guard stopped her. "And don't worry about what Remus said. He and his family are *never* getting out of here. The fairy godmothers ensured their magic prevented that."

Gemma took a deep breath. "I hope you're right. Anyway, thanks for letting me in. See you around."

The guard said goodbye, then Gemma left the dungeons. She remembered she had a potion in her pocket that her fairy godmother had given her long ago. It made heavy suitcases much easier to carry. Her suitcase grew magical legs, like thin sticks, and followed her as she headed toward the storm drain, requiring her to no longer carry it. The storm drain had a small, silver ladder that extended, leading up to the surface. A completely different world.

One that Princess Esme had done just fine in. Maybe that would be true for Gemma as well.

Just as she prepared to leave, she heard a familiar voice. "You ain't leaving without saying goodbye to little old me first, are you?"

Gemma dropped her head and took a calming breath before turning around to see Fairy Godmother Blanche walking toward her. She still wore the same dress she'd had on at the wedding, throw-up stains and all. Bags darkened her eyes, and she swayed unsteadily on her feet. She paused near the ladder, looking Gemma up and down.

"You're going in *that*?" she asked, gesturing at her dress. "You're going to stick out like a sore thumb."

"It worked just fine for Princess Esme. Why should I be any different? Besides, I like the way I dress. I don't want to change it now. Anyway, if you're here, I assume you heard I'm leaving."

Fairy Godmother Blanche nodded, then belched, making Gemma wince. "Yeah, I did. It's the talk of Fairhaven at the moment. Not many go up to the surface, you know."

Talk of the town? Gemma didn't like that. Remus had been right—she was just a nobody. But she was a nobody on a mission to see her mother again.

"Anyway, I'll bid you goodbye," Gemma said. "I'm not sure when I'll be back. Maybe soon if I don't like the place."

"Yeah, it can be a real tough world to live in. Sometimes those humans can be dangerous." Fairy Godmother Blanche shook her head. "You need me to go with you? Or give you any potions? I can whip up an anti-anxiety elixir if you'd like."

"Thanks, but no. I still have the other ones you gave me. And I want to try to make it on my own. My father already gave his blessing, so I should be on my way now."

"All right, all right. I won't stop you." Fairy Godmother Blanche looked up at the storm drain. "Just ... be careful, yeah? I know you think I don't care about you—or that I'm a bad fairy godmother or whatever. But I *do* want you to be safe. And I've already cast a spell to make you appear more human on the surface. Because I'm thoughtful like that. Ain't you glad to have me?"

Gemma chortled. "Well, actually—"

"Don't answer that. Now, if you need anything else, just come get me, okay? I'm here for you."

Gemma smiled, reaching for the ladder. "Thank you, Blanche. That's kind. Wish me luck."

"Good luck, Gemma!" Fairy Godmother Blanche called out, waving as she watched her climb the ladder. "Don't eat yellow snow. Oh, and look before you cross the street! Don't end up like Princess Esme who got hit by a car."

Gemma tried to remember all the advice, pulling herself farther up the ladder. When she reached the storm drain, she used all her might to push it to the side, then climbed through with her suitcase. She immediately grabbed her things and looked around.

She was standing on a busy street, one with lots of cars and humans. The hot summer air made sweat form underneath her big dress. The nearby sign read DUNDAS STREET, and there were hundreds of little shops lining the roadway. She looked both ways—following Blanche's advice—before heading to the sidewalk. People walked past her, glancing down at her dress but saying nothing.

"Not bad," Gemma whispered to herself. "I haven't gotten hit by a car. Maybe I'm doing better than the princess."

She quickly went over her to-do list in her head. One—find her mother. A total longshot, but she had to try. That was the whole point of coming to the surface; why she had agreed to Princess Esme's plan. It wouldn't just help Gemma but also help her father get closure.

Two—find a way to survive up here and be more independent. Just to prove she could, like the hero in a beloved story would.

And three—perhaps find love, if her anxiety didn't get in

the way. She needed something new. Something more exciting. She would know what it was when she found it.

Gemma took a deep breath. "Let's do this."

The sky was bright and blue, making Gemma wince. It was certainly different from the darkness and magical lights of Fairhaven. And the smells were different too. The stench of food, people, and sweat mixed together, nearly making Gemma gag. She didn't know how the princess had put up with it all.

With a hand over her mouth, Gemma reached down to grab her suitcase. It was having difficulty sprouting legs. One leg would pop out, then vanish. Magic was still compatible on the surface—but just barely. It seemed unpredictable. Gemma made a mental note to not rely on it, forcing herself to live as a human, and picked up her suitcase to carry it instead. She promised not to use magic, after all.

She walked down the street, people bumping into her shoulders. None of them said sorry. As she brushed it off, she passed a construction zone, then heard a few whistles in her direction.

When she turned, she saw four men staring at her. They were dressed in bright orange uniforms and eating sandwiches while on break. It looked like they were building something for the humans—maybe a playground. Gemma paused, wondering if they were talking to her.

"Excuse me, are you speaking to me?" she asked.

"Looking good!" one of the men yelled. "What time does that dress come off?"

Gemma scoffed. "I'm sorry ... what?"

"You live around here?" one of the other men asked. "Maybe we could grab a drink later."

Those men were giving Gemma a bad vibe. And why would they whistle at her? She wasn't a griffin or a phoenix. She shook her head and picked up her suitcase without bothering to say goodbye. They continued to whistle as she rushed down the sidewalk through the throng of people.

Was this what the outside world was like? Full of harassment, danger, and rudeness? Gemma wasn't sure she would like this world at all.

She took a deep breath, leaning against the side of a building. She could feel it coming on again—the anxiety. It started as a tingle in her stomach that spread through her whole body. Before she knew it, her hands began to shake, her tummy felt sick, and her head spun. And those lecherous men had brought it on.

Had she made a terrible mistake by coming up here? That question wiggled around in her brain.

When she felt like her heart would explode, beating erratically in her chest, she grabbed her suitcase and knew she needed to get off the street. The large crowd of unfamiliar humans weren't helping her anxiety at all. She slammed open a nearby door, then rushed inside and took a deep breath.

When she looked around, she realized she was in a bar of some kind. It had a dozen shelves with a large collection of alcohol, brown paint on the walls, some chairs and tables, and a dartboard near a set of washrooms. The place was empty without a person in sight.

"Hello?" she called out, her hands still shaking. "Is anyone here?"

Footsteps sounded, then a man came out of the back room. He was carrying a box with bottles in it that he started putting away behind the bar. He glanced at her, noticing her outfit before gesturing at the door.

"Sorry, we're not open yet," the man said. "Not for another hour."

"Oh. I'm sorry," Gemma murmured. "It's just ... I was having anxiety, and these construction workers started harassing me and ... and ...”

When she burst into tears, the man must've felt sorry for her because he jumped over the bar and rushed to her side. “Hey, you all right? Just take deep breaths. There you go.”

Gemma did as he asked, taking deep breaths in and out. Her anxiety began to calm itself as she wiped away a tear. “Sorry. I didn't mean to come in here and—”

“It's okay. I don't mind.” The man smiled, gesturing at the bar. “Why don't you have a seat? I'll get you some tea. On the house.”

Gemma nodded, sniffling as she headed to the bar. She sat down on one of the black stools as the man stepped behind the bar again. As he boiled some water for tea, Gemma took a good look at him.

He was handsome—dark, curly hair, piercing green eyes, and a thick beard. He wore a blue shirt with jeans and a name badge that read IAN. He had tattoos up and down his arms of familiar creatures. Dragons, phoenixes, and griffins. Gemma took it as a good sign. Maybe this human was different—maybe he could be trusted.

He spun around, setting her tea down on the bar. Steam billowed over the cup. “There you are. And like I said, it's free of charge.”

Gemma was relieved about that. “Thank you. That's sweet.”

“Nah, don't mention it. I own this bar—I can do whatever I want.” The man reached for a nearby rag, wiping down the counter. “So, you feeling better now?”

Gemma took a deep breath, warming up her hands on the steaming cup. “Yeah. Yeah, I think so. Thanks for being so nice. Ian, is it?”

“That's right. Ian Whitman.” The man held out a hand. “And you are?”

"Gemma Solace," she replied, shaking his hand. He had a firm grip but a soft touch. "Enchanted to meet you."

The words tumbled out of her mouth before she could stop them. Enchanted to meet you—what was that? It sounded like something out of a fairytale. As she blushed, Ian continued to wipe down the bar with a little smile.

"Never heard a greeting like that before. It's definitely unique," he replied. "Enchanted to meet you too, Ms. Solace. Now, if you don't mind me saying, you look out of place around here. You new to the city or something? Or are you entering a beauty pageant?"

Gemma looked down, realizing he was talking about her dress. "Oh—oh, yeah, I'm not from around Toronto. I come from a place far, far away. You wouldn't know it."

"Any place that wears ballgowns in the morning sounds fun. What brings you to our city?"

Gemma sipped her tea, thinking. "Adventure, really. I'm trying to live a bit more. Experience things before I die. A friend of mine gave me some money to go out and have fun. She wants me to live more too."

And finding her mother was always on her mind. Not wanting to tell a complete stranger everything, no matter how ruggedly handsome he was, she kept that to herself.

Gemma pulled the money out of her pocket, placing it down on the bar. As she did, she knocked over some of her tea, coating the bills with the hot liquid. She gasped and moved the slightly wet papers away. Without magic, the bills didn't fix themselves.

"Oops," she murmured. "Guess I ruined it."

"Wow, that's a lot of money. You'd better be careful with that around here. Wouldn't want to get robbed." He used his rag to wipe the tea from the bills and set them back in front of her. "Anyway, the money's still good. And that was nice of your friend. I think you'll like Toronto. Here, I'll give you a free guide to the city."

Ian reached under the bar. He set down a pamphlet for the city that listed all the fun things to do. "Check out the helicopter tour if you have a chance. Maybe I'm biased, but they're pretty fun. There's nothing like looking down at all the parks and buildings to make you feel alive."

"I will. Thank you." Gemma took the pamphlet, stashing it into her pocket. "You said you own this bar?"

"That's right. It's called the Horizon Bar—I opened it myself not that long ago. It's doing pretty well. And if you ever need to come back, either to stop a panic attack or for another cup of tea, my door is always open."

"Thanks. As I said, that's very kind." Gemma drank the rest of her tea, placing the cup down. "I really should get going now though. I have a lot to do."

He nodded, stepping around the bar. "All right. I'll walk you out. Be careful in these streets, Gemma. You seem like a nice woman. I wouldn't want you to get hurt. And if those construction workers bother you again, you let me know, okay? I'll deal with them."

Gemma thanked him and took her wet money back, stepping outside. The cool breeze blew her red hair over her shoulder. "Okay, sounds good. See you around, Ian."

He waved, watching her walk own the street. Gemma was just relieved that she had managed to find one nice human after that awful first introduction.

Maybe her luck was changing after all.

CHAPTER 4

For some reason, Gemma couldn't get Ian out of her mind.

She thought it was maybe because he was handsome—which he definitely was. Like a tattooed bad boy out of all those romance novels she read and loved, but with a kind soul who had helped her through anxiety. But it was more than that.

She felt drawn to him. He gave off good energy—almost like magic—and fascinated her. There was a magnetism to him, so powerful that it quieted Gemma's fears of heartbreak and abandonment. Maybe the whole 'enchanted to meet you' slip-up had been a preview of what was to come.

Shaking her head, she forced herself to stop thinking about Ian and focused. Right now, she was lost. She needed to at least get to Noah's apartment—a safe place where she could relax.

She saw someone on the curb lifting their hand, and a yellow car stopped and let them get in the backseat. She'd seen taxis on human television, but they were much bigger than she imagined. She heard the woman through the opened window give the driver an address and they took off. Getting an idea, Gemma leaned on the edge of the sidewalk and raised her hand.

"Taxi!" she called out. "Over here, please!"

One finally pulled up, bright yellow with black streaks. "Good morning, miss." The driver got out and helped her load her suitcase into his trunk, then opened her door and helped her climb into the back seat. "That's a nice dress you got there." He helped her cram the layers of tuille and lace into the back seat.

"Oh, thank you. It was my mother's." Gemma felt a twinge of sadness when she said that, then he slammed the door and Gemma fumbled with her seatbelt. How had they done this in the movies? Finally, after a couple of failed attempts, she pushed the metal clasp into its connector and heard a click. *Success!*

The man was back in the front seat and looking back at her expectantly.

"Thank you for driving me." She smoothed her skirts and pressed a hand to her stomach. She was *in* a *car.*

"You're welcome. Do you have the address for your destination?"

"Oh, right! Sorry." Gemma reached into her pocket, pulling out the note that Noah had given her. "Here—I'm heading to this place. An apartment."

The driver nodded at the note, his eyes lit with something Gemma couldn't define, and he looked at her with renewed interest. He turned his gaze back out the front window, and the car inched forward. Riding in a car was much different than riding a dragon back home. At least the taxi had seatbelts, something Gemma was grateful for.

The taxi took off and blended with the traffic. Everything was quiet when they stopped at a red light, then Gemma glanced out the window. How did people survive in a city this big without getting lost? She searched the faces of the passing people, hoping to see her mother.

"So, what brings you to Toronto?" the driver asked. "Are you a local or new in town?"

"Definitely new," she said, glancing down at her dress. "I guess my outfit gives it away. I just got here. And I'm eager to see the city. Any pointers?"

He smiled. "Sure—there are a lot of great places. The CN Tower, Ripley's aquarium, the baseball stadium. Toronto's got some amazing restaurants and live entertainment too."

Gemma doubted she would enjoy it as much as the food and music back in Fairhaven, but it was worth a shot. She knew Princess Esme's guards would check on her soon and she didn't want to disappoint.

"I personally recommend the Toronto Zoo," the man said, taking a right at the corner. "My daughter, Abby, loves going there."

"The zoo! How lovely. I adore that place too. What's her favorite animal? The dragon? The hydra?"

The driver gave Gemma a funny look in the rear-view mirror. "I don't know what zoos are like where you're from, but we don't have those animals here. No, my daughter's favorite animal is the giraffe. Because they're so tall."

"Gir ... affe." Gemma sounded the name out, but it didn't sound right. "Never heard of them. We don't have animals like yours where I'm from."

"And where would that be, miss?"

The name Fairhaven was on the tip of Gemma's tongue before she remembered how she was supposed to keep their magical kingdom under wraps. The world had come too close to learning the truth about them already.

"Oh, uh ... it's far away from here. Trust me, you wouldn't

know it. It's lovely though—and I miss it so much. I might be going back really soon."

"Well, I hope you stay a while. This city can be great if you give it a chance. Lots of people, yes, but also lots of adventure and good times."

Gemma perked up at that. Maybe Toronto would be the exciting break she needed.

He pulled into the small parking lot and put the car in park. She looked over her shoulder at the traffic behind them. She hadn't been paying very close attention, but it didn't feel like they'd gone very far. If she wanted to visit Ian in the future, she'd just walk. Gemma wrestled with her seatbelt for a few seconds before pushing a button that released the clasp, then stepped out.

The man unloaded her bag, their hands brushing as he passed the handle to her. He didn't release it right away, and Gemma looked up at his hopeful face. "You didn't pay your fare."

"Oh, sorry. Like I said, I'm new around here." Gemma followed him to the window where he pointed to an electronic box on the dashboard flashing the total. She reached into her pocket, pulling out a single hundred-dollar bill. "Here you are."

He took the money, grinning, and handed her back her change. "Thanks, miss. Say ... would it be all right if I got your number? Maybe I could take you out sometime."

"Take me out? What for?"

He blinked. "Come on, don't you have dates where you're from? We could get coffee. Or maybe dinner."

Gemma took a good look at the man. He was handsome with blond hair, blue eyes, and a casual shirt and jeans. His stubble made him look older, but Gemma would've pegged him for early thirties. She blushed, stepping away from the taxi.

Going out with that man just didn't seem right. Especially when she was still thinking about Ian.

"I'm sorry, but I don't have a phone. And I won't be in town long enough. But thank you anyway." Gemma turned, then began walking toward the apartment building. "Have a good day!"

The man sighed in disappointment, then nodded and put the taxi in reverse. He pulled out of the parking lot and into the flow of traffic. Once he was gone, Gemma opened the door to the apartment building and stepped inside the lobby.

It wasn't as cozy as her home, but at least it was a safe place to rest her head.

Following the note's instructions, she headed toward the elevator and pressed the button. It took her to Noah's floor, and she walked down the hallway, watching the numbers on the door get higher as she went. Then she paused at the right door, unlocking it with the key.

When she entered, the apartment was beautiful—lots of natural light, comfy couches, and privacy. But it still didn't feel like home. She missed her own bed, her own kingdom. Gemma felt like she was intruding in someone else's home even though she had permission.

Sighing, she set her suitcase down and then began to unpack. She eventually decided to use Ian's room as a makeshift closet and the couch as her bed. Gemma stripped the blankets and pillows from his bed and carefully laid out her clothes on it.

Once she had figured out how the nozzles worked, Gemma showered. Now, fresh and clean, there was one last thing Gemma wanted to do.

Sleep.

She curled up on the coach and drifted off almost immediately. When she woke up, it was dark outside, and her stomach grumbled. She needed to eat.

Remembering that she didn't have magical potions on her side to help cook, Gemma entered the kitchen and looked through the cupboards at the supplies. She found a simple recipe for macaroni and cheese that looked interesting. And, luckily enough, Noah had all the ingredients in the apartment. She dumped the noodles into the pot, put it on the stove, and turned it on. Then she frowned when it wasn't cooking.

"Okay, I'm missing something," she muttered. "Oh, I know! It needs water."

She filled the pot with water, then tried to get it to boil. She turned a bunch of nozzles on the stove. Just when she thought she had gotten the hang of it, she caught a glimpse of a single spark on the burner.

And then the entire stove went up in flames.

Gemma screamed, jumping back from the fire. She didn't know what to do. If a fire broke out in Fairhaven, a fairy godmother was on the scene to put it out with magic in the blink of an eye. But that didn't happen on Earth. All the rules she knew were changed—and she'd have to adapt to survive.

As she scrambled around, looking for something to put out the fire with, an alarm above her head began to blare. She screamed again, taking cover behind the kitchen island while covering her ears.

"Stop!" she cried. "Please, stop!"

All the uncertainty was enough to give her a panic attack. With her heart pounding, she ran toward the kitchen sink and turned on the tap. A nozzle caught her eye, and she pulled it free and aimed it at the stove. When she squeezed the trigger, a blast of water hit the flames, and she sprayed until the fire was out and she was soaked. But the kitchen was still smoking, and the stove itself was completely destroyed.

So much for Noah's stove—and the macaroni and cheese.

With the fire alarm still going off above her head, something she had seen malfunction on a comedy show from the surface called *Friends,* Gemma reached for a dish towel and fanned underneath the alarm for a few minutes. Once it had finally stopped, she cracked open a window, letting the smoke escape. Then a loud knock came at the door.

"Toronto Fire Services" a manly voice called out. "Is everything all right in there?"

Gemma ran to the door, opening it to find a handsome man standing on her welcome mat. He was tall with dark skin, chocolate eyes, and curly hair. Not to mention muscles that bulged out of his firefighter's uniform. She blushed, then forced herself to calm down to speak with him.

"Yes, yes—everything's fine. So sorry to worry everyone," Gemma said, noticing the other renters down the hall had opened their doors to see what was going on. They were murmuring about her while keeping a safe distance. "Had a small fire break out while I was cooking. But I managed to put it out. I think."

Gemma coughed, then noticed her robe was singed. The firefighter nodded. "All right then. One of your neighbors heard the smoke alarm go off and called us. You mind if I check out the place?"

"Sure, of course. Come on in."

The firefighter entered, taking a quick scope of the apartment. When everything seemed fine, he walked back to the door, nodding. "All right, looks like we're good. Just be more careful next time, okay?"

"I promise. Have a good evening."

The man gave her a small smile before she closed the door. Gemma sighed and slunk to the floor while chastising herself. She had barely been in the human world for a few hours and had already started a fire—one that could've hurt someone.

She just didn't think she was cut out for this life of adventure that the princess and Gemma's father wanted for her.

Trying not to cry, Gemma showered for the second time, trying unsuccessfully to scrub the smell of smoke from her hair, then dressed in a burgundy gown and put her hair up into a twist. She suddenly wasn't in the mood for dinner anymore. She was in the mood for Fairhaven, for her dad's music, Cal's cake, and the security of her library. After double checking the kitchen, she left the apartment and locked the door behind her. People walking down the hallway peered at her, murmuring about the fire. Heat burned her cheeks. Coming to the surface was a huge mistake.

She hurried down the hallway, taking the stairs so she wouldn't run into anyone on the elevator. Once she was outside, the evening breeze blowing through her hair, she glanced down the street and found the nearest storm drain. The fairy godmothers used magic spells to keep it hidden from humans and connect them all to Fairhaven. Gemma ran toward it and opened the grate before sliding it back above her head and descending the ladder.

Once she made it back into Fairhaven, the dark and dampness all around her, she felt much better. Like she was finally in control again. She hurried down the golden streets of Fairhaven to her little home in the distance.

When she opened the door, she found her father sitting on the couch, practicing an instrument. It sent out little ripples of magical light as he played a heavenly tune. Half-eaten dinner sat across from him. As she entered the room, he looked up, noticing her with wide eyes.

"Kiddo, you're back," he said, setting his instrument aside. "So, how did it go? Are you enjoying your time on the surface?"

With him staring at her, looking so hopeful, Gemma burst into tears. For the second time that day.

Her father gasped, rising to his feet and rushing to her side. He pulled her in for a big hug. "Gemma, what's wrong? Why are you crying? Are you hurt? And is that ... smoke I smell?"

Gemma nodded, pulling away. "It is, Papa. It all went wrong —first these big men yelled at me on the street, then I had a panic attack in a bar. The bartender was nice actually. Then when I made it to Noah's apartment, I tried to cook dinner and almost burnt down his place! Oh, why did I ever think I could do this?"

Her father watched her with sad eyes as she plunked herself on the couch, hiding her face in a pillow. He walked over and rubbed her back while bending down next to her.

"That does sound awful, but everyone makes mistakes. Those men were just idiots and plenty of humans have started fires too. Don't beat yourself up over it."

Gemma removed her face from the pillow, staring up at him. "Maybe. But I think it's a sign I'm not ready to go to the surface. I'm awkward and anxious and bad at being human. I should just stay in the library forever and never come out again."

"But what's the point of that? Gemma, I want you to live. I want you to experience everything you can. That's why I agreed with Princess Esme when she shared her idea with me. I know you can handle it—you're smarter than you think. And finding your mother and hearing her side of things would help us both. I want to know why she chose to believe in someone like Senator Remus."

"Yeah. I hear you." Gemma sniffled. "Look, Papa, it's nice of you to try to cheer me up, but it's not working. I should go tell Princess Esme and Noah that the surface world isn't for me. I belong here—I see that now."

Her father sighed, rising to his feet. "Gemma, I really wish you would give it another shot. Besides believing in you and wanting you to get out more, do you know why else I agreed with Princess Esme?"

Gemma shook her head, her dress bunched up around her.

"Because your mother was just like you. Isolated, shy, nervous. She had a very limited view of Fairhaven and the human world. And I believe that's how Senator Remus' ideology was able to poison her mind. One political rally was all it took to sway her. He took advantage of her ignorance, her naivety. And now she's gone."

Gemma paused. "Do you think I'll follow in her footsteps?"

"No, no—of course not. You're a bright young woman who couldn't hurt a fly. I just ... I want you to see all that this world has to offer. Ours *and* the humans. I want you to live more than your mother and I have. Now, I know you have anxiety, but don't let that convince you you're not strong enough to do this. Anxiety is a liar. You always have been strong and always will be, kiddo. I know that in my heart."

Gemma appreciated his speech, but she was still unsure. She sat up and frowned. "Oh, I don't know, Papa ..."

"Wait here a moment. I think someone else has a better chance of convincing you."

Before Gemma could respond, her father took off, opening the door and running into the street. She watched from the window as her father headed toward the castle. Ten minutes later, he returned with Princess Esme and Noah by her side. He let them into the house where Gemma was blushing in embarrassment.

"Your Majesties, hi," she said, then remembered Esme's preference. "Oh, sorry. Esme and Noah."

Princess Esme nodded, dressed in a casual, red dress. "Hello, Gemma. Your father tells me you had some difficulties in the human realm."

"Something about my stove catching on fire?" Noah added, raising an eyebrow.

Gemma nodded. "Yes, it did. I'm so sorry! I tried to make macaroni and cheese, but the stove caught on fire. I haven't even had a chance to do anything besides screw things up—"

Noah shook his head. "It's all right, Gemma. I'm not upset. I expected you to be clueless about the surface world—just like my wife was once. You've never been there, after all. You only know what you've seen in books and human movies. I figured some mistakes were bound to happen. But we knew you were smart and strong enough to figure it out on your own."

"And there's nothing to forgive. It was an accident," Princess Esme added. "We believe you can do this. We just wish you would believe in yourself as well."

When she looked at her father, he was nodding along, trying to give her some encouragement. Gemma didn't know what she had done to get the princess of Fairhaven to believe in her this much. But she was grateful—and hoped that faith wasn't misplaced.

Princess Esme stepped forward, placing a hand on Gemma's shoulder. "Look, I know being in an unfamiliar environment is stressful, especially for someone with anxiety. I know I had lots of fears about whether I would survive or not up there. But I did —which means you can do it too. And maybe, just maybe, if you give it long enough, you'll see there's much to be gained up there."

"Like friends, good deeds, adventures," Noah added. "I know me and my wife had our fair share. We want that for you too."

"You should listen to them, kiddo. They speak wisdom," her father said, stepping closer. "So, what do you say? Will you go back to the surface and try again?"

Gemma's anxiety screamed at her—telling her to stay in

Fairhaven because it was safer. But when had safe ever helped someone grow and experience new things? As nervous as she was, she *did* see the appeal of the surface world. Of all the possibilities that were there and chances to break out of her shell. Not to mention the chance to find her mother for her *and* her father's sake. It was clear those nightmares weren't going to stop by themselves.

So, for once, she swallowed her anxiety and nodded. "Okay—I'll go back and try again. But this is the last time. I don't know how many fires I can take."

CHAPTER 5

For the second time, Gemma said goodbye to her father and hugged him tight. Then she followed Princess Esme, Noah, and her father toward the ladder that belonged to the storm drain in the distance. Before she left, Princess Esme fetched a few books from the library, promising they would help her.

"Here—this is a cookbook from the surface. The meatloaf is especially good," Princess Esme told her. "And this is a book on human culture. With these, you should have an easier time. I should've given these to you earlier, I think. I'm sorry."

Gemma took them, stashing them safely in a satchel. "No worries, thank you. I'm still really sorry about your stove, Noah. I'll try to be more careful this time."

Noah shook his head. "I'm not mad at all. Just take care of yourself, all right? And I'll arrange to have a new stove put in with my landlord. Maybe you can try again."

Gemma nodded, hoping so too. She found the fact that a stove was her biggest enemy a bit ridiculous. As she turned toward the storm drain, a lone guard stood there, nodding at her.

"Trying again?" he asked.

Gemma sighed. "Yes—and hopefully, I'll have better luck this time. Goodbye, everyone. And thanks for the pep talk."

As the others said goodbye, Gemma reached toward the ladder, slowly pulling herself up. She noticed Fairy Godmother Blanche lying in the gutter a few feet away. She looked drunk again, holding some magical concoction of a drink in her left hand. Her wand sat in her right, and her dress was wet and muddy from the ground.

The woman noticed Gemma, lifting her head with a gentle sway. "You again—you're back already. Couldn't beat your anxiety, eh? Well, no worries. Fairhaven is a safe place for you. Maybe you're better off just staying in that library of yours."

For the first time, Gemma wasn't so sure. She wanted to prove to everyone—including herself—that she could do this. That she could survive on the surface for at least a little while and have a good time.

And that stubbornness to succeed was going to fuel her. Maybe it was the nudge she needed.

"Not this time, Blanche. I won't be back for a long, long time," Gemma said, pulling herself up the ladder. "Trust me on that. See you later!"

Her fairy godmother didn't look like she believed her, but she was too drunk to argue. Gemma waved one last time to her father before opening the storm drain above her head. She looked, making sure there was no oncoming traffic, and then pulled herself up onto the street.

It was dark outside now—and very late. There were fewer cars and people on the streets, making Gemma sigh in relief. Maybe she'd have to become a night owl to get around and ease her anxiety. She looked both ways before crossing the street, then made it safely to the sidewalk.

"Okay, here I am again," she whispered to herself. "I can do this."

"Gemma?"

When she spun around, she spotted a familiar face. Ian. He was dressed in the same outfit as before and his eyes twinkled under the streetlights.

He was downright dreamy. She understood the appeal Noah had for Princess Esme. There was something about the humans—something magical, despite the fact that they didn't have magic at all.

"Oh, um, hello," Gemma replied, shifting uncomfortably. "Nice to see you again."

"You too. What an *enchanting* evening," Ian teased, making her blush. "What are you doing out here? It's pretty late. I was just leaving early for the night. There's only so many drunken idiots I can take, and I've reached my limit right now. Left Barney, my employee, in charge."

She couldn't very well tell him the whole truth—and the cooking incident. So, she just shrugged.

"I went for a walk," she lied. "Wanted to explore the neighborhood a bit."

"Well, going out at night can be dangerous. Where are you staying? Do you want a ride home? I can drop you off on the way to my apartment."

Gemma remembered all the stranger-danger talks her father had given her, but something about Ian was very trustworthy. Almost like how Princess Esme had once trusted Noah. Gemma had heard their entire love story at the wedding from her window seat, something that made her sigh dreamily.

"That would be great, thank you," she replied. "I'm staying at an apartment in the city. Just borrowing it from a friend."

"Sounds good. Toronto can get dangerous at night, especially for a woman, so I want to make sure you get back safely." He gestured at a small sedan parked on the street. "Follow me."

As she headed toward his car, he opened the passenger side door for her. She thanked him and ducked her head inside before buckling up, this time with much more ease. Ian walked around the side of the vehicle, getting into the driver's seat and starting the engine.

"It's no carriage, but it makes getting around easier," Ian joked. "You'll have to point the way."

Gemma remembered the streets the taxi driver had taken, so she nodded. "No problem. And thanks for the ride."

Ian smiled, giving her butterflies as he pulled into traffic. "It's no trouble at all."

As he drove down the dark streets, Gemma wanted to find out more about him. She knew so little. She racked her brain, trying to think of a conversation starter when Ian spoke first.

"So," he began, turning the corner, "are you liking Toronto so far?"

Gemma shrugged. "It's growing on me. Not sure how long I'll stay, but I'll give it a shot. How long have you lived here?"

He stared straight ahead as he continued to drive. His eyebrows furrowed before he spoke. "My whole life, really. I've traveled a bit around the world but always came home. There's nothing like home, after all."

Gemma nodded. "I understand that perfectly. What kind of places have you traveled to?"

"Oh, just about everywhere. The United States, France, Ireland, Germany. All for my dad's work."

He winced like he hadn't meant to admit that. Gemma didn't know about any of those places. "Sounds like a fun adventure. Why did you open your own bar?"

"I wanted a change of pace, you know? To make it on my

own. My parents don't really approve, but that's too bad. This is my life and I'm going to live it the way I want."

Gemma could relate to that. From Princess Esme to Gemma's father, everyone had an opinion for her life. But the only one that mattered was her own.

"Good for you, Ian. I'm happy for you."

He gave her a small smile, staring at her out of the corner of his eye. "Thanks. I'm pretty happy here. After all, you just never know who you're going to meet in my line of work."

Did he mean her? She didn't have a chance to ask as they pulled into the parking lot of Noah's apartment building. She unbuckled her seatbelt, then turned back to Ian.

"Well, thank you for the ride. Probably much safer than walking," she said. "Maybe I'll come back to your bar sometime."

He nodded. "I'd like that—and I'll have a cup of tea waiting for you. Have a good night, Gemma. Oh, let me get that door for you."

Ian opened his car door, then rushed around to the other side. He opened Gemma's door for her before she stepped out. As she went to close it, her fingers brushed against Ian's. She felt those familiar butterflies again but he jumped back like he had gotten burned.

"Are you all right?" Gemma asked.

Ian laughed nervously, shutting the door. "Yeah, yeah—I'm fine. Just chilly out here. See you around."

He rushed back to his side of the car, then hopped in and drove off. She found his behavior strange as she entered the apartment building but shook her head. Ian had seemed so into her—so keen to know more. But why had he jumped back when their hands finally touched?

With a sigh, Gemma walked toward the elevator and

pressed the button. She had been a fool to think she was going to find love on the surface world. That was only for the lucky few—like Princess Esme—not for an average, boring girl like her. The elevator arrived a second later, then Gemma stepped inside. It was almost surreal that she was up on the surface, in an elevator, riding in cars. How her life had changed in the last 24 hours.

"Hold the elevator, please!"

Gemma held out a hand, stopping the elevator from closing. A woman in her thirties in jeans and a t-shirt stepped on. She had dark hair, freckles, and green eyes. A little girl followed, around ten or eleven, wearing a pink skirt with a yellow top and carrying a chocolate ice cream in her hand.

"Thank you," the woman said to Gemma, then pressed a button on the wall.

Gemma nodded as the little girl looked up at her with wide eyes. She had hair as red as a rose, her skin soft like porcelain. "Wow ... Mom, look. A real-life princess. With hair just like mine!"

When Gemma wondered what she was talking about, the woman turned to her. "My daughter means your dress. She thinks you look like a princess."

Gemma laughed, shaking her head. "Oh, no, no, no—not a princess. Never me. I just really like dresses."

"It's beautiful," the little girl said, eyeing it as she licked her ice cream. "Mom, can I get a dress just like that?"

The woman ruffled the girl's hair. "Sure, sweetie."

Gemma smiled at the little girl and gestured to her wrist. "That's a pretty bracelet you have on."

The girl's brow furrowed. "This? It's my hospital bracelet."

"Hospital bracelet?" Of course. Gemma had seen them on television, but they didn't have them in Fairhaven. She just couldn't stop putting her foot in her mouth.

The woman held out her hand, a tight smile on her lips. "Say, I don't believe we've met. I'm Carly Brenton."

"Gemma Solace," she replied, shaking her hand. "I just got here today. I'm staying at a friend's apartment while exploring the city. I'm actually not from Toronto."

"Really? Well, I think you'll like the city. Always something fun to do." The woman gestured at the little girl. "This is my daughter, Abigail. But everyone calls her Abby."

"Hi," the little girl said, still licking her ice cream.

"Nice to meet you both," Gemma said. "It's awfully late. What are you two still doing up?"

Carly hesitated, staring down at her daughter. "We just got back from the hospital, actually—"

When the elevator jostled, the ice cream went flying out of the little's girl hands. It fell onto Gemma's dress and splattered across the fabric. Carly gasped, picking up the ice cream.

"Oh no! I'm so sorry," she said, reaching into her pocket to pull out some tissues. "I have some Kleenex right here to clean you up."

Carly tried patting the ice cream out of Gemma's dress, but she only ended up smearing it even more. They both knew it was going to stain. If Gemma had been in Fairhaven, she would've had her fairy godmother clean it up with a simple spell. It seemed she'd have to do laundry in the real world.

"Your pretty dress," Abigail murmured. "I'm so sorry."

Gemma shook her head, forcing a smile. "Really—It's all right. I have plenty more. Don't worry about it at all."

Thanks to the fairy godmothers' magical potions, Gemma could fit dozens of dresses in her suitcase. They came out neatly one at a time when she unzipped it. She knew Abigail would've found that exciting—if only she could've told her.

Sometimes, the secret of Fairhaven could be a burden.

Carly nodded, stuffing the ice-cream-covered tissue back in her pocket. "Thank you, that's kind."

When the elevator arrived on their floor, it dinged. Carly gestured for her daughter to step off. Gemma waved as they headed out. "No worries. I hope to see you two again."

Carly smiled, her hand on her daughter's shoulder. "We'd like that. Have a good evening, Gemma."

As she thanked them, the two walked off, heading down the hallway. Despite the ice cream smeared across her dress, that interaction had gone well. Maybe Gemma would have friends on the surface world like Princess Esme had in no time.

When the elevator arrived on her floor, she stepped off, then followed the familiar hallway to Noah's apartment. She unlocked it with her key and entered. The stove was still in the same spot, singed and dirty. At least the smell of smoke was gone from opening the windows.

"I'm back," Gemma said to the stove. "And I won't let you stop me again. Everyone's going to see what Gemma Solace can do."

After that little talk with the stove, Gemma locked the door and headed for bed. She changed out of her messy dress and into the pajamas she had brought. She fell asleep on the couch, then her eyes opened to sunlight.

The city was loud and boisterous out the window, something Gemma wasn't used to. Fairhaven had always been so quiet. As she stretched and yawned, then put on another dress in the shade of emerald green, she glanced out the window. Hundreds of people were on their way to work and school, honking at each other in their cars, and construction workers drilling in the distance made Gemma's teeth rattle.

It wasn't anything like home. Back in Fairhaven, there were no intersections, cars, or traffic. The fairy godmothers made sure of that. Toronto was louder, crowded, and had less magic, but maybe that was what Gemma needed. Something different —and a challenge.

When her stomach grumbled, sounding like a roaring dragon in her tummy, Gemma knew she had to make something. She pulled out the cookbook that Princess Esme had given her and carefully read the instructions. She finally decided on cereal, something that she had seen eaten in many human TV shows. It required no effort and she safely made it without causing another fire.

The food wasn't as good as back home without all the magic potions to spice it up, but it was something to soothe her hungry stomach. Once she finished, she washed the dishes after reading the guidebook again, then a knock sounded on the door. When she opened it, two burly men in uniforms stood there with a clipboard and a new stove.

"Is this the apartment of Noah Crawford?" one of the men asked. "He asked for a stove to be delivered to this address. As soon as possible."

Gemma nodded, stepping aside. "Yes, it is. You can take the old stove away too. It kind of ... went up in flames."

The men shared a look, then entered the apartment. Gemma watched from the doorway as they hooked up the new stove and took the old one away. It had been her biggest obstacle so far—but she was determined to conquer it.

If only she could rub it in her drunken fairy godmother's face.

It took the workers about thirty minutes to finish, something that could've been done much quicker with magic back home. Thinking about Fairhaven, she then remembered her dirty dress. After ushering the men out the door, she picked up the dress and found a laundry card sitting on Noah's coffee table. She wandered until she located the communal laundry room just down the hall. Then she figured out how to do the laundry by knocking on a neighbor's door and asking for advice. Struggling to understand a world without magic, she finally got the basics after twenty minutes and thanked the neighbor.

The washing machine cycle said it would take an hour, and Gemma didn't want to stand around for that long. So, she got into the elevator, then rode it down to Carly's floor.

When she stepped out, she headed down the hallway, finding Carly leaving her apartment with Abigail. She was fixing her daughter's backpack while the little girl played with some video game device. Just as she was about to say hello, a man came out of the apartment behind them and gave Carly a kiss.

Gemma almost gasped. She recognized the man—he had been her taxi driver. The same one who had wanted to take her out on a date.

He was wearing a wedding ring now, dressed casually for another day at work. Gemma didn't recall him wearing it before, so he must've removed it for work to hit on women. She made a face, thinking it was pretty low of him. Despite recognizing the building where she was going, and knowing the risk of his wife finding out, he had flirted with her anyway—so brazen and inappropriate. Did these humans not believe in loyalty? Or was he so despicable that he didn't care?

He placed his arm around Carly's shoulder and walked the two of them to the elevator. Gemma hid behind the corner to watch them. And she was pretty certain the man hadn't been wearing a ring when he was driving her around and flirting with her.

"I'm going to be at the dance studio all day, then Abby has another appointment tonight. Same hospital," Carly said, pressing a button on the elevator. "I know you're busy with work, but I'm supposed to have a late client. A man who wants to learn how to dance before his wedding. Do you think you can drive Abby to her appointment? I can meet you two there when I'm done work."

The taxi driver—who seemed to be Carly's husband and Abigail's father—frowned. "Oh, I don't know. It gets really hectic in the day. I'm not sure I'll have time."

"No time? But Abby needs these treatments." Carly huffed. "Come on, John, you haven't even taken her once. I'm not asking for much—"

"Hey, don't get mad at me! I haven't done anything wrong. Besides, what's this with you working with a male client?" John crossed his arms. "Not sure I like the sound of that. What if he tries to hit on you?"

Carly shook her head. "You're unbelievable. Nothing is going on."

Abigail placed her hands over her ears, trying to block out her parents' argument as the elevator doors closed. Gemma couldn't hear the rest of their conversation—but it definitely sounded like trouble in paradise. Did Carly know that her husband was flirting on the job?

She would have to tell her. As hard as that was going to be.

CHAPTER 6

Once the washing and drying had finished, Gemma took her dress out, examining it on the table. The dress was a bit wrinkly, but like magic, the stain from Abigail's ice cream had washed right out. Maybe those washer things weren't so bad after all.

"And I did it all by myself with no disaster," Gemma whispered, smiling. "I think I'm starting to get the hang of this human thing."

She picked up her dress, carrying it down the hallway back to Noah's apartment. When she entered, she placed it in her suitcase, then glanced out the window. Gemma still felt bad that Carly's husband had flirted with her—even though she had done nothing wrong.

Gemma would have to find a gentle way to tell her the truth. Nothing hurt worse than finding out your love was behaving inappropriately behind your back. She assumed, of course, thanks to all those heartbreak plots in the fantasy romance novels she had read.

Wanting to find her mother but not knowing where to start, she needed something to do in the meantime. There had to be some fun activities in Toronto to get her used to the city. Thanks to the money Princess Esme had given her, she could afford to do some of them. But she didn't want to completely rely on the princess. She wanted her own money—to be proud of herself for earning something.

"How do I get money?" she asked herself. "I'll need more than what Princess Esme and Noah gave me. For rent, for food, and to find my mother."

When she looked out the window again, she saw more people driving away for work. Some of them were dressed in doctor's outfits, mail carrier clothes, and fancy suits. She already had nice clothes—now she just needed a job.

"Guess I'm getting one of those," she murmured. "Just like Princess Esme did. If she can do this, so can I."

After stuffing the paper bills deep into her pocket, she left Noah's apartment and locked the door before heading down to the lobby. It was mostly empty with everyone off to work and school. She walked out of the building, squinting underneath the hot sun as she wandered down the street.

When she saw a HELP WANTED sign in the window of a small restaurant, she opened the door, entering. There were a few tables and chairs with a counter where an older man in his late sixties stood. Behind him, pizzas were cooking in fancy pizza ovens. Gemma sniffed the air and her mouth watered. She had read about pizza in a novel once and it sounded so good that she knew she wanted to try one.

"Welcome to Luigi's Pizzeria," the man said. "My name is Luigi De Luca, the owner. How can I help you?"

Gemma pointed at the sign in the window. "I need one of those job things."

The old man looked her up and down. "You sure you want to work in that outfit? Might get a bit messy. You'll need to put on a uniform."

"Okay, that's fine."

"Good, good. You have experience making pizzas before?"

Gemma winced. "Um, not really. I've read about them in books, though. If that helps."

"It does not." He folded his arms across his chest.

She shifted, glancing down at her dress. Maybe she should have taken her friends' advice and had some jeans made for her. "Oh. Well, um, do you think you can show me the basics?"

He hesitated so long, Gemma thought he'd turn her away, then finally, "I'll try my best. We'll have to be quick—I have my grandson's recital in an hour and my other employee called in sick. Thank goodness you showed up." The old man opened the door that led into the kitchen. "Come on in, your shift starts now. Your name is?"

"Gemma. Gemma Solace. You know, I don't think I've ever had pizza before."

The old man shook his head, looking skeptical. "Never had pizza? Lord, help us."

For the next twenty minutes, the man ran through the basics of making pizza. He showed Gemma how to roll the dough and where to find the ingredients in the kitchen. She was then instructed to oil and put pizza sauce on, then add whatever toppings the customers ordered. Gemma also received a quick crash course with the cash register and Luigi counted the money inside.

It was overwhelming, but Gemma was trying her best.

"You'll want to familiarize yourself with our menu," the old man said, grabbing one and handing it to Gemma. "We serve basic pizzas—pepperoni, Canadian, deluxe. That kinda stuff."

Gemma wasn't sure what those terms meant but she nodded. "Okay, I think I understand. Anything else?"

The old man reached into a cupboard, pulling out a uniform. "Yeah, put this on. Looks to be about your size. That big dress doesn't really belong in a kitchen anyway. Good luck —I gotta get going now. Don't burn the place down."

Gemma hoped she wouldn't, not having had the best luck with stoves.

The old man grabbed his keys, then scurried out of the restaurant. Gemma was all by herself—only her and her anxious thoughts. She went into the bathroom, quickly changing into the uniform. She was glad to have it, noticing some pizza sauce splotches on her dress. She'd need that washer and dryer again. The uniform was a black shirt with matching pants and a pizza logo on the breast pocket. It came with a matching hat that smelled like old pizza.

"Well, it's different from what I usually wear, but this'll do," she murmured to herself in the bathroom mirror. "Pants feel ... weird. How do you move in these?'

After doing some lunges and squats, Gemma got the hang of them. Even though she missed her pretty dresses. She forced a smile and tried to give herself a pep talk. "Gemma Solace, pizza chef, coming through!"

When she opened the door with her dress in hand and headed into the dining area of the restaurant, she found three teenagers snickering near the cash register. They looked to be around fourteen or fifteen and were carrying backpacks. She quickly tucked her dress in a cubby in the kitchen before walking out to greet them.

"Um, hello," Gemma said, heading toward the register. "Are you here to place an order?"

"We were just looking around," one of the kids said, his gaze darting to the front door and back.

Gemma's gut churned with unease.

The boys shared a weighted look, then headed toward the door. The first boy said, "See you."

"Wait, don't you want some pizza?"

They had already made it to the door, leaving the restaurant. Gemma sighed. Was business always going to be this slow?

Ten minutes later, after tapping her nails on the counter and waiting for anyone to show up, the door opened again with a chime. A frantic-looking man in his mid-forties entered. His eyes lit up when he saw Gemma, then he rushed toward the register.

"Oh, thank God you're open," he muttered. "Hey, where's Luigi? He's usually here running the place."

"He had his grandson's recital," Gemma explained. "He left me in charge. Is there something I can do for you?"

The man nodded, pulling a long list out of his pocket. "Yes—I could really use the help. You see, my wife asked me to call ahead and place a pizza order. Her grade five class is having a pizza party for lunch, and I promised her I'd pick them up."

Gemma knew the feeling of anxiousness very well, and the man was the perfect embodiment of it. She nodded and took the list. "It's okay, sir—take a deep breath. Everything will be all right."

She was trying to convince herself of that too. After her fiasco with the stove, she really wanted to prove to herself she could do this.

He took a deep breath, then exhaled. "Yeah, okay. Maybe you're right. I just don't want to let my wife down. Anyway, do you think you could make ten large pizzas as fast as you can? I wrote down all the different orders."

Gemma glanced down at the list, reading what the man had written. He wanted four pepperoni pizzas, two vegetarian, three Hawaiian, and one Canadian. Gemma briefly looked over the nearby menu to see what they contained and nodded.

"I think I can do this," she said. "Have a seat. I'll get started right away."

"Oh, thank you, thank you!" the man cried. "You've made my day."

He took a seat, scrolling through his phone as Gemma entered the kitchen with the list and the menu. She stared into the pizza oven with hesitation. Could she do this?

That man out there—and Luigi, the owner—were counting on her, so she had no choice. She picked up some dough and got started on making the pepperoni pizzas first.

Forty minutes later, after many mishaps, tears of frustration, and burnt pizzas, all ten were ready—thanks to the multiple pizza ovens and plentiful ingredients—and Gemma was covered in sauce splotches and flour dust. She was grateful Luigi had given her a uniform.

After placing the pizzas in boxes, she walked toward the cash register, finding the man still seated at one of the tables. He looked up with a smile before he rose to his feet and walked over. Gemma set the ten pizzas on the counter in a tall tower.

"Oh my gosh, you did it!" he cried, opening the top box. "Mmm, smells delicious. You did a fantastic job, thank you. How much do I owe you?"

"Let's see ... it's fourteen dollars for a medium pizza, times ten." Gemma quickly read through the menu prices to make sure she was right, then fiddled with the register. "Sorry, let me figure out the buttons. It's my first day. Okay, then add tax ... it'll be a hundred and sixty dollars."

"Good thing I went to the bank before this. Damn inflation prices." The man reached into his pocket, pulling out a wallet. He placed a bunch of cash down on the counter. "Here you go— and a nice tip for helping me. Thank you."

"My pleasure. Have a good day!"

As the man nodded and picked up the boxes, he smiled at Gemma before leaving. She felt pretty good about herself. She had succeeded at yet another task and even made a tip.

She pocketed the tip money, then placed the rest for the pizza in the cash register. But as she opened it, the bills Luigi had counted were gone. Where had all the money gone?

She put the man's payment in the till, then wandered into the backroom. Luigi had shown her the surveillance system before he left. She figured out how to rewind the footage. It was strange watching herself carrying her uniform—like she was a star she'd seen in human movies. Then she came across the teenage boys from earlier.

And she gasped as they reached behind the register, taking all the money they could fit in their pockets while she was changing in the bathroom. No wonder they had been snickering when she had come out. They were thieves—and at such a young age.

Gemma turned the footage off, feeling sick to her stomach. She'd almost had a perfect day at work if it weren't for those boys. How was she going to break the news to Luigi?

She rushed back to the cash register, not wanting to repeat her mistake. She waited by the counter for another half an hour until the door opened with a chime. Luigi entered, followed by a boy around nine or ten.

"... and you did so well, buddy," Luigi was telling him. "Your old Pop is very proud of you."

The boy beamed. "Thank you! Can I have my pizza now?"

The old man laughed, deep and hearty. "Of course, you can. Come on."

Gemma winced as Luigi walked toward the register, followed by the boy. She cleared her throat and decided to just tell him. "Um, sir ... I have some bad news."

Luigi frowned. "What is it? You didn't burn down the kitchen, did you?"

Not this time.

"Uh, no. Something else. When I went into the bathroom to

change into my uniform, some teenage boys stopped by. I didn't notice until another customer came in, but … they stole a lot of money from the register. It's on camera too. I'm so sorry."

Luigi's face dropped. "What? Stay here."

He ran into the backroom, playing the footage for himself. The little boy looked up at Gemma, and she forced a smile.

Luigi ran back into the dining area, shaking his head. "No, no, no … this is awful! How could you leave the register unattended like that?"

"I'm so sorry. I had no idea the money would be stolen."

Things like that just didn't happen in Fairhaven. It seemed Gemma was going to have to get used to the idea that humans were thieves and couldn't be trusted.

Luigi sighed. "Thankfully the rest of my money is still in my safe, but this is terrible. If I can't trust you to watch over the restaurant while I'm gone, then I'm afraid you can't work here anymore. I'm sorry."

Gemma nodded, removing her hat. "I understand. And I'm very sorry. Let me change out of this uniform."

She grabbed her dress from the cubby, then walked into the bathroom, removing the uniform and putting her dress back on. Gemma was grateful to finally be back in the dress—it felt familiar and comforting, like a warm hug. She then walked out and handed the clothes to Luigi. He took them, handing her money in return.

"Here, for a day's work," he said. "Thank you for your help. Good luck in your job hunt."

Gemma took the money as the little boy watched her, then headed toward the door and walked out into the street. At least she had made some money—giving her a chance to try some activities—but she was disappointed in herself. Again.

Why couldn't anything just go right?

As if on cue, thunder roared in the distance. A gray cloud

began to lightly spritz rain on her head. She sighed, throwing a hand up to avoid it from pelting her hair and continued trying to find a job.

She eventually found a hardware store down the block that was hiring. They thought it was odd she wore a ballgown but Gemma promised she'd use their uniform if she was hired. Gemma was put through an interview first with a tall man— the manager—who kept looking at her breasts. When he licked his lips at her, she'd had enough.

"I need a job, but not this badly," she said, rising to her feet in his office. "You're a disgusting creep. Goodbye."

His mouth dropped open and he gaped as she scurried out of his office. Who knew finding a job in the human world would be so difficult? In Fairhaven, everyone was given a job that best-suited their needs. No one was left behind.

But the surface? Things were different here. *Too* different.

Trying one last time, she found a call center in a tall building up ahead. It seemed simple enough when the lady who was hiring people brought her to a desk and explained the rules. She even complimented Gemma's dress, making her hope this was meant to be.

"All you do is pick up the phone, call someone from this phonebook here, and ask them survey questions," she said, showing Gemma the buttons. "That's what our company does. Go ahead—call someone. I'd like to see you in action."

Gemma nodded, taking a deep breath before picking up the phone. She dialed a random number from the phonebook and waited for it to ring. A few seconds later, a gruff-sounding man picked up the phone.

"Yeah?" he answered. "Who the hell is this?"

Not off to a great start.

"Um, hello. My name is Gemma. I'm with a survey company." Gemma cleared her throat. "I'm calling to ask you a few questions—"

"You listen to me," the man snarled, "I'm sick of you telemarketers! If you call me one more time, I'm gonna hunt you down and kick your ass. You understand?"

Gemma was speechless. Before she could find the words, the man hung up. She put down the phone and turned to the woman. "I'm sorry, but I don't think this job is for me. I don't really like talking on the phone. Especially when people are so rude."

The lady nodded, sadly. "I understand. Good luck finding a job that suits your needs."

At this rate, Gemma was going to need *all* the luck in the world.

As the hiring lady walked away to coach someone else, Gemma looked down at the phonebook, noticing the thousands of numbers in there. Was it possible she would find her mother after all this time?

She browsed through the listings, though she didn't see Katherine Solace. And she wasn't sure what her mother was going by these days. What if she had changed her name? Or moved out of Toronto entirely? Her mother could be far away by now, living a new life in another country. Gemma sighed and closed the book.

Did her mother ever miss Gemma, like Gemma missed her mother? Did she regret sympathizing with a man like Senator Remus? Gemma had so many questions. And if she never found her mother again, they would go unanswered forever.

Before her mother allied herself with Senator Remus, things were amazing. Growing up, her mother read Gemma to sleep, cooked dinner, and ate with the family. They went on hikes and strolls across Fairhaven together. Gemma wanted that back so badly—to be a family again—but right now, those memories seemed so far away.

She rose to her feet, collecting her things before leaving the building. It was still drizzling as Gemma took cover under a nearby awning. The pizza shop owner had given her forty dollars, add that to the twenty-dollar tip, and she had a good start, but she'd eventually need more. Not just for activities around town, but also for groceries and finding her mother.

"Come on, there's gotta be one job I'm good at!" she cried to the sky, making people walking by stare at her. "This can't be it. Can it?"

As Gemma trudged down the sidewalk, cursing her bad luck, a cloud parted above her head. It sent a streak of light down onto a small building at the end of the road. As her eyes adjusted to the sign above the door, she couldn't believe her luck.

The sign read ENCHANTED TALES BOOKSTORE. And there was a hiring sign in the window, covered by tall books on either side. She grinned widely, an excited squeal ripping its way out of her throat.

Gemma had hit the jackpot.

As she ran down the street, heading toward the bookstore, a car drove by and splashed the nearby puddle onto her dress. Soaking wet and frustrated, Gemma hoped that bookstore would be the job of her dreams.

She was sick of struggling in the human world.

CHAPTER 7

Gemma reached the door of the bookstore, soaking wet and panting, but she made it. And only an hour before closing time. When she opened the door, a bell rang overhead, and she stepped into heaven.

White and blue walls stole her attention, with hand-drawn characters from popular books. Dozens of shelves lined with new books had that earthy, fragrant smell, making Gemma stop and inhale the aroma for a few seconds. Light jazz music played overhead and a female voice spoke up.

"Hello there, can I help you?"

Gemma turned, noticing an older woman standing near the cash register. She held an open romance novel in one hand, and a pile of books stood on the table beside her. She looked to be in her mid-sixties with graying hair, a blue dress, and red lipstick.

"Um, hi," Gemma began, approaching the desk. "I saw your help wanted sign in the window. Are you still looking?"

The old lady nodded, putting her book face down on the counter, place marked. "I certainly am. Do you have any experience working in a bookstore?"

"Not a store, no. But I worked at a library back home. I live and breathe books."

The woman smiled, holding out a hand. "Now that's what I like to hear. What's your name? I'm Barbara Danvers."

"Gemma Solace," she replied, dripping water onto the tiled floor. "Sorry—I got sprayed by a puddle on the way here."

"Oh, you poor dear. Wait here—I'll get a towel to dry you off."

Gemma nodded, browsing the books on the desk as Barbara flitted into the back office. She came back a few seconds later and wrapped a large towel around Gemma's shoulders. As Gemma dried off, wiping down her dress, she found the old lady staring at her with a smile.

"What is it? Is there something on my face?" Gemma asked.

Barbara laughed, shaking her head. "No, no, dear—you look great. I love your dress. It's just ... you remind me so much of my daughter, Mackenzie. Even down to your red hair. She loved dressing up too, especially as a child."

Gemma handed the towel back. "Really? I'll have to meet this doppelganger then."

Barbara's face fell as she took the towel. "I'm afraid you can't. My darling girl passed away six months ago. She was a soldier who was killed in action."

"Oh. Oh, no." Gemma paused, fearing she had said something wrong. "I'm so sorry for your loss."

Barbara looked down. "Thank you—It's been very difficult. For me *and* my grandson. He's not the same since she passed. He's been acting out, getting into trouble. It's been very hard."

"I bet. Do you have a partner to help you through?"

"No, sadly. My daughter's passing put a strain on our marriage. We divorced just last month. I haven't seen him at all —and neither has my grandson. And my daughter's husband serves in the military too, so he's always away on duty and never calls. Me and my grandson are really all we have."

Gemma felt so bad for the old lady and her grandson. She wished there was some way she could cheer her up.

"Well, I'm really sorry. I sort of lost my mother, actually. So, I understand loss very well."

"Then I'm sorry for your loss as well." The old lady sniffled, then put the towel down. "And I'm sorry to put all that on you. It did feel good to talk about it, though. Anyway, let's go into my office and interview you for the position."

Gemma nodded, following Barbara into the small office. She sat across from her as she brought up some interview questions on her computer. They were simple—Barbara just wanted to know about Gemma's experience, her knowledge of the filing system, and how many books she had read.

"Oh, tons," Gemma said with a smile. "Books are my closest friends. Romantic fantasy is my favorite, actually. I get my love of books from my mother."

"Funny coincidence—I do too. Well, that concludes our interview. I think you'd be a great employee. I haven't had any other applications, actually. I guess no one wants to work at a bookstore these days."

"Their loss. They don't know what they're missing."

"Exactly. Now, let's talk about payment. Can I have your social insurance number? And what bank are you with? Where should I send your earnings?"

Gemma shifted nervously in her seat. "I, uh, I'm still working on getting a social insurance number and all that stuff. Long story. Could you just pay me in cash? That would be the best way."

"Of course, whatever you need. Are you … are you in some kind of trouble? Do you need my help to get on your feet?"

Gemma laughed nervously. "That's sweet of you, but no. Just new to town and still setting things up."

"Got it." Barbara rose to her feet. "Would you be able to start right away? I do need some help around here. Only an hour before closing and I need to finish up some things."

"Yes, absolutely. What do you need me to do?"

Barbara led her out of the office, then showed Gemma around the bookstore. All the books were neatly organized by genre and alphabetized. All Gemma had to do was make sure they stayed that way, sweep the floors, and put more books on the shelves while Barbara handled the more complicated cataloging. Barbara watched Gemma work for a moment and nodded.

"You're very good at this," she said. "I have no doubt you'll do a great job. I'll be at the front desk if you need me."

Gemma nodded, returning to work. She let her mind wander as she stocked the shelves with new books. Being surrounded by them made her feel like she was back home in Fairhaven. She thanked her lucky stars that the bookstore had been hiring, giving her the perfect job.

In the hour before closing time, a few customers came in. Gemma helped them out and sent them in the right direction. Barbara rang them up as Gemma swept the floors, making sure the bookstore stayed neat and tidy. She was finally enjoying her time on the surface.

When the bell rang again, Gemma lifted her head, noticing a boy around fifteen entering the bookstore. She recognized him immediately. He was one of the boys from the pizza parlor—the one who had stolen from the cash register. With her broom in hand, Gemma followed the boy, making sure he didn't have a chance to steal anything here.

Now that she had found her dream job, she was going to work as hard as she could to make sure she didn't lose it.

She watched from behind a tall bookshelf of fantasy novels as the young boy approached the cash register. Barbara was still there, reading a book. As he got closer, Barbara put the book down and blinked at the kid.

"What are you doing here?" she asked, checking her watch. "Didn't Mr. Brennan give you detention after school for that fire alarm stunt you pulled last week? You should still be there right now."

"Whatever, Nana. Detention is stupid anyway."

Nana? Gemma raised an eyebrow, surprised that the young boy was Barbara's grandson. She *had* said that her grandson had been acting out since his mother's death. Poor kid.

Barbara sighed. "We talked about this, Jake. You need to do better—"

"Yeah, yeah. Look, I came here to get some money. My friends want to go to the arcade."

"On one condition." Barbara reached into her pocket, pulling out a few dollar bills. She handed it to the boy who eagerly took the money. "Promise me you'll go to the detention tomorrow, at least. Or no more arcade money."

"Fine."

"Good. I'll be calling Mr. Brennan to make sure. Now, don't stay there too long, all right? You still have some homework from last night to finish. School comes first."

The boy rolled his eyes. "Whatever. See you later."

As he walked to the door, Barbara shook her head and focused on the book. Gemma set her broom aside and rushed after him. When he stepped outside, grinning at the money in his hand, Gemma followed and reached for his shoulder.

"Hey! Get the hell off me," Jacob snarled, turning around.

"It's all right, Jacob. My name is Gemma—I'm a friend of your grandmother's," Gemma said. "I just got a job at her bookstore. And we need to talk."

Jacob scoffed, putting the money in his pocket. "About what? I don't even know you. And my friends are waiting for me."

Gemma looked over his shoulder, noticing a couple of boys across the street. They were the same ones who had stolen the money from the pizza parlor along with Jacob.

"This won't take long. Don't I look familiar?" Gemma asked. "I'm pretty sure I still smell like pizza."

Jacob took a second, then blinked. "Oh ... you were working at Luigi's, weren't you?"

Gemma nodded as she crossed her arms. "That's right. And I know what you and your friends did, Jacob. Luigi was so upset that he fired me. You need to return the money you stole."

"Can't. We already spent it on McDonalds."

Gemma scoffed. "Then you'll have to work to pay it off. Or I'm going to march back in there and tell your grandmother what you did."

"No! Please, don't. My Nana ... she's been through a lot. I don't want her to know."

"I can see why. She told me she lost her daughter—your mother. I'm very sorry. I have no doubt this is a hard time for you."

Jacob sneered. "What do you know? You didn't know my mother at all. You don't understand."

"I lost my mother too, Jacob. I know the feeling of emptiness it brings—the anger, the pain. We're more alike than you think." Gemma shook her head. "But really, you have to pay back Luigi at some point. He's a nice man who didn't deserve to be stolen from. I know you're hurting because of your mother's death, but you have to stop acting out. It's not helping you *or* your grandmother."

Just when she thought she might get through to the boy, Jacob backed up. "Just leave me alone, okay? I don't need this."

He took off, running to catch up with his friends. They greeted him with smiles when he showed them the money his grandmother had given him. As they walked off, Gemma shook her head.

So much for getting through to the boy.

She turned, heading back inside the bookstore. Barbara looked up from the desk and frowned. "Oh, Gemma—there you are. I thought you were sweeping?"

"I am, Ms. Danvers. I just wanted to meet your grandson."

"Please, call me Barbara. And you met Jacob, hmm?" Barbara sighed, glancing out the nearby window. "That boy is a handful. I hope he was polite, at least."

Gemma debated telling Barbara the truth about him stealing from the pizza parlor, but she didn't want to upset her. That woman had been through enough. And she wanted to give Jacob the chance to be honest and make up for his mistake.

"He was fine," Gemma said, reaching for her broom. "I'll get back to work now."

For the rest of the time before closing, Gemma cleaned up and put books away while helping the customers find what they were looking for. Barbara was very impressed with her work ethic. She shared her dinner with Gemma, enjoying some sandwiches and tea she had made in the office.

"Have you ever been married, Gemma?" Barbara asked, pouring tea for her. "Any kids?"

"Oh, no," Gemma said with a blush as she reached for her cup. "No kids. I've had a few crushes here and there, but I've never been in love. I'm way too anxious and shy for that."

Barbara smiled, nibbling on a cracker. "Well, don't give up. You're beautiful and intelligent. Any man would be lucky to have you. Trust me, the anxiety will get better as you age. I had some when I was a young girl too—ages ago. And it got better for me. Maybe it'll be true for you?"

"I hope so. What about you? Have you considered falling in love again after divorcing your husband?"

Barbara sighed. "Not really, no. I just don't think it's in the cards for me. Right now, I'm looking after my little bookstore and my grandson. The two most important things in my life."

"I get that. My father is doing the same—looking after me and working hard. He's a talented musician, actually. Ever since my mother left, he's really thrown himself into his work."

Barbara looked intrigued. "A musician? Sounds interesting. He must be a lovely man. From what I can tell in the brief time since I met you, I know he raised an amazing daughter."

Gemma smiled. "Thank you. I'm really glad you were hiring here."

"Me too."

As they finished dinner, footsteps entered the shop. Gemma craned her neck to see who it was. It wasn't Jacob like she thought, but a *very* familiar face. Ian.

He headed straight for the sign that read FANTASY ROMANCE and began browsing the shelves. Barbara rose to her feet, collecting the scraps from their dinner.

"Another customer," she said. "I'll go see what he's looking for."

"Let me." Gemma stood, trying to suppress a smile. "I can handle this."

Barbara nodded, throwing out their napkins as Gemma walked out of the office. She approached Ian who was flipping through the pages of a romantic fantasy novel. Exactly the kind Gemma would've chosen.

"That's a good one," she said as she walked up behind him. "You won't be disappointed."

Ian spun around, noticing Gemma with a smile. "Gemma! What are you doing here?"

"I work here. Just got a job here today, actually."

"Really? Huh. That's a funny coincidence." Ian clutched the book at his side. "Because this is my favorite bookstore. I come in here all the time."

All these meetings with Ian—and now the bookstore itself—were beginning to feel like fate. And Gemma didn't mind it one bit.

"Well, that's good to know. Get used to seeing me—I'll be working here a lot."

"I have no problem with that." Ian held her gaze, grinning. Then he blushed and glanced down at the book. "Anyway, I was looking at this one. You recommend it, you said?"

Gemma nodded, walking him through the storyline and characters. Ian listened quietly and held her gaze. He was standing so close to her that she could smell his sandalwood cologne.

"... and I think you'll really like it," Gemma finished. "It's got a happy ending, some magic, and two people who love each other. What more do you need?"

"I'm sold," Ian said with a laugh. "I'll go pay for this. And I'll let you know what I think about it when I'm done."

"Sounds great—you know where I am."

He nodded, heading toward the cash register. Gemma got back to work but peeked around at him from the side of the shelf. He reached into his pocket, pulling out a wallet that was loaded with money and credit cards.

He paid for the book, then thanked Barbara for her help. Gemma liked that he was so polite and respectful. His eyes scanned the bookstore, landing on Gemma before he waved. She waved back as he headed toward the door.

Maybe something was brewing there—something special. Gemma hoped so after everything she had been through.

When she saw Barbara staring at her with a smile, she looked up. "What is it?"

"The way that man was looking at you … my goodness, you would've thought you were pure magic," Barbara said with a little giggle. "It was cute. He's a regular in here—always checking out the romance section. I have no doubt you'll see him again."

Gemma knew she would too. It felt like destiny, after all.

A second later, the door opened again. Gemma looked up just as Ian strode inside with the book in his hand. She frowned, hoping nothing was wrong as she walked toward him.

"Ian, is everything okay?"

"What? Oh, yeah—everything's good. Perfect, actually." He smiled. "I came back to see if maybe … you'd like to have dinner with me. Tomorrow night? We can talk about books a little more then. If you aren't busy, that is."

Gemma paused, her heart pounding. As interesting as she found Ian, anxiety prickled at her spine.

What if he leaves me like my mother did? The fear was so loud that it stung her ears. With Ian still staring at her with those dreamy eyes, she took a deep breath and gave her answer. The one without fear.

Gemma smiled. "I can definitely make that, yeah. Will you pick me up at my apartment? You already know where I live."

"Absolutely. Say, around six p.m.?"

"Sounds good to me. See you then, Ian."

He nodded, turning toward the door when he paused. "I usually don't do this, you know. Ask women out on dates who I just met. Not after … not after what I've been through."

Gemma sensed there was a story there but she didn't want to pry. If he wanted to, he'd tell her what he meant in due time.

"Anyway, just didn't want you to think I'm some player or something," Ian said, turning back to her with a smile. "That's not what this is about."

"Well, that's good to hear. I don't usually accept dates from men I just met. I don't want you to think I'm a player either."

"Trust me, that's not how I see you at all." Ian paused. "I've … been hurt in relationships before. Really, really hurt. And while the fear side of my brain is telling me to stay away … my heart really wants to see you again. If that makes sense."

Gemma nodded. "It definitely does. I don't have much experience in relationships, but … I've been abandoned before. By someone I loved more than anyone else. So I get the apprehension."

Ian smiled again. "Then I guess we'll have to conquer our fears together, eh? Anyway, I'll see you tomorrow night. Have a good evening."

Gemma thanked him, wishing him the same as she watched him go. She was still staring out the window as his sedan pulled away. When she turned around, Barbara was grinning again.

"I'm going to need all the details about tomorrow, just so you know," she said. "I want to live vicariously through you."

Gemma laughed. "Deal."

CHAPTER 8

Gemma watched the sunset from the window as she put away some newer books. The sky looked so beautiful—and Earth had some incredible views—when Gemma took the time to enjoy them. And she was finally able to, now that things were getting better.

Barbara walked toward the door, putting the CLOSED sign in the window. "Well, we should close up for the evening. It's getting late. And I want to make sure my grandson got home without causing trouble."

"Sounds good." Gemma finished putting another book on the shelf, then approached Barbara. "Your grandson ... he seems like a troublemaker. If you want, I can keep an eye on him for you. I know how it feels to lose a mother."

Barbara's eyes lit up. "Would you? That would be great, thank you. You're a lot younger than me, so maybe he'll relate to you better. Sometimes I don't know what I'll do with that boy."

"He's just hurting. I'm sure with time, he'll get much better."

"Here's hoping." Barbara smiled. "For being so lovely and

working very hard, I'd like to give you a special gift. Come with me."

With curious eyes, Gemma followed Barbara to the back of the store. They entered the office where Barbara reached under her desk. Gemma noticed something that made her worry —a half-empty bottle of booze. It sent off warning bells in her mind. Not wanting to pry, she didn't bring it up as Barbara reached into her desk and pulled out some cash. She didn't have much.

"Here you go," she said. "A welcome bonus."

Gemma shook her head. "Oh, no—I can't take that. It's very generous of you, but you should keep your money. All I want is an hourly wage, that's all."

"Beautiful and humble. They do still exist." Barbara divided half the money, handing it to Gemma. "Here—at least take this. For doing such a great job."

"Well ... all right." Gemma took the money, pocketing it in her dress. "Thank you, I really appreciate it."

"Of course. I'm not sure how much longer me *or* this bookstore will be around, so I figure if I have the money, I ought to give it to you now."

Gemma frowned. "What do you mean?"

Barbara hesitated, looking like she wanted to tell her something before she paused. "Never mind. It's not your problem. Anway, have a good evening, Gemma. I'll see you bright and early tomorrow morning for your shift."

Gemma nodded, looking forward to it. She grabbed her things and left the bookstore just as Barbara was locking up. With her apartment building only a few blocks away, it didn't take her long to get home. By then, the sun had mostly set, taking the rain and cloudy skies with it.

After Gemma entered her apartment building, she heard arguing. It was none other than Carly and her husband—the taximan. All they seemed to do was fight. Shaking her head, Gemma hopped onto the elevator and rode it up to her floor.

She hoped if she ever got married, it would be much happier than that.

Minding her own business, she walked down the hall, then unlocked the door to Noah's apartment. She quickly changed into her pajamas and collapsed on the couch, exhausted from walking and working all day. A knock on the door an hour later woke her up.

Tightening the robe around her body, Gemma stood and walked toward the door. She peered through the peephole and saw a familiar face. Her father.

She opened the door, beaming. "Papa, you came! I can't believe this."

Gemma threw herself into his arms, making him laugh and hug her back. "Yes, I did, Gemma. Very few of us ever leave Fairhaven, and our fairy godmother had her concerns, but I wanted to see how you're doing the second time around. I begged Noah to give me your address and a map of the city. I got lost a few times, but I made it in one piece. Is everything all right?"

"Better than all right, Papa. Come on in and I'll tell you everything."

"Good, good. I've never been to the human world before, so you'll have to teach me some things. This place is so huge and unfamiliar. But I must ask first … did you find your mother?"

Gemma sighed. "Not yet. But trust me, it's never far from my mind. Now, come on in. Feels a bit silly talking to you in the doorway."

Gemma opened the door a little wider, letting her father enter the apartment. They chatted while she made them both some tea. To her relief, her father had brought her food he had cooked himself.

"Just stew," he explained. "Nothing fancy. But I figured you might be hungry—and scared to cook again after that last time."

"After that last disaster, you mean." Gemma took a long slurp of the stew, then nodded in appreciation. "It's very tasty, Papa. With fresh Fairhaven mushrooms. Thank you."

He sat back on the couch. "You're very welcome, kiddo. Now, what's been going up on here since you've been gone?"

Gemma wiped her mouth with a napkin. "Where do I start? I've met so many people ..."

She began with Ian, then got around to Carly, her daughter, and Barbara. Gemma beamed when she talked about the bookstore.

"Well, you look very happy," her father said with a smile. "I love to see it. And this is a nice apartment."

"I know, right? Noah was kind to let me use it. I'll have to do something to thank him. Maybe bake him a cake—once I get used to that stove."

"Sounds perfect." Her father turned silent, looking down. "I had an ulterior motive for coming here, actually. I wanted to see you, yes, but I was curious if you'd even caught a glimpse of your mother?"

Gemma shook her head, finishing her stew. "I haven't, Papa. I'm sorry. I tried to look her up, but I haven't found anything yet. As you said, the human world is huge. It could take a while. And truthfully, I'm not even sure where to start looking. It's a bit overwhelming, so I need time to think. In the meantime, I'm trying to get set up here."

"Ah, I see. I don't mean to pester you, of course. I understand this must be difficult for you." His eyebrows furrowed, his mouth turning down at the corners. "I just ... I miss her so much. All the time we spent together, her laugh, her warmth.

And then she met Senator Remus and was poisoned by his lies. That's when it all fell apart."

"I know." Gemma sighed. "I hate that man."

"Yes, I do too. I don't know, perhaps it's best if we never speak to her again. She chose her path, after all. People who look up to Senator Remus are too dangerous to live in Fairhaven."

Her poor father. He sounded like he was trying to convince himself that he was better off without his wife, but he was doing a poor job of it. "I'm not so sure, Papa. We must give her a chance to explain herself, at least. And before I left Fairhaven, I went to see the senator," Gemma replied, making her father's eyes widen. "Don't worry. I was safe. There was a guard there the whole time. Anyway, he said his plan wasn't over yet. That he still had tricks up his sleeve, especially as the one-year anniversary of his capture rolls around. Do you think he was telling the truth or just trying to scare me? That perhaps Mother is even involved somehow?"

"Hmm. He must be bluffing. There's no way he can escape from that prison. Princess Esme personally made sure of it." Her father shook his head. "The Senator's a liar and a jerk. I wouldn't pay much attention."

"Yeah, you're probably right. Still, Papa, be careful. Watch out for anything suspicious."

He smiled. "I could tell you the same thing, my brave girl. But it looks like you're doing well. I'm so very proud of you."

That brought a smile to Gemma's face. And if she were being honest, she was proud of herself too. She never thought her anxiety would let her come to the surface—and not just survive but thrive. It had been something that had plagued Gemma her entire life, pulling her down, but breaking through her shell was helping.

She was slowly becoming a whole other person, someone

more capable and confident. Step by step, day by day. She just needed to believe in herself and breathe.

"Thanks, Papa. How's Fairy Godmother Blanche holding up? She still drinking?"

"Of course," he said, snorting. "But she's doing well. I think she does miss you, in her own way."

"Hmm. If you say so. Anyway, how long can you stay? Do you have time to watch a movie? We can have a little sleepover."

He grinned. "With you? Of course, kiddo."

For the rest of the night, Gemma put movies on the television, taking some time to figure out the buttons. They watched Disney movies for the first time and loved them. Gemma fell asleep on the couch shortly after, feeling safe and comfortable around her father.

By the time the morning rolled around, the sunlight peeking through Noah's curtains, Gemma opened her eyes. She couldn't find her father anywhere around the apartment. When she stepped into the kitchen, she saw a handwritten note left on the counter.

Had to get home for another early performance and didn't want to wake you, her father had written. *You looked so peaceful sleeping. Anyway, I enjoyed our movie sleepover. We'll have to do it again sometime. Take care of yourself, kiddo, and see you soon. Love, Dad.*

Gemma smiled, holding onto the note. She might have lost her mother but at least she still had her dad. She didn't know what she would do without him.

Now that she had a job, Gemma realized she'd better get ready for work. She got dressed into another puffy gown, one as blue as the ocean. Then she brushed her teeth and made some cereal for breakfast again. It was the safer option, at least until her confidence improved.

As she ate breakfast, she turned on the television, finding the news station. A reporter talked about the weather and some fun activities in the city that were coming up—making Gemma think about the possibilities—before things turned somber.

"And authorities are still looking for information regarding a robbery at a downtown jewelry store," the reporter said. "An eyewitness said they saw a man in his mid-thirties with dark hair, blast open a door before making off with jewelry. They claim the man had some magical mist around him. If anyone has any information about this strange incident, the authorities urge anyone to call their hotline ..."

A magical mist? Gemma frowned, realizing that sounded like something from back home. Who was that man who stole the jewelry? Where had that strange mist come from?

Shaking her head, Gemma washed her dirty dishes and tried not to think about it for now. She had other things to focus on. Like her mother, for instance.

She tucked some money inside her dress pocket and left the apartment, locking it behind her. She walked down the hall and stepped into the elevator. As it descended, it stopped on a floor below hers where Carly, her daughter, and the taximan stepped on.

The taxi driver recognized Gemma immediately, his eyes widening. She could barely hold his gaze without feeling guilty.

Carly had no idea what was going on, smiling at Gemma. "Good morning, Gemma. Nice dress."

"It's so pretty," Abigail said, her eyes passing over the dress with a big smile.

Gemma laughed. "Good morning, everyone—and thank you, Abby. We'll have to get you a dress just like this one."

"I'd love that!" Abigail turned to her mother, putting on her best pleading eyes. "Can I, can I, can I? Please?"

Carly laughed, ruffling her hair. "Of course, sweetie. We'll look for it soon. Anyway, I wanted you to meet my husband. Gemma, this is John. John, this is Gemma."

John swallowed, looking Gemma in the eyes for a moment before his gaze darted back to the floor. "Uh, hello. Nice to meet you."

Gemma just nodded, saying nothing before she stared straight ahead. If Carly noticed their odd behavior around each other, she didn't say anything. Gemma was still wondering how she would break the news that her husband had asked her out.

"Mom, can I go to a birthday party after school?" Abigail asked. "Sarah invited me. She's in my English class. We're getting pizza for dinner before going to the movies."

Carly winced, pressing the button to head to the ground floor. "Sorry, sweetie, but you have another treatment session at the hospital this evening. Don't you remember? You won't make it in time."

Abigail crossed her arms. "No fair! Sarah was really excited. I hate this."

"I know," Carly said softly. "I do too."

Gemma glanced between them, wondering what was going on. When they had first met, Abigail had come from the hospital too. What kind of treatments did she need?

Her father said nothing, quietly stepping off the elevator when it arrived in the lobby. Gemma let Carly and Abigail follow before stepping off as well. As Abigail skipped toward a water fountain to take a sip, once again, Carly and John began arguing. Gemma felt a little awkward as she trailed behind them in silence.

"Some back-up would've been nice," Carly muttered. "Why do I always have to be the bad guy?"

"Huh? Oh, sorry. I was distracted," John replied, briefly glancing at Gemma. "I need to get to work. Excuse me."

He scurried out of the lobby, heading outside where he got into a taxi. He pulled away with a screech and didn't look back. While Abigail was still getting a drink, Carly turned to Gemma with a sigh, lowering her voice.

"I'm sorry you had to witness that," she whispered. "My husband and I … we've been going through a rough patch lately. Constantly arguing and at each other's throats. It's been awful, especially for Abby."

Gemma nodded. "I know—I heard you two arguing yesterday. I'm so sorry."

Everything was on the tip of her tongue. Gemma wanted nothing more than to tell Carly about her husband's flirting and ask about Abigail, but then the little girl skipped over.

"Where did Daddy go?" Abby asked, glancing around.

"Sorry, sweetie, but he had to leave for work. Don't worry— you'll see him again later. After your treatment." Carly placed a hand on her shoulder. "Go out to the car, I'll drive you to school in a sec. I just want to tell Gemma something."

The little girl nodded, heading out the doors to the lobby. The two women watched as she skipped to the family van and jumped in the backseat. She looked happy and healthy, certainly not the kind of kid who needed treatments at the hospital.

"I have to go—Abby gets impatient. But I wanted to tell you about a rooftop party later tonight," Carly said, keeping one eye out the window. "It would be late, about ten p.m. We do it every month in our building. A little get-together. I'd really like to see you there."

Gemma nodded. "I can do that, yeah. I got a new job at a bookstore yesterday, and I do have a date tonight, but I'll probably be back way before ten p.m."

"A job *and* a date?" Carly's eyebrow raised. "Look at you go.

Enjoy your date—I hope it involves less arguing than me and my husband's. Catch you later, Gemma."

Gemma waved goodbye, watching Carly leave the building to get into her car. They were becoming friends. And what kind of friend would Gemma be if she didn't warn Carly about her flirting husband?

Figuring out a plan in her mind, Gemma left the apartment building and began walking down the street. It was another busy work day in Toronto as hundreds of cars drove down the congested roads. To get her mind off her anxiety, she scanned the faces of the people she passed, hoping to see her mother's kind eyes. It took only the smallest trigger to push her over the edge, something she was trying to avoid.

She wanted the surface world to be a fresh start for her. She needed that.

Taking a deep breath, Gemma walked past Ian's bar. Ian was busy when she peered through the window. It seemed like he was preparing to open the bar later by washing the tables. She didn't want to bother him, so she kept walking, trying to hide from the nearby construction workers. They didn't notice her this time, as they continued working. When Gemma arrived at the bookstore, she saw a police car parked outside. They didn't quite have a police force back in Fairhaven, but Gemma would've recognized men in uniform anywhere.

She entered the bookstore, the bell chiming above her head. Barbara was standing near the cash register while speaking with two officers—one male and one female. Jacob and his teenage friends stood nearby, their faces looking as guilty as sin.

"And I'm terribly sorry, Officer," Barbara was saying. "My grandson has been ... difficult lately. I'm trying to watch over him, but it's been hard."

"We understand that, ma'am. We know it can't be easy losing a mother," the male officer said, stealing a glance at Jacob and his friends across the store. "But this is the third call we've gotten this month about your grandson. He's playing a dangerous game if he doesn't get his act together."

Barbara looked like she was on the verge of tears. Wanting to help, Gemma cleared her throat, stepping forward. "Um, excuse me, but what's going on?"

"This is a private conversation, miss," the female officer said. "Please, step away."

"It's all right," Barbara said. "This is my employee and friend, Gemma Solace. She knows my grandson is a handful. Jacob was caught egging someone's house this morning, I'm afraid. And cutting school. It just so happened it was the police chief's house."

Gemma winced. "That's awful."

And it reminded Gemma of Jacob stealing money from Luigi's. That boy was playing with fire. What if it graduated to something worse?

"It is. And the juvenile detention center will be in his future if he doesn't smarten up," the female officer said, pulling Gemma out of her thoughts. "One more incident and we'll be forced to take action. Consider this your final warning."

The male officer nodded. "Good luck, Mrs. Danvers."

"It's just *Ms.* now," Barbara said, sadly. "And thank you."

The officers nodded, smiling at both of them before leaving the bookstore. Barbara excused herself and went over to lecture her grandson and his friends. As usual, they were unapologetic and not listening.

But Gemma wished Jacob would apologize. If she told the police how he had stolen from the pizza parlor, it might've been the final straw that would get him arrested. And while Gemma cared too much about Barbara to let that happen, she was still worried about what Jacob would do next.

Between harboring secrets about her grandson and Carly's husband, Gemma had a lot on her plate these days. But thankfully, the thought of going out to dinner with Ian made her feel a lot better.

CHAPTER 9

The work day passed at an agonizingly slow pace. As Gemma skimmed the books on the shelf, all she could think of was her date with Ian later. He was on her mind more and more these days—a welcome reprieve from thinking about her mother and Senator Remus' next move.

She fell into a rhythm, cleaning up and helping the few customers who came in find what they were looking for. Then she had lunch with Barbara, sharing a charcuterie board in her office while going over some plans for the bookstore.

"I have a shipment coming tomorrow with the latest fantasy books," Barbara said, laying a list down on her desk, "and then an author signing next week. Local indie author. Should be fun."

Gemma nodded, finishing her lunch. "Looking forward to it. You know, I'm surprised you don't get more customers. Books are amazing! Why aren't more people coming in?"

Barbara sighed as she set aside her notes. "The truth is, Gemma ... my bookstore hasn't been doing well these past few months. Financially, I mean. People don't seem to want physical books anymore—e-books are all the rage. And thanks to inflation, I guess they don't have the spending money they used to."

"Well, that sucks. We need to do something about it." Gemma thought for a moment. "What about … a grand reopening? We can raise some money to keep you open, play board games, enjoy some baked goods, and so on. Maybe that would give people more of an incentive to come in, especially if game nights were regular."

They had games of magical potions and dragons back in Fairhaven. Gemma had never taken part though, always in her library.

"I've thought of that before, considering board games are so popular. You know, Monopoly, The Game of Life, Sorry. I've wanted to put in game tables, encourage people to come in. But it's too much for one person to handle. I wouldn't even know where to start—"

Gemma smiled, placing a hand over Barbara's. "Then let me. I'll plan the grand reopening night—don't you worry."

"Sounds great, thank you."

"Don't mention it. I should get back to work now. Got my date with Ian later too."

As she stood up, Barbara smiled. "Yes, I remember. Are you excited?"

"I am. And nervous." Gemma looked down at her hands, hoping they wouldn't start shaking. "I don't tell many people this, but … I have bad anxiety. And it can come out randomly."

"I'm sorry. That sounds very difficult." Barbara rose to her feet, giving her a reassuring smile. "I'm sure you'll do great. You're a lovely person, Gemma, and I have no doubt Ian will see that. He probably does already."

Gemma was still nervous, but that pep talk helped a little. "Here's hoping. If you don't mind, though … I have a question to ask you."

Barbara tidied up her office, throwing out her food scraps in the small garbage bin in the corner. "Of course—shoot."

"I didn't mean to pry, but I saw something yesterday. A bottle of alcohol. Is everything all right?"

Barbara froze, then slowly turned to face Gemma. "You saw that, eh? Well, no need to worry, though I appreciate it. It's for special occasions. That's all."

"But ... the bottle was mostly empty."

Barbara ignored that comment. "You should get back to work, Gemma. There are some mystery books at the front desk that need to be put away."

It was clear Barbara didn't want to talk about the contents of her desk. Not wanting to pry and lose her job, Gemma nodded and left her office, then picked up the books and got to work. But she had a feeling something was up with her boss— something serious.

After a few hours, when the final customer had come and gone, Gemma reached for her things and headed to the door. "Everything is done, Barbara. I'm heading home for my date."

Barbara looked up from her computer at the cash register. "Thanks, Gemma! I appreciate all you do. Have a great date!"

Gemma thanked her, then left. She pretended to walk away but then circled back around. As she peered through the window, trying not to get caught, she saw Barbara lock the doors and then disappear into her office. When she returned, she was chugging that half-empty bottle of alcohol that Gemma had seen.

Gemma shook her head, feeling sorry for Barbara, as she turned and walked through the busy streets. She knew it couldn't have been easy to lose her daughter in action, divorce her husband, run a struggling business, and then have the sole responsibility of raising a troubled grandson. Anyone would've been pushed to the edge.

As Gemma thought of ways to help Barbara with the grand reopening game night, she reached her apartment building. She rode the elevator up to her floor and walked down the hall to Noah's apartment. She looked up popular board games online, learning the rules and forming a plan in her mind. She had just enough money to buy the games and have them shipped to Barbara's store. Then she ran to her suitcase, choosing from one of many dresses to wear on her date.

"No, no, no ... not this one," Gemma muttered, setting them all aside. A sparkly gold dress with ruffles and a long train caught her eye. "Ah, perfect!"

She quickly showered, then did her hair and changed into the golden gown. When she looked amazing, a gentle knock sounded on the door. Gemma looked through the peephole and smiled before opening it to reveal Ian standing on her step.

He was holding a bouquet of flowers, looking handsome in a blue button-down shirt. He paired it with brown pants and black suede shoes, combing back his black hair. Gemma had to admit—he looked very handsome, like a prince in a fairytale.

"Wow, Gemma," Ian said, his eyes roaming over her outfit. "You look incredible. Do you always wear dresses?"

"Always," Gemma said with a little laugh, her eyes landing on the bouquet. "Are those for me?"

"They are." Ian held them out. "They're almost as sweet as you."

"That was cheesy, but thanks." Gemma laughed and took the flowers, sniffing them. "They smell amazing. Come on in while I find a vase."

Ian nodded, stepping inside the apartment as he shut the door behind him. He glanced around as Gemma rushed into the kitchen to find something to put the flowers in. She eventually found a white vase, one designed with dragons on the side. She put the flowers inside and filled it with water before turning around.

"Nice apartment you have here," Ian said, still glancing at the furniture. "Real cozy."

"Thank you. And thanks for coming to pick me up. I'm ready now—If you are."

He held out an arm, his shirt riding up a little. It exposed his tattoos underneath. "I definitely am. Follow me, my lady."

Gemma smiled, wrapping her arm around his before they left her apartment. Her stomach jumped with butterflies but in the best way. For once, excitement caused her anxiety, not fear. Ian had that effect on her.

She locked the door before Ian led her out of the building and toward his car in the parking lot. He even opened her door, helping her inside the passenger seat. Gemma thanked him and waited for Ian to get inside before he pulled away.

The city was beginning to get darker now with people heading home for dinner. They made chit-chat in the car as Ian drove, knowing his way around the city. He took them to a fancy five-star restaurant in the distance. He parked on the street, then helped Gemma out of the car when she noticed the long line around the block.

"Seems busy," she said. "How are we going to get a table?"

"I got us a reservation. No need to worry."

Gemma said nothing as Ian led her to the door, then the bouncer recognized him and let him inside. They were greeted by a hostess in the foyer near a water fountain. She smiled at Ian, then led them to a small table in the back.

"I'll bring you your menus in a second," the hostess said. "Please, get comfortable. Let me know if you need anything."

Gemma nodded. Ian pulled out her chair and she beamed up at him as she took her seat. He sat across from her and smiled. As Gemma played with the edges of their red tablecloth, she wondered if Ian was as nervous as she was. Soft music played overhead as people around them ate and quietly chatted, the sounds of a nearby fish tank filling the air.

"So, this is a nice place," Gemma said, getting comfortable in her seat. "I've never been here before."

"I have. It's one of the fanciest places in the city," Ian explained. "I wanted to take you someplace nice. I wanted it to be special."

"I appreciate that, thank you. No one's ever done that for me before. Tried to make things special, that is."

"No? That's a shame."

It really was. Gemma had gone too long without being properly loved and appreciated. Maybe all that would change now that Ian was in her life.

The hostess returned a minute later, setting down their menus. She took their drink orders and then vanished into the kitchen.

"You know, I realize I don't know you very well," Gemma said. "So, tell me something about yourself."

Ian paused for a moment, thinking. "Me? There's not much to tell. I'm not that interesting. I run a bar, live alone with my dog, and like to live a quiet life without much fuss."

"Nothing wrong with that. I didn't know you had a dog, though."

Ian reached into his pocket, pulling out his smartphone. He smiled as he opened his photo app and held it up toward Gemma. A big black lab was on the screen, chewing a bone. While pet dragons were more common in Fairhaven, Gemma had read in books that humans loved their cats and dogs. And Ian was proof of that.

"His name is Max," Ian explained, scrolling through some more photos of his dog. "I've had him since he was a puppy. He's my best friend."

"Oh, he's so cute!" Gemma cried. "I didn't have any pets, but a neighbor of mine had a dragon."

Ian put his phone away, lifting an eyebrow. "A dragon, huh? I wasn't aware they existed."

Gemma scrambled for words, mentally chastising herself. How could she let something like that slip? She had to be more careful around humans—no matter how much she liked them.

She laughed nervously, looking anywhere but Ian's eyes. "A stuffed dragon, I mean. Not a real one. That would be impossible. And silly."

Ian nodded. "That makes more sense. My dog has a stuffed dragon he loves. The stuffing's falling out, but he plays with it anyway."

Gemma breathed out, relieved that he bought her lie. Fairhaven was still a secret for now. If things went well between them, when should she tell him about her kingdom? And the magic inside it? She knew Princess Esme had struggled with that secret as she began a relationship with Noah.

When the waitress returned with their drinks, interrupting her thoughts, Ian ordered. "The salmon, please. It's amazing from here, Gemma. You should try it."

Gemma nodded, smiling at the waitress. "Then I'll have the salmon, too, thanks."

The waitress wrote it all down, then took their menus and vanished into the kitchen again. The table turned quiet as Gemma racked her brain for something to say.

"So, how—"

"You—"

They laughed, both speaking at the same time. Gemma blushed. "Sorry, didn't mean to interrupt you. Go ahead."

Ian shook his head. "Nah, you go. Ladies first, after all."

"Well, all right. I'm just curious about your reading habits. Have you always been a reader?"

"Oh, definitely—ever since I was a little boy. And I've always been into fantasy romance too. Where the brave knight saves the woman he loves, or vice versa. I'm a bit of a hopeless romantic in that sense."

Gemma smiled. "Funny—so am I. Favorite books?"

Ian threw out a bunch of titles, making Gemma nod along. "I like all fantasy romance, really," he said. "Not hard to please. I used to get teased by my friends for liking romance growing up, so I hid it for a while. They thought it was lame that a guy liked romance. Girly, even. But I just don't care anymore. I like what I like."

"Exactly. Good for you. I grew up reading books too. They were my escape, my safe place. They still are, really."

And the bonding with her mother mostly came from books. She missed her more as the days passed.

Ian's eyes lit up. "It was the same with me. I guess we have a lot in common, huh?"

Gemma sipped her water, nodding. "Seems that way, yeah."

They chatted while they waited for their meal, then it arrived a few minutes later. Ian had been right—the salmon *was* amazing. Gemma hadn't had dinner that good in a long time.

"We have to get dessert too," Ian said, taking another bite of his fish. "Dessert is one of the reasons I get up in the morning."

"Don't forget books," Gemma said, then they toasted to great fiction.

Once their salmon was finished, they each ordered a different dessert. Gemma went with the chocolate cake while Ian tried the strawberry cheesecake. He bit into it, nodding his head.

"Yep, this is the best thing I've ever tasted." He put a small piece of cheesecake on his fork, then held it toward Gemma. "You want to try?"

Gemma didn't even hesitate as she leaned forward, eating the bite off his fork. She nodded as she chewed. "Wow, that's amazing. I wish we had this kind of dessert where I'm from."

"Where *are* you from?" Ian asked, returning to his dessert. "You never told me."

Gemma laughed nervously. "Like I said, you probably wouldn't have heard about it. It's a very small town."

Ian looked like he had some questions before the waitress returned, placing the check on the table. "Here you go. Was everything okay?"

"Everything was fantastic," Gemma said, reaching into her pocket to pull out some bills. "Now that I have a job, I can afford dinner."

But Ian reached for his wallet, then placed his card on the table. "Don't worry about it—this was my idea. I've got it."

Judging by the large amount of money she'd seen in his wallet the other day, Gemma knew he could afford it. It seemed business was booming at the bar. She still felt bad not paying for anything but backed down once the waitress took the card and walked away.

"Thank you for dinner," Gemma said. "It was amazing. Next time, it's on me."

Ian smiled. "Next time, huh?"

Gemma realized what she had said, blushing. "Yes, next time. If that's okay with you?"

"Oh, it's more than okay with me. I had a great time. In fact, if you hadn't mentioned anything, I would've asked you on another date."

"Looks like I beat you to the punch, then. I'm glad we're on the same page."

Ian's eyes sparkled. "We are. Wait a second ... was that a book pun?"

Gemma giggled. "You know, I think it was."

As they shared a smile, people in the restaurant murmured around them. A couple diners pulled out their phones and began to record Ian.

"Okay, am I crazy or are all those people staring at you? What's going on?" Gemma whispered. "Why are they taking videos?"

"Uh, I don't know. They probably have nothing better to do." Ian tugged his collar, rising to his feet. "Come on—let's get out of here."

Gemma grabbed her things and stood. Ian led her out of the restaurant and didn't look back. People continued to stare and record them but no one said anything. Ian thanked the bouncer at the door, then walked with Gemma down the block.

"Sorry about all that," he said.

"No worries. It was still an incredible first date."

"Like something out of those fantasy romance books we love so much." Ian smiled. "There's a nice little park not far from here. Care for a late stroll?"

Gemma linked her arms with his and nodded. "Just try and stop me. Let's go."

CHAPTER 10

After walking a few blocks, Gemma and Ian finally made it to High Park, one of Toronto's largest and most popular parks. Ian played the role of the tour guide and showed Gemma around. Even after dinner, it was as busy as ever as kids ran around and played games, people walked their dogs, and cyclists sped past. The trees were tall and gave coverage from the spitting rain that had started.

Ian didn't talk about the people snapping pictures back at the restaurant and Gemma didn't want to ruin their date by asking. Whatever it was, she hoped it was nothing serious.

"I take my dog here sometimes," Ian said, breaking the silence as he walked close to Gemma. "He loves socializing with the other dogs."

"I bet. I'll have to meet Max sometime—he's a total cutie."

Ian smiled, glancing at Gemma. "I'd like that. Sometimes I even bring him to my bar as a mascot. The patrons get a kick out of him. Brings in more business too."

"That's so cute! What a good boy."

"The *best* boy. We're kind of a package deal, so if you don't like him or vice versa, this probably won't work out."

"Don't worry—I love dogs. From what I've read about them, anyway. I've never been around one before, but I'm sure they won't mind me either."

Ian raised an eyebrow. "Never been around a dog? That's a shame. My family used to breed them. Very expensive poodles they would train for competitions. My mother was always taking them to compete."

"You ever thought about doing that with Max?"

Ian laughed. "Hell no—I'm going to let him be a dog. Everything else in my family is done for the sake of a performance. I refuse to treat my dog that way."

"What do you mean?"

Ian paused. Just as he opened his mouth, a tweeting bluebird came down from one of the tall trees. The bird landed on Gemma's shoulder, singing its little song.

"Whoa! That was awesome." Ian smiled, gesturing at the bird. "Looks like you have a friend."

Gemma reached up and petted the bird's head. "Well, hello there, sweetie. How are you?"

The bird tweeted back in response. If Gemma had been in Fairhaven, she could've used a potion to help her speak with animals. But it didn't seem like the human world had anything like that.

When a squirrel came up to her, pausing at her feet, Ian laughed. "Wow, you've got the whole animal kingdom coming out to see you. Are you some kind of Disney princess?"

"I wish." Gemma shook her head. "Just a simple librarian who loves dresses and animals. They don't give me anxiety like humans do."

Ian nodded. "I hear that. Before opening my bar, I had some bad anxiety too, mostly caused by my family. It's gotten better now though. You ever have another panic attack, come to me. I'll sit with you until it's gone."

"I really appreciate that, Ian. Thank you. No wonder you knew exactly how to help me."

"Yeah, I definitely have experience with it. Unfortunately." Then he reached into his pocket and pulled out his smartphone. "Wait—stay right there. I want to get a picture of us with the animals."

Gemma nodded, waiting for Ian to snap the pictures on his smartphone. She watched as he moved in front and made sure the camera could still see Gemma, the bluebird on her shoulder, and the curious squirrel at her feet. When he snapped the photo, he turned the camera toward her; it came out perfectly.

"Nice," he said, pulling the phone around to look at it. "Proof of our first date."

Gemma gently shooed the bluebird and squirrel away. "And it was a great first date. The only one I've ever had, actually. Never been on a date before."

"Never?" Ian raised an eyebrow. "Well, I'm glad I could give you such a good experience. Anyway, it's starting to rain. Want to get back to the car? I'm worried that pretty dress will get ruined."

Gemma nodded, looking down as the rain spattered her clothes. "Sounds good."

Ian held out an arm for Gemma to take, then he walked her down the block before reaching his car. The people snapping pictures had vanished. He opened her car door first, helping her inside, then he walked around and got into the driver's seat. They sped off as the rain picked up.

"It's been really rainy in Toronto lately," Ian said, turning on the windshield wipers. "The weather's been messed up. I don't know what's going on."

Gemma shivered, feeling a cool breeze creep up her spine. "I'm used to cooler temperatures so I don't mind, but a little sunshine would be nice once in a while."

Ian paused at a red light, stealing a glance at Gemma. He removed his jacket and wrapped it around her shoulders. "There—so you don't freeze to death."

"Thanks." Gemma smiled, sinking into the jacket. It smelled like him—a scent she was coming to enjoy.

A few minutes later, Ian pulled into the parking lot of her apartment building. He opened his door before walking around to help her out. "Come on, I'll walk you up to your apartment."

"Thank you, that'd be nice." Gemma stepped out, removing the jacket and handing it to Ian. "Here you go."

He shook his head. "Nah, keep it. Looks better on you anyway. And I've got a hundred more back at home."

Gemma nodded, smiling before she led him into her apartment building. She wondered why so many of her neighbors were out and walking around until she remembered the rooftop party. She checked the clock on the wall, realizing it was about to start soon. She had stayed out longer than she thought.

"Hey, if you're not doing anything tonight," Gemma said, turning to Ian, "there's a rooftop party for the building. You want to come with me? I was invited and I really don't want to go alone. Bad for anxiety."

Ian nodded. "Sure, I'd like that. Lead the way."

"All right, perfect. I'll introduce you to a new friend I recently met. Carly and her daughter, Abigail. They live a few floors down from me. Very nice people."

Except for Carly's flirting husband. What was Gemma going to do about that?

She and Ian rode the elevator up to the roof, glancing at each other in comfortable silence. He would make her blush just by a look and she would do the same to him. It was cute.

When the elevator arrived on the roof, Gemma stepped off, gesturing for Ian to follow. Pop-up awnings covered a snack table and a handful of seating areas. Dozens of her neighbors sat on plastic chairs, eating snacks and listening to music. The kids had their own play area where Abigail and her friends colored.

Gemma spotted Carly and her husband arguing again, this time near the edge of the roof. Gemma pointed at the two of them. "Well, there she is—my neighbor, Carly. And her husband, John. We actually already met. He's a taxi driver who drove me around a few days ago."

"Small world." Ian winced. "Looks like a tense conversation. Everything all right between them?"

Gemma shook her head. "No, I don't think so. Let's go see if they're okay."

Ian nodded, following Gemma through the crowd of people toward the edge of the roof. She couldn't tell what they were arguing about because they hushed when Carly spotted them. Carly put on a big smile, turning to them and avoiding her husband completely.

"Hey, Gemma! Glad you could make it," Carly said. "And you brought someone. Who is this? A new neighbor?"

"No—he's my date, Ian Whitman. Ian, this is Carly Brenton."

"A pleasure," Ian said, shaking her hand. Then he turned to the husband. "And you must be John, the husband, I take it? Nice to meet you."

He held out a hand but John pushed past them. "I need a drink. Excuse me."

As he wandered off, Carly sighed. "Sorry about him. He's been in a sour mood all week."

"No, I'm sorry, Carly," Gemma said. "All you two do is fight. That can't be easy on you."

Carly looked down, her lip quivering. "No … it really isn't. Anyway, I don't want to ruin the party. Why don't we get you two some snacks and you can tell me how you met?"

Gemma nodded, gesturing for Ian to follow. They grabbed some cheese and crackers—a light snack since they were still full from dinner and dessert—and told Carly how they met. A panic attack in a bar, then another chance meeting at Gemma's bookstore.

"That sounds like fate if I've ever heard it," Carly said, beaming. "Such a cute love story. I wish you two happiness."

Gemma stole a glance at Ian, noticing he was already staring at her with a smile on his face. She hoped this fairytale would end on a happy note.

The rain had stopped, and a cool breeze danced around them.

"Come on, let's go see my daughter, Abby," Carly added. "She's right over here."

Gemma and Ian nodded, following Carly to the small section where Abigail was sitting. Her father was nowhere to be found. She was busy coloring a picture of a dragon with a woman in a bright dress who looked a lot like Gemma.

"Hey, Abby," Gemma said, staring down at the picture. "Nice drawing. That girl looks like me."

"She *is* you," Abby replied as she stared up at her with a smile. Then she pointed at the dragon and castle in the background. "This is your pet dragon and your castle. Where you live as a princess."

"That's really cute," Ian said, glancing at Gemma. "We just got back from a walk in the park where all the animals were flocking to her. Definitely sounds like princess behavior to me."

Abigail's eyes lit up. "Really? That's so cool!"

"I guess animals just love me," Gemma joked, trying not to raise suspicions. She guessed the animals were drawn to the smell of the magical potions lingering on her dress and the good energy that went with it. With sensitive noses, they could smell what humans couldn't. "Are you having a good time at the party?"

Gemma changed the subject, chatting with Abigail and Carly for a little while. When a little boy asked Ian to draw with him, Ian sat and picked up a crayon. Gemma stood a few feet back with Carly and watched over the kids.

"He's very good with children," Carly whispered to Gemma, staring at Ian as he drew a spaceship with the boy. "That's something you want in a partner. If you want kids, that is."

"I do. One day—if it ever happens." Gemma smiled. "Maybe it will soon."

"Well, I'm rooting for you. My marriage hasn't been the greatest but that doesn't mean I don't want others to be happy in love."

Gemma wondered if she should tell Carly about her husband now. But how would she bring it up?

"Speaking of my darling husband, where the hell is he?"

Gemma scanned the rooftop with Carly, not seeing him anywhere. "God, he disappears so much. It drives me insane. He should be here, hanging out with his family. And taking Abby to her appointments instead of me doing it all the time."

"I've been meaning to ask you about that. You mentioned treatments at the hospital before. What's wrong? Is Abby okay?"

Carly sighed, crossing her arms. "She's got a bunch of health problems, I'm afraid—mostly autoimmune diseases. So many allergies and things she can't do. Plus, lupus medications and weekly treatments that she needs."

"Wow. I'm so sorry," Gemma said, staring over at Abby while shaking her head. "That's rough for anyone, but especially a child."

"I know. And my husband's no help at all—It's like I'm practically a single mother. I have a life too, you know, plus a dance career. At a dance studio not far from here. If I miss any more work, I might not be able to pay rent. And my family needs it. My husband doesn't always make a lot of money as a taxi driver."

Gemma turned to her. "Well, if you ever need a babysitter, you know where to find me. Abby likes me already, and I won't charge you a dime."

"Really?" Carly's eyes lit up. "Oh my gosh, that would mean the world. Thank you, Gemma—I might just take you up on that offer. Since my deadbeat husband won't lift a finger."

Gemma nodded just as Ian walked over, still smiling from interacting with the kids. "I'm not the best artist, but I helped Abby draw a giant octopus monster. Then crayon-Gemma swooped in with a sword and a big dress and saved the village."

"Really? I'm a hero princess, I guess," Gemma joked. "You were great with those kids."

Ian shrugged. "Eh, it was nothing. I have a younger brother, so I've had experience. He's got some mental health issues, too, so I've had to be there for him a lot. Anyway, it's getting late and I should get home. Have a shipment coming in at the bar bright and early tomorrow."

"The bar?" Carly raised an eyebrow.

Gemma nodded. "Yeah, Ian owns a bar a few blocks from here. It's a nice place—we should go there for drinks sometime."

"God, I'd love that. Anything to get away for a little while. Anyway, it was nice meeting you, Ian. I hope to see you again soon. Get home safe."

Ian thanked her, then Gemma led him to the roof's exit door. "Come on, I'll walk you to the car. Like the hero princess I am."

Ian laughed, following Gemma to the elevator. Carly called out that she and her daughter would be waiting for Gemma to return to the party. She nodded, then on the way down, she and Ian talked about how cute the kids were and the warm welcome that Carly had given him. After they walked outside, they headed to his car in the parking lot and paused.

Gemma's mind wandered. Her hands were clammy as she nervously awaited a kiss from Ian. That seemed to always happen when the two love interests in her books were alone together. To her disappointment, it didn't happen.

"Well, I know I sound like a stuck record," Ian began, "but I really did have a great time with you. Best date I've had in a while, actually."

Gemma smiled. "Glad to hear it. I'm free again tomorrow night. If you are." She clasped her hands behind her back, peering up at Ian with what she hoped as an inviting look.

Ian nodded. "I am—and I think I have a date idea in mind. I'll pick you up around six p.m. again if that's okay."

"That works. Looking forward to it."

"As am I."

When Ian turned quiet, his eyes darting to Gemma's lips, she wondered again if they were going to kiss. Her first kiss— she could barely contain her excitement. But then he looked away, opening the driver's side door.

"Uh, I should get home now," he said, getting into the car and putting his hands on the steering wheel. "Sleep well, Gemma. See you tomorrow."

She nodded and said goodbye. He waved at her as he drove out of the parking lot and vanished down the road. She stood there for a few minutes, watching his taillights fade.

He hadn't kissed her. It looked like he wanted to, but then he made a quick getaway. Had Gemma done something wrong? The thought of hurting him in some way was like a dagger through her chest.

When she heard movement, she glanced down the street.

Someone in a dark hoodie escaped a dark alley and ran the other way. The street was too dark to make out who they were. But a spray of magic—purple, pink, and yellow with sparkly hues—followed after them.

That must've been a leftover effect from the time Senator Remus and his fairy godmother had made magic compatible on Earth. She knew Princess Esme's guards were heading to the surface to get rid of the remaining pockets of magical energy that lingered. But who was that man? And did he have any connection to that news report about the magical robbery that would somehow lead back to her mother?

Her stomach twisted in knots, fearing for her mother's safety. She really needed to double her efforts to find her. But how? She fruitlessly peered up and down the streets.

Shaking her head, Gemma entered her apartment building and hoped everything was all right in the human world. Princess Esme had stopped Remus—they had nothing to worry about. Or so everyone in Fairhaven thought.

As she approached the elevator, she spotted John standing there by himself, finishing a beer. He belched before throwing the bottle into a nearby garbage can. When he spun around, realizing Gemma was standing there and watching him, his eyes widened.

"It's you," he muttered. "The woman I drove home."

Gemma nodded. "It's me. Excuse me—I need to get back to the party. Carly and Abby are waiting for me."

But John reached for her arm, holding her back. "Not so fast. We have a few things to talk about first."

CHAPTER 11

Gemma pulled her arm away, disgusted. "Let go of me! Or I'll cry for help."

John released her and stepped back. "All right, all right—calm down, lady. I just wanted to talk to you."

"About what?"

"Don't act coy," he snarled. "We both know that I asked you out. And since you're growing closer to my wife, I'm worried you're going to tell her."

"I just might. What is wrong with you? Carly does a lot for you, you know, and your daughter is sick." Gemma shook her head. "You should be there for them more, not flirting with strangers on the job. You make me sick."

"Hey, don't judge me! My daughter's illness has been hard on me too. Besides, flirting ain't a crime. I just don't want my wife to find out, all right? She has enough on her plate. So please, don't tell her."

"You should be the one to tell her. She deserves better than a cheating husband. I bet I haven't been the only one, have I?"

John paused. "Just ... just mind your own business."

"That tells me all I need to know." Gemma's lip curled in

disgust, stepping into the elevator. "You have to break the news soon or I will. I can't stand by and watch anyone—especially a friend—stay in a relationship like this."

She pressed a button on the elevator, then the doors closed in John's face. She took a deep breath and clasped her shaking hands to her chest. But she was proud of herself for standing up to him.

When the elevator arrived on the roof, she stepped out. Carly beamed at her while holding a cup of fruit punch. "Hey, you're back! You should try the fruit punch—it's amazing."

Gemma nodded, forcing a smile as she grabbed a cup. Poor Carly was so oblivious to her husband's cheating.

John didn't return, staying away for the rest of the party. Gemma could tell it bothered Carly, but she didn't bring it up. Instead, she hung out with her daughter and Gemma all night, cracking jokes and putting on a brave face. Gemma knew it had to hurt.

Once the party had ended and it was very late, Gemma walked Carly and Abby back to their apartment. They could hear the television on inside. When John began yelling at the television over something, maybe a sports game, Gemma knew he had gone home.

Carly rolled her eyes. "He's probably drinking on the couch and watching hockey again. I tell you he wasn't like this when we first met."

"I'm sorry, Carly. If you ever want to talk, I'm here." Gemma turned to Abigail, patting her shoulder. "Have a good sleep, you two. And I'm planning a little surprise for you, Abby. I hope you like it."

"A surprise for me?" Abigial's eyes lit up. "Wow. I can't wait. Night, Gemma."

She skipped into the apartment, vanishing into her bedroom. Carly thanked Gemma and gave her a hug before heading home. Gemma took the elevator again, reaching her own apartment with no more confrontations or arguments.

Her mind drifted back to Ian as she fell asleep on the couch, wondering if he was thinking about her too. Despite John, it had been the perfect evening.

When Gemma woke up the next morning to bright sunshine, she brushed her teeth and got dressed in a magenta gown before attempting to make eggs for breakfast. To her delight, she hadn't burned down the stove this time. The whole apartment smelled heavenly as she made sure the stove was off and brought her cooked food to the table.

"It's no griffin's eggs, but it'll do," Gemma said, shoveling food into her mouth. "Tastes amazing."

When a knock sounded at the door, Gemma swallowed her bite and walked into the foyer. She opened the door, finding a newspaper on her front step. Someone must've been delivering the paper to all the apartments. Back home, a stork had the responsibility of doing that.

Bending down, she picked up the newspaper and gasped at the headline. It was her and Ian from last night—sitting at the restaurant, eating food off each other's forks. One of the diners had snapped the picture.

But why had it ended up as front-page news? Gemma was a nobody—and she thought Ian was too.

When she read the headline, it started to make more sense. IAN WHITMAN, BILLIONAIRE'S SON, ON DATE WITH MYSTERY WOMAN AFTER PUBLIC BREAK-UP.

Public break-up? Billionaire's son? Gemma's head spun. Just who was Ian, really? The newspaper seemed like a gossip column, something Fairhaven had back home too. She hated it then and hated it now.

She closed the door, setting the newspaper down. She walked toward Noah's laptop and turned it on. After taking a few minutes to figure out how to use it, realizing it was quite similar to the filing system back home in her library, she went to Google and typed in Ian's name. Their romantic dinner was the first article that popped up.

She briefly wondered how many people would see it. Would her mother be one of them? Maybe it would help Gemma track her down sooner. Her stomach tingled with butterflies at the thought of seeing her, then she was angry again that her private life was splashed across the internet for all to see.

But then it took Gemma to a Wikipedia page, one that described Ian's family. It said his father, Ralph Whitman, owned an oil company that had made him billions of dollars. His wife, Susannah Whitman, was a Hollywood actress. After looking it up, Gemma understood that Hollywood was a place for the rich and famous, the upper echelon of society. The internet said they met decades ago and had their son, Ian, and his younger brother Marcus. He looked only a few years younger, in his twenties like Ian.

Gemma was floored. Why hadn't Ian mentioned any of this?

Scrolling down, it only got better. Ian had dated a famous British actress named Ivy Bingham for a few years. They had a very public break-up with Ivy screaming in Ian's face, the pictures plastered all over the Internet. Ivy was gorgeous—long blonde hair, pale skin with freckles, baby-blue eyes, and the perfect figure.

Gemma flinched, feeling self-conscious. Why would Ian want to be with Gemma when he could've had someone famous like Ivy? There was a whole side to Ian that she hadn't known about. Maybe he would've felt the same if she told him where she was from.

Feeling too sick to eat, Gemma rose to her feet and threw out the eggs. She was just about ready to head to work when another knock sounded on the door. She walked over, looking through the peephole first and noticed a familiar face.

Ian. He was standing there, dressed for another work day at the bar while nervously tugging at his clothes. She hoped he had an explanation ready for her.

Gemma opened the door, coming face to face with Ian. She crossed her arms. "Hi."

"Hey," he began, sighing. "I take it you've seen the news? Beautiful dress, by the way. But you always look beautiful."

"Thanks. And yeah, I have. I wanted to know more so I looked you up on that computer thingy. The son of a billionaire and actress? Who dated another actress?"

Ian winced. "This is exactly what I was trying to avoid ... but yeah, it's all true. Can I come in? We should talk about this."

Gemma opened the door a little wider, gesturing for him to enter. "Of course. We'll have to be quick, though—my next shift at the bookstore starts soon."

"Yeah, so does work at the bar. I'll try to explain everything as fast and coherently as I can."

Gemma nodded, walking into the living room. "Okay. You want some tea? I sense this is going to be a big discussion, and my father told me tea makes everything better."

Ian smiled as he sat down on the couch. "Tea would be great, thank you. Your father's a wise man."

"That he is."

Gemma entered the kitchen, turning the kettle on. That was one thing she knew how to do. She waited a few minutes for it to boil, then poured two cups of green tea for her and Ian. She carried them out to the living room and placed them down on the coffee table.

"Thanks," Ian said, leaning forward and picking up his tea. "First off, I want to say I'm sorry. I never meant for our date to end up in the news. Or to make you feel like I've been lying to you."

"I just don't understand," Gemma said, sitting down on the couch. "Why lie to me about who you are?"

For a moment, Gemma felt a twinge of guilt. She was doing the same—lying about her identity. But she had better reasons than Ian.

"Because. My family ... well, they're toxic, to put it plainly," Ian said with a sigh. "Sure, they're rich and have everything they've ever wanted, but they're selfish and greedy and arrogant and cruel. They've looked down on my little brother for being mentally ill his whole life. Anxiety, panic attacks, and depression mostly. One day, I decided I had enough and stopped speaking to them. I left with some money, only my inheritance, and opened my own bar. I always wanted to run a business, and I've always been good at mixing drinks. Did it a lot for my father's clients once upon a time."

Gemma sipped her tea. "Hmm. I guess I can respect that— wanting to go your own way and get away from toxic people. What about this actress you dated?"

Ian turned silent for a moment, his mouth opening and closing. "Ivy ... I don't really like to talk about her. Let's just say that relationship was a trainwreck, full of gaslighting and abuse that went on for too long. She's tried to contact me since I left my family, but I haven't returned her calls. We're over—I've completely moved on."

Gemma nodded. "That's good to hear. I guess those people in the restaurant noticed you?"

"They must have, yeah. I can usually fly under the radar for the most part, but once in a while, someone who knows my parents or Ivy from the movies will recognize me. It can be hard to get away from sometimes."

"Well, if you ever need to escape it all, you know my address. You're free to crash here anytime to get away."

Ian smiled. "Thanks, that's sweet of you. So … you aren't mad at me?"

"No, I'm not. How could I be? Seems like you did the right thing getting away from your family. And your ex-girlfriend."

"Maybe I did. I'll admit, it was hard to leave all that money behind. I miss not having to worry about paying rent or affording food. But the mental cost was too high." Ian sipped his tea, then shook his head. "I don't regret getting away at all. I only wish my brother would too, but my parents have him under their spell. He's still living with them."

"I'm sorry, that's rough. Seems like you both have suffered a lot."

"We really have. My parents are awful, awful people. My father runs an oil company that's destroying the planet, and my mother has worked with some abusive producers without giving a damn. And my ex is just an awful person. I'm better off without them. If I had my way, I'd erase any and all connections I have to them."

"I think you've tried your best. What drew you to your ex in the first place?"

"Her beauty, of course. Her strong work ethic too. And I thought she was a good person. But she was a damn good actress and pulled the wool over my eyes." He shook his head. "Anyway, I'm much happier now that I found you."

"Same here. So, that's it, then? Nothing else I should know?" Gemma raised an eyebrow. "You're not secretly a superhero on the side, are you?"

Ian laughed. "I wish, but no. That's it—everything is out in the open. So, after hearing all that … are we still on for our date tonight?"

"Absolutely," Gemma said with a smile. "Looking forward to it, actually. Thanks for coming over to explain everything."

"I figured I should so you weren't wondering. If it isn't obvious ... I really care about you, Gemma." Ian hesitated, then finally looked at Gemma. "I didn't want my past to screw things up between us, so I knew I had to come clean."

"And I respect that. I just have one question."

"Shoot."

Gemma set down her tea, leaning closer. "Last night, when you were getting your car ... why didn't you kiss me?"

Ian blushed before he looked away. "Well, it's just ... you make me nervous. In a good way. And I guess I don't want to rush things. I'd rather take it slow, see how things unfold on their own. After my last disastrous relationship, I'm trying to avoid that happening again. Jumping into things too fast, I mean."

"All right, I understand. I don't want to pressure you or rush you into anything."

"I know. Thanks, Gemma." Ian rose to his feet with a smile. "And thanks for the tea—it was amazing. I should get to work now, but I'll see you tonight."

Gemma nodded, walking Ian to her door. "Sounds perfect. See you then."

He gave her another smile before walking down the hallway, then headed downstairs to his car. The truth hadn't been so hard to hear—not like it would be for Carly—but Gemma was still grateful Ian had come clean.

After doing her dishes, Gemma left her apartment building and walked to the bookstore. The board games she had ordered arrived quickly and sat on the doorstep. She picked them up, then entered the store with the chime of a bell and set the supplies behind the counter but couldn't find Barbara anywhere.

"Barbara?" Gemma called, glancing down the aisles. No one was inside the store. "Are you here?"

When she heard crashing from the office, Gemma ran toward the door and opened it. Instead of finding a burglar like she had thought—or Jacob doing something he wasn't supposed to be—she found Barbara on the floor, hissing in pain. A nearly empty bottle of Jack Daniels sat on her desk, and another empty bottle lay on the floor beside her.

"Damn it!" Barbara cried, rubbing her back and glaring at the chair.

"What happened?" Gemma held out a hand. "Come on—let me help you get up."

"Thanks." Barbara took her help, then sat down again. "I ... sort of fell out of my chair."

"Ouch. How did that happen?"

Barbara shrugged. "I guess I wasn't paying attention. Anyway, is it time to open the store? I got here an hour ago to take inventory. I think I lost track of time."

"Yeah, it's opening time. I bought the supplies for the grand reopening too." Gemma gestured to the bottle on the desk. "Did you drink all of that this morning?"

Barbara glanced at it. "Maybe I did. Just needed a little pick-me-up, that's all. Had a bad fight with Jake this morning. I love my grandson, but he's driving me insane."

"I'm sorry. But Barbara, I'm worried about your drinking habits. This isn't the first time I've seen you with alcohol." Gemma sat down across from her. "Are you okay?"

"Me? Yeah, yeah—I'm fine. Just a little tipsy. I can still work." Barbara rose to her feet, swaying. "Okay, maybe I should sit down for a little bit."

She plopped back in her chair as Gemma nodded. "I think you should, yes. You remind me so much of my fairy godmother."

"Your fairy ... *what?*"

"Uh." Gemma coughed to cover up that slip up. "Nothing, nothing. Look, I'll bet you started drinking to forget about your daughter, right? And cope with your grandson's bad behavior?"

Gemma could relate. When her mother fled, Gemma had drunk an entire bottle of magical alcohol called Essence. It was quite popular in Fairhaven. After spending a whole night throwing up, she swore to never do that again. To find healthier, better ways of coping with the loss. She became even more invested in her books and never looked back.

Barbara sighed. "Maybe. I know it seems concerning, but I'm fine—really. Now, there are a bunch of non-fiction titles on my desk that need to be put away. Do you think you can take care of that for me?"

Gemma nodded, rising to her feet. "All right—consider it done. But I'm still worried about you. I think you need to cut back on your drinking. Maybe even completely until you've passed the grieving process. And I understand, you know. I was once like you."

Barbara raised an eyebrow. "Really? How so?"

"I drank once. To cope with my mother leaving." Gemma closed her eyes. "It was awful—I ended up throwing up and swore off the stuff after a bender. I don't regret giving it up. Maybe it'll be the same for you."

"I'm glad you got sober. Not sure that'll ever happen for me," Barbara muttered, "but here's hoping."

Gemma left Barbara in her office, shutting the door. She saw through the small crack that Barbara had reached for the bottle again. What was it going to take to convince that woman to get sober? Her grandson needed her at her best, especially for what he was going through.

When Gemma approached the cash register, finding a pile of books there, the bell above the door chimed. A young, chipper woman in a blue pantsuit entered with a fluffy micro-phone. A cameraman followed her in and began filming parts of the bookstore.

"Hi there!" the woman said. "I'm a reporter with the local news, and ... wait. You look familiar. Don't I know you?"

She must've recognized Gemma from that newspaper article with Ian. And she really didn't want a life of fame when she was supposed to keep a low profile.

"No, I'm sure you don't," Gemma lied. "Is there something I can do for you?"

"Yes—I'm going around doing interviews with small busi-nesses. It's a tough time to own a business with all that infla-tion nonsense. Anyway, is the owner of the bookstore available for a chat?"

Gemma knew being interviewed would greatly help the bookstore, but Barbara was in no position to be on TV when she was so drunk. Gemma briefly glanced at the office before turning back to the reporter.

"She's here, but she's a bit under the weather, I'm afraid," Gemma lied. "I'm her only employee and I'd have no issue doing an interview. What do you want to know?"

A small knot of anxiety tightened in her stomach, but she did her best to push it down. If Gemma could give a good inter-view and raise the bookstore's sales, it would be one less thing for Barbara to worry about. As Gemma talked with the reporter, she brainstormed ways in her head to help Barbara—before she got even worse.

CHAPTER 12

The interview went well with Gemma answering as many of the reporter's questions as she could. She couldn't answer personal questions about Barbara's life or why she opened the bookstore, so she pointed out the books on their shelves and gave the reporter their business hours. She also mentioned that they were hoping to add game nights and activities for people of all ages—something to bring in even more business.

It was worth a shot.

"Thank you—you did great," the reporter said, gesturing for the cameraman to lower his camera. "It's a shame we couldn't speak to Ms. Danvers herself but we understand. You should see our interview on the news tonight in a segment on local businesses."

Gemma smiled. "Wonderful, thank you. Have a good day."

The reporter nodded, even buying a romantic fantasy novel on the way out. Gemma knew exactly what to recommend to her. Once they were gone, she walked to the office where Barbara was passed out at her desk. The now completely empty bottle of Jack Daniels sat across from her head.

"Poor woman," Gemma murmured, finding a blanket on one of the shelves. She draped it over Barbara's shoulders and turned off the light. "I hope things get better for you soon."

She left the office, closing the door behind her before getting back to work. It was a slow day—not many customers came around. Gemma hoped the TV interview would change all that. As she tidied up one of the aisles, the door chimed open, and fast footsteps entered the bookstore.

When she came around the corner, she saw Jacob and his friends hiding behind the cash register. A little old lady was hobbling down the sidewalk while shaking her cane above her head.

"You darn kids!" she cried. "When I catch you, I swear ..."

She faded down the sidewalk, then Gemma approached the cash register. Jacob and the other boys continued to hide there while snickering and holding onto pieces of fabric. They looked like materials you'd use to make a dress. When they didn't see her, Gemma cleared her throat.

"Excuse me, boys?" she asked. "What do you think you're doing?"

The boys' eyes widened as they stood up, murmuring. Jacob was the first one to speak. "Uh, nothing. What are *you* doing?"

Gemma crossed her arms. "I work here. What's that you're carrying in your hands? Some kind of fabric?"

"It's nothing. Come on, guys."

Jacob's friends scurried to the door, disappearing outside. But Gemma grabbed Jacob's arm to hold him back. "Wait a second, please. This is important."

He pulled away from her. "What do you want now?"

"You heard the police last time—one more incident and they'll be forced to take action. Now, I have a feeling you stole that fabric. If they caught you, you could go to jail. Do you understand that?"

Jacob paused, shrugging. "I don't care. It doesn't matter—nothing does anymore. Just leave me alone."

"What about your grandmother? Doesn't she matter? Because she isn't doing well right now, Jacob, and your bad behavior isn't helping. Will you stop for a moment and think about someone other than yourself?"

Jacob thought about that for a moment, looking sincere before his face changed to a snarl. "You don't know anything. So, stop lecturing me."

"Only if you stop being a brat! You're lucky to have a grandmother like her, kid."

Jacob scoffed. "What did you just call me?"

The door to the office opened, revealing a tipsy Barbara standing in the doorway. "I heard shouting. What's going on? Jake, is that you? You're supposed to be at school."

"I'm going." He rolled his eyes at Gemma, then stepped out onto the sidewalk. "Later."

Gemma chased after him, closing the door behind her so Barbara couldn't overhear. "Look, I'm sorry I called you a brat. But seriously, you need to get this bad behavior under control. You're going to ruin your life. Both your grandmother and mother wouldn't want that."

"Leave me alone!" Jacob called, walking down the sidewalk toward his friends. "I don't care what you think."

"Those boys are a bad influence on you! I don't know what their situation is, but you still have a future, Jacob. Don't ruin it!"

The boy still wasn't listening, catching up to his friends before they walked away. They threw the fabric in the nearby trash. Gemma shook her head, realizing they didn't even want what they had stolen—they just wanted to cause trouble.

She walked toward the garbage can, fishing out the folded fabric. They were soft in her hands. Gemma glanced around, looking for the old woman, but she had vanished. She eventually saw a store called FERN'S FABRICS down the block that seemed to be where the boys had stolen from.

Gemma headed down the sidewalk, entering the shop. It was small and crowded with racks of fabrics in different colors for sale. The same old lady she had seen before, presumably Fern, was sewing something near the front desk. She wore a purple sundress and was shaking her head while her cane sat on the counter.

"Rotten, rotten boys," she muttered under her breath, her hands working away. "We never would've treated the elderly like that in my day ..."

Gemma approached, clearing her throat. "Excuse me, ma'am?"

The old lady jumped before turning around. "Oh, you scared me! Hello there. Welcome to my fabric shop. My name is Fern but most people call me Mrs. Jones."

"Nice to meet you, Mrs. Jones. I couldn't help but overhear." Gemma held up the fabric. "Did a group of boys come in here and steal this from you?"

The old woman's eyes lit up, and she reached out to take the fabric. "Oh, yes—they did! They were awful. They came in, pretending to shop. When I turned my back, they stole what they could and ran away. I chased after them, but I'm in no condition at my age to catch them. Sadly, they escaped. Where did you find this?"

"In the garbage can outside. They threw it away. I'm so sorry, Mrs. Jones."

The old woman sighed, setting the fabric down on her desk. "Thank you, that's kind of you to fish it out. What's your name?"

"Gemma Solace. I work at the bookstore down the street. I just wanted to say—don't be so hard on those boys. I know one of them is struggling with the loss of their mother. A soldier in the army."

Mrs. Jones cocked an eyebrow. "Really? My husband served for forty years, so I appreciate her service. Losing a parent can be difficult, especially on a child. Still doesn't excuse theft, though."

"No, it really doesn't. Don't worry—I'm trying to turn that boy's life around."

"Good, good. Best of luck. Just make sure he doesn't come back, or I'll have to call the police. I can't have thieves running around, stealing from my shop. It's bad for business."

"Of course, I'll make sure of it. Thank you for your compassion, Mrs. Jones." Gemma had an idea, pausing. She noticed a child size mannequin a few feet away. "Say ... do you think you could make me a dress? Similar to the one I'm wearing, but for a little girl? Around the same size as that mannequin over there?"

Mrs. Jones adjusted the bifocals on her face, looking at the mannequin. "Of course I can! Dressmaking is my specialty. Yours is lovely, I might add. Something I would've worn in my younger days. Anyway, is the dress for your daughter? Or son?"

"No—just a friend's daughter. She loves the dresses I wear, and she's sick, so I want to do something nice for her. She has a lot of autoimmune diseases, the poor girl. Anyway, when can you have it ready?"

"If I start right away, by tomorrow. A dress for a child won't take long, and I've got the fabric I need right here—especially since you brought some back for me. Since she's a sick child, I won't charge anything. Just tell her to take care of herself."

Gemma gawked. "That's sweet of you, Mrs. Jones, but please—I want to support your business. Let me give you something. How about a hundred dollars?"

Mrs. Jones smiled. "If you insist, dearie. Thank you very

much. Come back tomorrow and I'll have it ready by then. I have no other orders at the moment."

Gemma thanked her again, then left the money on the table as payment. She quickly helped pick out a pattern before Mrs. Jones cut the fabric. As she walked toward the doors, she noticed a bulletin board with a bunch of posters taped to it. One of them caught her eye.

NIGHTLY COMMUNITY CENTER GROUP THERAPY, the pamphlet read. FOR GRIEF, ADDICTION, HEARTBREAK, COPING WITH ANXIETY, AND MORE. FREE AND OPEN TO ALL.

Gemma glanced over her shoulder. "Hey, Mrs. Jones—can I take this pamphlet? I think I'm going to recommend this group therapy session to a few friends of mine."

"Oh, of course! The grief group therapy really helped my husband when he lost his brother last year." Mrs. Jones continued working, not even looking back at Gemma. "It's all yours."

Gemma thanked her, then removed the thumb tack from the poster and slipped it into the pocket of her dress. She left the fabric store and headed down the street. When she entered the bookstore, she found Barbara near the cash register, looking tired and hungover as she leaned on the counter near a pile of books.

"There you are," she said, noticing Gemma. "Where did you run off to? And what did Jacob want?"

"Nothing—everything's fine. Just wanted to place a dress order before I forgot. You doing okay?"

"My head hurts and I'm still tipsy. My, that reminds me of my college days." Barbara let out a belch, making Gemma wince. "Oh, sorry. And thanks for watching over the shop while I was ... busy."

"Of course, you're welcome. A reporter even stopped by—

wanted to do a segment on indie stores to help them grow their business. I did the interview for you. Should air tonight on the evening news."

Barbara's eyes widened, slamming a book down on the counter. "You did? I was really hoping to give that interview myself. She's been poking around for a while now."

"Oh. Oops." Gemma had stolen the spotlight when it wasn't her intention. "Well, no offense … but you weren't in any position to be on TV. With your drinking and all. I just wanted to help."

Her words cracked like a whip. "I still could've done the interview. I can handle myself, thank you very much."

Her anger must've been the booze talking. Gemma nodded, not wanting to upset her even more. "Okay, you're right. I'm very sorry. I just wanted to bring in more customers."

"Well, I hope it helps. What did you say exactly?"

"I gave information on our hours and books, of course. Then the idea of hosting game nights and activities to bring in more customers."

Barbara's eyebrows furrowed. "My grandson keeps me busy. I'm not sure I have time to run all these game nights, you know."

"Well, then … I'll do it for you. I promise—It'll work out, Barbara." She patted her shoulder. "Take a deep breath."

Barbara did just that. "Fine, fine. I'm too tired to argue anymore. I'm sorry if you think I'm being harsh, I'm just concerned about logistics. Anyway, I hope all that you said helps because right now, this store is a ghost town."

Gemma looked around. She was right. Not a soul could be found inside the store—something that probably wasn't helping Barbara's alcoholism. Gemma remembered the pamphlet then, setting it down on the counter.

"Fingers crossed. Anyway, have you seen this? I saw it on the wall at the fabric store down the block."

Barbara looked at the flyer, shrugging. "Yes, I think I have. The community center has been a staple around here for a long time. What about it?"

"I'm going tomorrow night—I'm hoping it can help me with my anxiety. Maybe even help me cope with losing my mother. I was thinking you and Jacob could come with me. You know, so I'm not alone."

Barbara thought for a moment, then nodded. "All right, only because you've done so much for us. Which I greatly appreciate. We'll be there for you. I'll try to convince Jacob to come as well."

Gemma smiled, taking the flyer back. "Great—I'll meet you two there. Anyway, I should get back to work now."

As Barbara nodded, she seemed unaware of Gemma's true plans. She hoped she could get her *and* Jacob to counseling to help them solve their problems. They were both heading down dangerous roads.

Gemma continued stocking the shelves, then took a lunch break. She had lunch with Barbara as she always did in her office as they shared a few sandwiches. Barbara was still drunk, but at least she could talk and walk around. As she bit into a tuna sandwich, her eyes lit up.

"I'm so sorry, I completely forgot to ask," Barbara began. "How did your date go with Ian last night?"

Gemma smiled, finishing off a small bag of chips. "It went great. In fact, I'm seeing him again tonight. Don't know what he has planned, but it should be fun. I really, really like him. He's a wonderful man."

"I can tell." Barbara smiled. "I used to feel that way too, back when I started dating my ex-husband. Oh, how I miss those days."

Gemma frowned. "I'm so sorry, Barbara. I really am."

Barbara sighed, wiping her crumbs into the nearby garbage can. "Yes, well … things don't always work out the way we want them to. Anyway, let's get back to work, shall we?"

Gemma nodded, ending the conversation as she got back to work with Barbara. They helped each other stock the shelves, counted the money in the register, and cleaned the entire store. Gemma didn't mention Ian's background—just in case Barbara knew about his family. Wanting to lie low was something both she and Ian had in common.

A few hours later, once the working day was done, Gemma collected her things and her pay and left the bookstore. She quickly reminded Barbara to head home and watch the news to see her bookstore featured. Gemma hoped she could actually see it without getting wasted again.

Once she reached her apartment, Gemma passed Carly and Abby coming home, smiling and saying hello. She couldn't wait to surprise the little girl with a dress made just for her. She was still eyeing Gemma's dress as she turned the corner, vanishing from view while holding her mother's hand. That flirtatious father of hers was still nowhere to be found.

After riding the elevator up to Noah's apartment, Gemma quickly showered and put on another dress. It was silver with sequins this time and went to her knees—just in case Ian brought her somewhere where she had to walk. The last thing she wanted was to trip over a long dress and fall on her face in front of him.

When a knock sounded on the door around six p.m., Gemma answered it with a giddy smile. Ian stood there— looking handsome in a leather jacket and jeans. The jacket had the symbol of a small airplane on the breast pocket. And he was holding flowers in his hands again, this time red roses.

"Hey," he said with a smile. "You look amazing—as usual."

"Me? Have you looked in a mirror? This is your most handsome look yet," Gemma said, making him blush. "More flowers?"

"Of course. It's kind of a tradition now."

She took the flowers, sniffing them. "The best kind. Let me put these in water with the others and then I'll be ready to go."

He nodded, waiting for Gemma. She quickly put the roses in the same vase as the other flowers and rushed to the door. She locked it and headed downstairs with Ian, then got into his car after he opened the door for her like a perfect gentleman. Gemma was never going to get tired of that.

"So, where are we heading tonight?" Gemma asked, buckling her seatbelt. "You never told me."

Ian grinned, pulling out of the parking lot and into traffic. "It's a surprise. Don't worry—I think you're going to like it. Do they have fast food where you come from?"

"No, not at all. Our meals are always prepared fresh." With a little magical spell to ensure they last, but Gemma didn't say that. "What's fast food like?"

"Cheap, greasy, and not that good for you. But hey, it tastes delicious. This should be a new experience for you. Let's grab dinner first before our adventure begins. Tim Hortons, here we come!"

Ian drove them to Tim Hortons for dinner. According to Ian, it was a popular Canadian coffee chain. They also served donuts and simple meals like sandwiches and soup. They both got chili, then chased it down with some iced coffee afterward. Gemma was in heaven as they sat at a wooden table in the small restaurant.

"Okay, I think I love fast food," she said.

Ian laughed. "Same here. Now, before I show you the surprise, I wanted you to meet Max. Would that be okay?"

Gemma's eyes lit up. "Of course! Can't wait."

Ian nodded, throwing out their garbage before driving them back to his apartment. It was a small building on the edge of town—too cheap for a billionaire's son—but Ian spoke about it with pride. He opened her car door, then led her inside the building and into the elevator.

"This is the first place I lived that was my own, you know?" he explained as the elevator ascended. "My parents had nothing to do with this. I'm proud I was able to afford it and live here."

"I'm proud of you too, Ian. You've done well for yourself."

He beamed. "Thanks, Gemma. So have you."

She blushed, then stepped off the elevator when it arrived on his floor. Ian led her down the hall to his apartment where he unlocked the door and gestured for her to enter. The apartment was quiet and cheaply decorated, yet homey and serene at the same time. The furniture was mismatched and holey and the carpet looked chewed up from an animal, but Gemma didn't mind one bit. It was Ian's home—and she loved the smell of him in the air.

Photographs of Ian at his bar covered the walls, then some pictures with a man in his twenties who she assumed was his brother, Marcus. They looked happy as they beamed at the camera.

Gemma barely had time to react before something big tackled her to the floor, drooling all over her. A large black dog began licking her face and wagging his tail. Ian gasped, pulling the dog off her.

"Max, stop! What did I tell you about jumping on people?" he asked, holding him back and petting his furry head. "You knocked this beautiful lady down. And ruined her dress. Looks like he got some drool on you, Gemma. Sorry about that."

Gemma laughed, picking herself up. "I don't mind—not

when he's so cute. Nice to meet you, Max. I'm Gemma. And you're as handsome as your owner."

The dog barked, licking her hand. Ian watched with a smile. "Looks like Max likes you. That's always a good sign. I'm cautious of anyone a dog doesn't like."

"Me too. In my experience, animas have such great instincts. I think we're going to be good friends." Gemma petted his ears, blowing kisses at him. "Who's a good boy? Yes, you are!"

She petted the dog again, making him bark in joy. As Ian began petting him too, then rubbing his belly, Gemma hoped Ian was having the same good feeling about her that she was about him.

CHAPTER 13

After saying goodbye to Max, Ian led Gemma out of the apartment before locking the door behind them. Max was barking behind the door and seemed like he wanted to go out too. As they walked down the hallway, Gemma wiped dog hair off her dress and shook her head.

"Poor boy," she said. "He just wanted to spend time with us."

"Don't worry—we can arrange a doggy date or something. Max loves going for walks." Ian eyed Gemma's dress. "Sorry, did he get his hair all over you? I love that dog, but man, does he shed. Here, let me help."

He wiped off some of the dog hair, making her skin feel electrified when he touched her. But Gemma didn't mind. "It's all right—he's cute, so I'll let him get away with it. Maybe I should get a pet."

"You definitely should. They're great companions." Ian pressed a button on the wall, beckoning the elevator. "Max is my best friend—I tell him everything. Adopting him was the best decision I ever made since leaving my family. I knew I was taking him home when I saw his cute little face at the shelter."

When the elevator arrived, Gemma nodded and stepped on. "I hear that. And I feel the same with my books."

"Hear! Hear!" Ian said, pressing the elevator button. "But spending time with a beautiful woman is nice too."

Gemma blushed, riding the elevator down to the lobby. Ian led her out toward his car where he opened her door for her again. Once he had hopped inside, he drove down the street, still tight-lipped about their date. They chit-chatted on the drive until Gemma saw the airport sign in the distance.

"The airport?" She frowned, turning to him. "Are you taking me somewhere? I'm afraid I don't have a passport."

Or any identification. Gemma had read humans needed those when traveling in books and movies. But Fairhaven didn't have that kind of stuff, and Gemma hadn't been in Toronto long enough to register for anything. The thought of flying made her stomach twist into knots. What if they crashed?

Ian raised an eyebrow. "How did you get to Toronto? You came from somewhere far, didn't you?"

"Uh, that's right. I did," she stammered. "I ... took the train. And I was lucky no one asked for my I.D."

"Yeah, I'll say. Weird." Ian shook his head, pulling into the airport parking lot. "Anyway, we're staying in Toronto, don't worry. Besides books and dogs, I have another passion. Flying. If it's okay with you, I wanted to take you up in my private plane."

"Wow—I've never been in a plane before." Gemma unbuckled her seatbelt, nodding. "Yeah, I'd like that."

Ian smiled, opening her car door before leading her to a private hangar. "This is one of the only gifts I kept from my parents—my little private plane. Sometimes I feel guilty for not giving it back since I left, but I love it."

Ian opened the hangar door, letting Gemma enter first. When she spotted a small airplane, her eyes widened, it was red with white stripes—probably for Canada's flag she had seen blowing atop poles in the city—which could hold two passengers and some cargo in the back.

"If it makes you feel better, I've had rigorous training," Ian explained, walking toward the airplane. "I've taken over a hundred lessons since I was fifteen and haven't gotten into a single accident. Plus, I take Max out once in a while. He loves to fly too."

"Like father, like dog," Gemma joked, making Ian laugh. "I trust you, Ian. If you say you know how to fly, then I believe it."

And flying in a plane for the first time seemed like something exciting—exactly what she came to the surface to do.

Ian beamed from ear to ear. "Glad to hear it. Come on—you're riding shotgun. After you, my lady."

Ian opened the passenger side door of the plane, helping Gemma get inside. She looked at the straps attached to the seat; it was so different than a car's seatbelt. Ian chuckled and climbed up so he could reach her. His face was close to hers as he guided her arms into the harnesses. His sandalwood scent wrapped her in a cocoon of warmth. The air between them thickened with something Gemma had only read about in books. His gaze caressed her lips, her heart thudding in her chest. He swallowed, and her gaze was drawn to his throat.

"There you go." He clicked the final buckle, and their eyes met. Gemma licked her lips. "We've gotta take off in a minute," he whispered, breaking the spell.

Gemma nodded, leaning back in her seat. "Okay."

Then Ian walked around, getting into the pilot's seat. He seemed to know what he was doing as he buckled up and flicked a bunch of buttons on the ceiling.

"Are you ready?" he asked. "I love a good evening flight. It's really peaceful."

Gemma nodded. "With you? More than ready."

Ian reached for the controls, then put on a headset and piloted the plane out of the hangar. Gemma took one as well so they could communicate. He steered it down the private runway before it began to lift into the air. Gemma had ridden on a dragon back home, gliding around Fairhaven, but an airplane was different.

This airplane didn't breathe fire or accidentally throw Gemma off with the snap of his tail. Luckily, they weren't in the air when that'd happened so all she had to show was a bruised tailbone.

As she looked down at the city of Toronto, lit up by the streetlamps, she felt in awe. She could see everything so clearly —the CN Tower, the parks from overhead, and all the skyscrapers. The people down on the sidewalk seemed so small.

"Gorgeous, isn't it?"

It took Gemma a second to realize Ian was speaking to her. She was so transfixed by the view that she had barely heard him, then forced herself to nod. "Absolutely. I can see why you love flying."

"Like books, it was an escape for me. A chance to get away from my family." Ian stared straight ahead, steering the small plane. "My mother always thought my hobby was too dangerous, but I'm pretty sure it helped me stay sane all these years."

Gemma's breath caught in her throat. She had never seen something so mesmerizing. Back in Fairhaven, sunlight rarely made its way down the storm drains. The sunrise in person made it hard for Gemma to tear her eyes away from the glow. "I understand. Thank you for taking me up here, Ian. It's beautiful."

He grinned, then his voice went deeper. Like an announcer voice on the radio. "You're welcome. Attention, attention—this is your captain speaking. If you look to your right, you'll see Lake Ontario ..."

Gemma laughed at his narration, listening to all the exciting spots in Toronto. Ian really knew his way around. After his speech, he gestured toward the sky, a flash of light above their heads.

"Hey, look—a shooting star. Make a wish."

Gemma peered out the window. A shooting star exploded through the sky above their heads, similar to the ones she had read about in fantasy novels. They were supposed to be as magical as you could get in the human world. Gemma closed her eyes, wishing her life in the surface world would only get better from here.

When she opened them again, Ian was looking at her with a smile. She hadn't realized how close they were sitting. The cockpit had minimal room, making it feel cozy and intimate. He nudged her shoulder.

"I made my wish," he whispered, looking deep into her eyes. "Did you?"

Gemma nodded. "I did. What did you wish for?"

"I can show you right now. If you'd let me." Ian blushed. "I'd really like to kiss you, Gemma. Would that be okay?"

She laughed, trying to cover up her nervousness. Her tummy flipped, her hands shaking in her lap as Ian stared at her lips. "More than okay, Ian. You can even kiss me twice if you want."

He chuckled, then they both leaned in. His lips brushed hers, soft as a feather, his breath mingling with hers. It was perfect. Gemma pressed into him, wanting more almost hungrily, needing to feel him against her body. He groaned, cupping her cheek and angling his head. The kiss was exactly what she'd imagined her first kiss would be like. The sun setting behind them, shooting stars blazing across the sky, and fireworks exploded behind her closed eyelids.

She had no doubt in her mind then. Ian was the one for her —her fairytale.

Ian pulled away, turning back to look straight ahead. "Well, that was perfect. The date, meeting Max, kissing in an airplane. Ten out of ten."

Gemma nodded. "I agree. More than worth the wait."

"Definitely. Man, look at all the people down there." Ian pointed out the window. "All living their own lives, worrying about their problems. Being up here puts how many people are in the world into perspective."

Gemma watched the people below. Her mother was some-where down there? And if so, where? Was she living happily or miserable after being kicked out of Fairhaven?

Ian cleared his throat, dragging Gemma out of her thoughts. "Anyway, I'll take us back down now. It's getting late."

Gemma took one last glimpse at the city of Toronto from above, then Ian flew them back onto the runway. She missed the views already. He guided the airplane into the hangar before turning off the engines. Then he removed his headphones and gestured for Gemma to do the same, opened his door, and walked around before grabbing Gemma's waist and helping her down. She blushed, feeling his hands on her waist.

"You did well for your first flight. When I took my little brother, he was very anxious. Had to turn around." Ian shook his head. "You were a model passenger."

Gemma curtsied. "Thank you, I try. I have anxiety too—I know it's not pleasant. I'm sure he didn't mean to freak out."

"Yeah, I know. He's had it rough. My brother's the only one I like in my family. Maybe you two can meet sometime. Just not in an airplane," Ian joked. "Anyway, I'll take you home. We both have early mornings tomorrow."

Gemma nodded, walking arm-in-arm with Ian out of the hangar. They found his car where they had left it and hopped inside. They held hands on the drive back to her apartment, and Gemma relived the kiss all over again. Ian walked her up to her apartment to make sure she got in safely.

"So, are you free again tomorrow night?" Ian asked as Gemma unlocked her door and stepped inside. "Because I'd love to see you again. If it isn't too much."

"It's not too much. And I'd love to, but I have a group therapy session," Gemma explained. She turned in the open doorway and leaned against the frame. "Kind of a long story, but I think my boss has a drinking problem. I'm trying to get her help."

"Oh, that's nice of you. Okay, not tomorrow evening then. But I'll be in touch. Maybe I'll even drop by the bookstore. You know, just to browse."

Gemma smiled. "I'd like that, Ian. I'm trying to set up some game nights at the bookstore, actually. Barbara was a little upset about it—she thinks she's too busy—but I'll handle it all. Just need to work out some stuff. But you could maybe bring your brother, help the business grow?"

"That's a great idea. I'd love to—and I'm sure Marcus would as well. Goodnight, Gemma. See you soon."

Gemma didn't hesitate at all as their lips brushed. This kiss was hungrier, more passionate. Ian tangled his fingers in her hair and then rested them on her hips. She grabbed his lapels, pulling him in closer. She was utterly mesmerized by the scent of him—his sandalwood cologne, his aftershave. She never wanted it to end. To her disappointment, Ian pulled away. They were both breathless, saying nothing for a few seconds.

"That was ..."

"Incredible," Ian filled in, blushing scarlet. "Sleep well, Gemma."

He strode down the hall, heading into the elevator. Gemma watched him vanish with a wave before heading into her apartment. She closed the door and leaned against it, sighing dreamily. It had been a perfect second date.

But it seemed like whenever things heated up, Ian blushed and ran away. Had something happened that had made him so guarded? He had mentioned he was in a bad relationship, though Gemma wondered if there was more he wasn't telling her.

Pushing it out of her mind for now, Gemma changed into her pajamas and passed out on the couch, dreaming of Ian. She woke up to her alarm buzzing, then had cereal for breakfast and got ready for work. She decided on a puffy, brown dress with flowers along the hem.

When she passed Carly and Abby in the hallway, she could only smile, excited to show the little girl the dress later. It was going to be perfect.

After walking a few blocks to work, she made it to the bookstore, opening the door with a chime. Barbara was near the cash register, ringing up a few people with their books. She was humming to herself, and the place looked busier than usual.

"Full house," Gemma said, heading toward the desk. "And you look to be in a good mood. What's going on?"

Barbara finished checking out the customer, then turned to Gemma with a smile. "The interview aired, Gemma. It's brought in more customers already. Oh, I'm so happy!"

She reached out to hug Gemma, thanking her for giving the interview. Gemma was happy she had helped a little bit. And when they finally held the grand reopening, she hoped it would bring in even more customers to liven up the place.

As Gemma got to work, helping customers and filling the shelves, she noticed the door to Barbara's office was ajar. The new bottle of alcohol sitting there wasn't nearly as empty as the one from yesterday. It seemed Barbara wasn't drinking as much. Maybe her business' success was all she needed to get her out of her funk—or realizing she had missed an interview due to her drunkenness. Either way, there was some progress.

When lunchtime rolled around, they were still busy with customers, so they rang them up together and ate while they worked. Barbara was eager to hear the news about Gemma's second date.

"And then he kissed you? In his airplane?" Barbara smiled, checking out a romance novel. "How romantic. It's like you're in some kind of fairytale."

Gemma tried to hide her blush but her cheeks burned hot anyway. "I know. I can't believe this is real life. I used to dream about finding a man like him, and now, it's really happening."

"I'm so happy for you. And I'm still living vicariously through your dating life, by the way. I just want you to be careful. I saw in the newspaper that Ian's the son of a billionaire and he dated an actress. I don't want you to get hurt—or have his past come back to bite you."

Gemma was more worried about *her* past hurting Ian, but she nodded along. "I promise I'll be okay, Barbara."

"Good. Now, keep going, please. All this juicy relationship gossip makes me feel young again."

Gemma laughed, giving her even more details that Barbara soaked up like a sponge. When the customers died down a bit, Gemma ran down the block on her break, heading to Fern's Fabrics. Mrs. Jones had the beautiful, small gown sitting on the desk when she entered the store. It was a pink princess gown with ruffles around the cuffs and a silver streak down the middle.

Gemma's eyes widened as she approached, pointing at the dress. "Is this it?"

The old lady nodded as she looked up with a smile. "This is it. I hope it's all right."

"All right? It's better than that. It's gorgeous!" Gemma

picked up the dress, running her fingers along the fabric. It was soft and smooth. "Gosh, this is just like something kids would wear back in Fairhaven."

Mrs. Jones adjusted her glasses. "Back where, dear? I've never heard of such a place."

"Uh, no, you wouldn't have. It's far from here." Gemma shook her head. "Anyway, thanks for this. Can't wait to show Abby. Have a good day, Mrs. Jones!"

The old lady waved, then got back to her sewing behind the desk. Gemma carried the gown back to the bookstore and kept it in the office for safekeeping. She chastised herself for talking about Fairhaven out loud, hoping Mrs. Jones wouldn't bring it up ever again.

Gemma then headed back down the aisles, cleaning things up. A few hours later, it was time to close the bookstore as Gemma finished up a few last-minute things. Just as Barbara was about to lock the doors, Gemma heard a scuffle. It sounded like someone forcing their way inside the store.

"Get out of here!" Barbara yelled. "What are you doing?"

Gemma's head popped up, her heart pounding. She ran around the side of the bookshelf and saw the commotion. Barbara was standing near the door, holding her hands up in front of a man wearing a black mask. His features were unrecognizable but the gun in his hand was clear. Gemma's stomach twisted, then she froze in place out of fear.

"Give me all your money out of the register," he demanded, waving the gun around. "Hurry—I don't have all day, lady!"

Barbara nodded, rushing toward the register. She began to take out the money she'd made that day from the new customers—a few tears slipping out of her eyes—as Gemma hid behind the shelf, needing to do something.

It was now or never.

Just as she tip-toed toward the man, hoping to disarm him,

he turned his head and noticed her. He lifted a hand, then a magical wave of sparkling purple light tripped Gemma up, spun her around, and made her fall to the ground. She hit the back of her head against the floor with a groan. Her hands shook, both with anxiety and shock.

"Nice try," the man snarled, "but I knew you were there. Now, come on—I need my money. Or I'll start shooting your nosy little employee."

"Please, don't!" Barbara cried, rushing toward the door with the money in her hands. "This is all I have. Take it and go!"

The man grabbed the money out of her hands, then opened the door and ran down the road. He faded into the darkness. Gemma groaned as she forced herself to sit up, little particles of purple magic floating around her before fading to ashes on the ground.

It was no different than the spellcasting from down in Fairhaven. But how did that human have the power to do that? He could've been one of the Fairhaveners who escaped to the surface, but Gemma didn't recognize him.

Barbara rushed over, kneeling next to Gemma. "Oh my gosh, you're bleeding. Gemma, are you okay?"

"I think so. My head is killing me." Gemma rubbed the back of her head. "Are you okay, Barbara?"

"I'm fine, dear. I just wish I could've stopped this." She shook her head, pulling out a cell phone from her pocket. "Here, let me call you an ambulance. Just to get your head checked out. And I'll need to call the police as well."

Gemma nodded, hobbling over to the front desk where she sat down on one of the chairs. Barbara phoned 9-1-1 and asked for the paramedics and the police. The officers showed up first, scouting out the place before returning to them at the register.

"The coast is clear, ma'am. The thief is gone," the officer

said. "Do you have security cameras? We'd like to get video footage of the suspect."

"Of course—right back there in my office," Barbara said, pointing at the door. "Go ahead in, it's not locked. I'm going to stay here with my employee and make sure she's all right."

The officers nodded, heading into the office to review the footage. Barbara grabbed a paper towel and ran it under warm water in the bathroom before applying it to Gemma's head. She was taking care of her like any concerned mother would, making Gemma think of her own mom. She missed those days.

Was it possible the man with the gun knew where her mother was? Would finding him bring Gemma closer to her?

"I'm so sorry this happened, Gemma," Barbara said, on the verge of tears again. "This part of town is usually safe—we've never had a robbery before. Are you sure you're okay?"

"Yes, I'll be okay," Gemma said, forcing a smile to comfort her. "We're both alive and that's what matters."

Barbara wiped a tear away. "Yes, I suppose you're right. But the money we just made is gone. I still have the credit card sales, but that was it for the physical cash. Just when I thought my business was doing better, thanks to that interview, some jerk comes in and ruins it all. I can't believe this ..."

And neither could Gemma. She was just relieved it wasn't Barbara's grandson again. He was trouble, but robbing a place with a gun seemed to be too extreme for him. No—this had been someone else. And someone with magical knowledge.

But how? As they waited for the paramedics to arrive, Gemma knew she had to find out.

Before it became a threat to both the surface world *and* Fairhaven.

CHAPTER 14

The paramedics arrived five minutes later, shining a light in Gemma's eyes. They declared she was in good health—but told her to take it easy—before leaving. Gemma felt fine so she didn't plan to take that advice, and she could always go back to Fairhaven if she was seriously injured.

"I'm glad you'll be okay," Barbara said, watching the paramedics drive away from the window. "I'd never forgive myself if you got hurt at work, especially trying to defend me. It was brave of you but dangerous."

"It's all right, Barbara—it's not your fault. I'd do it again in a heartbeat." Gemma jumped off the desk, rubbing her head. "Just need to get better at sneaking up on someone next time."

"I hope there isn't a next time." Barbara shivered. "But this city has gotten so unsafe lately."

Two officers came out of the office, holding a USB drive. One of them took notes while the other spoke with Barbara and Gemma. "First off, are you two all right? He didn't hurt you, did he?"

Gemma weighed her options. She couldn't very well tell the officer the man had magic. He never would've believed her, and she was still supposed to keep Fairhaven a secret. So, she had no choice but to deceive the officer.

"He pushed me," Gemma lied, knowing she'd feel guilty later, "but the paramedics said I'll be okay. It's already starting to feel better, thanks to Barbara's TLC."

Barbara smiled. "Anything for you, dear. But I saw him push you—yet his hands didn't even touch you! There was some kind of mist in the air. It was pink and purple ... almost perfume-like."

The two officers glanced at each other, then the other wrote down their testimony. The first officer nodded. "Yes, we've gotten that report before. You aren't the only business to be robbed lately."

"I saw that on the news," Gemma said. "Something about an uptick in robberies?"

"That's right, miss. But no need to worry—we're looking into it. We've got the entire Toronto Police Department working together to stop this criminal. We believe it's only one man doing this."

"Well, the person who stole from me was definitely a man. Couldn't make out his features though," Barbara said with a sigh. "Sorry we can't be of more help, officers."

"That's all right, ma'am. We're just relieved everyone's all right. We'll have more cops on patrol in the area if it makes you feel better."

"It does, thank you. We'll let you know if anything else happens."

"Great, thanks. In the meantime, we've taken a copy of your surveillance footage. It matches the culprit we're after. His identity is still a mystery, but we'll get to the bottom of this soon enough. He can't hide forever, especially as he ramps up his crimes." The officer pocketed the USB drive, turning to his partner who was snapping pictures of the robbery. "Are you ready to go?"

The other officer nodded, then packed his camera into his bag. They shook Gemma and Barbara's hands before heading toward the door. Just as they opened it, a burly man with a detective's badge entered the shop. Gemma noticed the name CRAWFORD on his badge immediately.

She had heard Noah's father was a cop—a homicide detective to be specific, one investigating a string of murders caused by Fairy Godmother Zamira where she had magically removed organs without making any incisions. It was all part of her experiment to make magic compatible with the surface world, which she eventually had. And some of that magic still lingered. She was dead though, so Gemma knew it wasn't her causing these incidents.

"Hello, gentlemen," Detective Crawford said. "I was in the area and saw the cop cars. Another robbery?"

"Yes, Detective," one of the officers replied. "We've got it under control though. The shop is secure, and we've taken all the evidence pictures and testimonies that we can."

The other officer turned around, glancing at Barbara. "Speaking of which, Ms. Danvers? You'll want to call your insurance company. Perhaps you can get some of the stolen money returned."

Barbara hesitated, then nodded. "Yes—I'll do just that, Officer. Thank you."

"Good. In the meantime, we'll get back to the station and keep working on this case. We want to catch this bastard sooner rather than later." The cop nodded at Detective Crawford. "See you around, Detective."

As they left, Gemma caught Detective Crawford's eye. He held her gaze for a moment before frowning. "Excuse me, but … do I know you?"

He must've recognized her from the crowd at the wedding. She laughed nervously, glancing at Barbara and hoping she wouldn't overhear. "Nope, never seen you before. You might've seen me on TV—I gave an interview to a reporter about this bookstore yesterday. Anyway, let me walk you out. Barbara, I'll be right back."

Barbara nodded, cleaning up around her cash register. Little particles of magic—like glittering dust—had fallen onto her desk. As she busied herself, Gemma headed toward the detective and gestured outside. He followed her and shut the door behind them.

When it was just the two of them out on the darkening street, Gemma spoke up. "You probably have seen me around, Detective. At Noah's wedding. You are his father, aren't you?"

"Yes, I am." Recognition flashed across his face. "Does this mean … you're one of them?"

"From Fairhaven? Yes, I am. I was in the crowd at Esme and Noah's wedding. Beautiful ceremony, by the way."

"It really was—I'm happy for them. I knew you looked familiar. I just didn't want to ask you about Fairhaven. I know all that crap is supposed to be kept quiet. Noah gave me a long talk on the way to the wedding."

"Yeah, and for good reason. Humans might freak out if they learn about a magical world underground. Or misuse our magic if they get their hands on it. Look at what's already happened— Senator Remus tried to bring magic to the surface and his fairy godmother succeeded. Then they placed humans from Toronto under their spell. Their memories were all wiped, of course, after Princess Esme saved the day, and it was business as usual for Earth. But there's still pockets of that magic around the city."

"Which someone is exploiting. One of my people. Humans," Detective Crawford filled in. "Yeah, I know. It's been happening for a little while now—a bunch of thefts and assaults. It's the same man, I'm pretty sure, since he looks similar on all the surveillance footage we've gathered."

Gemma nodded. "Exactly. This guy, who I think is a human since I don't recognize him from Fairhaven, obviously had access to a pocket of magical energy. The very kind that was left over when Remus' fairy godmother made magic compatible on Earth. Princess Esme is sending guards to the surface to remove most of them, but maybe she didn't get one in time. Once he figured it out, he learned how to use it—for a life of crime. When he pushed me, it was with magic. No hands used at all."

Detective Crawford winced. "This isn't good. The officers have heard eyewitnesses mentioning magic, though they don't really believe it. I'm the only one on the force who knows the truth about Fairhaven and all this magical crap. Even though I work homicide, I've been trying to help out the guys on the theft squad."

"Well, I wish you luck. I'll keep an eye out. Maybe if we put our heads together, we can stop this guy."

"Boy, that would be nice. Magic is dangerous—I know that much. But soon enough, small robberies ain't gonna cut it for this criminal." Detective Crawford reached into his pocket, pulling out a card. "Here, you see anything dangerous, you call my number immediately. I got a feeling this guy is gonna escalate."

Gemma took the card. "Yeah, I feel the same. Something big is going on—and everyone's in trouble. And one more thing. Unfortunately, some of Remus' sympathizers escaped to the surface before we could jail them. With the senator behind bars, I guess they thought they would be next and fled. Anyway, keep an eye out for them too. They could be behind this. Or gave this human magic in the first place."

"Yeah, definitely." Detective Crawford sighed. "That makes

my job a bit more complicated. These people could be anywhere. Damn, this is one big mess."

"Tell me about it, Detective. Anyway, it was nice to meet you. We'll be in touch soon."

"Hey, that's my line," he joked. "Take care now."

Gemma wished him the same, then watched as the detective walked to his unmarked police car and drove off. Gemma looked down the block, making sure no other stores were affected, and it was only the bookstore that had gotten robbed. She felt so sorry for Barbara after everything she had been through.

But then a dark feeling filled the pit of her stomach. What if one of the sympathizers was behind this somehow, like she had suggested to the detective? And had ties to her mother? Senator Remus *had* said he was planning something special for his one-year anniversary ...

Words that now haunted her.

When she entered the bookstore, fighting away anxiety, she found Barbara sweeping up the dust, then throwing it in the garbage. She looked relieved when she saw Gemma. "Oh, there you are. You got the detective's business card?"

Gemma looked down, still holding onto the card with his information. "Yeah, I did. Just in case. I don't know if this robber would be stupid enough to return to the scene of the crime, but if he does, I'll call the detective immediately."

"Good, good. God, I hope he doesn't come back. He's already taken everything I have." Barbara set her broom aside, sighing. "And I can't even call the insurance company. Mainly because I never took out insurance. The monthly fees were too much. And if anyone found out, I could be kicked out for violating the lease agreement."

Gemma pocketed the card, frowning. "Oh, Barbara ... I'm so

sorry. So, does that mean you can't recover the money that was stolen?"

"Exactly. Not unless they track this thief down and get it back." Barbara leaned against the desk, looking defeated. "Gemma, I'm telling you … I can't lose this bookstore. It's all I have. Without it … I don't even know what I'd do."

Gemma approached her, placing an arm on her shoulder. "Don't worry—we'll find a way to raise the money that was stolen. I'm still working on a grand reopening-slash-game night. The first of many game nights, I hope."

Barbara sniffled, trying not to cry. "Okay—thanks, Gemma. You're such a sweetheart. You know, I've been alone for so long. My grandson barely talks to me these days. So, I'm glad you're here."

"I'm sorry. That's rough." Gemma shook her head. "Well, I'm not going anywhere—no matter what. We're going to get your bookstore on the right track again and get justice. Mark my words."

Barbara smiled. "I admire your optimism so much, Gemma. My daughter was like that too. When she set her mind on something, it was going to happen. She had a real fire inside of her. God, I miss her so much."

When the bookstore turned silent, Gemma didn't know what to say. She just wrapped Barbara in a big hug and they both cried for a little while. Once they pulled away, Gemma grabbed Abby's dress, then they locked up the bookstore and walked out onto the sidewalk.

"Do you need a ride home?" Barbara asked. "I want to make sure you get back safely."

"Sure, that would be great. Thank you."

Barbara nodded, then the two of them got into her small sedan. After she gave Barbara her address, they chit-chatted on the way to Gemma's apartment. Neither of them spoke about the robbery. Gemma was still processing that it had even happened.

Once Gemma arrived home, she thanked Barbara who was heading home to her grandson, then entered her apartment building. Once she had ridden the elevator to her floor, she used Noah's home phone that was only for emergencies to call someone special.

Ian answered on the third ring, the sounds of his loud bar in the background. "Hello? You've reached Ian. If this is about my family or my date, you can piss off. My life is private."

"Ian, it's me," Gemma replied. "The bookstore … someone robbed us at gunpoint."

Ian's heavy breathing lasted for a few seconds. "Holy shit, Gemma. Are you all right?"

"Yes, I'm fine. So is my boss. We're both shaken up. I don't know why I'm calling, really." Gemma sighed. "I guess I just needed to hear your voice to feel better."

"Aw. Well, I'm glad you're okay. Are you at home now?"

"I am. My boss just dropped me off." Gemma looked out her window at the dark sky, watching the people on the sidewalk. Any of them could've been the thief. "Not sure how I'll sleep tonight. I probably won't—not after what happened."

"Yeah, I bet. Stay there—I'm coming over. I don't want you to be alone."

"Ian, that's sweet of you, but it's not necessary. What about your bar?"

"Barney is here; he can close up. You're more important. I'll be over as soon as I can. First, I've gotta stop at home and feed Max."

Gemma smiled, finding it sweet that Ian would make her a priority. She really did have a good man. "Okay. See you then. And thanks again."

They said goodbye, then Gemma got ready for bed. She

changed into some silk pajamas, brushed her teeth, and assembled some blankets on the couch. Forty-five minutes later, a knock sounded on the door. She looked through the peephole first to make sure it wasn't anyone dangerous, but it was only Ian.

When she opened the door, he pulled her into a bear hug. It felt warm and comforting. When he pulled back, he took a good look at her. "Your forehead—ouch. That looks painful. What happened?"

Gemma led him into the apartment, locking the door before telling him everything over tea. He shook his head once she had finished telling the story—leaving out the part about the magical energy. Ian didn't need to know that, not yet at least.

"I'm so sorry," he whispered. "This is awful. I can't believe anyone would do that—and to a bookstore."

"I know. It was pretty shocking." Gemma set down her tea, sighing. "It'll be hard to go back there without thinking about the robber, but I've got no choice. Barbara needs me—she's already fragile after losing her daughter in combat. I have to be there for her."

Ian smiled. "You're a good woman, Gemma. That's kind of you. If you wouldn't mind ... I'd like to stay the night. You know, just to make sure nothing bad happens to you. I can sleep on the couch if that's all right."

Spend the night? That was a big step, and the thought sent a flutter of baby dragon wings in her stomach. But Gemma really liked Ian. And after the evening she'd had, it was a big comfort. She would just have to sleep in Noah's bed after all. It was the only sleeping spot left.

"Yeah, that would be great. Let me know if you need anything. Plenty of spare toothbrushes in the bathroom."

Ian thanked her, getting ready for bed. He changed into a pair of pajamas bottoms and a tank top that Noah had left before they ordered takeout for dinner. Ian knew the number of a local Chinese food place by heart, one that was delicious. They ate it on the couch while watching a romance movie on Netflix, one that had been adapted from a popular book that Gemma hadn't read.

"You're right—this food is amazing!" Gemma cried, scarfing down another eggroll. "I can't believe I've never had Chinese food before."

"First time for everything." Ian's eyes darted down to her mouth, then he leaned forward to wipe her lips with the edge of his thumb. "You had some plum sauce on your lip. There—I got it."

When he sucked the plum sauce off his finger, making eye contact the whole time, heat spread through Gemma's belly. She wanted nothing more than to pull him closer and kiss him again until they were both breathless. But she didn't know if he was ready for that when he had pulled away before—or even if she was ready. It was a big step.

So, she just smiled and thanked him, then went back to her delicious dinner. They finished eating, and Ian let Gemma keep the leftovers. Since she was still worried about cooking, she was thankful for the pre-made food.

"Want to watch another movie?" Ian asked, scrolling through Netflix. "There are more book-to-movie adaptations."

Was he really oblivious to her desire or just being a gentleman? She took a deep breath and nodded. "Sounds great. Put it on."

They sat next to each other on the couch, their fingers brushing the entire time. Halfway through the movie, Gemma felt her eyes becoming heavy, then she faded into dreamland. She had nightmares of the robbery again—and how much damage the thief could do to the world if he continued using that magic.

There was a reason humans didn't have magic on the surface, and it had to go back that way— to before Fairy Godmother Zamira made magic compatible on the surface. Gemma knew why it never worked now—these humans couldn't handle it. It was too dangerous in the wrong hands. That was true about Fairhaven too, though their population was far fewer than Earth. Gemma didn't know how they could handle billions of humans suddenly using magic potions for their own nefarious purposes.

When Gemma's eyes opened, she was still lying on the couch in a sitting position. She glanced around, noticing the sunlight outside. It was early morning when she checked the clock on the wall. But where was Ian? He wasn't next to her on the couch.

Had he really left in the middle of the night? Had their closeness scared him again and he had fled? Gemma checked the kitchen for a note but couldn't find any. She was disappointed, hoping he would've stuck around to say goodbye at least. But maybe the bar needed him, and he had to go.

Speaking of which, Gemma needed to use the bathroom. She walked across the apartment and opened the door without knocking. And she finally solved the mystery of where Ian had gone.

He was drying off from a shower with a spare towel, completely naked in her bathroom.

CHAPTER 15

Gemma paused for a second to take in the handsome view in front of her.

Ian had large biceps, accentuated by his tattoos. Even his abs were toned—most likely from lifting boxes of alcohol all day at his bar. Droplets of water clung to his skin, gently falling onto the floor as he wiped himself dry.

"Oh my gosh, I'm so sorry!" Gemma cried, forcing herself to move. She shut the door and leaned against it from the other side. "I thought you had left."

Ian laughed, opening the door to face her. A towel was around his waist. "It's all right—probably my fault for not locking the door. Did you really think I would leave without saying goodbye? And especially when you were asleep?"

Gemma shrugged, blushing. "I don't know. I'm glad you didn't."

"Me too. What kind of gentleman would I be?" Ian joked. "I hope you don't mind that I used your shower."

Technically, it belonged to Noah, so Gemma just shrugged. "I don't mind at all—make yourself at home. While you get dressed, I'll make us some breakfast. I've been meaning to try cooking omelettes."

"Mmm, my favorite." Ian pushed past her and walked into the living room. He pulled a t-shirt from a duffle bag and pulled it over his head.

Gemma blushed, heading into the kitchen. She wanted to stick around and watch the rest of the show, but she'd promised omelettes, and she would deliver. She hoped she wouldn't burn the stove down again as she prepared the ingredients: two eggs, some cheese, and chopped onion and peppers from the fridge. Noah had been kind enough to fully stock the entire apartment.

After making the first one without an issue, Gemma was pretty confident in herself. She fried the next one and set it aside just as Ian entered in a tight-fitting black t-shirt and jeans. He sniffed the air, then grabbed a seat at the kitchen island.

"Wow, that smells amazing," he said. "Didn't know you were such a good chef."

Gemma snorted, bringing the plates and forks to the island. "I'm not, trust me—I'm still getting the hang of it. You don't even want to know how bad my first attempt at mac and cheese was."

Ian laughed, taking a plate. "I'm sure it wasn't that bad. Thank you—It looks delicious."

She sat next to him, enjoying her omelette. As she chatted with Ian, she realized she could get used to this—their daily breakfasts. If he never left, Gemma wouldn't mind one bit.

After breakfast, they did the dishes. Gemma then quickly dressed in a pastel-pink gown and walked out to greet Ian in the kitchen. She checked the clock, then gestured at the door.

"If you have to go, I totally understand," she began. "I have to get to work soon too."

"Actually, I was hoping to spend the day with you. You

know, come with you to work to make sure the place doesn't get robbed again." Ian scratched the back of his neck, looking nervous. "Call me paranoid, but I want to make sure you're okay. If you don't mind."

Gemma smiled. "I don't mind at all—that's very sweet. But what about your bar?"

"Don't worry, my employee will look after it. I trust him. So, shall we get a move on?"

"Definitely. There's just something I need to do first."

Gemma rushed toward the front door, picking up the small dress that she had ordered the day before. Ian frowned when he walked over and noticed her holding the gown.

"Who's that for?" he asked. "Looks a little too small for you."

"Oh, definitely. It's for my neighbor's daughter, Abby. You met them at the rooftop party. She's always commenting on my dress, plus she's sick, so I had this made for her."

Ian smiled. "That's really sweet of you, Gemma. I'm sure she'll love it. Lead the way—I can't wait to see her face."

Gemma stepped into the hallway with Ian and the little dress. She locked her apartment door before they headed to the elevator. They rode it down to Carly's apartment and knocked on her door.

Carly opened the door a second later in a red salsa dress with tassels around the hem. Her hair and makeup were perfectly done. When Gemma saw her smoky eyeshadow and red lips, she beamed. "Carly! You look so beautiful. What's the occasion?"

She smiled. "Aw, thanks! I'm getting ready for work. Didn't expect to see you this morning. What's going on?"

"I have a surprise for Abby," Gemma said, holding out the pink dress. "I had this made for her."

Carly's eyes lit up, and she reached out a hand feeling the

fabric of the dress. "Oh my gosh—how beautiful! Abby's going to be so happy. She's been bugging me every day for a dress like yours, but I just haven't had time. Anyway, come on, she's just eating breakfast."

Gemma nodded, stepping inside the apartment with Ian. He closed the door as Carly led them into the dining room. Abby sat there, eating a bowl of cereal while playing on a Nintendo Switch. When the little girl didn't look up, Carly cleared her throat.

"Sweetie? Gemma's here," Carly began, "and she's got a very nice gift for you. Look what it is."

Abby looked up, and when she noticed the gown, she set her Nintendo Switch aside. Her eyes widened as she rose to her feet. "Is that ... is that for me?"

Gemma nodded, smiling. "It is. Here you go. Go on, try it on. I want to make sure it fits."

Abby squealed, taking the dress out of Gemma's hands. Then she wrapped her arms around Gemma's waist in a big hug. "Thank you, thank you, thank you! It's so pretty!"

Gemma laughed, patting her shoulder. "You're very welcome. Everyone should have their own princess dress."

Abby squealed, then headed down the hall to her room to get changed. Carly, Ian, and Gemma were smiling at each other when a door down the hall opened. John stepped out, dressed casually for another day of work. He put his taxi hat on and walked into the kitchen.

When he saw Gemma, his face dropped. "Oh, it's you. What are you doing here?"

"John!" Carly chastised. "No need to be so rude. What's the matter with you?"

John crossed his arms. "Nothing—I just didn't expect to have an audience when I woke up. Carly, I think you've been seeing this woman too much."

Carly rolled her eyes. "Hardly. She just popped over to give Abby a princess dress. She was so happy."

"A princess dress? Why would she need that?" John shook his head, pouring a glass of orange juice off the table. "Stupid."

As John sipped his juice, Carly looked like she wanted to say something to him, then Abby opened the door to her room. She came out in the dress, fitting perfectly into it. Gemma's eyes widened with delight as Carly and Ian clapped. John scowled, keeping his head low. Abby twirled and danced around before prancing over to Gemma.

"Look, look—it fits!" she cried. "And it's so beautiful!"

"*You* are beautiful," Gemma corrected, bending down to her level. "And don't you ever forget it."

"I won't," Abby said with a smile. "Hey, there's still time before school. We should have a princess tea party. Come on!"

Before Gemma could respond, Abby grabbed her hand and dragged her down the hall. Gemma looked back at Ian and Carly with a laugh. They were smiling at her but John wasn't. His hard gaze was scary.

For the next half hour, Gemma sat with Abby in her room at a small table on plastic chairs. Teddy bears were scattered around them, wearing crowns and attending the tea party. Abby poured Gemma an imaginary cup of tea before sipping her own.

"Thank you for the dress," Abby said. "I feel like a real princess now."

"You are," Gemma said with a smile, pretending to sip the cup. "And you're welcome. I'm glad it made you happy."

"It did. I just wish Mom and Dad would be happier."

When Abby sighed, Gemma leaned closer. "What do you mean?"

"Well, they're always fighting. Always arguing. It makes me sad." Abby grabbed one of her teddy bears, clutching it tight to her chest. "So, I stay in my room a lot with my teddies. They come with me to the hospital too."

"Yes, your mom told me about that. About your autoimmune conditions. I'm sorry, Abby. I wish I could make things better for you—with your health *and* your parents."

Abby smiled. "You already have, just by giving me the dress. I'll never forget it."

As Gemma smiled back, the door creaked open. Carly stuck her head inside the bedroom. "I'm so sorry to interrupt this royal tea party, but school is starting soon. Are you ready to go, Abby?"

Abby rose to her feet. "I am—and I'm going to wear this dress all day long. Then all my teachers and friends will know I'm royalty."

Carly laughed. "Sounds great. Come on, I'll drive you to school. Your father's just about to head out too."

Gemma stood, tucking her chair under the desk. "You look so lovely in your dress, Carly. You should wear it more often."

Carly smiled. "Thank you, Gemma. This is the look I wear when teaching my salsa classes. You and Ian should come to my studio, you know. At least once. Dancing can bring people closer together."

"We might do just that. Thanks, Carly."

Abby skipped out of the room, leaving the two women behind. As Gemma went to follow her, Carly grabbed her arm, holding her back. "I wanted to say I'm sorry about my husband's behavior earlier. I don't know what's gotten into him lately, but he's been so cruel."

Gemma nodded. "I know—and I'm sorry you're dealing with this. You have nothing to apologize for, though."

"Don't I? He's *my* husband. I just wish I knew what was going on."

Gemma wanted to tell Carly so badly what was going on,

but then she saw Abby's smiling face in the hallway. She didn't want to ruin such a happy moment with her and her new dress, so she kept silent.

"I hope you figure it out soon. Whatever you need, I'm here for you," Gemma said with a smile. "It's what good neighbors do."

Carly looked up at her, smiling back. "The city was lucky when you chose to move here, Gemma. And so was I. Come on, I'll walk you to the door."

Gemma nodded, leaving Abby's bedroom. They walked down the hall where Abby and Ian were chatting about dragons. Gemma just laughed, watching them interact. Ian had a special way with kids.

John stood in the kitchen, sipping some coffee and still glaring at them. Gemma just ignored him like he wasn't there at all. When the four of them stepped into the hallway, John followed, then locked the door behind them.

Abby turned to Ian with a devious smile. "Last one to the car is a rotten egg!"

When she took off running in her dress, Ian laughed, then chased after her. "Hey, no fair—you had a head start!"

Carly giggled, picking up the pace to catch up with them. It left Gemma alone with John. He turned to stare at her. Gemma found his gaze uncomfortable.

"What?" Gemma asked. "I believe the words you're looking for are, 'thank you for buying a pretty dress for my daughter who's sick. It made her happy. You're the best.'"

John snorted. "I don't care how happy it made her—I want you to stay away from Abby and Carly from now on. I don't want you talking to them anymore."

"Or what?"

"Don't play games," John growled. "Just stay away from them, all right?"

"You're still afraid I'll tell Carly the truth, aren't you? About what you've been doing behind her back?" Gemma shook her head. "I'm not going anywhere. Like I said before, you should be the one to tell her, John. This is your mistake—your doing. Find a way to tell her before I do."

John's jaw clenched, then it looked like he was going to say something nasty before a nearby door opened. Several kids from another apartment clamored into the hallway. Gemma just shook her head, pitying John before scurrying off down the stairs. She finally caught up to Ian, Carly, and Abby outside.

Ian was huffing, bent over near the van. "You win, Abby. You're a fantastic princess *and* runner."

Abby smiled, clapping her hands. "I won, I won, I won!"

Carly laughed while unlocking the doors to their van. "Come on, Your Royal Highness—school time. You can see Ian and Gemma later."

"Okay. Bye!" Abby called out, then hopped into the backseat of the van. "I'm going to show everyone my princess gown today!"

Gemma smiled, then she and Ian waved as Carly got into the van and backed up. She mouthed a 'thank you' out the window before the van pulled out of the parking lot and headed down the street. John came out of the apartment building a few moments later, still glaring at Gemma before he got into his taxi and left too.

"Well, that was nice. Good to see her so happy," Ian said. "You did a great thing, Gemma."

Gemma shrugged. "It was nothing. I just wish her father wasn't as grumpy. Abby told me she's sad because they fight a lot."

"Poor girl. I used to be the same—my parents argued all the time too. Not even all the money in the world can make people happy. I hope things get better for Abby and Carly." Ian shook his head. "Anyway, I'll drive you to work. I hope Barbara won't mind me hanging around all day."

"Nah, I don't think so. She'll probably be relieved. I know I'm still spooked from the robbery yesterday."

"Yeah, I know. I'm sorry." Ian unlocked the doors to his sedan, opening the passenger side for Gemma. "Hopefully the police will find the culprit soon, and Barbara can get all her money back."

Gemma hoped so too—or they just might lose that beloved bookstore.

Gemma and Ian quickly stopped by his apartment to check on Max and feed him. After some pets, Ian drove her to work and they chatted about normal things, then Gemma brought up Carly's invitation to the dance studio. Ian seemed interested even if he wasn't the best dancer. They arrived at the bookstore ten minutes later, then entered and found it empty except for Barbara near the front desk.

She slid another bottle of Jack Daniels under the counter, smiling at them. Her eyes were a bit bloodshot, and Gemma wondered if she had been drinking all night.

"Hey, you two," Barbara said. "What are you doing here, Ian? Looking for another book?"

"Actually, I'm here to stand guard all day," Ian said, the bell chiming above the door behind them. "If you don't mind. I'd be upset if that robber came back."

"So would I. No, I don't mind at all—stay as long as you'd like," Barbara said with a smile, then it faded. "Unfortunately, you two are the only ones here. Once people heard about the robbery, they've been too scared to come in. I had a couple a little while ago who refused to shop here. I asked them to come in, but they refused and left."

Gemma sighed. "I'm so sorry, Barbara. I thought the TV interview would help your business."

"I did too, but I guess that's life." Barbara looked on the verge of tears, then turned around. "I have some work to do in my office. Make yourself at home, Ian—and thanks for coming."

She vanished inside her office, shutting the door. Gemma shook her head and turned to Ian. "Poor Barbara, that woman has been through a lot."

"I know, I hope she'll be all right. Anyway, now that I'm here, I may as well work too."

Gemma smiled. "Aw, thanks, Ian. Okay—we just need to sort through these sci-fi titles …"

After working for a few hours, laughing as they went along, Gemma and Ian took a lunch break. Barbara still hadn't come out of her office, and Gemma wanted to give her some space. Barbara convinced Gemma to try shawarma from a small shop down the block, then they ate their food at the restaurant and returned to work.

"Barbara?" Gemma asked, entering the bookstore. "We're back now. Are you here?"

She looked around, searching for the woman in her office and down the aisles, but she was nowhere to be found. And that was when Gemma grew really worried. Her chest tightened, and her hands became sweaty. It wasn't like Barbara to just vanish and leave the bookstore unlocked.

Was she in some kind of trouble? Gemma knew she had to find out.

CHAPTER 16

Gemma left Ian in charge at the bookstore, asking him to guard the cash register and take care of any customers. When she told him she had to go looking for Barbara, he was hesitant to send her alone but finally agreed when Gemma insisted. She walked out the door of the bookstore and looked down.

After asking a few other people on the street if they had seen a woman matching her description, someone finally said she went east. As Gemma continued walking, she saw a bottle of Jack Daniels in the nearby garbage can and knew she was going the right way.

After walking a few blocks, Gemma spotted a small bridge over a lake up ahead. It looked like the perfect spot for cyclists and hikers. The darkening sky made it hard to see, then when the clouds formed and the rain pelted her, Gemma struggled even more. But she was certain she saw someone standing on the bridge that resembled Barbara's hunched profile.

As she walked closer, she realized it was Barbara. She was hanging around near the edge while clutching the handrail on the right side. She stared down into the water, saying nothing. It looked like a far drop.

"Barbara?" Gemma asked, walking up behind her.

Barbara startled before turning around. "Oh, Gemma! You scared me. I didn't even hear you come up."

"Sorry. But what are you doing out here? I came looking for you. I was worried."

Barbara forced a smile, then turned back to staring at the water. "That's sweet of you, Gemma—thanks. Just needed some fresh air. The bookstore was starting to feel suffocating, especially since the robbery yesterday."

"I know—I'm sorry. But you left the bookstore unlocked. Anyone could've walked in while I was gone. Fortunately, it was only me and Ian."

Barbara shrugged. "What does it matter anymore? The robber took all my money. There's nothing left to steal. And thanks to that thief, I might have to close my bookstore. I just can't afford it these days."

"Don't say that. We'll find a way—I know we will." Gemma stepped closer, placing a hand on Barbara's shoulder. "Something else is going on, isn't there? I can tell something's wrong."

Barbara sighed, taking a minute to compose herself before responding. "I had an awful fight with my grandson earlier. And every night, I dream of my daughter. She's always there, just out of reach. I miss her."

"I know. Is that why you came out here?"

"Yes. Yes, it was." Barbara finally turned around, coming face to face with Gemma. "I've been coming to the bridge a lot on my breaks. I guess ... I guess I've been working up the courage to jump off one of these days, but I haven't quite gotten there yet."

Gemma's eyes widened. "No, Barbara. Please don't do that!

You have so much to live for. Your daughter wouldn't want you to die."

"I know. But those thoughts remain, no matter what." Barbara turned, a tear slipping out of her eyes. "I just wish I could take all the pain away. Bring my daughter back, make my grandson happy again. And save my bookstore."

"Well, maybe we can do two out of three," Gemma said softly. "Your grandson needs you. *I* need you—along with so many other people. You're a wonderful person, and I don't want to lose you."

"I will admit, the day you came into my life, things got a lot better. You remind me so much of Mackenzie." Barbara turned to Gemma with a smile. "Kind, thoughtful, beautiful. Thanks for coming to find me. She would've done the same."

"Of course. She sounds like an amazing woman, and I'm sorry I couldn't meet her. And please, whenever you feel tempted to come to this bridge, come find me instead. We'll talk, drink tea, watch movies. Whatever you need to keep going."

Barbara pulled her in for a hug, one Gemma didn't resist. They were both drenched from the rain. "Thank you. Thank you very much. Anyway, that's enough sadness for one day. Let's get back to the bookstore and out of this nasty rain, hmm?"

Gemma agreed, her arm around Barbara's shoulders. She led her off the bridge and down the street. "You know, you really should come with me to the community center tonight. You and Jacob. I think you could benefit from a group therapy session there."

Barbara sighed. "If you think it'll help ... then all right. I haven't really had time for therapy."

"Well, we'll make time. Me and Ian are both here for you."

"That's so sweet. And it was nice of him to stay at the book-store all day—it definitely made me feel better."

Gemma nodded. "Me too. He left his bar to spend time with me."

Barbara raised an eyebrow. "Indeed? You really have a keeper there, Gemma. Don't let him get away."

Gemma had no intention of doing that—or letting Barbara slip through her fingers. She was going to keep both of them in her life, no matter what.

When they made it back to the bookstore, Ian was standing guard over the cash register, making sure no one stole from it this time. He smiled when Gemma and Barbara entered the store with their squeaky shoes.

"There you two are," he said. "Everything okay?"

Gemma nodded. "Everything's perfect. We're heading to the community center later tonight—there's a group therapy session. Since we were busy last night with the robbery and all. Want to come?"

"Of course, whatever you need." Ian walked around the desk, heading toward Barbara. "Gemma told me about the loss of your daughter. I'm so sorry, Ms. Danvers."

Barbara sighed. "Thank you, young man. I miss my daughter very much. Anyway, let's dry off, hmm? I've got some spare towels in my office for rainy days just like this one."

When she returned, Barbara had two towels for her and Gemma. They quickly dried off before Barbara got back to work. As she scurried down the aisle, putting books onto the shelf, Ian glanced at Gemma in concern. She gave him a thumbs up before cleaning the shop. At the end of the day, Barbara led them toward the door before putting the CLOSED sign in the window.

"Well, thank you both very much for helping me today. I really appreciate it," Barbara said. "How about you two come over for dinner with me and my grandson? It'll be a welcome reprieve from the painfully awkward dinners we usually have."

"I'd like that," Gemma said, glancing at Ian. "You?"

He smiled. "A free meal? I won't say no to that. Lead the way."

Gemma laughed, leading them out of the bookstore. Barbara locked the door before getting into her sedan. Ian and Gemma followed in his car, heading to a suburban part of town. Barbara lived in a cozy, blue bungalow with her grandson. When she pulled into the driveway, Ian did the same.

"Hopefully her grandson will agree to come to the group therapy session tonight," Gemma whispered, unbuckling her seatbelt. "That boy needs help too."

"Fingers crossed," Ian said before stepping out. "Let me get your door for you."

Gemma smiled, waiting for Ian to open her door. She thanked him before they walked up the driveway to reach Barbara. She looked through her purse for her keys, then inserted them into the locks on the door. When she opened the door, then gestured for Gemma and Ian to follow, it was dark inside.

"Jake?" Barbara called, flicking the light switch. "Are you here?"

The back door slammed open, and then feet scurried to a bedroom down the hall before the door closed. Barbara sighed, setting her purse down and turning around to look at Ian and Gemma.

"I should go see what that boy is up to now," she muttered. "Have a seat anywhere you'd like—I'll be back soon to cook dinner. I hope you like spaghetti."

"My favorite," Ian said, rubbing his stomach in anticipation.

Gemma shrugged. "I've never had it, actually."

"Never?" Barbara stared at Gemma with wide eyes. "My goodness. It's such a common dish!"

Gemma laughed. "Not that common, apparently. But I'm sure I'll love it. Thanks, Barbara."

She nodded, then vanished down the hallway. Ian and Gemma walked inside and sat on the leather couch in the living room. A minute later, they heard shouting down the hall. It sounded like Barbara and Jacob had gotten into another argument.

"... and what were you doing this time?" Barbara demanded, chasing Jacob down the hall. "There's red paint all over your clothes!"

"Leave me alone, Nana. Jeez!" Jacob called out, then noticed Gemma and Ian in the living room. "Oh, it's you."

"They're our guests for dinner tonight, Jake. You would've known that if you had listened to me," Barbara said. "Then we're heading to the community center afterward."

"What? Why?" Jacob demanded. "I'm playing Fortnite with my friends later."

"It can wait one evening. Now, come on—I need your help making spaghetti, please. I'll let you eat some of the parmesan while we wait for it to cook."

Jacob rolled his eyes, then followed his grandmother into the kitchen. He boiled the water for pasta while Barbara fried the ground beef, added a jar of sauce to it, then some green pepper, onion, and delicious-smelling spices. Gemma and Ian sat quietly on the couch as they watched Barbara's grandson argue with her the entire time.

"That boy doesn't know how lucky he is to have such a loving, patient grandmother," Ian whispered. "I wish I would've had Barbara instead of my parents."

"I know. But he *is* still grieving," Gemma said, eyeing them in the kitchen. "Maybe some group therapy will help. Before one of his antics lands him in jail."

As Ian nodded, the pasta finished cooking. Gemma and Ian

helped Barbara set the table before the four of them sat down. Barbara's cat, Tickles, a Himalayan, came around and ate some cheese that Jacob threw for her on the floor. Gemma was used to house pets that were more of the mythical kind—dragons, unicorns, and hippogriffs. She reached under the table, petting the cat's soft fur and fell in love instantly as it purred beneath her.

"What an adorable creature," Gemma said with a smile, then picked up her fork. "I must get my own cat. Anyway, Jacob, how was school?"

Jacob ate with one hand and petted his cat under the table with the other. "Fine."

"Do anything exciting today?" Barbara asked.

"Not really."

The table turned silent. As Gemma ate, she watched Jacob play with the cat, a smile on his face the whole time as he ignored them. Was that the secret to turning his life around? Something to do with animals?

Gemma thought about it as Barbara collected their dirty dishes, then added them to the dishwasher. Once the cycle was started, Barbara gathered her purse, then walked to the door.

"Time for the community center now, Jacob," she said. "Gemma and Ian invited us. Are you coming?"

Jacob looked like he wanted to argue, his mouth snapping open and closed, then eventually nodded and put on his shoes. "Fine. Whatever."

After petting his cat to say goodbye, the four of them left the bungalow, then got into their cars. It was a twenty-minute drive to the community center downtown. They parked and headed inside, finding the place busy with people playing sports, working out, and attending programs. Gemma found a sign that read GROUP THERAPY SESSION THIS WAY on the wall and pointed.

"Here we are," Gemma said. "Follow me."

The three nodded, following Gemma down the hallway. When they reached the group therapy room, it had already started with several people sitting in a circle. A therapist sat in the middle with a clipboard. The four of them snuck in, finding some empty chairs.

"… and it's been really hard losing my mum," an elderly woman said, sniffling. "Just because she was in her nineties doesn't make it any easier."

"At least you had lots of time with her," Jacob muttered.

"Shh," Barbara chastised, glaring at her grandson.

Fortunately, the old woman hadn't heard. The therapist nodded and scribbled some things down. "Yes, losing someone —especially a parent—is never easy. And it comes with so many emotions. Sadness, anger, regret."

Gemma cleared her throat. "How do you deal with all of those emotions?"

"Well, nothing will completely ease your pain. But some things can help," the therapist replied. "Spending time with the family you still have, letting yourself cry, and coming to therapy are all good things. Honoring your loved one is important on your journey to healing. Can anyone relate to what Betsy has said?"

Barbara nodded, staring down at her hands. "Yes … yes, I can. I lost my daughter in action a few months ago. Since then, me and my grandson's lives have been turned upside down. We miss her so much."

Gemma expected Jacob to have a snide comment, but he didn't say anything. He sat there quietly, avoiding eye contact.

"To deal with the pain, sometimes … I drink. Way too much," Barbara said, shutting her eyes. "I'm trying very hard to stop, but it's a challenge."

"I do that too," Betsy said. "A glass of wine turns into the whole bottle. It does ease the pain, if only for a little while. Sometimes, I … even think about ending it all. My life. So, I can be with everyone I've lost."

Barbara looked like she could relate as tears gathered in her eyes, her chin quivering. "I do too. Too often. Fortunately, a good friend saved me from doing something stupid today."

Gemma placed a hand on Barbara's shoulder. "Anytime."

Jacob finally looked up, glancing at his grandmother. "I think about that too. Ending my life. I just … I miss Mom so much."

"Oh, Jake," Barbara said, turning to her grandson. "I'm so sorry. This isn't the life I wanted for you."

As Gemma glanced at Ian, she wondered if he was thinking the same thing—that this was good. Getting all their emotions out in the open was good for Barbara and Jacob. Only then could they begin to heal—and maybe treat each other a little better too.

"My, I'm so sorry," the therapist said. "What a loss you've suffered. Suicidal thoughts are very common after losing someone so important, as well as unhealthy coping mechanisms. I think you need to focus that energy into a healthier outlet."

"Like the bookstore," Gemma added, glancing at Barbara and Jacob. "Both of you should come in and do something fun. Maybe arts and crafts in the back or something while spending time together."

Barbara nodded. "I'd like that. Jake, what do you say?"

Jacob looked around the room and rose to his feet, pushing in his chair with a squeak. "I think nothing's going to bring back Mom so what's the point? I'm outta here."

"Jake, wait!" Barbara cried.

Her grandson ran to the door, then vanished down the hall. Gemma sighed and slunk in her seat. So much for therapy. Just when she thought she was getting through to Jacob, he had pulled away.

"That poor child," the therapist said. "He's been through a lot. We should give him some space to process his emotions. Now, who would like to go next?"

As other people in the session spoke about their losses, Barbara grabbed her purse, then rose to her feet. She chased Jacob down the hall. Gemma sighed and stood, figuring they should go after them too. Ian gave an apologetic smile to the group therapy session before following.

When they had made it out into the hallway, Jacob and Barbara were nowhere to be found. Gemma figured they both must've left after that deeply personal group therapy session. She turned to Ian, sighing.

"Well, I tried to help by bringing them here tonight," she began. "Seems I only made it worse."

"No, you didn't. You did your best—and I think you *are* getting through to them. Slowly." Ian smiled. "You saved Barbara from ending her life today. That's a victory, Gemma. Don't forget that."

"Yeah, I guess you're right. I'm worried about Jacob having the same thoughts as his grandmother. I feel so bad for that boy." Gemma shook her head. "Anyway, it's getting late. We should both get home."

"Good idea. I'll drive you back to your place. Got an early day tomorrow at the bar."

Gemma was disappointed Ian wasn't going to stay another night, but she was just grateful he had stayed at all. She had enjoyed her time with him—even when dealing with other people's problems. When they arrived back at Gemma's building, Ian gave her a peck on the lips before walking her up to her apartment.

"Tonight was interesting, but I'm glad we had a chance to

spend time together," Ian said with a smile. "You should come over to my apartment tomorrow night. I want to cook dinner for you. I've got a recipe I've been dying to try. And Max wants to see you again soon."

Gemma laughed. "Just Max?"

"Okay, me too. Guilty." Ian grinned. "I'll pick you up after work, if that's good with you."

"Sounds perfect. Goodnight, Ian. And thanks for coming today."

He nodded, then pulled her in for another kiss before saying goodbye. Gemma was grinning to herself like an idiot as she unlocked her door and entered the apartment. The effect Ian had on her was almost enough to make her forget about Carly's husband drama, Barbara and Jacob's problems, and the robber who had access to magical energy.

That last one really scared Gemma. But she needed to find out the truth before it was too late.

CHAPTER 17

Gemma left her apartment building, making sure she wasn't seen. As she crept outside, noticing everyone was too busy with their own lives to pay any attention to her, she removed the grate off a nearby storm drain and climbed down.

The smell of magic elixirs, plants, and Fairhaven food filled her nostrils as she descended the ladder. When she looked around the underground city, with pulsating magical particles in the air, she smiled. Nothing was better than coming home.

Much like on the surface world, it was late. Everyone in Fairhaven had retired to their homes to rest for the evening. But Gemma wasn't here for a reunion. She scurried to the castle, finding a light on in Princess Esme's bedroom.

Once the guards recognized her and let her pass, she headed up to the room, then knocked on the door. It opened a few moments later to Princess Esme and Noah, both in their pajamas. Gemma curtsied out of instinct.

"Gemma, it's you," Princess Esme said, tightening her robe around her waist. "Why are you here? I thought you were on the surface."

"I was. So sorry to disturb you, especially at night," Gemma began, "but I came because I have something important to say."

"It's no problem at all." Princess Esme said and opened the door a little wider. "Come on inside."

Gemma thanked her, then quickly entered the bedroom. It looked like Noah and Princess Esme had been watching something on Netflix—a human tradition—after the fairy godmothers used magical to summon the internet. Fairhaven had adopted some human practices several years ago. Feeling out of place and nervous, Gemma's hands shook.

"Something's going on up there on the surface. Something bad," Gemma murmured, pacing. "The bookstore I got a job at was just robbed. By a human with magical energy around him. He pushed me but ... without using his hands."

Princess Esme nodded. "Yes, we've heard reports of that. I've got people looking into it."

"Including my father," Noah added. "He's a homicide detective up there and the only one on the force who knows about Fairhaven. He'll crack this case—I know he will."

"Yeah, I spoke with him," Gemma replied. "Nice man. He's worried too. That it might spiral out of control, I mean. Before I left, I spoke with Senator Remus—"

"You did *what*?" Princess Esme interrupted. "It's probably best to stay away from him. Even I haven't dared to return to the cells."

"I know, I know. But I wanted to ask about my mother. He didn't know anything, unfortunately, but he told me he wasn't done with Earth. What if there's a connection here? What if ... what if he knows this human and he's helping him?"

"Impossible," Noah said. "We just confirmed with our guards Remus and his family haven't gotten out of the cells. They've had no outside contact."

That was what Gemma kept being told. Why did she have a hard time believing it?

"All right, all right. I just thought you needed to know." Gemma sighed. "Humans are dangerous enough without giving them magic to make matters worse."

Princess Esme placed a hand on her shoulder. "It's sweet that you're worried but trust me—we've got patrols out investigating these magical pockets. We hope to have it all contained soon. Including this criminal who's found out how to harness magic from our world, thanks to Fairy Godmother Zamira making it compatible up there."

Gemma took a deep breath, forcing herself to stay calm. "Okay—I trust you, Esme. Good luck."

"Thank you, Gemma. In the meantime, I take it the Earth world has been good for you?"

"Besides the robbery? Sure." Gemma blushed when she thought of Ian. "Very good to me, yeah. Anyway, I should get going. Just wanted you to know what happened."

"Thank you for telling us," Princess Esme said, leading Gemma out of the room and down the stairs. Noah trailed behind. "We'll let my father know in the morning. He hasn't been feeling well lately."

Gemma paused. "Oh? What's wrong with the king?"

Noah shrugged. "Not sure yet—but the witch doctor looked at him and didn't see anything wrong. Esme's fairy godmother did the same. It could just be a cold."

"Or old age," Esme added. "My father *is* getting older. It's why I've been trying to take on more royal duties. Anyway, get back to Noah's apartment safely, Gemma. We'll take care of all this strange business. Just enjoy your time on Earth, yes?"

Gemma nodded, thanking her before heading to the ladder. She didn't want to wake up her father at this hour. She hoped

Princess Esme could get to the bottom of things—and that her mother and the sympathizers weren't involved in any way.

As she prepared to climb, a familiar face slipped out of the back of the castle. When she looked closer, it was Cal. He noticed her and then walked over with a smile.

"Gemma, you're back! Nice to see you," he said. "I guess Earth wasn't right for you?"

"I mean, it hasn't been easy," Gemma said, thinking back to all her mishaps, "but I'm making a life there. I have a job, an apartment, some friends. I even went on a few dates with someone special."

"You did? Wow. That's … that's unexpected. Where did you meet this lucky guy or gal?"

"His name is Ian—and funny enough, I just walked into his bar while having a panic attack. Things kinda evolved from there."

Cal smiled. "Huh. Well, that's great. I'm happy for you. He'd better treat you right or I'll have to have a talk with him."

"Don't worry—he's been a perfect gentleman."

"Good, good. I'm glad you're living a new life up there. Anyway, I should get home now. Late night at the castle. Baked a bunch of cakes ahead of schedule for tomorrow."

"I bet they're amazing. I should get back to Earth too. Hey, did you hear King Tedros is sick?"

"I did, yeah. Poor guy. I keep bringing him some special chicken noodle soup—the humans say it can cure anything—but he's still ill. I don't know what's going on."

"Hmm. Keep me updated, okay?" Gemma gestured above. "Some strange things are going on back on the surface world too. Some guy robbed the bookstore I work at the other day with—get this—magic on his side."

"Cal's eyes widened. "Sheesh, that doesn't sound good. Be careful, Gemma."

"I will. See you around, Cal."

When she turned, he grabbed her arm. "No, I really mean it—you need to be careful. Maybe you just oughta stay low in that apartment Noah gave you. Take time to relax. Fairhaven will still be here later."

"Yeah, I guess so. I like the fact that I can drop by anytime though. Anyway, be careful too, Cal. See you."

He nodded as she climbed the ladder, heading back up to the surface. Gemma could still feel his eyes on her back as she opened the grate and pulled herself up onto the street. Gemma headed home through the darkness, trying to push all her worries out of her mind. She fell asleep on the couch again and awoke to her very loud alarm. After turning it off, she followed the same routine—shower, get dressed in another gown, then eat breakfast and head to work. She didn't want to miss a single shift, not when Barbara needed her.

When she made it to the bookstore, it was empty as usual. Barbara stood near the cash register, wiping off the counter. When the bell chimed, she looked up excitedly, then frowned.

"Ah, Gemma—It's you. Not that it's not nice to see you, I was just hoping you would be a customer. A paying customer."

Gemma nodded, frowning. "I know, I'm sorry. There's been no one?"

"Not since the robbery, no. I told you—this place is done for. It's only a matter of time. I suppose I'll have to start looking for another job soon. And maybe declare bankruptcy."

Gemma didn't want that to happen. She thought about the grand reopening, wondering if Cal could make desserts to lure people inside the bookshop. Who didn't like pastries? That was something the humans and Fairhaveners had in common, at least.

"Anyway, thanks for taking us to the group therapy session last night. I appreciate you trying to help," Barbara said, organizing the books on her desk. "I haven't had a drink this morning. Maybe that's progress."

"It is. I'm proud of you, Barbara. What about Jacob? Any luck getting through to him?"

Barbara shook her head, sighing. "No—he's a real tough nut to crack. Just when I think I'm making progress, helping him grieve or repairing our relationship, he pulls back. I just wish I could get through to him. Help him overcome the loss of his mother and stop with his antics. I think he was graffitiing something yesterday, you know. That explains the red spray paint on his hands and clothes."

"Oh no, that's not good. I'm sorry, Barbara. I hope he comes around soon."

"I do too—or Lord only knows what'll happen. And sorry we left before saying goodbye last night. My grandson stormed out to the car and wanted to head home. It was a tense evening, to say the least."

"I bet." Gemma frowned. "Really, I wish there was a clear way to help you. Both of you."

"Sometimes we all need someone to talk us off a ledge. I'm grateful you did that for me." Barbara smiled. "Now, do you think you could help me put away some romance novels? I know they're your favorite."

As Gemma nodded, sorting through the books with Barbara, she thought back to Jacob's interaction with their cat. The smile on his face had been genuine—she could tell he loved animals. Maybe there was something animal-related they could do to get him on the right track.

The day went by slowly with lots of cleaning, but no customers. Barbara's mood was low the entire time. Still, she didn't reach for a drink on the job, and Gemma was proud of her. Getting through to just one person might've been enough.

Once closing hours came, Barbara put the CLOSED sign on

the window and said goodbye to Gemma. As Gemma waved at her car, Ian's car pulled up in front of the shop. Gemma smiled at him and hopped in the passenger seat.

"Hey there, cutie," Ian said with a smile. "How was work?"

"Eh, could've been better." Gemma put on her seatbelt as Ian drove away from the curb. "Didn't even get one customer. Barbara's really upset—keeps talking about shutting her business down. We need to get that grand reopening going before it's too late."

"All right, I'm in. And I hate to say it, but ... I know someone who's great at grand reopenings and fundraisers."

Gemma turned to Ian as he stopped at a red light. "Who?"

"My mother—she and my father were always putting on one. If I ask them, maybe they'll help."

"But you haven't spoken to them in such a long time."

"I know." Ian's hands tightened around the steering wheel. "But I bet they could help raise a lot of money for Barbara's shop. And my brother has been bugging me about seeing him again. There's a party tomorrow night, actually. At my parents' mansion in town. If we go, maybe we can plead our case. Get them to spread the word about the grand reopening to all their annoying rich friends."

"*We?* You want me to go with you?"

"Yes, please," Ian said, stealing a glance at her as the light turned green. "I'll need some back-up. And as much as I have issues with my parents, I do love my brother. I'd like for you to meet him."

Gemma nodded. "Okay, then I'll be there. Whether or not we can get help for Barbara."

"Thanks, Gemma. You're the best." He cleared his throat. "So, I was wondering ... You know about my money-hungry family. When will I get to meet yours?"

"Well, like I said, my mother left us. I don't know where she is. But you could meet my father—maybe even my friend Esme. She's practically royalty where I'm from. She just got married."

Ian cocked an eyebrow. "Sounds interesting—I'm in. Just name a time and place. Now, why don't we talk about something more pleasant, shall we? Mentioning my parents leaves a bad taste in my mouth."

Gemma quickly changed the subject, talking about what was going on in Toronto. Butterflies flitted around in her stomach when she thought about Ian meeting her father. Him being so willing was a good sign—and a step in the direction of becoming more serious.

When she thought about it, Gemma liked that idea very much.

Ian pulled into his parking lot a few minutes later, opening Gemma's door for her. He led her into the building and up to his apartment where Max started barking behind the door. Ian laughed, unlocking the door before he was tackled by the black labrador. The dog came over to say hello to Gemma with his tail wagging.

"Hello to you too, Max," Gemma said, laughing when the dog licked her face. "It's nice to see you again. I just have one question ... who's a good boy?"

As she petted the dog, making him roll over for more, Ian locked the door with a smile. "Cute. Go ahead—make yourself comfortable. I'll get started on dinner."

Gemma nodded, heading into the living room. As she watched Ian happily humming to himself, she realized he had made a life for himself here, away from his family. In a way, that was exactly what Gemma was trying to do—for different reasons. No wonder she felt herself drawn so much to him. They were two of the same, both forging their own path.

"Do you want garlic in the sauce?" Ian asked, leaning into the living room.

"Sure, I'd love that." Gemma turned around, noticing his KISS THE CHEF apron. "Ha, that's a cute apron. And on that note ..."

She crossed the living room, pulling him in for a kiss. He kissed her back, moaning into her mouth, and Gemma lost herself in him again. It was easy to do with Ian. She suddenly remembered he was cooking and pulled away to let him check on the food just as the water began to boil. Ian turned as well, noticing at the same time.

"I really hate to stop doing that, but I gotta put the pasta in now," Ian said, turning around to head back to the kitchen. "But I wouldn't mind more of that later."

"Noted," Gemma said with a laugh, then jumped up to sit on the counter. "If I can help, just let me know. I'm a newer chef, but I'll try my best."

"All right then. If you'd like to chop up an onion, that would be great. Just shield your eyes—those things will make you cry."

Gemma nodded, chopping ingredients next to Ian. He made sure the pasta cooked and poured them two glasses of wine. The smell of creamy Cajun chicken pasta filled the air. With Max underfoot, doing tricks and amusing them while begging for scraps, they both had a great night of good food and each other's company. As he walked her to the door, she didn't want it to end.

"Well, the food was amazing. You're a fantastic chef," Gemma said on the doorstep. "Thanks for everything you do. I mean it."

"Hey, no problem. And I'll pick you up for the party at my folks' house tomorrow night. I know you have lots of those dresses, so I don't even need to ask if you have fancy attire."

Gemma laughed. "I have nothing *but* fancy attire. I'll be

ready tomorrow. And hey, if it isn't too much trouble, could I ask a favor?"

"Of course. Name it."

Gemma pointed at Max over his shoulder who was chewing on a toy bone. "Maybe we can show Jake your dog—take them both to the park. It's clear the boy loves animals, so maybe that's a good way to help him heal."

A smile spread across Ian's face. "Yeah, good idea. I like the way you think, Gemma. Come on—I'll drive you home. Then I should check on Barney and make sure everything's okay at the bar. You want to rest before the party tomorrow. Trust me, you'll be emotionally and mentally drained after a night with the Whitmans. My parents can be exhausting."

The more Ian told her about his parents, the more nervous she became. But with Ian, she'd go anywhere.

Ian drove her home, then walked her up to her apartment door and kissed her on the step. It was more chaste this time—less heated than the one at his apartment. Gemma wondered when their relationship would progress to the next step. She didn't want to rush things, not when they were so perfect, so she kissed him back sweetly before he waved and headed down the hallway.

He got into the elevator, vanishing downstairs with a smile. Gemma sighed dreamily as she turned to unlock her door. As she did, she heard footsteps approaching from the staircase.

"Gemma! There you are. I've been waiting for you to get back," Carly said, stopping at her door. "I'm ready to take you up on that drink offer. I need to get out of here—like ASAP."

CHAPTER 18

Gemma looked Carly up and down, noticing a small cut on her cheek. "Hey, Carly. You doing okay? You're bleeding."

When Gemma motioned at her cheek, Carly reached up, prodding her jagged skin. "Oh, yeah—I'm fine. Just a little clumsy. Anyway, are you free to go out for a drink right now?"

"Yeah, sure. We'll head to Ian's bar—he was on his way there after we had dinner together."

Carly smiled. "That's so sweet. You've been on a few dates with him now, huh?"

Gemma nodded, walking down the hallway with Carly. "We have—and I really like him. I'm meeting his family tomorrow night, then I'm planning for him to meet mine."

"Wow, that sounds serious." Carly pressed a button on the elevator. "I'm happy for you. Really."

"Thanks. So, where's Abby?"

"Fast asleep—she has school tomorrow. Finally, Friday. You know she sleeps in that princess gown you got her? She absolutely loves it."

Gemma smiled, getting into the elevator when it came. "That's good to hear. She's a sweet girl—she deserves the best."

"She really does. I wish I could give it to her," Carly mumbled as the elevator descended. "Anyway, thanks for agreeing to go out with me. I just need to get away sometimes, you know?"

Gemma understood perfectly. When the elevator arrived in the lobby, they left the apartment building, the night air blowing a chill up Gemma's dress. They walked down the block to Ian's bar.

"Busy place," Carly said, glancing around as she reached for the door. "Seems like Ian's doing well for himself. Good for him."

Gemma nodded, proud of ... what was he? Not quite her boyfriend yet, but something more. Whatever they were, she was glad to have him in her life.

The bar was rowdy as they entered and headed to the bar. Burly men were sipping beers at their table while others were playing pool. Ian was serving a glass of wine to a woman at the bar, then looked up with a smile as Gemma and Carly approached.

"Gemma! Nice to see you again," Ian said. "I thought you were heading to bed?"

"I was—then Carly here wanted to go out for a drink," Gemma said, sliding onto a bar stool. "You remember Carly, right?"

"Of course, I do," Ian said, turning to her with a smile. "What can I get you?"

"The strongest thing you got," Carly said as she sat down next to Gemma. "A shot of tequila would be nice."

Ian nodded, turning his back to the row of drinks. "Tequila coming right up. Gemma, you want anything?"

Gemma wasn't much of a drinker, except for an occasional

glass of wine, but she wanted to stay sober to make sure Carly was okay. "Just a ginger ale, please. With extra ice."

Ian nodded, getting them both their drinks. Carly downed her tequila quickly and asked for another. Ian glanced at Gemma, raising an eyebrow, then brought her some more shots on a tray. Gemma sipped her ginger ale, then Ian walked away to serve another person at the bar. Gemma glanced over and saw a man in a hoodie—and he seemed oddly familiar. When he reached out to grab a drink, little magic particles pulsated around him, but no one else noticed. Gemma had a sinking feeling she knew who it was.

The bookstore robber—and the same man responsible for all the other thefts. His magic was growing stronger, just like his criminal inclinations. She could feel the magical buzz emanating through him. But he was no fairy godmother, the only ones who could do magic. Everyone else had to use magical potions.

So, how had he gotten that magic?

Gemma rose to her feet before she could stop herself, making her way over to the man. He slurped down his drink and turned around to head to the door. Gemma caught only a glimpse of his face which was pale and bearded. As he walked past her, Gemma knew she was losing him. Just as she reached out, attempting to grab his shoulder, a drunken man staggered between her and the robber.

"Hey, pretty lady." The drunk man hiccupped. "You come here often?"

"Out of my way, please!" Gemma called out, pushing the man aside. He scoffed and swore at her as she rushed to the door.

But when she made it outside, the robber was gone. She sighed. How could she let him slip away?

Returning inside, Gemma was mad at herself but hoped she

would find him again. If he frequented the bar, maybe she could catch him another time. As she returned to her seat, Ian was still busy serving drinks to others, and Carly was quickly becoming drunk.

She swayed in her seat, hiccupping before turning to Gemma. Her words were slurred when she spoke. "Hey, you're back. Where'd you go?"

"Uh, nowhere," Gemma said as she sat down. "You doing okay?"

"Yeah, yeah—I'm just fine. You know, you really are lucky to have a man like Ian. He practically worships you. That's hot. Not like my husband who doesn't give a damn about me."

She downed another shot, making Gemma wince. "Carly, maybe you've had enough alcohol for one night. I don't want you to be hungover for work tomorrow."

"Ah, who cares?" Carly slurred. "Ian, keep those shots coming!"

Ian turned around, a towel across his shoulder. He looked at Carly and narrowed his eyes. "I really think you've had enough. How about a coffee instead? Or water or tea?"

Carly waved her hand. "Eh, you're no fun. Come on, Gemma —let's go to different bar. I need another drink."

When Carly stood, she nearly fell over. Gemma reached for her and held her up. "Whoa there—I got you. Come on, we should get you home. See you later, Ian."

He waved. "Let me know how she is tomorrow, okay?"

Gemma nodded, leading Carly to the door. She was still swaying and trying to argue. "I don't want to go home! Home sucks. I want another drink. Why couldn't your little boyfriend just give me another damn shot of tequila?"

"Because you've had too many," Gemma said, opening the door to the bar. When they stepped onto the quiet street outside, Gemma could hear herself think again, quietly sighing in relief. "Okay, what's really going on, Carly? You aren't being yourself. I'm worried about you. If you need to talk about anything, I'm here."

Gemma gently set Carly down on the curb, then she started crying on her shoulder. "He hit me tonight, Gemma. That's why my face is all cut. It's John's fault. We were arguing again and then he just ... hit me. His wedding ring smacked me in the face."

Gemma winced. "Oh my God—Carly, that's awful. You can't stay with him. You and Abby need to get out."

"I know, I know." Carly sighed. "Things have gotten so complicated, Gemma. I wish they didn't have to be."

As Carly kept her head on Gemma's shoulder, she knew she needed to tell her about the flirting. But not now—not when she was so drunk and already in pain. When Gemma heard snoring, she looked down, realizing Carly had fallen asleep on her.

Just great.

"Come on," Gemma whispered, pulling Carly to her feet. "Let's get you home. You can crash on my couch."

Carly was barely conscious, still drunk as Gemma pulled her down the sidewalk. She hauled Carly the two blocks to her apartment building and brought her to Gemma's apartment. After unlocking her door, she put Carly on the couch, tucking her in with a nearby blanket.

"Poor woman," Gemma whispered. "See you in the morning, Carly. Get some rest and sleep off that tequila."

Gemma headed into Noah's room, having no choice but to sleep in his bed. When morning came trickling through her curtains, Gemma stretched and rose to her feet. She left the bedroom and found Carly on the sofa drinking coffee. She had bags under her red eyes, looking exhausted and terrible with bedhead.

When Gemma entered, Carly lifted her head. "Hey, Gemma. Hope you don't mind I borrowed some of your coffee."

Gemma shook her head. "I don't mind at all. You feeling okay?"

"I've got a pounding headache. And I can't remember a thing." Carly rubbed her temples, setting her coffee down. "What happened last night?"

Gemma sighed, walking over and sitting across from Carly. "You wanted to go out for drinks. When we did, you drank way too much tequila, then cried on my shoulder. And told me John hit you."

Carly looked down. "Yeah, he did. We were arguing and … one thing led to another. I'm sorry I put all that on you, Gemma."

"What are friends for? I told you I'd be here for you, and I mean that." Gemma leaned closer, reaching for Carly's hand. "Not to make matters worse, but … there's something I need to tell you. Something important."

Carly looked up. "What? That I need to leave John?"

"Yes, but besides that. The first day I came to Toronto … your husband picked me up in his taxi. He asked me out, Carly. And he wasn't wearing a wedding ring. He's been cheating on you with his passengers. When I confronted him, he basically admitted it."

Carly ripped her hand away. "I can't believe this! Why did you wait so long to tell me?"

"I'm sorry. I was waiting for the right moment. Then John cornered me, threatening me to stay away—"

"I thought you were my friend. Friends wouldn't keep secrets like this," Carly hissed, rising to her feet. "I need to go get Abby ready for school. Excuse me."

"Carly, wait!"

But she had already stormed out of the apartment, slamming the door behind her. Gemma sighed. That so hadn't gone the way she wanted it to.

Gemma did the only thing she could—got ready for work and hoped Carly would come around. John was the villain here, not Gemma. She hadn't done anything wrong.

She just hoped Carly would realize that too.

After getting dressed in another gown, Gemma left her apartment and locked the door. She went to Carly's floor, but they had already left—John included. She didn't even see their cars in the parking lot when she walked past. Sighing, she walked to the bookstore and entered.

When she did, she saw Barbara at the front desk, sipping a glass of wine. She looked up and nodded. "Hey, Gemma."

"Hi, Barbara. Drinking again? I thought you were quitting."

Barbara sighed. "Yeah, I did too. Then I got into another argument with my grandson and the police came by. They told me they had no leads about the robbery—that it was a dead end. And next thing I knew, I had a drink in my hand. Again."

Gemma frowned. "I'm sorry, Barbara. I really am."

"I know. And I appreciate you trying to help, but everything's so screwed up." Barbara shook her head. "Anyway, enough of my problems. The mystery aisle is a bit dirty. Can you sweep the floors?"

Gemma nodded, grabbing a broom and getting to work. As usual, no one came in that day. More people across the city were being cautious and staying inside since the string of robberies. Gemma hoped someone—hopefully Princess Esme's soldiers—would find the culprit soon. Why was it taking so long?

The day passed quickly with nothing new happening. Gemma said goodbye to Barbara, then headed home through the streets at dusk. She hadn't bothered to tell her that she spotted the robber at Ian's bar but lost him in the crowd. She didn't want to give Barbara a reason to drink even more than she already had. And Gemma knew she should've told the detective, but she was ashamed she had lost the robber.

This man was using magic somehow. It was made possible by Fairhaven, Gemma's people. And she felt a responsibility to stop him. When she had better news—like the man's name, his address, or anything concrete at all—then she'd tell the police.

With a little luck, she'd find the man *and* her mother and could return to Fairhaven a hero. Just like the endings of all those fantasy novels she loved.

When Gemma made it home, she spotted Carly and Abby getting into the elevator. It looked like they were coming home from another hospital appointment with a bracelet on Abby's wrist. She was still wearing the dress Gemma had bought her, licking an ice cream cone. The dress was getting filthy from constant use.

"I really should wash that dress, sweetie," Carly said to her daughter. "It's starting to smell."

"No! I'm never taking it off." Abby licked her ice cream again, then spotted Gemma. "Oh, hi, Gemma!"

As soon as Carly saw Gemma, she shut the doors to the elevator in her face. Gemma sighed and decided to take the stairs. When she reached her apartment, still sad about the fallout with Carly, she changed into a lilac gown for the party at the mansion. It fit into her suitcase like magic. When she was done fixing her hair, a knock sounded on the door.

When she opened it, Ian stood there, wearing a tux with a blue bowtie. It made his green eyes pop. He held out another bouquet of flowers—lilacs this time. They went perfectly with Gemma's gown.

She took them, smiling. "Beautiful flowers, Ian—thanks. And you look amazing."

He smiled back. "Just trying to keep up with you. Ready to go?"

Gemma nodded, putting the flowers in water before reaching for his arm. "I am. After you."

He led her down the hall once she had locked her door, then they stepped into the elevator. "I'm nervous about you meeting my family. Like I said, they … aren't the nicest people. Way too into their money. But my brother will be there."

"I'm sure I can handle it," Gemma said, giving him a smile. She hoped so at least. "I got Carly home safe last night, by the way. She was pretty drunk."

Ian nodded as the elevator descended. "Yeah, it's why I decided to cut her off. Everything okay?"

Gemma sighed. "No, not really. Her husband hit her. And when I first arrived in Toronto, he wasn't wearing his wedding ring and wanted to take me out on a date. He's been cheating on her too. With his passengers."

Ian's hands clenched into fists and his jaw worked. "Wow. Poor Carly. John's a scumbag." When the elevator reached the lobby, they stepped out. "Did you tell her?"

"I did this morning when she sobered up, yeah. I was waiting for the right moment. But now she's not speaking to me. She's mad I waited so long. I just didn't know how to break the news, you know?"

Ian nodded. "I understand. That's a hard situation to be in. But you did nothing wrong, Gemma. She's angry at the wrong person. She should be divorcing John, not getting mad at you. I have no doubt you've been a good friend to her and Abby."

Hearing Ian say it made Gemma feel better. She thanked him, then stepped outside and got into Ian's car. They chit-chatted and listened to the radio as he drove them into what Ian described as a rich part of Toronto. Bridle Path, a private, gated community full of mansions, pools, and pristine lawns, came into view as they passed. It looked nice, but it was nothing compared to Fairhaven. Her kingdom was dark, lit by magical lanterns, and underground with townhouses. This place was full of mansions and sports cars.

"So, this is where I grew up," Ian said, heading toward a gate. "Still remember the code and everything."

"Big place," Gemma said as Ian inputted the code. Then the gate opened before he drove through. "But I like your apartment now much better. It's way cozier."

Ian smiled. "Yeah, I think so, too."

He parked in the courtyard, his sedan wedged between dozens of luxury vehicles. The lights were on, and gentle jazz music played from inside. The party had already started. Ian stepped out of his sedan, then held out an arm for Gemma to take.

"This way, my lady," he said with a smile. "To the ball we go."

Gemma took his arm, beaming. "Now I'm *really* starting to feel like a princess."

"To me, you absolutely are."

Gemma blushed as they reached the front door. An elderly butler answered, letting them inside. He looked Ian up and down and then finally Gemma.

"Ah, Ian—you've returned," the butler said. "Your parents will be pleased. They've missed you, you know."

"I know. But there's a reason I left. I'm only here for two things—to have Gemma see the house I grew up in and meet my brother. That's all." Ian turned to Gemma. "Gemma, this is Mr. Collingsworth. He was my family's butler growing up."

"Nice to meet you," Gemma said.

The butler said nothing, sneering as he stared her up and down.

Ian cleared his throat. "And Mr. Collingsworth, this is Gemma Solace. My girlfriend."

His girlfriend? That was the first time they had ever used that term. Gemma liked the way it sounded, reaching for his hand and squeezing it. Ian smiled back at her and squeezed her hand too. It was amazing how one glance from him could make the entire world fade away.

Mr. Collingsworth scoffed. "Girlfriend? Oh my. Your parents won't be happy to hear that. Anyway, they're in the dining hall with the rest of the guests. They'll be glad to see you again. Do be on your best behavior, Ian. And you too, Emma."

"Her name is *Gemma*," Ian corrected, his jaw clenching. "And don't get used to me being back, Mr. Collingsworth. I have no intention of staying. Excuse us."

Ian gently tugged on Gemma's hand, pulling them past the snooty butler. He sneered at them and shut the door. Judging by his reaction, this was going to be a long night.

CHAPTER 19

The mansion was spacious on the inside with dozens of bedrooms, long hallways with crystal chandeliers, and dining rooms for parties. Hand in hand, Ian kept Gemma close to him as they walked down the carpeted hallway, passing maids and butlers. They whispered about Ian as they walked by, unable to believe he had returned after all this time.

"Just ignore them," Ian said to Gemma. "I know, I plan to."

Gemma nodded as he led her into a large dining hall, one with several buffet tables full of five-star meals. People in glamorous gowns and tuxes with diamonds and jewels on them stood around, sipping champagne and chatting. Ian and Gemma paused in the doorway to take it all in.

"Is this how you grew up?" Gemma whispered. "With all this glitz and glamor?"

Ian nodded. "Yeah, but it never felt right. That life wasn't for me. And being back here makes me realize how glad I am that I escaped. Not everyone was so lucky."

A woman in her sixties with dyed-blonde hair, dark eyebrows, and heavy makeup glanced over, noticing Ian. She wore a designer black gown with a matching blazer and heels. Her diamond-encrusted purse glittered off her shoulder. A smirk tugged at her crimson lips as she sauntered over, gesturing at someone in the crowd to follow her.

A tall man with a black suit, a bald head, and a gold watch headed toward Ian and Gemma. They had to be Ian's parents—he resembled them in looks and nothing else. Sipping their champagne for a moment, they stared at Ian and Gemma.

"Well, well, well," the woman said. "Look what the cat dragged in."

"Have you finally come back to us, my boy?" the man asked.

Ian shook his head. "Only for a night, Dad. Marcus invited me, and I didn't want to be rude. Where is he?"

"Upstairs, lying down," Ian's mother said, rolling her eyes. "He's having another one of his episodes. A panic attack, I think. That boy does it for attention, I swear."

"*No one* has a panic attack for attention," Gemma interrupted. "They're uncomfortable and awful—you feel like you're dying. You should be glad you don't have them. He needs and deserves your support."

"Harumph." The woman studied Gemma for a moment. "And who might you be? I don't recall your name on the guest list."

"This is Gemma Solace, my girlfriend," Ian introduced proudly, clutching her hand tight. "We met a little while ago. Gemma, meet my parents—Hank and Chelsea."

"Girlfriend?" His dad laughed. "Everyone knows you belong with Ivy. Even the public is rooting for you."

Gemma felt Ian's grip tense. Either his parents didn't know about Ivy's abuse or didn't care, and Gemma didn't want him to go back to that awful woman.

"Me and Ivy are over. I'm with Gemma now," Ian said

calmly. "Now, if you don't mind, I'm going to check on Marc upstairs. Excuse me."

"Wait just a moment, son," Hank said, placing a hand on his shoulder. "We have some people you need to meet. Come on."

Before Ian could refuse, Hank tugged on his arm, leading him to a group of people. Ian lost his grip on Gemma's hand, and she followed, feeling uncomfortable. Her heart pounded at what his parents might say next. His parents led Ian to a well-dressed man in the crowd.

"We've heard you opened your own bar. I question why a bar of all things, but being a businessman runs in the family," Hank said, then gestured at the man. "This is Dan Gable—he runs a successful bar chain across North America. He's willing to partner with you to take your business to new heights. More money, more fame. That sort of thing."

Dan smirked as he held out a hand. "Anything for a Whitman. Glad to see you came back, Ian."

Ian pulled away from his father, sneering. "I didn't come back—and I don't need anyone's help. I'm more than happy living my own life, thank you very much. Now, Gemma and I are going to see my brother. Don't get in my way again."

His parents scoffed as Ian turned, reaching for Gemma's hand. He led her toward a spiral staircase.

"Really, we apologize for our son's rudeness," Chelsea said. "We don't know where he gets it from—or why he's with that tart in the awful dress. We have his best interests at heart, and he still disrespects us. His life went downhill when he and Ivy broke up ..."

Gemma's heart ached. His parents had no idea what he'd been through.

"Don't listen to them," Ian said, tugging Gemma up the stairs. "They don't know what they're talking about."

Gemma nodded. "You weren't lying before—they seem like awful people."

"The worst. Ignorant, snooty, know-it-alls. Their money and privilege make them blind to the real problems of the world. I'm glad I know better." When they reached the upper level, Ian began walking down the hall. "This way. My brother's room is over here. Mine is right here, untouched. I'm surprised Mom and Dad didn't turn it into a bank vault or something once I left."

Ian opened a door to his right, then led Gemma inside. It was a luxury bedroom—complete with a king-sized bed, a large television, all the technology and toys a child could want, and a balcony with a view of the city. Gemma sat on the bed, sinking into the comfy mattress.

"This is nice," Gemma said. "The room, I mean."

Ian nodded. "Oh, it's a nice house. I spent hours in this bedroom, trying to get away from my parents and their functions. Teenage me would be very glad I got out. Anyway, Marc is just down here."

Gemma rose to her feet, following Ian out of his room and down the hall. He knocked on a door with golden trimmings. When no one answered, Ian pushed the door open, finding it unlocked.

"Marc?" Ian called. "Are you in here?"

As Gemma entered the room behind Ian, she found it similar to the other bedrooms. A person she assumed was Marcus—looking like Ian, but younger—sat in the corner, playing with a fidget toy. The room was dark and the door to the balcony was open to let the air inside.

Marcus lifted his head, dressed in a fancy suit. His eyes widened when he noticed Ian. "Oh my God, Ian! You came. I can't believe it."

"I came for you, not Mom and Dad. I wanted to see you

again." Ian sat on his bed, gesturing at Gemma. "This is Gemma Solace. My girlfriend. She works at a bookstore not that far from my bar."

Marcus' eyes lit up. "A bookstore? My brother loves his romantic fantasy. I guess that explains how you two got together. Nice to meet you, I'm Marc."

Gemma shook his hand, glad he was a lot more polite than his family. "You too, Marc. Ian's told me a lot about you."

"Like how you're the only one in my family that I can stand," Ian joked. "How are you doing? Mom said you were having a panic attack up here."

Marcus nodded, setting his fidget toy aside. "I was, but I think it's calmed down. I just ... I hate parties so much, and Mom and Dad constantly drag me to them. It was getting too much so I came up here to get away."

It seemed Ian and his brother had a lot in common. Gemma nodded. "Good idea—sometimes you just need a moment to breathe. You know, I have panic attacks, too."

Marcus looked surprised. "You do?"

"That's how we met, actually," Ian added. "I was working at the bar when this beautiful woman in a gown waltzes in. She was having a panic attack, so I gave her a cup of tea and helped her calm down. I knew what to do since I grew up with you, Marc."

Marcus smiled. "Well, that's nice. It's helpful to have someone to calm you down when you're going through a rough time. I wish Mom and Dad would be there for me, but they're the type of people who think anxiety isn't real."

"Idiots." Ian shook his head. "Why don't you leave them, Marc? Come live with me. I've got enough space in my apartment, and I'm sure my dog would love you. Mom and Dad are toxic, you know that."

"Yes, I do," Marcus said with a sigh, "and while I appreciate the offer, I can't. How am I supposed to support myself? I can't work—not with my anxiety. And I don't want to take advantage of you and force you to take care of me. With Mom and Dad's money, at least I'm comfortable. Without them, I'd be on the street."

Ian frowned. "Marc, please—"

Footsteps sounded in the hallway, then Ian's parents poked their heads through the doorway. Their mother was the first one to speak. "We knew you were up here. Why don't you come back downstairs, Ian? There are other people who are dying to see you."

"People with exciting business opportunities," his father added. "Or you could always come work for me at my company again. The other employees miss having you there."

"So you can boss me around and keep me under your thumb? All the while denying Marc's anxiety *and* polluting the planet with your oil production?" Ian shook his head. "Hard pass. I like my life with my apartment, bar, dog, and Gemma in it, thank you very much. I don't need anything else."

"How disappointing," his mother hissed, glancing at Gemma. "You should be ashamed of yourself, young woman. Encouraging our son to turn his back on us. How do you sleep at night?"

"Gemma had nothing to do with that," Ian insisted, rising from the bed. "I can think for myself and make my own decisions. But Gemma supports me wholeheartedly."

Gemma nodded. "I do. I think if you really love your son, Mr. and Mrs. Whitman, you'd give him the freedom to do whatever he wants with his life. He's a good man—you should be very proud."

Gemma couldn't believe she had the courage to stand up for Ian. She never would've done that before coming to Toronto. He was helping to bring her out of her shell, to make her more confident. And she loved it.

Ian smiled at her, sending butterflies shooting through her stomach. Gemma was amazed at how little it took from him to make her swoon.

His mother scoffed, turning to Ian's father. "She's known us for a few minutes and she's already making demands and assumptions. Our son sure knows how to pick 'em, hmm?"

"Don't talk about Gemma like that," Ian snapped. "She's my girlfriend, and she deserves respect. Now that I'm done seeing my brother, it's time we leave. Come on, Gemma. Marc, we'll be in touch."

His brother nodded, waving as Ian guided Gemma to the door. His parents mumbled about him as they headed down the hallway and toward the staircase. Gemma could feel Ian's anger, a stark contrast from the usual calm, easy-going energy he gave off.

"Sorry about that—all of it," Ian whispered, leading Gemma down the stairs. "And for not asking them for help with the grand reopening thing. I just need to get out of here."

"I totally understand," Gemma said. "We'll find another way to spread the word and raise money for Barbara. Let's just go."

Ian thanked her, leading her to the door when a gorgeous blonde woman in a tight red dress and heels entered the foyer. Gemma recognized her from the Google search. When her eyes settled on Ian, she smiled. Then she walked over and touched his arm.

"Ian, there you are," she said with a smirk, her British accent thick. "I was hoping you'd come to the party tonight. How have you been?"

"Fine. Not in the mood to catch up, Ivy," Ian said, stepping to the side. "Excuse me."

Ian's ex-girlfriend in the flesh. She was beautiful, famous, and glamorous, yet Gemma knew the truth—she was abusive. She was like poison ivy. Maybe that was how she got her name.

"Don't be that way, Ian," she purred. "We had good times together, didn't we? Remember our trip to Bali? Or our walk around Paris?"

Those two had done a lot of expensive, romantic things together. Ian didn't look like he wanted to go back to those days.

As he scowled, Gemma noticed a group was forming. Ian's parents and brother had come down from upstairs. After hearing their voice, even the guests inside the dining hall had poked their heads out. Some pulled out their smartphones, taking videos of the two.

"Sure, we had a lot of great times ... when things were good," Ian said. "But then you'd get jealous or grumpy. And we both know what would happen then."

Ivy scoffed, glancing around. "I don't know what you mean. I don't remember that at all."

"Probably not. Abusers never remember, only the victims." Ian shook his head. "I wish I had taken pictures of all the times you hurt me. Attacked me with your nails or hit me with things because you thought I was cheating or going to leave you. You're just like my parents—abusive in different ways, but still abusive. And I'm glad I got the hell away from you. You can all rot in hell for all I care."

Ivy scoffed, saying nothing as Ian stormed out of the mansion. Gemma kept her head down and followed him as the guests murmured louder and snapped pictures. The butler at the front door glared at her as Gemma headed outside, then slammed the door behind her.

Ian stood on the grass a few feet away, bent over and

clutching his knees. Gemma ran to his side and rubbed his back. "Hey, are you okay? I had no idea Ivy was *that* abusive."

"She was," Ian whispered. "So, so abusive. Society thinks men can't be abused, so I tried to hide it for so long."

"Oh, they definitely can. Abuse is never okay. And what you did back there was pretty brave, outing all your abusers. It had to be hard."

"Yeah, it was. And I'll be okay. Let's just go back to your place." Ian stood up straight. "I want to get as far away from here as possible."

"Okay, no problem. I'm right behind you."

Ian smiled. "I know—and thank you for being there tonight. With everyone staring at me, then Ivy confronting me ... I knew I had to tell the world what she did. My parents, too. It felt good to get it off my chest."

"Of course, Ian. I'm here for you. And I'm happy for you, too. Hopefully, you can start to heal."

"With you, I already have." He reached for her hand, gently leading her to his car. "They can keep their money and fame. The way you look at me, Gemma, makes me feel like I'm worth a billion dollars."

She smiled, blushing as she got into his car. He pulled out of the courtyard and passed through the gate before heading back to her apartment. Gemma noticed his parents and the guests had walked out onto the lawn, but they hadn't followed. Good riddance.

"You know, you told everyone in there that I was your girl-friend," Gemma said, breaking the silence in the car.

Ian glanced at her. "Yeah, I did. I know—we haven't discussed labels yet, but ... I'd really like for you to be my girl-friend. Now that you've seen my messed-up family, would you still say yes?"

"Of course. You can't choose your family, Ian, but you *can* choose who you are. And you became a wonderful person." She kissed his cheek. "I'll happily be your girlfriend any day of the week."

Ian beamed, staring straight ahead. "Phew, that's a relief. I was worried you'd say no. I don't know how you do it, Gemma."

"Do what?"

"Make my heart skip a beat every time you look at me." When he stopped at a red light, Ian finally looked at her. "But it makes me feel like I'm on top of the world."

"The feeling is mutual," Gemma said with a smile. She briefly considered telling him about her mother, then stopped. She'd have to find the right words first. "What do you say we order takeout and watch movies tonight?"

Ian nodded. "That sounds perfect to me."

When they arrived back at Gemma's apartment, they did just that—ordered pizza and watched Netflix, cuddling all night. When Ian leaned in to give Gemma a goodnight kiss, she poured all of her emotions into it. He deepened the kiss and lifted her, carrying her to the bedroom. They spent all night showing how much they cared for each other.

And when Gemma woke up in Ian's arms, then traced his abs in the morning light, she wasn't even thinking about all the danger the surface world was in. Or that she still needed to find her mother somehow.

Maybe that was wrong, but for now, Gemma was happy to be with someone who she cared for and who cared for her just as much.

CHAPTER 20

Gemma never knew love like this existed.

The kind that made you feel wanted, seen, heard. Alive. She had only read about it in books. Yet, when lying in Ian's arms, she felt it all.

Ian peppered kissed along her neck, and she giggled, turning over to look into his eyes. Even with bedhead and morning breath, he still looked fantastic.

"Hi," she whispered.

"Hi," he whispered back.

In that moment, she was glad that this wasn't a dream.

"So, last night was ... incredible," Ian said with a smile. "It was everything I thought it would be."

Gemma nodded. "Me too. Thanks for making my first time so magical, by the way."

"You're welcome. The only other woman I've been with was Ivy, but ... that never felt right. Not like it does with you."

"I know what you mean." Gemma caressed his face. "I wish I could lie here with you forever."

"Don't tempt me." Ian turned his head, looking at the clock.

"I guess we should get up. My bar and your bookstore won't run themselves."

Gemma reluctantly got up, throwing on some clothes. Ian did the same after grabbing a quick shower. When they were dressed and ready, they had cereal for breakfast and drank coffee in front of the television.

When Gemma turned on the news, she gasped. The headline read MYSTERIOUS MURDER PUZZLES TORONTO POLICE. The video on the screen showed a crime scene taped off with investigators walking around, including Noah's father. A news reporter stood in front of the tape while talking into a microphone.

"... and Toronto Police believe it's connected to the wave of recent robberies," the reporter said. "Eyewitnesses claim they saw a flash of light before a man was stabbed around midnight. The eyewitnesses claim that the knife just flew from a man's hand and into the victim's chest—without being thrown—and that this was a case of wrong place, wrong time. The police urge anyone with information to come forward. Back to you in the studio."

The screen changed, and a pair of news anchors appeared. The man said, "Police are still investigating the mysterious murders a year ago where organs went missing from victims with no incision marks—"

Gemma picked up the remote and turned off the TV.

"Man, that's messed up," Ian said, sipping his coffee. "First these robberies, now murder?"

"It's the same guy who robbed the bookstore, Ian. I just know it," Gemma said next to him.

Ian tensed. "Well, now I'm even more worried about you. And who knows—they never found the person who stole all those organs, so maybe it's the same guy."

Gemma knew it wasn't—that Fairy Godmother Zamira had

been behind that. But this new wave of crime was deeply concerning.

"Promise you'll be safe at the bookstore?" Ian asked, breaking her train of thought.

"I will. We were fortunate he didn't kill us that day."

"I'll say. What's with this bright burst of light thing? And the knife magically flowing to the victim's chest?" Ian asked. "I saw on the news that other witnesses said the same during the robberies. Some magical light or whatever. Sounds like something out of a dark fantasy novel. Did that happen when he robbed the bookstore?"

Gemma hesitated. "Uh, I can't really remember. I was just trying not to get shot."

"Right, I understand. What the hell is going on?"

Gemma knew perfectly—that a human had gotten his hands on magic after Senator Remus and his evil fairy godmother made it compatible on Earth. She still wasn't sure how it was possible. Not wanting to scare Ian, she kept her mouth shut, hoping there was something Princess Esme could do. The situation had already gotten out of control.

And it was more vital than ever that Gemma find her mother and see if she knew anything. To just make sure she was all right. But she still had no idea where to start.

"I wish I knew," Gemma said, standing to take her dishes to the sink. "I should get to work now—make sure Barbara's okay. Take care of yourself at the bar, all right?"

"I always do." Ian leaned in, kissing her. "I'll be over tonight if that's okay. We can just order takeout and watch movies."

Gemma smiled. "Sounds like heaven to me. I'll walk you outside."

Ian nodded, rising to his feet. Gemma led him out of her apartment before she locked the door and then stepped into the elevator. As they rode it down to the lobby, they spotted John leaving with a suitcase.

Gemma nudged Ian. "Look—seems like Carly finally kicked out her husband."

"Good riddance," Ian said, making her nod.

They walked outside, following John. Just as they turned to head to Ian's car, John noticed them. Unlocking his taxi, he shoved his suitcase in the backseat before walking over to Gemma with a scowl.

"You!" he yelled. "You told my wife, didn't you?"

"I did," Gemma admitted. "And you're lucky all she did was kick you out. If you ask me, you should go to jail for hitting her."

"You stupid bitch," John sneered. "You ruined everything—"

"Hey! Watch your mouth," Ian said, stepping in front of Gemma to protect her. He was inches away from John's face. "If I were you, I'd get in your taxi and drive off. Don't make this worse for yourself."

"Are you actually defending this harlot?" John asked, gesturing at Gemma. "It was her fault I flirted with her, you know. She's always wearing those dresses, looking tempting—"

Before Gemma even knew what had happened, Ian punched John in the jaw. He staggered back with a groan and fell into the side of his taxi. Clutching his face, it started to bleed as he glared at Ian.

"Shut the hell up," Ian said. "Just get out of here. I never want to hear you harassing Gemma or Carly ever again, you hear me? Or I'll do worse to you than that punch."

John said nothing as he opened his car door, then got into the driver's seat. He sneered at them as he backed away and drove off down the road. Everything was quiet as Ian watched the man flee. Some people on the sidewalk looked over, murmuring as Gemma touched his shoulder.

"Hey, you all right?" Gemma asked. "That was some punch."

"I'm fine. Barely hurt," Ian said, glancing down at his fist. "I've had to break up some nasty bar fights, so I was prepared. Are *you* okay? What he said to you wasn't cool."

"Yeah, I'm fine. I just hope he's gone for good. Carly deserves better."

"Me too. Let me know if he comes back, and I'll teach him another lesson." Ian shook his head. "Man, I hate abusers. If I can put one in their place, I'll gladly do it."

Gemma nodded. "Hear! Hear! Thanks, Ian. I really appreciate it."

"Anything for my girl." Ian kissed her forehead, then opened the passenger side door. "Come on, I'll drive you to work."

Now that's how you treat a lady, Gemma thought as she got into Ian's car. *John has a few lessons to learn.*

After chit-chatting on the drive, Ian pulled into the parking lot of the bookstore. The store looked empty with no visitors as usual. Gemma kissed Ian once more, then got out and waved, looking forward to seeing him again later. He waved back before vanishing down the road to head to work.

Gemma entered the bookstore, finding the door unlocked and all the lights off. She flicked the switch by the door, but nothing happened. "Barbara? Barbara, are you here?"

When Gemma walked toward the front desk, Barbara was there, lighting more candles. It was the only light in the store. She looked up, her gaze landing on Gemma.

"Oh, good morning, Gemma," Barbara said. "Unfortunately, our power was turned off this morning. I couldn't pay the bill. So, I guess we'll have to do things the old-fashioned way around here. Lots of candles and lighters."

Gemma sighed. "Barbara ... I'm so sorry."

She forced a smile, lighting another candle. "Hey, it's all

right—It's not your fault. A part of me knew one day I'd lose this bookstore. Times are tough for small businesses, especially after those robberies."

"What about the credit card transactions? Can you use that money to pay for the lights?" Gemma asked.

"I had to use it to pay rent, unfortunately." Barbara frowned and looked around helplessly.

"That stupid robber."

"And I saw on the news that it's gotten worse."

Gemma nodded. "Murder now. Yeah, I know. It's just awful."

"Very. I worry about my grandson. He's always out getting into trouble. What if this killer runs into him? All it takes is one late night with Jacob out somewhere where he shouldn't be—"

"Don't think like that," Gemma interrupted. "He'll be okay. I believe it."

"God, I hope so. I'd tell him to be careful, but I know he won't listen to me. Not since his mother passed." She shook her head. "Anyway, do you think you can take some of those battery-powered candles and place them in the windows? If someone walks by, I want them to know we're open."

Gemma picked up the fake candles. "Got it. Whatever you need, Barbara."

As she set up the candles, then swept the floors and put books away over the course of the workday, Gemma knew something needed to be done. She couldn't watch Barbara lose her business and sink deeper into depression. And if Ian's rich family wasn't going to help her, then she'd have to do it herself.

When the end of the workday came around with no customers at all in the store, Barbara sighed. "Well, I guess we should lock up. And Gemma, I won't be offended if you want to quit and find a new job. I'm not sure how much longer I can keep paying you. Or my rent. Having my power turned off is only the start, I'm sure. The last payment I made was just enough to cover last month's rent. I'm still behind. Without customers, there's no need for employees."

Gemma put her hand on Barbara's. "No, I'm not going anywhere. I'm going to help you save this bookstore, Barbara. I swear it. I'll work for free if I have to. I'm hoping the grand reopening will bring in more customers."

Barbara smiled. "You're sweet. Sadly, I think it's a lost cause. It wouldn't be the first thing I've lost. And I doubt it'll be the last." Barbara shook her head. "Anyway, get home safely, Gemma. These streets have gotten more dangerous lately."

They had—and Gemma's people were to blame. She felt guilty even though this was Senator Remus' fault.

After leaving the bookstore, Barbara locked the door and sped off in her car. But Gemma didn't head home right away. She hailed a taxi, then asked the driver to take her to the nearest news studio. To her relief, it wasn't John who had picked her up again.

She never wanted to see that man again in her life.

When she arrived at the news studio, she headed through the doors and a secretary greeted her at the front desk. Journalists, assistants, and cameramen were walking around, all very busy. Dozens of offices and newsrooms sat down the hall.

"Hello there. Can I help you?" the squeaky-voiced secretary asked. "Do you have an appointment?"

"Not exactly," Gemma said. "But I was interviewed by a journalist not that long ago. She was doing a segment on supporting small businesses. I was wondering if I could talk to her. Or get on TV at all. That same small business is really struggling after a robbery, and I need to get the word out about a grand reopening-slash-fundraiser-slash-game event tomorrow. Wow, that was a lot of slashes."

"While I have sympathy for a struggling business," the secretary said with a frown, "I'm afraid our reporters are very busy. But you can submit a request to be interviewed."

"All right, I'll do that. How long will it take to receive a response?"

"Well, there are many people in the community who are in need. Our current wait time is at six months."

Six months? Gemma knew Barbara didn't have that long. She was lucky if the bookstore would stay open another six *weeks*.

Gemma backed away from the front desk, shaking her head. "It's all right, thank you. I'll find another way."

The secretary nodded, returning to work as Gemma left the news station. She had an idea as she stood on the sidewalk. If that human was using magic for evil, surely Gemma could use it for good—especially now that it was compatible on Earth. Even though she wasn't allowed, she knew she had to.

Desperate times called for desperate measures. That was how that charming human idiom went. Putting up flyers and trying traditional advertising would take too long now, so it seemed like magic was the best way forward.

Finally deciding to do it, Gemma walked down the street, then opened the grate covering the storm drain and climbed down. She put the grate over her head before sliding down the ladder. The earthy smells of Fairhaven greeted her, making her feel at home. Dozens of her own people were heading home after work and school and smiled at her as they passed.

She quickened her pace, walking through the dark streets as she headed toward the castle in the distance. The guard recognized Gemma and let her through. She gazed longingly at her empty library for a moment, then walked toward the kitchen.

Cal was wearing his chef uniform and hat while finishing up for the day.

When he noticed her, he spun around with a smile. "Gemma! Nice to see you again. What are you doing back here?"

"Hey, Cal. I need some help. A friend of mine is in danger of losing her bookstore, the place I work at, and I wanted to do a grand reopening fundraiser tomorrow for her. Think you can whip up some tasty treats? Then the money raised could go to save her shop."

Cal smiled. "Anything for you, Gem. It'll only take a moment."

Gemma watched as Cal turned toward the counter, then removed a potion from his pocket. He waved it over the counter before dozens of baked goods filled the kitchen. Everything from cookies to donuts to muffins and croissants. Cal inspected the food, making sure it was all baked properly, then nodded.

Gemma looked around, wide-eyed. "Wow—this all looks amazing. Thanks, Cal."

"Don't mention it. I barely broke a sweat. Here, I'll get you a basket." Cal used another potion, then a basket large enough to fit all the desserts flew toward him. All the desserts magically placed themselves neatly into the basket. Thanks to the potion, which enchanted the basket, it was deep enough to hold it all. "Here you are. Hope you can save the bookstore."

"Thanks again. I really appreciate this." Gemma took the basket, holding it at her side. "One more thing. You got any elixirs to charm someone? It's not for evil, I swear. Just to help out the bookstore."

"I don't, but the fairy godmother workshop is just around the corner. Come on, I'll show you."

Gemma nodded, following Cal out of the kitchen with her basket in hand. She spotted several witch doctors leaving the castle as they headed down the hall. She frowned, turning back to Cal.

"What's with the magical doctors?" she asked.

"Oh, King Tedros is still very sick. Princess Esme hasn't given up on him, though." Cal shook his head. "Everyone in the kingdom is very upset."

"I bet. Poor king—and Esme too. She must be a mess."

Cal nodded, leading Gemma into a small workshop. "She really is. Don't worry, I'm sure he'll be better soon. Anyway, take whatever you need. I guess you should be thankful for Senator Remus, huh?"

Gemma browsed a shelf of magical elixirs, reading the labels carefully. "Thankful to him? Never. He's a traitor—with some dangerous ideas—and he conned my mother into believing it too. She fled to the surface with the other sympathizers because of him. Because she was afraid she'd go to jail with him."

Cal leaned against the doorway. "True enough. But without him, magic wouldn't work on the surface. You wouldn't be able to use these elixirs up there for whatever it is you're doing."

Gemma nodded, taking a charming potion off the shelf. "You're right—as much as I hate to admit it. I still don't trust the Senator, though. He's still in his cell, right?"

"Yep. Trust me, he's never getting out. Not under the watchful eyes of those guards."

"Good. I hope it stays that way." Gemma tucked the elixir into her pocket. "Anyway, thanks again, Cal. I should get back to the surface."

Cal hesitated, looking like he had something to say. Gemma knew him well enough to know when he was hiding something.

"Cal?" she asked. "Is everything all right?"

"Well ... I wasn't going to tell you this," he began, "but

there's something you should know. I don't think you should come to Fairhaven anymore. You're happy on the surface, aren't you? I think you should just stay there. Permanently."

Gemma was taken aback. "I am happy up there, yeah. Especially with Ian. But this place ... it's my home. You and my father are still here."

"I know that. And you know I love having you here. But since you've been gone ... your father's had some things to say about you. And they haven't been very nice."

Gemma's father? He had been nothing but loving and supportive all throughout her life, especially when her mother left.

"No," she whispered. "I don't believe that. Papa loves me."

"Come on—I'll show you. He was talking about you not that long ago. He's probably still there."

Confused, Gemma followed Cal when he turned and began walking down the hallway. He led her out of the castle and to a small performance hall where her father was playing. The hall was empty, and the performance was over, but her father remained to chat with a guard. Cal pressed a finger to his lips as they hid behind the wall, gesturing for Gemma to just listen.

"... and every time I look at my daughter, I see my wife. And her betrayal. It's very difficult," her father was saying. "In a way ... I'm glad Gemma decided to go to the surface. I've been doing much better since she left. I know that's harsh, but ... it's the truth."

The guard nodded. "I understand that. And Gemma was an outsider—even Princess Esme thought she was odd. She never really seemed to fit in. I heard the princess only gave Gemma some money and Noah's apartment to get her to leave Fairhaven. She and that library obsession of hers were making people uncomfortable."

Her father shook his head. "I really don't know where I went wrong with that girl …"

Gemma couldn't stand to hear anymore. She turned and ran, tears blurring her vision. Why would my father say that about me? And Princess Esme and Noah?"

She had thought they were her friends. Was it possible they were judging her and laughing at her all this time?

I really am a nobody, Gemma thought.

"Gemma, wait!" Cal rushed after her, grabbing her arm and spinning her to face him. "I'm sorry. I just thought you should know," Cal said, putting an arm around her shoulder. "Your father's been talking about you nonstop since you left. Some of the others, too. I've been defending you, and that really hasn't made me popular. Especially with Princess Esme and Noah."

Gemma wiped her tears and sniffed. "Well, I'm glad someone is. Thanks, Cal. I guess you're the only one I can trust around here." Gemma gestured at the storm drain above her head. "I really should get back to the surface. Maybe you're right—maybe I shouldn't come back here. Where I'm not wanted."

Cal nodded and wrapped her in a friendly hug. "I'll miss you but I understand. You take care of yourself up there, okay?"

"I promise, Cal. You, too. Goodbye."

Gemma climbed up the ladder, looking at Fairhaven one last time. She promised herself she'd never return again.

CHAPTER 21

As Gemma walked through the streets at dusk, she couldn't believe what she had overheard. Her father had never mentioned any of that stuff to her—resenting her for looking like her mother after her betrayal. It felt like a kick to the gut. And even Princess Esme and Noah had issues with her.

Maybe coming to the surface world had been a good idea all along. She had finally met people who were glad to have her in their lives—from Ian and Barbara to Abby and Carly.

They had become her true family.

When she reached the news station, she opened the door, finding the same secretary sitting there. She had finished hanging up a phone call and glanced at Gemma with a frown. "You again. If you're back for an interview, I'm afraid little has changed—"

Gemma opened the vial in her pocket, throwing the contents all over the secretary's desk. Pink, purple, and silver wisps spread throughout the office. The secretary coughed, then her entire face changed to a blank expression.

"I'd like to give a TV interview," Gemma said. "Where should I go?"

"Down the hall," the secretary said in a monotone voice. "First door on the left. I'll phone ahead and let the reporter know you're coming."

Gemma smiled, putting the empty vial away. "Thank you very much."

She headed down the hallway as the secretary nodded, then phoned ahead. Gemma knew she wasn't supposed to use magic in the surface world, that it was frowned upon by Princess Esme and King Tedros, but what other choice did she have? Barbara needed her help. She hadn't used it for evil, not like Senator Remus or that human criminal.

When she reached the door down the hall on the far left, Gemma opened it and walked into a news studio. A reporter in a pantsuit was giving the evening news at a desk in front of a camera crew. When the cameraman motioned for a commercial, the reporter took a break, flipping through her papers as a hair stylist and makeup team touched her up.

Gemma approached the cameraman, clearing her throat. "Um, excuse me? The secretary should've phoned ahead. I need an interview on the evening news."

The cameraman nodded. "Yeah, she did. I have no idea why it was so important, but she seemed pretty insistent. Head on up there—the reporter has been briefed. You'll be on after the commercial break."

Gemma nodded, smiling to herself for getting this far. Cal's potion had worked perfectly. As she glanced down at the basket, she hoped his delicious-smelling desserts would work too.

When she approached the desk, a hair stylist told her to sit down, then they got to work on Gemma. She tried to swat them away but they were insistent she be touched up for the evening news. The reporter turned to her, looking down at her notes again.

"So, I was informed I had to take this interview," the woman said. "Last minute but my secretary swore it was urgent. Something about a dying bookstore?"

Gemma nodded as the hair stylist finished. "That's right—we need to help my friend, Barbara. I only need a minute of your time."

"Well, you certainly got it. Not many people walk in from off the street and get to do an interview, you know. You're lucky the secretary is a good friend of mine."

Gemma just smiled. The empty vial jiggled in her pocket.

When the cameraman began counting down, signaling that they were coming back from the commercial break, the reporter smiled and turned to the camera. He gave her a thumbs up before she spoke.

"Welcome back to Channel Seven news. All the stuff that matters," the woman said, repeating the company slogan. "I'm sitting here with Gemma Solace, a local bookstore employee with an important message. Gemma?"

When the reporter turned to her, then the camera switched to her face, Gemma gulped. She had never been on live air before. What if she messed up?

With sweaty hands, Gemma wracked her brain for something to say as she turned to the camera. Barbara was counting on her—she couldn't screw this up.

"Uh, right. Thanks for having me," Gemma said, then cleared her throat. "I'm here because a local business is dying in front of our eyes, but we can save it if we work together. Barbara Danvers is the kindest woman I've ever met, and she's had a rough year after losing her daughter ..."

Gemma went through the entire story, trying to make the

public feel sympathy for Barbara like she did. Then she briefly touched on the robbery incident.

"... and after her store was robbed at gunpoint, Barbara wasn't able to pay her electricity bill. She desperately needs help," Gemma continued. "And I think, as a community, we should help her. So, I'm throwing a fundraiser-slash-grand reopening at the Enchanted Tales Bookstore tomorrow between the hours of eight am and six pm. I've already got all the baked goods here. The proceeds go to help a lovely woman keep her shop afloat and support her grandson. We're planning on doing regular weekly events too—like board games, sales, and raffle prizes. Still working out the kinks, but we're getting closer. Anyway, thank you for listening and I hope to see you there."

"And ... we're out!" the cameraman yelled.

The reporter nodded, turning to Gemma. "Nice work—you did well."

"Really? I was so nervous." Gemma took a deep breath. "But thank you. I just hope this grand reopening will help."

Or Barbara could kiss her shop goodbye—and Gemma would be out of a job. Her *perfect* job.

After saying goodbye to the reporter, Gemma left the studio. The secretary was still out of it at the front desk. Soon, the potion would wear off, and the secretary would just forget the whole thing.

When she got home, she made dinner, then watched a replay of her interview from earlier. She hoped it would draw in as many people as it could for tomorrow. After doing the dishes, a knock sounded on the door.

Gemma opened the door to Ian standing there, dressed casually in jeans and a white t-shirt. Although she missed him in a tux, he still looked good dressed down. They kissed and hugged before she let him inside.

"I saw your TV interview," Ian said, entering the apartment.

"That was really nice what you did for Barbara. And I'll be there tomorrow, of course. For the grand reopening."

Gemma smiled. "Thanks, Ian. I knew I could count on you."

"I never break a promise. Though I don't think you really need me—seems like you know what you're doing. And those desserts look amazing." Ian pointed at the basket on the table. "Did you make them all yourself?"

"Uh, yeah," Gemma lied, wondering if she should finally tell Ian about Fairhaven. Just the thought of what she'd overheard there brought her pain so she stalled for a little while longer. After overhearing her dad call her a burden, she never wanted to go back. "Took me a while but they're ready for tomorrow. And I'm grateful the TV studio was cool enough to interview me."

"I'll say. I'm proud of you, and I hope it works out." Ian sat down on the couch. "So, what do you want to do tonight? Movie marathon? We could always watch the Alien movies."

As nice as cuddling on the couch with Ian sounded, Gemma thought of Carly. She was already helping Barbara, and she didn't want to stop there. She hoped she could patch things up with the first person who welcomed her to Toronto.

"Actually, I was thinking we could go out," Gemma said. "If you're in the mood for it."

Ian rose to his feet. "Gemma, I'll go anywhere with you. Even to the center of the Earth."

Gemma laughed. "We don't have to go that far, trust me. I wanted to go to Carly's dance studio. I want to see if her offer to teach us salsa is still available."

"I don't have a problem with that, but ... isn't Carly still mad at you?"

Gemma sighed. "Yeah, she is. I'm hoping to patch things up between us, especially now that John's gone. What do you say?"

"I wish I'd brought my dancing shoes, but these will have to do," Ian joked, winking at her. "Lead the way."

Gemma nodded, thanking him for coming as she locked her apartment door. She and Ian rode the elevator downstairs before heading out to his car. He looked up Carly's dance studio on Google, then drove to the building downtown. Several cars were parked outside for tonight's lesson.

"Seems busy in there," Ian said, parking the car. "Good for Carly. She'll need the money for a good divorce lawyer."

Gemma nodded, opening her door. "And to pay for her daughter's treatments. Come on, let's head inside."

Ian followed her, locking the car as they headed toward the door which was in the shape of a dance shoe. Ian opened the door for Gemma, then she headed inside the studio. Large mirrors dominated one entire wall, and the massive wood floor left plenty of space for dancing. The studio filled with the squeaking of shoes as an elderly couple did the salsa in the middle of the room.

People watched on, cheering. Carly stood a few feet away, wearing her red salsa dress as she gave them tips. She adjusted their posture and showed them how to dance. Abby sat in the corner, coloring a picture with another hospital band around her wrist.

When she saw Gemma and Ian enter the studio, her head lifted with a smile. "Gemma, hi!"

Carly's head turned, noticing the two near the door. She glanced at the couple and the other guests in the studio. "Take five. I'll be right back."

As Carly approached, Gemma gulped. She really didn't want a confrontation in front of Abigail.

"Hi, Carly," Gemma said as Carly reached them. "I know this is out of the blue, but I wanted to come and say I'm sorry—"

"It's all right," Carly interrupted. "You don't owe me an apology. If anything, *I'm* the one who should be sorry."

Gemma paused. "Really?"

"Really. I was so rude to you when you didn't deserve it. You've treated me better than John, and I just threw your friendship away." Carly shook her head. "Now that I kicked him out, I can finally think clearly. And I'm really sorry for how I treated you."

"That's a relief," Gemma said, breathing out. "Because I miss being your friend. And I really am sorry I took so long to tell you about John."

"It's okay, Gemma, it's not your fault. I'm not sure what I would've done if the roles had been reversed. Anyway, John agreed to leave, and I've hired a divorce lawyer. I'm requesting full custody, alimony, and child support for Abby to keep us afloat."

Gemma smiled. "Glad to hear it. So, are we friends again?"

"Definitely," Carly replied. "If you'll forgive me."

"Nothing to forgive." Gemma beamed. "Hey, if you and Abby aren't doing anything tomorrow, I'm holding a grand reopening fundraiser at the Enchanted Tales Bookstore. Want to come?"

"Sure. I don't have anything planned. Just waiting to hear back from the lawyer on how to divide up our assets. I saw you on the news, by the way. It's nice that you're trying to save the bookstore."

"Someone has to. It's been tough for small businesses around here—especially with the robberies."

"Turned murderer now," Carly said with a shiver, glancing out the window. "I worry about my studio getting broken into. And me and Abby's safety. Eyewitnesses keep saying the guy is magical or something. I just don't understand. How is that possible?"

"I heard the same thing," Ian said. "I don't get it either. Maybe the eyewitnesses were high?"

Gemma feared the expression on her face might give her away. Her eyes dropped to the floor, grateful no one could read her mind. She knew the criminal had gotten magic from her people, just not how. Obviously, a cloud of magical dust from Fairy Godmother Zamira's experiment. Now, all she needed to do was figure out his identity.

Luckily, Abigail skipped over, so Gemma wouldn't have to respond. She held up a cute painting of the dance studio. As always, she was still wearing her princess dress. "Look what I drew!"

Gemma took the picture, smiling at the drawn dancers. "Very good, Abby. Maybe you have a future career of being an artist."

"I always tell my girl she can be anything she wants to be," Carly said, ruffling Abby's hair. "I truly believe that."

Abby took her picture back, looking at the hospital band. "I just wish I wasn't so sick. Going to the hospital all the time sucks."

"I know, sweetie," Carly said with a frown. "And I'm sorry. But you've done so well."

"And we're all proud of you," Gemma said with a nod. "How are you doing besides that, Abby?"

She shrugged. "I'm sad Dad's gone, but I won't miss him always fighting with Mom. He had a scary temper."

Gemma knew that the best—she had seen it.

"Don't worry," Ian said, glancing at Carly. "I put him in his place. Gave him a little ... present on his chin."

When he made a fist, Carly seemed to understand. "Really? Thank you. I have no doubt he deserved it. Now, I have to get back to work, but I'd love to welcome you to the dance class. Ever tried salsa before?"

"Never," Gemma said, glancing at Ian, "but we'd love to give it a shot."

Gemma and Ian followed Carly to the dance floor, listening to her instructions. Abby and the others in the studio watched from the sidelines. Carly was a great teacher, and after an hour, Gemma and Ian had slowly picked up how to do the salsa. Carly turned on the salsa music on her CD player and the two tore up the dance floor. They fumbled through the steps, tripping a few times, but they enjoyed each other's company. And that was all that truly mattered.

As Ian spun her around, Gemma laughed harder than she ever had in the past. But her father's betrayal and her mother's location were still on her mind. They were both impossible to escape from.

When they finished, everyone in the studio clapped, including Carly. "Well done, you two! That was a pretty good start for beginners. With a little more practice, you'll get even better."

She and Ian both panted as Gemma nodded. "I'd like that. What do you think, partner?"

"I think we've found a new date idea," Ian said with a smile. "I'm in."

"Perfect!" Carly said. "I've been looking for new members to join this studio. I'm going to need the extra money."

"I bet. Don't worry, this is on me. Business has been good at the bar," Ian said, paying Carly for the lesson. "Consider this the first donation to a better life for you and your daughter."

Carly took the bills, beaming. "Thank you, Ian, and you too, Gemma. You two looked great out there together, by the way. Your chemistry is off the charts. And I'm not just talking about dancing. I hope you're together for a very long time."

As Gemma looked at Ian, sharing a smile, she hoped so, too.

If all the craziness from Fairhaven and the robber-turned-murderer wouldn't screw it up.

After a few more dance lessons, Carly danced with the same handsome firefighter Gemma had met. She told Gemma she wasn't quite ready for a relationship just yet but that getting to know someone new couldn't hurt. Flattered Carly would share her thoughts with her, Gemma completely understood.

Gemma and Ian said goodbye to Abby and Carly and left the studio. Ian took Gemma back to her apartment, where she collapsed on the couch, exhausted.

"Whew, that dance lesson took everything out of me," she said. "It worked muscles I didn't know I had."

"Tell me about it." Ian sat on the couch next to her, wrapping an arm around her shoulder. "I'm just happy to be back home with you."

Gemma smiled, kissing his cheek. "I feel the same. And I'm glad I worked things out with Carly. I really do like her, despite her husband trying to tear us apart. Anyway, thanks for coming out tonight and taking part in my last-minute plan. Movie time?"

Ian nodded. "Yes, please. But before you put it on ... there was something I wanted to ask you."

"Shoot," Gemma said, turning her television on and scrolling through Netflix.

He cleared his throat. "Okay. Well, I don't want you to think I'm pressuring you or anything ... but I really would like to meet your family soon. Since you've met mine and seen what they're like. They can't be worse than my parents."

Gemma's throat bobbed. She had seen a cruel side of her father she hadn't thought was possible. It had been a devastating blow, one that made her stomach sick to think about.

"Anyway, I just wanted to meet your father. You know, to get closer to you," Ian continued. "I know we talked about this yesterday but I'm ready now. Maybe we could set something up for tomorrow evening? Have dinner together?"

Gemma turned to him. "I know I said I'd like that, but that was before my father and I had an ... argument. We aren't really on speaking terms right now."

"Oh. I'm sorry. What happened?"

He's happier without me. He's glad I'm gone. Those awful thoughts filled Gemma's mind, beating on her like a drum.

"I don't really want to get into it. But I'm not sure now is a good time to meet him—or anytime soon. Not even sure if *I* want to see him again."

Ian gave her a look, then turned to the television. He had suddenly grown tense. "Hmm. Okay."

Gemma paused. "Are you all right? You look upset."

"It's just ... are you telling me the truth or do you just not want me to meet him?" Ian asked. "Because I'll understand. Sorry, I know I sound paranoid, but my ex would do this. Lie to me and play mind games—"

"I'm not your ex, Ian," Gemma said, a little harsher than intended. "And no, I'm not lying to you. My father and I really aren't on speaking terms—not after I heard him saying some unkind things about me behind my back. That's the honest truth."

Ian still looked skeptical but dropped the issue. As Gemma put the movie on, she wondered—was Ian always going to be like this? Mistrusting everything she said because of his past relationships? At some point, he would have to let go. But she didn't know if he could.

Or if *he* would forgive *her* for lying about her magical past. Would it trigger his trust issues when it all came to light? That was another issue altogether.

"I'm sorry," Ian finally spoke up. "I hope I didn't ruin the mood."

"No, you didn't," Gemma said, pausing the movie. "At some point, Ian, you have to get over what your ex did to you and realize I'm not the same type of person."

"I never said you were." Ian sat up, growing defensive. "Look, maybe I should just go home. Maybe I screwed things up—"

A knock sounded on the door, making both their heads snap around.

CHAPTER 22

Gemma walked toward the door. When she opened it, she expected it to be Carly and Abby, coming over for something. But her eyes widened when she saw Fairy Godmother Blanche standing there. She had her dress on, her magic wand in hand with a devious smile.

"Ah, Gemma—there you are!" Fairy Godmother Blanche cried. "Everyone told me you were staying at Noah's apartment. I wanted to come visit—"

Gemma panicked, shutting the door in Fairy Godmother Blanche's face and not locking it. Her fairy godmother made a noise of disapproval on the other side.

Ian stood, walking over with a frown. "Hey, who was that? Why'd you close the door? And who's Noah?"

Gemma hesitated. "Oh, um, Noah? He's just a friend of mine who lent me this apartment. And that was ... never mind who that was. She's not important—"

The door unlocked by itself, then a magical spray of energy opened it. Fairy Godmother Blanche still stood there with a frown. "Well, good to see you too, Gemma."

"Seriously, who is this?" Ian asked, studying the woman. "She even wears the same kind of dress as you. And what was with that glittery stuff? It sounds like the way people described that murderer."

"There was no glittery stuff," Gemma said quickly. Guilt crept up her spine of having to lie to Ian again, but she thought it was for the best. For now. "You must be seeing things."

Ian frowned. "But—"

Fairy Godmother Blanche stood straighter. "You must be Ian, the man Gemma has fallen for. I've heard good things about you. My name is—"

"She's my aunt," Gemma interrupted. "Aunt Blanche. Who I didn't know would be dropping by this evening."

Fairy Godmother Blanche shrugged, pushing her way into the apartment. "Yes, well, you know me. I'm not much of a planner. Having a quiet evening together, I see."

"We were," Gemma huffed, "until you showed up. Um, Ian, maybe it *is* a good idea that you go home. Me and my aunt have to have a long talk about privacy."

Ian glanced at Fairy Godmother Blanche, noticing her wand before turning back to Gemma. "Uh, all right. It was nice to meet someone in your family, at least. See you later, Gemma."

Ian left the apartment, walking down the hallway. Gemma sighed and shut the door. She felt like she had made everything worse between them—especially after their argument.

"What was wrong with him?" Fairy Godmother Blanche asked, grabbing an apple off the kitchen counter. She took a bite and then spat it out. "Bah! Surface food is so plain. Seriously, why'd he leave?"

"We kinda had our first fight. Ian wanted to meet my family but I hesitated. Me and Papa ... we're not on speaking terms right now."

Fairy Godmother Blanche set the apple down, checking

things out in the kitchen. "Oh, no? My, that's a surprise. You two were always close, especially after your mother was banned from Fairhaven. What a loon. Anyway, what happened?"

"You haven't heard? Apparently, he's been telling everyone how glad he is that I'm gone. That I remind him too much of Mother. Cal showed me the truth the last time I came to Fairhaven. I heard Papa say it from his own mouth. Even Princess Esme and Noah were gossiping about me. And it wasn't nice. They think I'm weird."

Fairy Godmother Blanche turned around. Her eyes widened. "My goodness ... that's awful. I'm sorry, Gemma. I thought your father was better than that. I haven't heard him say a single unkind thing about you, you know. Though, I *do* spend a lot of time drinking." She tapped her chin. "I'll have to have a talk with him when I get back. As well as Princess Esme and Noah. They should know better as royals."

"What's the point? I don't want to cause any unnecessary drama. Just leave it alone." Gemma leaned on the kitchen counter. "Anyway, that's why I didn't want Ian to meet Papa. After I learned all that. And I'm not thrilled he met you tonight, either. What were you thinking? Just showing up on my doorstep?"

"What?" Fairy Godmother Blanche asked, opening the microwave and peering inside out of curiosity. "Ooh, very nice. Any-hoo, I didn't think it would be a problem. Or that you would have company so late. You've changed a lot since you left Fairhaven, hmm? The old Gemma barely left the library. And she most certainly didn't have a boyfriend."

Gemma shrugged. "Yeah, well ... I guess the surface world *did* change me. After tonight, I don't know. Maybe Ian will still be mad at me. He's got a lot of baggage from his last relationship. He was abused by some famous actress."

"Oh, how awful. Want me to poison her?"

"No! And no magic on the surface." Gemma thought back to using that potion on the secretary, then blushed out of guilt. "Uh, at least, from now on. And in case you haven't heard, there's some human going around, stealing and killing with the help of magic. Which Senator Remus made possible. We don't need any more around here than we already have. No more sneaking up to the surface or breaking down my door with magic if I shut it in your face."

"Oh, fine," Fairy Godmother Blanche grumbled. "I didn't mean any harm. I wanted to get away from Fairhaven for a while. The place gets stuffy—especially for a boring, old fairy godmother. Anyway, now that I'm here and Ian's gone, let's have some fun, shall we?"

Gemma raised an eyebrow. "What kind of fun? You might think I've changed a lot, but—"

"Oh, come on, girl!" Fairy Godmother Blanche cried, rushing to the door. "You must live while you're alive. I've tried to teach you that your entire life! Follow me—we're going to make the most of tonight."

Gemma sighed, knowing her fairy godmother wasn't going to drop it. And she really didn't want the woman going out alone. Who knew what kind of trouble she would get into on her own?

"All right, all right," Gemma muttered, catching up to her. "One night only. I mean it."

Fairy Godmother Blanche nodded, grinning as Gemma locked her door. She led the woman out of the apartment building where they stepped onto the street. The sky was dark, and Ian's car had vanished. Gemma hoped she hadn't ruined things between them.

That was the last thing she ever wanted to do.

Gemma showed her fairy godmother around, going for a

walk in the dark streets. Blanche was transfixed by all the human sights with wide eyes. As if fate had pulled Gemma's feet that way, they ended up near Ian's bar a while later.

"Ooh, there's an interesting bar over there!" Fairy Godmother Blanche said, pointing down the street. "Let's see what kind of human drinks they serve."

"That's Ian's bar. He owns it," Gemma explained. "We should stay away—I don't want him to see us. He might've already seen the magic you used to open my door."

Fairy Godmother Blanche rolled her eyes. "You worry too much, dear. These humans are too naive to seriously believe in magic. But fine, we'll do things your way. Where should we go instead?"

Gemma led her fairy godmother down the street, trying to block the woman from view. The few people that were out on the dark streets weren't paying attention to them—just the way Gemma wanted it. After her public dinner date with Ian, she knew the photographers might come back.

And she didn't want them snapping a picture of magic in action. Now *that* would be hard to explain, just like this robber-turned-killer.

Gemma found a quieter bar, leading Fairy Godmother Blanche inside. It was run by an elderly man who smiled at them as they took a seat at the bar. Fairy Godmother Blanche slammed her fist down on the counter, then gestured at the rack of drinks.

"I want the strongest alcohol you have!" she cried. "Make me really feel it."

"Oh, brother," Gemma muttered.

"You got it," the elderly man said, pouring some concoction into a glass that smelled awful. "Here you go."

Fairy Godmother Blanche grinned, bringing the cup up to

her mouth. She made a face as the liquid went down. She burped, then pushed the cup forward. "More!"

The bartender laughed, glancing at Gemma. "She's a tough cookie. Another glass, coming up."

Three mugs later, Fairy Godmother Blanche was drunk—just the way she spent her days in Fairhaven. Gemma sat next to her, unamused as the woman rambled on.

"... and this human world is very strange. The smells are all off," she muttered. "How did you get used to it?"

"I managed. Can we go now? You've had enough to drink. And you should probably get back to Fairhaven before someone realizes you're gone, like the Fairy Godmother Council."

"To hell with them!" At her outburst, some patrons in the bar looked over. "I never wanted to be a fairy godmother, you know. God, I had so many dreams ..."

"Then why didn't you refuse?"

Fairy Godmother Blanche shook her head. "I tried. Because I was so talented with elixirs, I was nearly forced to join. And you needed a fairy godmother—everyone in Fairhaven does. How could I refuse when I saw your cute little baby face all those years ago? You were so small, so helpless. And adorable."

It was then that Gemma realized why the council had paired her with Fairy Godmother Blanche. Maybe, even deep down, they knew the women were more alike than they realized. Both dissatisfied in Fairhaven, both craving something more.

And maybe, with a little luck, they both could turn their lives around.

Gemma placed a hand on Blanche's shoulder. "Look, I'm grateful for all the help you've given me over the years. And for looking after me as a baby. But if you don't want to be a fairy godmother, then quit. Petition the king to move to the surface and start a new life. One you really want. I can speak to Princess Esme on your behalf, too."

"But … I can't do that. Fairy Godmothers never quit their post—It's unheard of. And you wouldn't have one anymore."

Gemma shrugged. "I can live without one, Blanche. Trust me. If I've learned anything on the surface, it's that I'm more capable than I think. I was wrong to doubt myself. And although we haven't always seen eye to eye, especially when it comes to your drinking, I want you to be happy. Ask the Council to free you and start living a new life. You have my blessing."

Fairy Godmother Blanche leapt into Gemma's arms, hugging her tight. She hugged back in surprise. "Oh, thank you, thank you, thank you! I'm not sure how the process is going to work, but I'll get it started right away. Maybe … maybe I'll even get a fairy godmother of my own and not have to worry about this crap anymore!"

"Maybe," Gemma said with a smile. "So, are you ready to leave now? Did you get everything off your chest?"

Fairy Godmother Blanche let out a loud belch, then nodded. "*Now* I got everything off my chest. Come on, dear. I'll walk you home at least. Even when I'm not your official fairy godmother anymore, I'll still look out for you."

"Thank you, Blanche."

She nodded, stumbling a bit as she rose to her feet. If that had been magical liquor, she would've been in the gutter again. Maybe once Blanche was freed of her responsibilities, her drinking would stop.

Just like Barbara. Humans and Fairhaven citizens weren't so different after all.

Gemma led Fairy Godmother Blanche out of the bar, then started walking with her down the dark street. "So, I heard about King Tedros' illness. Is he getting any better?"

"Unfortunately, no. I've tried healing him with some

potions, but it's a mystery. I'm worried about the old fart. No one wants him to die."

But maybe someone did. "Hmm. Is anyone looking into this as a possible poisoning? Or are they just assuming it's natural?"

"Natural, of course. Perhaps a case of the Basilisk flu. Remember that nasty pandemic we had a decade ago? Perhaps it's back, who knows. Though the king is the only sick one. All the fairy godmothers are keeping an eye on the situation." Fairy Godmother Blanche paused, turning to Gemma. "With Senator Remus and his crooked family in jail, we don't really have any other enemies. You don't seriously believe his mysterious illness was caused by someone, do you?"

Gemma shrugged. "I mean, it's worth investigating. Especially with this human on the surface using magic for criminal activities—"

Just then, someone in a dark hoodie burst around the corner, waving a gun in their faces. He spoke with a deep voice as he aimed it at them. Magical particles burst around him, shrouding the air with purple and pink wisps. "Hand over all your money, ladies. Now!"

Gemma held up her hands. "All right, all right. Let's just stay calm, okay?"

As she reached into her pocket, digging around for her money, she realized this had to be the same guy from the bookstore and Ian's bar. The hoodie, gun, and magical energy were all similar. And he had just recently murdered someone. Gemma gulped, hoping they wouldn't be the next target.

Especially when she hadn't made up with Ian yet. In the face of death, their arguments seemed so small. She wanted nothing more than to make things right with him and run into his arms for comfort.

"What do you have there, hmm?" Fairy Godmother Blanche asked. "Is that one of those human guns? Truly despicable, they are. Look, I don't appreciate you threatening my charge, so step back—"

"Are you stupid, lady?" the man demanded. "Hand over all your money. Now—or I'll kill you both!"

"Fine," Gemma said, throwing her cash onto the ground. "There it is. Take all of it and leave us alone."

As the man bent down, reaching for the money, Gemma knew this was her time to strike. She had to figure out who this guy was before he hurt someone else. And the police had no leads so far.

Gemma tackled the man to the ground, kicking and punching him. He dropped the gun as the money went flying. "Blanche, get the gun. Kick it away!"

As Fairy Godmother Blanche reached for the gun, the man slapped Gemma, making her groan. His sleeve rode up a bit and showed off a snake tattoo.

As she struggled to get her bearings, her face aching, the man dove for the gun. He reached it before Fairy Godmother Blanche and then grabbed the money before stepping back. "Stupid women! Gambling with your lives when I've got magic and power on my side. I should kill you right here."

"What you don't know, little thief," Fairy Godmother Blanche said, reaching for her wand, "is that magic is a good friend of mine as well. Long before it was yours, in fact. Abracadabra, strike this man down—"

Before Fairy Godmother Blanche could finish speaking the spell, a bullet exploded from the pistol and pierced Blanche's chest. She gasped, then looked down. Blood bloomed from the wound, and she collapsed to the ground.

"Blanche, no!" Gemma cried.

The man paused, glancing down at Gemma for a moment. She wondered if he'd shoot her, too. But then he turned around and started running. Gemma knew she should've chased after him, but her fairy godmother needed her more.

She couldn't die before she got a chance to live the life she always wanted.

"Oh my God," Gemma murmured, falling beside Blanche. Her blood was all over the sidewalk. Gemma had to get her to the storm drain so they could get her to Fairhaven where she could be healed.

A couple turned the corner, and a woman gasped. "What happened? We have to call 9-1-1."

"No, that's really not—" Gemma started.

"Nonsense. We're here to help."

The man started dialing as the woman dropped by Blanche's side. "Help is on the way. Hold on."

With these people here, there was no way Gemma could take Blanche to the storm drain. This was not good.

The couple thwarted every attempt Gemma made to move Blanche, and the fairy godmother was no help, muttering incoherently.

Paramedics showed up an eternity later and put Fairy Godmother Blanche on a stretcher, then carted her into the back of an ambulance.

Gemma was allowed to ride with her, holding her hand the entire way. She kept pestering the paramedics about if Blanche was going to be okay, but they couldn't make any promises. The paramedics kept her stable as they hooked her up to a beeping machine. Blanche was still bleeding from the bullet wound above her chest, but the men wrapped it to stop the blood loss. One paramedic examined the bullet wound, frowning.

"What's wrong?" Gemma asked, leaning forward. "Something with the bullet?"

"Strange," the paramedic replied, "it's ... pulsating. Like, with energy. The only other time I saw this was on the murder victim from yesterday. But it was a knife wound, not a bullet. We tried to transport them to the hospital, but it was too late. I believe it could be the same killer."

Gemma gulped. She knew her fairy godmother was strong, and her people healed fast. She had to survive this—she just had to.

The paramedic frowned as he examined Blanche's blood. "I've never seen blood like hers before. It's thicker. Glittering, even. How weird."

Gemma knew why—because Blanche wasn't human. But no one else needed to know that.

"Do what you can for her, please," Gemma urged, squeezing Blanche's hand. "I can't lose her."

The paramedic nodded. When they arrived at the hospital, the paramedics wheeled Fairy Godmother Blanche inside for surgery. Gemma sat in the waiting room to hear the news. About an hour later, the doctor came out with a clipboard.

"We managed to get the bullet out, but it was coated in some kind of dark energy that hit her chest," the doctor said. "She's stable but we'll need to keep her here for observation. And to watch over that strange DNA of hers. Our lab couldn't make heads or tails of it. Her blood type wasn't even recognized in the system. Anyway, in the meantime, the police will be arriving to get your statement and take the bullet for processing. I already called them."

"Okay, Doctor. I imagine they'll want it—I think it's the same killer from yesterday."

The doctor sighed. "I do too. While I've never believed in the paranormal ... something odd is going on here. And I hope the police solve it soon before I end up with more victims."

The doctor walked away, heading back to check on Fairy Godmother Blanche. Gemma sighed and sat again as she thought about the culprit. Who was he? And why had he gone mad with magical power?

The doors to the hospital opened, then Detective Crawford and several officers entered. When he spotted Gemma, he ordered them to check on Fairy Godmother Blanche while he walked over to talk to her. His face was tight and somber.

"Hello, Gemma. Sorry to see you again under these circumstances," he said. "We got a call about a mugging turned shooting. And judging by the doctor's testimony, magic was used again."

Gemma nodded. "That's right—I saw it myself. The same guy from the bookstore. It's been him all along."

"Just wish I knew who he was," Detective Crawford muttered. "Damn it. Our leads have gotten us nowhere."

"I only know one thing—he's got a snake tattoo on his arm. I saw it when his sweater rode up a bit. After I tackled him."

Detective Crawford's eyebrow raised. "Really? Well, that isn't exactly helpful, but it's better than nothing. Thanks, Gemma. I'll go check on the victim now. She was described as wearing a dress and carrying a wand? She was gripping that thing pretty tight. Surprised she still had it through all the pandemonium."

Gemma nodded. "Wands are sacred to fairy godmothers. They'd never misplace them. And she's *my* Fairy Godmother, Blanche. She came out to explore the surface world."

"Ah, I see. I think Esme has one too. Anyway, I'll help smuggle her back into Fairhaven once my questioning is over. The hospital will never know her true identity."

"Thanks, Detective. After she got shot, I was going to take her down the nearest storm drain, but some humans showed up and called 9-1-1. With this guy going around, causing all these crimes and now escalating to murder, it's getting harder to keep Fairhaven a secret. People are bound to find out sooner or later—and maybe they'll even follow in this killer's footsteps once they discover how to use magic. And without having to say a spell or use a potion like the rest of us from Fairhaven, this human is unusual. That magic ... it's strong. Unheard of."

"And scary as hell," the detective said, making Gemma nod.

Right now, things seemed bleak. But one thing was certain.

A criminal was still out there, one who shouldn't have had magic. And someone needed to stop him.

CHAPTER 23

Gemma checked on Fairy Godmother Blanche before she left the hospital, making sure she was okay. She approached her hospital bed once the doctor had finished chatting with her. The bullet had been removed, a bandage over her chest where the shot had pierced her skin.

Fairy Godmother Blanche forced a smile, wearing a hospital gown instead of her dress. It was tossed over the side of the nearby chair. "Hello Gemma. Here to check up on me?"

Gemma nodded, reaching for her hand. "I am. You were pretty brave to take a bullet for me, you know. Thank you."

"As I said," Blanche began, placing a hand over hers, "whether or not I'm your fairy godmother, I'll still look out for you. And maybe getting shot was a good thing."

"What do you mean?"

"It showed me that life is short—both on the surface *and* in Fairhaven. I need to stop drinking and start living ASAP. You aren't the only one who needs to change."

"Well, I wish you luck. Let me know if you need anything."

She nodded. "I will. Once the doctors discharge me, I'll be

heading back to Fairhaven to resign as a fairy godmother and tell them what happened. They'll have potions that can help me heal faster, but they also need to know about this dangerous man with magic on his side."

"I told Princess Esme. She has a group of guards on patrol to look for him. I don't think it's going well, though. Maybe I need to look into it. I'm the one on the surface, after all."

"True. Just be careful, Gemma—this man is dangerous. We both saw that tonight. Don't get yourself killed. I might not be there next time to take another bullet for you."

Gemma promised she'd be careful, then wished her fairy godmother well before leaving the hospital room. Detective Crawford paced in the waiting room while keeping an eye on things. Gemma walked over to him, gesturing at the room over her shoulder.

"Thanks for agreeing to stay. I feel much better with you here protecting her," Gemma began. "She'll be leaving for Fairhaven once the doctors let her go."

Detective Crawford glanced around, as if to make sure no one listened. "Good, good. I'll escort her like I said. Glad to hear she'll be okay. I don't know much about you Fairhaven folk, but I don't want any of you hurt. My son doesn't either."

"Thanks, Detective. In the meantime, I'll keep an eye out for the human with magic and let you know if I find anything. Before I go … could I ask you a question? Well, two questions, actually."

"Of course. What is it?"

"I'm wondering if you know how I can track someone down. My mother, Katherine Solace, fled Fairhaven months ago. She was a sympathizer of Senator Remus' plan to bring magic to the surface and dominate all humans. The former happened, but the latter didn't, fortunately. Thanks to Princess Esme."

"Oh, that senator idiot? Noah told me about him. I know all about his plans." Detective Crawford shook his head. "Glad he's behind magical bars. And I'm real sorry your mom got caught up in all that."

"I am too. Anyway, do you know how I can track her down? Find out where she's living? I want to see her again—to talk to her. Maybe I can convince her that her family is more important than Senator Remus' plans." Even saying those words made her throat burn.

Detective Crawford pulled out his phone. "I'll write her name down and do a search at the precinct later. I'll let you know what I find. In the meantime, get home safely, Ms. Solace. You've had one hell of a night."

He could say that again.

"Thank you. One last thing." Gemma cleared her throat. "Has Noah ever said anything about me? Anything rude?"

Detective Crawford frowned. "What? No, of course not. Why do you ask?"

Because Cal told me he had. "Nothing, never mind. See you around, Detective."

Gemma thanked him again, then left the hospital. She hailed a taxi outside and took it back to her apartment building. Inside Noah's apartment, she collapsed on the couch and fell fast asleep, exhausted after a late night.

When she woke up that morning to her alarm, she debated telling Ian everything that had happened. That her so-called aunt—secretly her fairy godmother—had been shot by the same man who robbed the bookstore and got away at his bar. But until she found out more, she didn't want to alarm Ian. And they still weren't on good terms after their little fight last night. Just another thing she was worried about.

The human with magic was a Fairhaven matter, one she needed to fix before it got even worse for people on the surface.

Her own kind had caused this problem—and they needed to fix it. Somehow.

Yet another thing to add to her ever-growing to-do list.

She got up, then had breakfast and got dressed. After grabbing the basket of treats that Cal had magically whipped up, she left her apartment and headed outside. She took the busy sidewalks to work, trying to stay in large crowds in case the shooter came back. She didn't know what else he had planned, but it probably wasn't good.

When she reached the bookstore, Barbara was just putting the OPEN sign in the window. She nodded at Gemma and let her inside. The power was still out, candles scattered everywhere to bring in some light.

"Morning, Gemma," Barbara began. "I saw you on the news last night promoting the grand reopening fundraiser. I'm grateful, but I'm not sure it'll change much."

Gemma smiled, setting the basket of desserts down on the front desk. "Have a little faith, Barbara. We're going to save this bookstore—I just know it. And look what I brought."

Barbara peered inside the basket. Her eyes widened. "My goodness … so many desserts! They look amazing. How did you make all of this in time? And get on the news again?"

Gemma smiled, grateful for Fairhaven's magic. "I have my ways. Don't worry about today, Barbara—I'll handle it all. Just sit back and relax, okay?"

Barbara nodded. "All right, Gemma. And thank you. You really are such a dear."

"Don't mention it, Barbara. I invited a few people to the grand reopening fundraiser, Ian included. Hopefully he'll show up. We … sort of had a fight last night."

Barbara's smile dropped. "Oh no. I hope you two work it out. You're adorable together—and so compatible. If anything, getting into a fight was a good thing. If you can get through that, you can get through anything."

Gemma's stomach flipped with both doubt and hope. "Yeah, maybe you're right. We'll see. Will Jacob come to support you?"

"I asked him to, but I just don't know. If he isn't too busy causing trouble as usual." She shook her head. "Anyway, I'll just be piddling around and putting things away. Let me know if you need me for anything."

Gemma nodded, setting out all the baked goods on the desk. She pulled over some tables and tried to make the place look presentable. Ten minutes later, people began to trickle in. Gemma overheard them talking about the news station she had been on.

"This place is nice," one woman said. "And look at all these desserts! How much?"

Gemma told them the prices, then the desserts—and books—began flying off the shelves. After she set up the table with the board games and activities, people came in, intrigued, and began playing. They even said they would come back if it became a regular occurrence. Gemma was making so much money and safely storing it in the backroom to avoid another theft incident. Barbara came around the corner, noticing how many customers were coming in and out.

"Wow, I haven't seen this kind of traffic in a long time," she said with a smile. "Gemma, I think you might be onto something."

"I told you to stay positive," Gemma said, grinning back as she checked out another customer's book. "Here you are— enjoy reading."

As the customer thanked her, more people poured into the bookstore. The place was packed. As Barbara chatted with everyone, accepting their condolences over her daughter's loss and the robbery, Gemma had never seen the older woman so happy. And that made Gemma happy too.

The bell above the door chimed, then Ian entered. His face lit up when he saw all the people inside the bookstore and Gemma checking out people at the register. He walked over, grabbing a muffin and a fantasy romance novel off the shelf.

Seeing his face again made their argument fade away. Gemma wanted nothing more than to make up with him, though she forced herself to stay cool.

"These two for me, please," he said, handing Gemma some money. "And this place has some gorgeous employees."

Gemma blushed, handing Ian his change. "Here you go—and thanks for coming, Ian. Me and Barbara really appreciate it."

"Of course—whatever you need. This place is packed. Good to see it." Ian scratched his neck. "Look, about last night ... I'm sorry. I had no right to speak to you like that. You were right—you're not Ivy."

"Well, I felt bad about it all night. The truth really is that me and my father aren't getting along right now. But if that changes, then yes, I'd love for you to meet him. I have no doubt my family would love you."

Just like I do. She caught herself just in time. She feared it might be too soon for the L-word—though she did feel it. And strongly.

Ian smiled. "Then that works for me. When I got home, I realized how stupid I was to pick a fight with you. I mean, you're the best thing in my life. I don't want to mess this up. I need to work through my insecurities and let them go before I lose you. I mean, you've never given me any reason not to trust you."

Yet.

Gemma thought she would melt on the spot, leaving Fairhaven's big reveal for another time. "I feel the same way. But don't worry—you're not going to lose me. And if I wasn't working, then I'd totally kiss you right now."

Ian laughed. "Raincheck for later, then. Anyway, I'm glad we made up. I don't like fighting with you. It feels wrong."

"It really does. Promise to never do it again? Or, at least, to hear each other out and make up quickly?"

"Pinky swear," Ian said with a smile, linking his pinky finger with Gemma's. He gestured around the store. "Need my help? I left Barney in charge of the bar in case you needed another hand today. I figured it'd be busy with the grand reopening and all."

"Yes, please, thanks. Do you think you can put these books away?"

Ian nodded, taking the books and helping out around the store. He didn't complain once. Gemma was happy they had made up—especially after the night she'd had. Being face-to-face with a gun really put things into perspective.

When the door chimed again, Gemma looked up with a smile before it faded. Ian's parents and brother had entered the store. They looked around, checking people out with a scowl on their faces. Marcus was the only one she liked—he seemed normal and not snooty like his parents.

"This place has too many candles. They reek," Ian's mother said, waving a hand in front of her face. "Why don't they just turn a damn light on?"

Ian's father shrugged. "I have no idea, dear. This place is … charming, I suppose. In a poor kind of way."

Marcus rolled his eyes, then headed to the front desk to get away from his parents. "Hey, Gemma. Nice to see you again.

And I saw your interview on the news—managed to convince my parents to come out and support the store. It's for a good cause."

Gemma smiled. "Thanks, Marcus. Ian is here somewhere. You can go chat with him if you'd like."

"Will do. I'll find a book too, even if I'm not a big reader. Just want to support the store. See you again soon."

Gemma nodded, ringing up a few customers. Without power, they had to go back to the old days of using cash, calculating taxes, and logging the purchases in a book. Fortunately, Barbara had brought a portable credit card reader, so they didn't have to turn away any customers. Then Ian's parents stepped forward in line. They didn't have any books or desserts in their hands. What were they really here for?

Gemma faked a smile. "Hello, Mr. and Mrs. Whitman. Here to support the bookstore?"

"Not really. Marucs encouraged us to show up. We've come with a proposition, actually," Ian's mother said, glancing over her shoulder as if to make sure Ian and Marcus weren't standing there. Then she turned back to Gemma. "How much do you think it would take to save this miserable place?"

Gemma forced herself to stay polite. "I'm not sure, but Barbara is behind on bills and rent. Anything would help, really."

Ian's mother nudged her husband, then he reached into his jacket pocket and pulled out a check. He wrote down one million dollars and handed it to Gemma. She took the check out of his hand, looking it over. She wasn't used to human money, but that seemed like a lot to her.

Enough to save the bookstore and maybe even expand.

"Um, wow. That's a lot of money," Gemma said, wide-eyed. "What is this for? A donation?"

"A transaction," Ian's mother began. "You leave Ian alone and convince him to get back with Ivy, and the money is yours."

"Oh," Gemma said, putting the check down. "It's a bribe. To get me to stop seeing your son."

Ian's father nodded. "That's right. Listen, Gemma, we both know you're not right for him. He deserves so much more. And since he trusts you for some reason, we know you can convince him to close down his bar, return to us, and date Ivy again. Even marry her."

"It's for the good of his future," Ian's mother added. "And all this money could be yours if you agree. Don't be selfish, dear. If you care about Ian, you'll do what's right for him."

Gemma stared at the million-dollar check. It would really help Barbara, but the price was too high. She couldn't force Ian to go back to an abusive partner and an equally abusive family.

"It's because I care about Ian that I refuse to do this," Gemma said, reaching for the check. "Ivy abused him and you two aren't any better. He's happier now with his bar and new life—trust me. And I am completely in love with him."

Gemma tore up the check, scattering the pieces on the counter. Ian's parents glanced at each other in shock before glaring at her.

"You'll regret that, girl," Ian's mother said. "What a fool."

"We'll get our son back, one way or the other," his father added.

"Hopefully not," Gemma said. "You're banned from this store, by the way. Goodbye."

His parents sneered, then headed toward the door and left. Gemma gestured for the next person in line to step forward so she could ring their items through. She then tossed the scraps from the check into the garbage.

There had to be another way to save Barbara's bookstore—

one that didn't involve signing away Ian's future. He was worth more than all the money in the world.

As Gemma turned around, she saw Ian standing there with a smile on his face. He must've been there all along. "So ... you love me?"

Gemma blushed. "How much of that did you hear?"

"All of it. Marcus told me our parents were here, then I rushed to the front to make sure they didn't harass you. I paused to listen when I saw my father writing that check." Ian stepped closer. "You could've taken it—you and Barbara would've been set for life. But you didn't. And you don't know how much that means to me, Gemma."

"I'd never force you to go back to Ivy or your family. Sometimes, leaving really is the best thing to do," Gemma said, making her think about her own life. "And I want to see you happy. No amount of money in the world is worth jeopardizing all that."

Ian smiled. "Thank you. And just so you know ... I am completely in love with you too."

Gemma's face broke out into a massive smile. She couldn't believe it. She had found love. She found a place to belong in the surface world. Now, all she needed to do was stop that human terrorizing the city with magic, find her mother and repair their relationship, and everything would be perfect. As much as it could be.

"I'm going to kiss you now if you don't mind," Ian said, cupping her face. "All the people in here be damned."

"Yes, please," Gemma said, making him laugh.

As they kissed in the middle of the bookstore, people glanced over, murmuring and staring. But Gemma didn't care. She had Ian back—that was all she wanted. When someone in line cleared their throat, Gemma pulled away and got back to work.

"Sorry about that," she said with a blush, ringing up the customer. "That'll be twenty-two dollars and fifty-three cents."

As she accepted the cash, Ian stayed by her side, ringing up more customers. With him around, Gemma felt like she could do anything—even save the bookstore and help Barbara without that million-dollar check.

And, you know, save the surface world and find her mother in the meantime.

CHAPTER 24

Thoroughly kissed, Gemma worked hard with Ian and Barbara to process all the orders. The money raised continued to grow. Barbara couldn't believe it. She stood near the door with wide eyes, thanking everyone for coming.

Marcus walked up to the desk with a mystery novel. "I'd like this one, please. It's supposed to have good mental health rep. And a donut for the road."

Gemma nodded, calculating the total. "Eighteen dollars and seventy-three cents, please."

Marcus reached into his pocket, pulling out a check. "Here —for dealing with my parents. Put the money to good use."

Gemma's eyes widened as she reached for the check. From living on the surface, she knew that was a lot of human money. "Ten grand ... oh my gosh. I can't accept this."

"You can and you will. That was my allowance for last month. With Ian gone, I'm getting even more now. So, take it— use it to save this lovely bookstore and keep Ian happy. That's all I ask."

Gemma smiled. "Now that's a deal I can say yes to. Thank you very much, Marcus."

"Hey, no problem. My parents have so much money that they won't even realize it's gone."

Ian came around the corner after sweeping the floors, noticing Marcus checking out. "Hey, Marc—good to see you with a book. Whoa, is that check yours?"

"He's donating it to save the bookstore," Gemma said with a smile. "Isn't that sweet?"

"Very," Ian agreed. "But you don't have to do that."

"Don't I? I think I do," Marcus said with a smile. "And I've never said it before, but … I'm proud of you, Ian. For getting away and finding a good woman. You two deserve to be happy."

"And we are. Very happy," Ian said, wrapping his arm around Gemma's shoulders. "You can be too, you know. You can leave Mom and Dad."

Marcus paused. "It would be nice to get out from under their thumb. To have them stop questioning my anxiety every minute of every day. I'll think about it. Not sure if I have the same strength that you do, though."

"Of course, you do. Don't insult yourself," Ian replied. "Mom and Dad are poison. And if you get away, maybe your anxiety will improve. You never know."

"It just might. Who knows." Marcus took his book and donut. "For now, though, I'm heading home. I'll grab a taxi since it appears Mom and Dad abandoned me. Catch you later, Ian."

They said goodbye, watching as Marcus left the store and politely nodded at Barbara. She finished saying thanks to the people at the door before walking over to the cash register. Gemma smiled, handing her the check.

"Look—this is from Ian's brother," Gemma said. "Ten thousand dollars to save the bookstore."

"My goodness!" Barbara took the check, inspecting it. "This looks real to me. Why would he do that?"

"Because my brother is nothing like my parents. He's a good man," Ian explained. "And I hope it'll help."

"As long as you promise to quit drinking and get your life cleaned up, then the check is all yours," Gemma added. "Focus on your grandson, your mental and physical health, and the bookstore. That's what's important."

Barbara paused. "Deal. It won't be easy, but I have to try. For Jacob's sake. How generous—all of you," Barbara said, smiling at Gemma and Ian. "I'm going to put this in the safe so no one steals it. I don't think we'll get another second chance if that robber returns. Be right back."

Gemma nodded, watching Barbara scurry to the office. As they continued working, the door chimed open and Carly and Abby walked inside. Abby was still wearing the dress that Gemma had bought her, though it looked like she had taken it off long enough for Carly to wash it. She was licking another ice cream with a hospital band on her wrist.

Carly walked over with Abby trailing behind, smiling. "Ooh, this is a cute bookstore. And judging by all the people coming in and out, I'd say the grand reopening fundraiser is going well."

"It really is." Gemma beamed. "How are you two doing today?"

"Wonderful, actually. Abby's doing much better," Carly said, placing her hand on her daughter's shoulder. "Her autoimmune system hasn't been flaring up as much lately. Fingers crossed it stays that way, but the doctor was very happy. Got her some ice cream to celebrate."

Gemma smiled. "I'm happy for you, Abby. Here's to good health."

Abby licked her ice cream. "Thanks, Gemma. Do you have any books here that I could read?"

"Certainly—follow me, please. Ian, can you watch the cash while I'm gone?"

Ian nodded, setting his broom aside. "Sure, no problem. Hope you find an awesome book."

Carly stayed with Ian to chat as Abby followed Gemma down the aisles. Gemma knew her way around the bookstore, pointing out famous authors and books that were popular. The middle grade section was bursting with new worlds to enjoy.

"This one is very good," Gemma said, handing Abby a middle grade fantasy. "I think you'll enjoy it. It has a strong female character—just like you."

Abby smiled, taking the book in her other hand. "Thanks. And I wanted to talk to you in private."

"Oh, okay. Is everything all right?"

Abby nodded. "Yeah, actually. Mom's been really happy since Dad left. I miss him, but he was mean to her. A lot. I'm actually glad he's gone."

"I am too, Abby. I want you both to be happy."

"We are. Thanks to you." Abby glanced over her shoulder, then back at Gemma. "And Mom's been talking about that guy from the dance studio. I think she really likes him."

Gemma smiled. "I'm happy for her. The firefighter?"

"Yeah. He's a nice guy. He smiled at me when I came by the studio that one time." Abby smiled. "I like seeing Mom happy."

"She deserves it—and so do you. Come on, Princess Ice Cream," Gemma joked, gesturing at the cash register. "Let's get you that book. My treat for our favorite customer."

Abby happily skipped back to the cash register, letting Ian calculate the total before handing it to her in a bag. Then Carly bought her a cookie for later. They thanked Gemma and Ian, then left the store with the chime of a bell.

"Carly's doing much better," Ian said once they were gone. "She's got a crush already. Some firefighter?"

Gemma nodded. "I know—Abby told me. I'm happy for them. Their lives haven't been easy."

"Neither have ours, but everything worked out," Ian said with a smile. "You can't stop fate. I believe that."

And now, Gemma was starting to believe that too as she smiled back.

Barbara came out of the back office, welcoming several new customers to the store. She gave a thumbs up to Gemma before helping them find what they were looking for down the aisle. At this rate, they were going to need to order more books and desserts or they would run out soon. Gemma wondered if Cal would help her out again or if she should stay away from Fairhaven altogether.

Cal had been pretty insistent she move on. He had never been that forceful before. But maybe he was right—maybe she needed to leave Fairhaven in the past and embrace her new life.

As she mulled it over, the door opened again, and Jacob came in. He browsed the selection before finding something on animal facts. He walked over, setting it down on the cash register.

"Heard about the grand reopening or whatever," he said. "I want to buy this. To support my grandma."

"That's nice of you, Jacob," Gemma said, checking the back of the book for the price. "That'll be ten dollars and fourteen cents."

Jacob nodded, reaching into his pocket to pull out his allowance, then he paid for the book. Barbara's eyes widened when she noticed her grandson.

"Jake, you came," she said. "Thank you—that was sweet of you to support me."

Jacob shrugged. "I just needed a new book, that's all. See you later."

As he turned, heading to the door, Barbara glanced at

Gemma, her mouth gaping. They were both shocked Jacob had come to show his support, but maybe it was a good thing. Maybe it meant he was changing for the better.

Just as he reached up to push the door open, a new customer came in. It was Luigi—the man who ran the pizza place down the block. He glanced at Jacob.

"You look familiar, young man," Luigi began, studying him for a moment. "Have I seen you around before?"

"Uh, no," Jacob lied, putting his head down. "I gotta go."

"Wait a minute!" Luigi blocked the door and stopped him from leaving. "Now I remember. You're one of the punks who stole from my cash register. I've got it on video. You're in big trouble, young man!"

Jacob sneered. "I don't know what the hell you're talking about, boomer. I'm outta here."

As he tried to dart around Luigi, the pizza owner grabbed Jacob by his backpack, holding him in place. "I don't think so. I'm going to call the police, and you're going to pay back what you owe me."

"Let go of me!" Jacob screamed, making everyone in the bookstore look over.

Jacob tried to get away, but Luigi continued to block his path, keeping the door closed. Barbara ran over with a look of concern. Gemma turned to Ian, sighing.

"This isn't good," she whispered. "Jacob's in a lot of trouble."

Ian gave her a look of confusion. When Barbara reached Jacob, she stood in front of him. "Excuse me, why are you grabbing my grandson?"

"He's crazy, Nana!" Jacob cried. "He just started accusing me of stuff and then wouldn't let me go."

"Your grandson is a thief, ma'am," Luigi replied. "He stole from my cash register."

Barbara scoffed. "Look, I know my grandson can be a troublemaker, but he wouldn't do that. Are you sure you've got the right boy?"

"Yes. I'm one hundred percent sure. And I can prove it. So can your employee over there. She was working for me when it happened."

Barbara glanced over her shoulder, her gaze landing on Gemma with a frown. "What on Earth is he talking about?"

Gemma sighed, heading toward them. Ian continued to watch in shock from the cash register. "Sadly, Barbara … Luigi's right. Before applying here, my first job was at Luigi's pizza restaurant. It didn't last long, though. When he went to a recital with his grandson, he left me in charge. A few boys came in and stole money from the cash register—Jacob included—while I was changing into my uniform in the bathroom. I lost my job over it."

Barbara's face scrunched in sadness as she turned to her grandson. "That's … that's awful! Please, tell me you didn't do this, Jake. That you wouldn't steal from a business owner who's only trying to survive out here like I am."

Jacob hesitated, glancing between his grandmother and Luigi. Gemma cleared her throat. "Jacob, I think you should be honest. Lying is only going to make it worse."

Jacob sighed. "Yeah … yeah, I did it. I'm sorry, Nana. But my friends would've called me a wuss if I hadn't!"

"Then those aren't your real friends. Those boys are a bad influence." Barbara shook her head. "I just can't believe this, Jacob. What am I going to do with you?"

"Maybe you ought to raise your grandson a bit better," Luigi sneered. "Because you've raised a little thief."

"Excuse me?" Barbara asked, offended.

"Yeah, don't talk to my grandma like that, you prick!" Jacob cried.

"Jacob, language!"

Gemma stepped forward. "Everyone, please—let's calm down. Luigi, Barbara's done a fine job raising her grandson. He's just had issues since his mother died."

"That's no excuse." Luigi crossed his arms. "I lost my wife too—someone very important to me—and I didn't rob anyone."

"That may be true, but grief is harder on children. Try to have compassion and see it from our point of view. And I'll pay for the money Jacob stole. Now that I have a paycheck, I can afford it."

But Luigi shook his head. "No, that won't do. It's clear this boy is out of control—and I don't want my own grandson learning from this bad influence. Something needs to be done before another small business is stolen from."

"Something like what?" Barbara asked. "He's just a child. Surely there's no need to call the police."

"I think there is." Luigi pulled his phone out, dialing 9-1-1. "Stay right here where I can see you. The cops will be here soon."

Luigi stepped off to the side, speaking into his phone. Jacob tried to run out the door, but his grandmother reached for him and pulled him back. She whispered something in his ear, then he nodded.

"Yeah, okay," he muttered. "I guess I should own up to it."

"Good, thank you. Running will only make it worse." Barbara turned to Gemma, looking upset. "Why didn't you tell me as soon as you realized my grandson was involved?"

"I'm so sorry, Barbara. I wanted to tell you," Gemma began, "but you had your own issues, and I didn't want to make things worse. I was hoping Jacob would confess what he did on his own time. Even pay back what he and his friends stole."

"But he didn't." Barbara sighed. "Jake, Jake, Jake ... what am I going to do with you?"

Jacob looked down, saying nothing. Gemma was just relieved Barbara didn't seem too mad at her. She had almost lost Carly; she would've been devastated if she lost Barbara after everything they had been through.

"There, the cops are on their way," Luigi said, walking back toward them. "They can deal with you. Hey, everyone, this kid stole from my shop!"

When people began to murmur, Barbara turned to Luigi. "Stop that, please! There's no need to take out your frustration on the bookstore. Why don't we go outside and wait for the police, hmm?"

Luigi reluctantly agreed, heading outside with Barbara and Jacob. Jacob sat down on the sidewalk and put his head in his hands. Although he had stolen the money, Gemma felt bad for him. The boy had his whole future ahead of him—and now, it was in even greater jeopardy.

When she walked back over to the cash register, Ian was ringing up another customer, then sending them on their way. "Hey you. What's going on over there? Something about Jacob stealing money or something?"

Gemma sighed. "Yeah, he did. I was actually working at the pizza place when he stole from the cash register. I was in the back changing into my uniform and wasn't watching."

Ian's eyes widened. "Jesus. I know the kid's been through a lot but that's awful. What's happening now?"

"The pizza shop owner called the police to report him. I need to do something and should probably go with Jacob. Can you stay here and watch the bookstore?"

Ian nodded. "Yeah, of course. Whatever you need. Let me know how it goes."

"Will do."

Ian turned back to the cash register, ringing up another customer as Gemma left the bookstore. The same two officers who had given the boy his last warning pulled up in their police car. They stepped out, looking disappointed as they approached Jacob on the sidewalk.

"Hello again," one officer said, glancing between Barbara and Luigi. "We received a phone call about a theft?"

"Yes, Officer—I found the boy who did it. I've got the security footage on my phone," Luigi replied. "I want him prosecuted to the fullest extent of the law."

"No, please!" Barbara cried, on the verge of tears. "Jacob's only thirteen. Have some compassion."

The other officer sighed. "We've given him that, ma'am, and warned him that his next offence would be serious. He didn't listen. I'm afraid we'll have to bring him into the station."

Barbara buried her face in her hands. "Oh, my goodness, this can't be happening ..."

"I'm sorry, but the law is the law." The police officer pulled out a set of handcuffs. "Don't resist, Jacob. We'll take you to the station where you'll be detained and questioned, then you'll await a trial."

"Good," Luigi said, crossing his arms. "Hopefully the little punk will learn his lesson."

"Can I go with him?" Barbara asked. "To the station, I mean? I don't want him to be alone."

The police officer nodded, putting the handcuffs around Jacob's wrists. Jacob didn't resist as they led him into the back-seat of the police car. He looked miserable as they placed the seatbelt around his waist.

"Yes, you can. Meet us there," the officer said, closing the door. "We'll read him his rights. And you'll want to hire a lawyer. If you can't afford one, one will be appointed for you. But there's an office that does pro-bono work downtown if you'd rather find your own."

"I'll do that, thank you." Barbara sniffled. "Just let me grab my purse."

Barbara ran back inside the bookstore to grab her purse. Gemma was left alone with Luigi as she stared at Jacob in the back of the car. Barbara headed outside, already on the phone.

"Yes, hello. My grandson was just arrested for theft. I'm afraid there's video proof," Barbara said into the phone, scurrying to her car. "I'm on my way to the police station. I'd like a lawyer to meet me there ..."

As Barbara and the police car took off, Luigi looked pleased, heading back to his pizza shop. But Gemma knew she couldn't let this happen. She had to do something before Barbara lost one more thing in her life—her only grandson.

CHAPTER 25

Leaving Ian in charge at the bookstore, Gemma hailed a taxi and asked the driver to take her to the police station. Officers chatted at water coolers, worked at their desks, and processed criminals down the hall.

Jacob was one of them. The officers had beaten her there. Barbara was conversing with a lawyer off to the side, going over their options. Gemma shook her head as she approached the front desk.

"Excuse me, but I'd like to speak with someone who was recently arrested," she began. "Jacob Danvers. Can I see him?"

The secretary pointed down the hall. "He's being finger-printed and booked down there. Don't be too long—he's meeting with a lawyer soon."

Gemma nodded, walking down the hall. She passed other criminals in jail cells, searching for the robber who stole from the bookstore and shot her fairy godmother, but he wasn't there. Not yet.

He had a knack for escaping the police—and Princess Esme's guards—but Gemma wanted to find him. And soon.

When she saw Jacob pacing in a cell, she approached the bars, clearing her throat. "Hey, Jacob. How are you doing?"

He glared at her from behind the bars. "How do you think? I'm scared. And tired. But mostly scared."

"I understand that. And I'm really sorry you're in here. Is there anything I can do to help?"

Jacob glanced down the hall. "Yeah, maybe. Tell my grandma I'm really sorry. That if I get out of here ... I'll do better. I'll stop hanging out with those boys, start listening to her. I mean it."

Maybe Jacob really was changing, and getting arrested was the only way to teach him a lesson. She still felt bad all of this had happened.

"Okay, I will. She's out there speaking with your lawyer right now. I'll go talk with her."

Jacob nodded. "Thanks. Gemma ... they're going to send me away, aren't they? To juvey? That pizza owner dude seemed pretty upset."

Gemma winced. "They might, yes. But your grandma and your lawyer are going to help. And I will, too. Hang in there in the meantime, Jacob. We're all here for you."

"I probably don't deserve it. But thanks." Jacob sniffled. "I really miss Mom."

"I know you do, Jacob. And you *do* deserve it—you mean a lot to us. No matter what you do, that will never change. Especially for your grandma. She loves you to pieces."

"I love her, too," Jacob whispered, then turned silent.

Gemma patted his hand before he sat down on the little bench inside the jail cell. The prisoners awaiting trial stared at Gemma as she headed down the hall. Barbara and the lawyer were still near the doors, whispering as she wiped her eyes.

"... and I just can't believe it's come to this," Barbara said. "I wanted so much better for my Jakey."

"I know you do. I'll do everything in my power to ensure the judge shows leniency," the lawyer said, carrying a briefcase. Papers poked out the side with legal jargon written on it. "I'll try to help Jacob in any way that I can."

Gemma cleared her throat. "Hey, Barbara. How are you doing?"

Barbara glanced over, still drying her tears. "Just awful. My only grandson, in chains like a common criminal. Oh, I can't believe it."

"I know. I'm so sorry. I take it you found a lawyer?"

Barbara nodded. "Yes, one of the pro bono ones the police officer suggested. I can't afford one of those expensive criminal defense lawyers."

"Is there anything I can do?"

Barbara shrugged. "Other than going back in time to stop my grandson from stealing, I'm not sure. Things seem so dire."

"They really do. I just spoke to Jacob; he said he was sorry. He wanted me to tell you that. That he wants to change, and he loves you."

"I love him, too. And I appreciate his apology, but it seems like it's too late." Barbara sniffled one last time, turning to the lawyer. "Anyway, thank you for coming, Gemma. We really appreciate all the support you've given us."

Gemma smiled. "Of course. Anytime. Ian's watching over the bookstore while I'm here. We're both here for you."

"That makes me feel better. I'll need that strength through Jacob's trial. I even tried calling his father, but he didn't pick up. My ex-husband, either." Barbara shook her head. "I'm truly alone in all this. Jacob is mine to deal with."

Gemma stepped closer, reaching for Barbara's hands. "You're *never* alone, Barbara. I've been trying to show you that all this time."

Barbara forced a smile, her eyes and nose red from crying.

"Hearing you say that does make me feel a little better, funny enough. Maybe it's because you resemble my daughter so much. Anyway, the lawyer and I should go speak with Jacob. We need to think of our defense."

"Okay. Good luck," Gemma said, watching them walk toward the cells.

Once they vanished around the corner, Gemma gave them some privacy. She left the police station and hailed a taxi outside. When it arrived, she rode it back to the bookstore, though she didn't go inside to greet Ian. She walked down the block to the pizza parlor and opened the door.

Luigi stood behind the cash register, waiting for customers. His grandson was coloring at a small table a few feet away. The delicious aroma of pizza filled Gemma's nostrils, making her remember her first job in the surface world.

"Hello and welcome to—" Luigi paused, his face dropping when Gemma walked closer. "Oh, it's you. What are you doing here?"

"I need to speak with you," Gemma said, walking toward the cash register. "I hope you have a moment."

Luigi crossed his arms. "I really shouldn't, not while the legal proceedings are still going on. I trust you understand."

"I really don't, Luigi. Yes, what Jacob did was wrong. He'll even admit that. But if he goes to juvey, it'll ruin his entire future. As I understand it, he'll have a record, and he'll never have a chance of correcting his mistakes."

"Not my problem," Luigi said, reaching for a rag and wiping the counter down. "He should've thought about that *before* stealing from my restaurant. And I hear he's been doing other criminal things too. Perhaps juvey is the best place for him—It'll teach him a lesson. Now, if there's nothing else, I really should get back to work."

When Luigi turned around, ignoring her, Gemma thought

about heading back to Fairhaven to ask for another charm potion, much like she had to get that television interview. But this was different.

She wanted to change Luigi's heart on her own—without magic on her side. To prove she could live among the humans in the surface world, just like them. She had already used it once at the news station and didn't want to get in trouble.

So, she cleared her throat, trying again. She stole a glance at Luigi's grandson for a moment. "That's your grandson over there, right? The same one you took to a recital?"

Luigi turned around, nodding. "Yes, that's right. His name is Angelo. Where are you going with this?"

"How would you feel if he was taken away by police? Would you want to see him go to juvey?"

Luigi rolled his eyes. "My grandson would never do such a thing. He was raised better than that. And I'm doing it on my own, too, so don't give me that spiel of how Barbara is a strained, single grandmother. That's no excuse. Jacob did the crime, and now he's going to answer for it. That's that."

"Is it? Look, Luigi—please, try to have some empathy for a child. Losing his mother in the line of duty wasn't easy on him *or* Barbara. Yes, he did something wrong, but he told me he wants to change if he ever gets out of jail. I believe he should have the chance to—"

Luigi froze. "What did you just say?"

"That he promised to change if he gets out of jail?"

"No, no—before that. The part about his mother."

"Oh ... that she served in the military? She was killed in the line of duty. Since then, Jacob has acted out, getting involved with the wrong crowd." It appeared she was finally getting through to him, so as much as she hated to share information that was given to her in confidence, she was pulling out all the stops to help change Luigi's heart. "And Barbara began drinking. Both of them have had suicidal thoughts, sadly. I was getting through to her, but I was still trying to help Jacob."

Luigi reached under the kitchen counter, pulling out a picture frame. He was in the picture with his wife who was in uniform—also serving in the military. *How serendipitous.*

"That's how I lost my wife recently," Luigi began softly. "She was serving overseas and had just shipped out. Her commanding officer tried to get her to retire since she was older, and so was I. Me and my grandson wanted to spend more time with her. One more tour of duty, she promised me. And then she'd retire and come back to helping me at our pizza parlor while spending more time with our grandson. But ... things didn't go that way. She stepped on a landmine and ... that was it."

"I'm so sorry for your loss, Luigi. How tragic."

He nodded, tucking away the picture frame beneath the desk. "Thank you. We miss her terribly. My son, unable to cope with the pain, died of an overdose after that. My daughter-in-law got involved with the wrong crowd and went to jail. Me and my grandson are just like Barbara and Jacob, in a way. I guess we just have healthier coping mechanisms. Or we were luckier. I don't know."

"Maybe. Look, this can't be a coincidence that you both lost people in the same way. Your wife and Jacob's mother died bravely in service to this country, and I don't think either of them would want to see a boy sent off to jail, do you?"

Luigi paused for a moment, sighing. "No ... I don't think they would. Maybe I was too harsh. Especially considering Barbara and Jacob have had mental health issues too. That's common among soldiers, something my wife struggled with as well. I appreciate you telling me about that. But it's hard to be a business owner, you know. And I wanted to teach those boys a lesson. I really was trying to help."

"I know you were. And trust me, Jacob *has* learned his lesson. I think this experience has changed his mind about a lot of things. Now, will you head to the police station and drop the charges? Official ones, at least? Maybe Jacob could do something else to earn your forgiveness. Like … volunteer here and pay back the money he stole."

Luigi rubbed his chin where gray stubble had formed. "Yeah … I like that idea. If he agrees to that, I'll drop all the charges. You have my word."

Gemma smiled. "Thank you, Luigi—you have no idea how much this will mean to Barbara and her grandson."

Luigi nodded. "I'm just glad the boy is going to turn his life around. Next time, I won't be so lenient."

"Right—I'll make sure he knows that. I'll head back to the police station and tell them the good news."

"And I'll call the station myself and tell them I'm dropping all charges. I want them to release Jacob immediately." Luigi paused. "But Gemma? Can you take a message for me?"

She reached for the door, pausing. "Of course. What is it?"

"Tell Barbara and her grandson I know the pain of losing someone in the line of duty," Luigi said softly. "And that I hope they both heal, despite all this."

Gemma smiled. "Will do. Thanks again, Luigi. See you around."

He nodded, returning to wiping down the counter as Gemma left the pizza parlor. She was proud of herself as she hailed a taxi and rode in it to the station, giddy and beaming. She had saved Jacob, all with the power of words. No magic needed.

When the taxi arrived at the police station, she paid the driver and headed inside. Barbara, Jacob, and the lawyer were standing in the foyer, speaking with an officer.

"And you're very lucky Mr. De Luca had a change of heart.

Otherwise, you would've been sent to juvey for sure," the officer said. "Don't waste this second chance, young man."

"I won't," Jacob said, rubbing his wrists. "Thanks."

The officer nodded, walking away. Gemma headed toward them with a smile. "Hi everyone. So nice to see you free again, Jacob."

"Gemma, you're back!" Barbara cried. "Have you heard the good news? Luigi just called and asked the officers to drop all the charges. I can't believe it. My grandbaby, free!"

When she reached down, pulling Jacob into a big hug, he blushed and looked embarrassed. "Nana, please. People are looking."

"Oh, sorry, dear. I'm just so happy." Barbara turned to the lawyer. "Thank you for your help, but we won't be needing your services. It seems Luigi changed his mind all by himself. Thank goodness."

The lawyer nodded, shaking her hand and leaving the station as Gemma smiled. "Actually, I spoke to Luigi. After some convincing, I got him to drop the charges."

Barbara's eyes widened. "You did? But... how? The man seemed pretty insistent that my grandson go to jail to pay for what he did."

"He found out you lost your daughter in the line of duty. Luigi's wife also died while serving. I guess realizing that helped him find some compassion." Gemma turned to Jacob. "But you're not completely off the hook. Luigi wants you to volunteer at the pizza parlor—to pay off the money you stole."

Jacob sighed. "Okay. I guess it's better than going to jail. Thanks, Gemma."

"Yes—thank you so much. I don't even know what to say anymore," Barbara said, tears welling in her eyes. "Without you ... I don't even want to think about how much worse off we'd be. You're the best thing that's happened to us in a while."

When Barbara leaned in to hug her, Gemma hugged back with a smile. She gestured at Jacob to join, who rolled his eyes but leaned into the hug anyway. From the corner of her eye, Gemma saw him smile. Once the group hug was over, Barbara pulled back, wiping tears from her eyes.

"I'm over the moon. And we should do something to celebrate," she began. "I know money is tight but let's go out for dinner. We all deserve it. After checking on Ian and the bookstore, of course. I need to tally how much money we've made. Come, I'll drive you back, Gemma."

Gemma nodded, following Barbara and Jacob out of the police station. She let Jacob ride in the front as she hopped in the back. Barbara took them back to the bookstore, watching as more customers came in and out. When the three of them walked in, Ian's jaw dropped.

"You're back," he began, adding more money to the till. "And soon. What happened with Jacob?"

Barbara patted Gemma's shoulder. "Gemma intervened before it could escalate to trial. She got Luigi to drop all the charges."

Ian smiled at Gemma. "Is that so? Sounds like something she'd do. Congrats, Gemma. You saved the day. Like a true princess."

In that moment, watching Jacob and Barbara bond again, Gemma felt like she was on top of the world. Nothing would take away that accomplishment—not even the human using magic for evil still on the loose.

"It's been a good day and we're both fortunate," Barbara said with a nod, patting her grandson's shoulder. Then she checked her watch. "Almost time for dinner—we should go out and celebrate. I'm just about to close up. Do you know how much money we've made, Ian?"

Ian smiled. "Enough to save your bookstore for a long, long time, Barbara. See for yourself."

Barbara walked toward the cash register, then counted all the money from the grand reopening fundraiser. They had made several thousand, plus the generous check that Marcus had left. Barbara burst into happy tears again.

"My goodness—this is the best day I've had in a while!" she cried. "My grandson is free, and the bookstore is saved. I'll go call the electrical company and pay for the power to be turned on. Gemma, Ian—I know I'm repeating myself, but I can't thank you two enough. You've truly saved my family."

As they nodded with a smile, Barbara headed into the back room to make a call. Ian checked out the last few people who were buying books and desserts, nearly clearing out the shelves. Gemma made a note that they'd need to order more inventory as soon as possible—and they certainly had the money to do so.

She turned back to Jacob, noticing he was staring at his mother's picture that Barbara had recently hung on the wall. She wore her uniform and smiled at the camera with the Canadian flag behind her.

"Hey, Jake," Gemma said, approaching him. "Long day. How are you feeling?"

"Glad to be out of that cell. I never want to go back there again." Jacob shivered, still staring at the framed picture. "If Mom was here, she'd be so upset with the way I've treated Nana. And all the things I've done."

"She would be, but she'd forgive you. A mother's love is forever," Gemma said, thinking about her own mother and hoping it was true. That she hadn't forgotten about Gemma on the surface, and they could finally reunite and make things better. "So, what's next for you?"

Jacob turned to Gemma. "I guess I have a part-time job at Luigi's now. And I'll tell those boys I can't hang around with them anymore. Besides that ... maybe me and Nana could hang out. I could teach her how to play *Call of Duty*."

Gemma laughed. "Cute. I'm sure she'd appreciate that. I'm really happy you've gotten a second chance, Jacob. I know it still isn't easy. Losing a mother ... it's a pain like no other."

Jacob said nothing, though Gemma knew he felt it too. And if Detective Crawford wouldn't help her, she'd need to find a way to track down her mother—and make sure she was safe, despite her betrayal.

CHAPTER 26

Barbara got off the phone with the electric company, sharing the good news that the power would be turned on in twenty-four hours. No more candles—finally, real lighting. All made possible because of the successful grand reopening.

Barbara locked up the bookstore, making sure to take the money with her so it wouldn't get stolen again. They headed to a nice restaurant in town—Ian helped them get past the long line—and found a private table in the back. Gemma and Ian sat next to each other, holding hands as Barbara and Jacob sat across from them.

"Bring us a round of your nicest champagne," Ian told the waiter. "It's on me, so don't worry."

The waiter nodded, then hurried to grab the bottle. When he returned with three glasses, attempting to pour one for Barbara, she held up her hand. "None for me, thanks. I'm on the path to sobriety. I've decided to turn my life around for the better."

She glanced at Jacob, then they shared a smile. Gemma was proud of Barbara and everything she had been through.

"I'd still like to make a toast, though. To good friends," Barbara said, holding up her glass of water as the waiter left. "And to Gemma. She came into our lives unexpectedly but changed them in the best way."

"That she did," Ian said with a wink, lifting his glass. "To Gemma."

After they clinked their glasses together, they enjoyed a good meal and dessert. As Barbara set money down on the table to pay, a conversation a few tables away caught Gemma's attention. A man in a trench coat handed a document across the table to an elderly woman.

"It's all here, Mrs. Mortimer," the man said, sipping a martini. "Everything I could find on your son. He's not dead or nothing—he just doesn't want to speak to you. Something about you being a narcissist?"

The elderly woman sneered, looking through the folder of photographs and addresses. "How dare he! He doesn't know what he's talking about. Are all these addresses where he lives?"

"Yep—also places he frequents. Cafes, gyms, libraries. That sort of thing. He didn't seem too interested in hearing from you, but you can try anyway. Now, my payment?"

The elderly woman nodded, slipping the folder into her purse. "I'll e-transfer it to you by the end of the week. Thank you for your help, Mr. Schultz. I'll make sure to tell my friends about you."

The man grinned, finishing his martini. "Thank you—and thanks for the drink. You take care now."

The woman wished him the same, grabbing her purse before she left the restaurant. The man ordered another martini and took a few phone calls. When Ian noticed Gemma staring, he nudged her.

"What's up?" he asked.

"Who is that man?" Gemma pointed at his table. "In the trench coat?"

"Oh, him? Local private investigator for hire. I've seen a few of his television commercials. I think my parents hired him once to track me. Despicable." Ian shook his head. "His name's Lenny something. Lenny Schultz, maybe?"

"Hmm. He seems good at finding people."

"The best, yeah. Why did you want to know?"

Gemma sighed. "I think it's time I found my mother. Ever since she walked out on me and my dad, there have been some things I've wanted to ask her. Do you think the private investigator would help me?"

"For a price, sure. You want to go talk to him?"

Gemma nodded, bidding goodnight to Barbara and Jacob. Then she and Ian walked over to the private investigator's table. He looked up, sipping another martini as his phone continued to buzz.

"Can I help you?" the man asked.

Gemma nodded. "I hope so. Are you a private investigator?"

"What? The trench coat give me away?"

"Real funny," Ian said. "Remember me? My parents hired you to track me around the city?"

The private investigator looked at Ian, nodding. "You know, I do. Your daddy's that rich oil billionaire, ain't he?"

"Unfortunately," Ian grumbled. "Look, my girlfriend, Gemma, wants to hire you to track down her mother. Think you can help her out?"

The private investigator grinned. "Finding people is my specialty. What's her name?"

"Katherine. Katherine Solace. And she won't be easy to find. She's ... not exactly from around here."

"No? Well, I do like a challenge. Here, take my card." The man set down a card on the table with his phone number, confirming he was Lenny Schultz. "Call me tomorrow and see if I got anything on your mother. I promise to try my best—If you got the money."

"I have money." Gemma nodded. "If you do find her, don't say anything to her. I don't want to scare her off. She looks like me, just older."

"A real beauty, then," Lenny said with a smirk, making Ian tense. "Ooh, your boyfriend didn't like that. Anyway, I'll get on it ASAP. You two have a good night."

Lenny chugged the last of his martini, then slammed some dollars down on the table before leaving. Ian watched him go while shaking his head. "Personally, I don't like private investigators—especially that one. They're always sticking their noses where they don't belong."

"Maybe, but I really want to find my mother again. It's been a while. I even tried asking a detective, but I haven't heard anything back yet. I'm starting to think I'll never know."

"Huh," Ian said, leading Gemma out of the restaurant. "Well, I hope Lenny delivers, then. Now, let me drive you home. Would it be okay if I spent the night again? I left Max with Barney, hoping you'd say yes. I'll have to give him a raise after this past week." He chuckled.

Gemma grinned. "More than okay. And Ian ... I really do want you to meet my mother. I don't want you to think I don't. It's just ... things are strained between us, much like my father. I think I should speak with her first before introducing you two. If she even wants to be in my life anymore."

"I understand. Really—I won't get mad like last time. I know you're not like my ex—and thank God for that." Ian leaned in, kissing Gemma's cheek. "I hope you find your mom and you get all the answers you're looking for."

Gemma did too.

To Ian's relief, no one snapped pictures of them at the

restaurant. He took Gemma back to her apartment, where they cuddled on the sofa while they watched old movies. They spent the night together, their bodies intertwined in ecstasy before the morning rolled around. Ian got up first and made Gemma pancakes and bacon that he found in the cupboards and refrigerator.

"You're a great chef," Gemma said, putting a bite of pancake in her mouth while sitting on the couch. "Mmm. I've never had these before."

"Never had pancakes?" Ian laughed. "First the spaghetti, now this. What do your people even eat where you come from?"

A dozen magical foods came to mind, but Gemma just shrugged. "Oh, you know. This and that. Simple foods. Anyway, I think this is my new favorite."

"I aim to please," Ian said with a wink, flopping on the couch with his plate.

As they ate breakfast, Gemma turned on the television and set it to the news channel. She was eager to see if there was any information on the human with magic. When they didn't mention anything, Gemma was disappointed, feeling like he was slipping through her fingers. But the next news story shocked them both.

"Of course I'm not abusive," Ivy said, sitting in a chair with a reporter across from her. "I know the video of my ex-boyfriend accusing me has gone viral, but I promise—he's just upset I dumped him. None of it is true."

"Bullshit," Ian said, sitting up on the couch. "Our whole relationship was abusive. It took forever for my cuts and bruises to heal. God, I should've taken pictures. And when she begged me to take her back, I refused. She's spreading lies!"

"It's okay, Ian. I believe the truth will come out," Gemma said, patting his shoulder. "It always does."

She hoped that was true for her mother and the robber on the run, too.

After breakfast, they both got dressed before Ian took Gemma to Barney's apartment to get Max. She said hello to the dog as he licked her and wagged his tail. He was eager to see his owner after a night apart. Gemma went with Ian as he walked Max, heading through the downtown park.

"You know what we should do? Let's invite Barbara and Jacob here," Gemma said. "Jacob seemed to love animals. Maybe that can be a comfort while he's still grieving. I know he's got a cat already, but from what I've heard, there's no loyalty like a dog."

Ian nodded. "True. And that's a wonderful idea. Here—I'll call them. You really need to get a phone, you know."

"I really do. I'll go soon and find something."

Now that Gemma's stay was going to be more permanent than planned, she would need some things to fit into society. A phone, some casual clothes, and maybe even a driver's license for starters if she could fake a birth certificate and blend in. Fairhaven was becoming a distant memory these days.

Barbara and Jacob showed up ten minutes later, happy to have gotten an invite. The bookstore was closed on Sunday, and Barbara had put all her money into the bank where it was safe. She paid Gemma some of her owed wages with the cash. Gemma beamed at the money with pride, knowing how hard she had worked for it.

Barbara chatted with Gemma and Ian, then Jacob's face broke out into a smile when he saw Max. The two of them hit it off, playing fetch while Barbara, Gemma, and Ian watched from the park bench. Other dogs and their owners walked past, birds chirping in the trees.

"It feels so good to see him smile," Barbara said, her eyes fixated on her grandson. "And to be free of that God-awful jail cell. I'm going to send Luigi a thank-you card in the mail for dropping the charges."

"Good idea," Gemma said, watching Max roll over on the grass for Jacob's belly scratches. "Has he started working at Luigi's yet?"

"Yes—he was just there this morning, sweeping the floors. Luigi was very kind and impressed. Jake's going to pay back every dollar he stole and then some. It's the least he can do. And it'll teach him responsibility until it's time for him to get a job."

"Good for him," Ian said with a nod. "I'm glad to see Jacob doing better. And if he needs a male role model at all, I'm here. I don't know everything, but *I do* know what it's like to be a young man, trying to make his way in the world. I can answer any questions he might have."

"Would you? That would be wonderful. Thank you. Thank you both so much," Barbara said, beaming. Then she turned back to Max chasing Jacob and laughed. "My, he really loves your dog, Ian. Thanks for inviting us."

"No problem," Ian replied. "You ever think about getting Jacob a dog? His own, I mean?"

"His face just lights up whenever he sees an animal," Gemma added. "I think animal companionship could help him get through his mother's loss. Maybe he could channel that grief into a healthier outlet. And having a dog of his own would teach him responsibility."

"You know what? You're right. Now that I'm making more money, I might be able to afford for Jacob to have a pet of his own." Barbara nodded. "I'll visit the animal shelter today and see what dogs they have. Jacob's going to be *so* happy. I can't wait."

When Jacob came running back over with Max, out of breath and laughing, Barbara told him it was time to head home. His shoulders slumped with a frown as he begrudgingly said goodbye to the black lab. Barbara just winked at Gemma and Ian.

"Come, Jake, let's go visit your mom's grave before heading home. We haven't been in a while," Barbara said, leading her grandson down the path. "It might be good for both of us."

As they faded from view, Ian placed the leash around Max's collar. "I guess we should head home too. Again, nice job on helping Jacob and Barbara. They seem to be doing much better these days—both of them."

Gemma nodded. "Agreed. And thanks. It wasn't easy, but it was worth it. Hey, before I head home, can I call that private investigator real quick? I just want to see if he found anything on my mom."

"Yeah, of course." Ian reached into his pocket, pulling out his smartphone. "Here you go. Take as long as you need—we'll give you some privacy."

Gemma thanked Ian, taking the phone and dialing the private investigator's number from the card he had given her at the restaurant. She still had it in her pocket. Ian walked away, petting Max under a shady tree as the phone rang and rang.

On the fourth ring, Lenny picked up. "Yeah, who's this? I'm on a stakeout right now."

"Oh, I'm sorry to bother you," Gemma said, pacing in the park. "It's me—Gemma. Gemma Solace. We met at the restaurant last night. Anyway, I wanted to know if you found my mother yet?"

"Oh, her? Yeah, that case is closed already. Found her last night. Right now, I'm on a stakeout for a mafia boss' son."

Her mother had been found? And so soon? Gemma's heart pounded. This had been the moment she was waiting for; what all her nightmares in Fairhaven were leading up to. If she found her, then maybe she could get to the bottom of things and finally tell Ian about her past.

"You did?" Gemma could hear her heartbeat pounding in her ears. "Why didn't you tell me?"

"I was gonna. Swear it. Just got busy, that's all."

"Right. So, it was easy to find her, I take it?"

"Too easy. Well, it was dumb luck, actually. I stopped at this amazing diner last night—right on the edge of town. It's got the best cherry pie. Anyway, the waitress was your mother, Katherine. Noticed her badge and asked for her last name."

Gemma was floored. Her mother was in town, this whole time? And working as a waitress—a normal job? She couldn't believe it.

"She got paranoid and afraid when she realized I knew things about her," the private investigator continued. "I assured her I was only there on behalf of you, her long-lost daughter, and that she wasn't in trouble or anything. Had to tell her the truth before she freaked out on me. She said she was glad I wasn't a Fairhaven guard. You know what the hell she was talking about?"

"Uh, no—sorry. Which diner was it?"

"Pelican Diner. She said she was working again all day today. Something about her being poor and needing the money. Speaking of which, what about my payment?"

"Yes, right. I'll e-transfer it to you soon to the email on your card. I'll have my boyfriend show me how to do it. Anyway, thank you very much. Good luck with your stakeout."

The P.I. thanked her, then she hung up. She walked back toward Ian and Max who were hiding in the shade. She handed him his phone, nodding.

"Well, he did it. You were right—he *is* good," Gemma said. "My mother works at a restaurant called Pelican Diner."

"They have the best cherry pie there. Trust me." Ian tucked the phone away in his pocket. "Do you want me to take you there? I can drive you. It's no problem at all—and I don't need to meet her until you're ready. I'll just sit outside in my car and wait for you."

While Gemma was flattered—and glad Ian wasn't pressuring her to meet her family again—she hesitated. She had spent all this time trying to find her mother, but she hadn't planned her next step. What would Gemma say to her? What would her mother say? So much was uncertain.

"Uh, no. Not right now," Gemma said, feeling her heartbeat quicken. "I think I need to go home and lie down. Process all of this before I have a panic attack."

Ian rubbed her shoulder. "Yeah, okay—whatever you need. Come on, I'll drive you home."

Gemma thanked him, following Ian and Max to the car. She petted the dog and stared out the window on the entire drive home. She couldn't believe it—her mother was so close. And yet, she was still a traitor, allying with Senator Remus and supporting his wicked plan. Gemma wasn't even sure if she wanted to see her again.

Ian pulled into the parking lot of the apartment building, then unlocked the doors. "Here we are. I have to get to the bar and open for the day—It's pretty busy on a Sunday. Will you be okay here alone? Because you could always come with me to work."

Gemma smiled, kissing his cheek. "I'll be okay, Ian, but thanks for asking. Just going to watch some TV, enjoy my day off, and think about my mom. If I even want to see her again. Some wounds ... well, some can't be fixed."

Ian nodded. "I understand that. You've seen my family. Well, try to have a good day. I'll pop back for another date soon. You know I can't get enough of you."

"The feeling is mutual," Gemma said with a giggle, then kissed Ian.

As she stepped out, Ian leaned out the window. "Bye, beautiful! Oh, and before I forget, I'm having a bar trivia night tonight. You want to come? It could be fun. Get you out of the house for a little bit. Or the apartment."

Gemma nodded. "Sure, I don't have anything planned. See you then, Ian."

Ian waved, then backed out of the parking lot and drove down the street. Max leaned out the passenger side window with his tongue out, and the wind blowing through his fur. Gemma laughed at the image, then headed into her apartment and up the elevator. She flung off her shoes and flopped on the couch as soon as she stepped through the door.

For now, Gemma wasn't going to think about her mother. She was just going to watch some movies and eat ice cream and zone out before the trivia night later. It sounded fun—like a perfect distraction. Something Gemma needed.

CHAPTER 27

Not even the funniest movies in the world could distract Gemma from thinking about her mother. She had to see her today—she couldn't waste another second. So, Gemma turned off the television, locked her apartment door, and left the building.

She hailed a taxi outside, telling the driver to take her to the Pelican Diner. It was in a rough part of town—low-income households, rumors of shootings, and no help from the community. When she paid the driver, she stepped out, staring up at the Pelican Diner.

It was painted red and white, mimicking the Canadian flag. People walking by glared at Gemma. She must've looked out of place in her gown. She ignored their glances, took a deep breath, and opened the diner's door.

A record player sat in the corner, belting out some old tune. The floor was checkered, there were plenty of booths to sit at, and regular customers ordered coffee and food at the bar. There were only two employees—a burly chef making the food in the back who kept sticking his head out to accept orders, and a waitress at the bar, filling another man's coffee.

Gemma almost didn't recognize her at first. Her mother. Instead of a dress, she had a red and white uniform on—a plain shirt with a skirt and heels. Her eyes were tired; she had lost weight and wore heavy makeup. She smiled at the man, then finished pouring his coffee and wiped down the bar.

Gemma froze. What should she say? What should she do? She didn't know. This was the first time she had seen her mother since she'd fled, and Gemma was speechless.

When a woman entered the diner behind her, forcing her to move, Gemma decided to step forward. She cleared her throat, approaching the bar. Her mother refilled ketchup to a bottle and seemed preoccupied.

"I'll be right with you, love," her mother said, in the same sweet voice she would use to sing Gemma to sleep. "One sec."

Gemma nodded, playing with the edges of her dress as she waited for her mother to finish and recognize her. Her heart pounded, her hairline sweating. Everything came down to this moment.

Her mother looked up, her eyes landing on Gemma. "What can I get—oh."

Both women were speechless. Gemma cleared her throat, forcing herself to speak. Her voice came out soft and strained. "Hi, Mom."

"Hey, Kathy—can I get another refill?" a truck driver at the bar asked, holding up his coffee mug.

Her mother nodded, reaching for the coffee pot. When she had filled the man's cup to the brim, she turned to Gemma. "You, me—backroom. Now. We can talk in private back there. I'll be right back, everyone."

The diners nodded, returning to their meals and coffee while chatting with each other. Gemma's mother opened the side door to the bar and gestured for her to join her. In confusion, Gemma followed her mother through the bar and into the backroom.

It was freezing in there—packed with food and other supplies for the diner. Gemma shivered, clinging to her gown. Her mother closed the door once they were both inside, then turned to her.

Gemma itched to feel her mother's arms around her. Find comfort in the sound of her voice. It had been so long with so many words unspoken. They stared at each other, as if waiting for the other to make the first move. Her mother spoke first, something Gemma was grateful for.

"How … what are you doing here?" she asked. "The last I knew, you were in Fairhaven, working in that library."

Gemma nodded. "I was. But Princess Esme thought I should get out more—see what the surface world has to offer. I've been up here for awhile now. My life has completely changed."

"Oh, yeah? How?"

"I met someone. Ian. I'm in love," Gemma said, unable to stop herself from smiling. She briefly wondered if she should tell her mother all this, they were practically strangers after the past year apart, but the words tumbled out before she could stop them. "I work at a bookstore now and have amazing friends. I'm staying at Noah's apartment too. You know, Princess Esme's new husband? To be honest … I don't think I'm ever going back to Fairhaven."

Her mother sneered. "Well, at least you have the choice. I had to leave. Me and the sympathizers feared we'd be prosecuted for agreeing with Senator Remus' plan. We hadn't even done anything! It was ridiculous. What about free speech?"

"The senator's ideas were evil. King Tedros just wants to make sure no one follows in his footsteps."

Her mother rolled her eyes. "Whatever. God, I can't stand the royal family."

"Hey, don't talk about my friends like that," Gemma said with a frown. "You're the one who sided with Senator Remus. What else were they supposed to do?"

"Oh, I don't know. Maybe listen to us instead of throwing us away?" Her mother's face was bright red, scrunched in anger. "But King Tedros never listened. It was always his way or no way."

The anger and betrayal in her mother's words hurt Gemma. She'd hoped to help her mother see the error in her ways, plead with Princess Esme to allow her to come back. But now? It all seemed so impossible. "I mean, he *is* the king for a reason," Gemma murmured. "I hear he's changed since Princess Esme came back. That he's willing to listen to different ideas now. You know, as long as they're not dangerous."

"Not good enough," her mother said with a fire behind her eyes. "It's too little, too late."

Gemma didn't like how angry her mother had become. Was there any hope of changing her mind?

"Mom, Senator Remus wanted to take over the human world," Gemma began. "He made magic possible up here and almost enslaved everyone. Now, it's led to a human using magic for criminal stuff. Don't tell me you think that's okay."

Her mother hesitated. "I didn't at first. But after speaking with Senator Remus ... I don't know. I felt myself drawn to him. His plans make sense."

"That's because he was manipulating you, Mom. And his other followers. I'm really sad you've chosen this path. I needed you in Fairhaven. I needed my mother to guide me." Tears clogged her throat and she swallowed to regain her composure.

Something in Gemma's words must've softened her mother. She took a deep breath, changing her tone. The change was so sudden that it raised Gemma's suspicions. "You're right. I'm sorry, Gemma. I didn't want to leave. But it was clear my political viewpoint didn't make me welcome there anymore. I don't regret fleeing to the surface. It was better than ending up in a jail cell. I'm doing much better up here too, just like you."

Gemma sat down on a bunch of crates, nodding. "I see that. When did you get the job at the diner?"

"As soon as I could. We needed money and couldn't return to Fairhaven. So, me and the other sympathizers banded together, found some cheap housing, and all got jobs. Working at a diner was the best choice for me."

"And you haven't used magical potions at all since coming here? You don't know anything about the human who has?"

Her mother rolled her eyes. "No, Gemma. I don't. I've been trying to stay alive, make enough money for rent. That's it. Nothing's going on."

For some reason, Gemma didn't believe her mother. There was a glint in her eyes that had formed ever since she began to believe Senator Remus' lies. But without proof of anything going on, Gemma just nodded.

"Okay. I believe you." It was a lie, but for now, Gemma was going to play nice. Mainly so her mother would let her guard down. "But if you break that trust, I'm going to be really upset."

Her mother paused. "Nothing's going on, Gemma. Really. I'm just a regular human now, working my butt off and living in their society."

"I see. I used a private investigation to find you, by the way. It was a fluke—he stopped by for a coffee and saw your nametag."

"Oh, right. That guy. Maybe I should've changed my name," her mother grumbled. "Not that I'm not happy you're here, of course. It's so good to see my darling daughter again. I just don't want to draw any attention, you know? I'm trying to live under the radar. So the king won't find us. You won't tell him I'm here, will you?"

Gemma was tempted—especially since she still didn't completely trust her mother. She could've been up to something as they spoke. But she decided to play along for now. "I won't, no. Like I said, unless you break that trust. So, now that I've found you … what comes next?"

"Well, you're an adult now, Gemma. I'm leaving it in your hands. Do you still want me in your life? Even if we disagree about many things?"

Gemma paused, thinking. "I do. Maybe … maybe we could meet for coffee. Try to repair our relationship."

And maybe, Gemma hoped, she could change her mother's mind on Senator Remus—maybe even find a way to get her able to return to Fairhaven. Just because Gemma didn't want to go back there didn't mean she wanted her mother banned forever. She knew her father would've been grateful to have her back.

Her mother nodded. "I'd like that. Why don't we meet tomorrow? I'm off work. And I live just down the block. Here— I'll write down the address for you. I want to hear everything about your new life, including your boyfriend. I never thought you would ever date. You were always so invested in your books."

Her mother scribbled her address down on a napkin, handing it to Gemma as she nodded. "Yeah, me either. I guess we've both changed. Well, I'll let you get back to work. I've got some stuff to do today. And Mom, despite everything … it's good to see you again. Can I hug you?"

Her mother leaned in, hugging her tight with a smile. "Of course you can. In a way … I'm relieved you're on the surface. You were too good for Fairhaven, anyway. I'm happy you've made a new life here."

"Me too, Mom. Me too."

"Here's to new beginnings," her mother said, pulling back. "And your father ... how is he doing? Does he still hate me?"

"Hate you? No. Pity you? Definitely. I think you broke his heart," Gemma replied. "But ... I haven't spoken with him in some time. He said some hurtful things while I was gone."

"Really? That isn't like him." Her mother sighed. "I guess we've all changed lately, hmm?"

Truer words had never been spoken.

Before Gemma could say anything else, the chef opened the door, peering into the backroom. Gemma recognized him as one of the other sympathizers. He, along with her mother and a handful of other Senator Remus supporters, had fled to the surface.

"Hey, Kathy—we need you out here," he said. "More customers arrived, and they want their orders ASAP."

Her mother nodded. "I'm coming, Archer. See you tomorrow, dear."

Gemma said goodbye, then followed her mother and the chef out of the backroom. He wasn't lying—the diner was busy, and her mother had her hands full. As her mother took more orders, Gemma slipped out of the diner, looking back at the building.

If she really wanted to know if her mother was up to something or not, there was only one way to find out. She'd have to follow her. It was clear her mother wasn't going to be honest—she never was. Not since Senator Remus had polluted her mind.

Gone were the days when she could trust her.

So, Gemma hid in the bushes, waiting until sundown. Another waitress arrived to begin her shift and her mother left the diner with her keys and purse in hand. As she began walking home, she didn't know Gemma was following her. She stayed a few blocks back so she wouldn't get caught.

Her mother turned left, heading down a side street into a

neighborhood of townhomes. Children played outside as her mother walked toward a small townhome at the back of the neighborhood. She unlocked the front door, then entered. Gemma crept over, sticking to the bushes as she peered through the window.

There was a group of other people in the living room—and they had dozens of barrels in there, leaking some kind of black fluid onto the floor. Her mother set her purse down and approached the group. They were all sympathizers who had fled Fairhaven and had banded together to survive up on the surface.

"Is it almost ready?" her mother asked the group.

One man nodded, patting the side of the barrel. "Yes, it is. We should be good to go soon."

"Perfect. And I thought I should tell you all the good news. My daughter, Gemma, is on the surface too. She's started a new life here and seems happy. So, she'll be all right—she won't be affected at all. Which I'm grateful for. It'll save me a lot of worry."

Affected by what? Just what were all those barrels for?

Before she could hear anything else, Gemma moved and stepped on a branch, making it crackle loudly underneath her feet. Her mother and the rest of the sympathizers looked around for the source of the sound. Not wanting to get caught, Gemma took off, heading back to the main road.

She quickly hailed a taxi, then gave the driver her address, narrowly avoiding a confrontation with her mother. Gemma knew she wouldn't have been happy to see her spying on them. She thought about the barrels the whole way home, wondering what was going on—and what she was going to do about it.

Especially with Senator Remus' one-year anniversary coming up—and the threat he had made.

When she arrived at her apartment building, she paid the driver with her small paycheck and headed upstairs. After she and Fairy Godmother Blanche were robbed, she really needed to watch her spending. She paced for a while, then realized it was almost time to head to the bar for the trivia event. A knock on the door scared her, making her pause.

Was it her mother? Had she found out that Gemma had been there, spying on whatever plan they were putting into motion?

When Gemma opened the door, it was only her father. He held up a basket of magical fruit and stood on the doorstep with a smile. "Hello, Gemma. Just wanted to visit you and make sure you're okay."

Gemma swallowed hard. It was difficult looking at her father after hearing him say all those awful things about her. She took the basket, nodding. "Um, thanks, Papa. That's nice of you."

He frowned, studying her face. "Is everything all right, Gemma? You look upset. Are things still going okay with your boyfriend and the bookstore?"

"Things are great on the surface, Papa. For me, at least. I just … I really want to be alone. Is that okay?"

Her father frowned, stepping back. "Oh, uh … of course, kiddo. Whatever you need. I'll come back at a better time, okay? Have a good evening."

He turned, heading down the hallway and stepping into the elevator. Gemma felt bad for sending him away—and equally bad for not telling him about her mother and whatever plan she had concocted—but what had he expected? For her to embrace him after he had insulted her behind her back? It felt like a betrayal.

Just another parent who had let her down.

She wanted to run after her father, to tell him what she had overheard. But then tears formed in her eyes and she stopped. To have two loving parents, then end up here? Gemma couldn't believe it.

Sighing, Gemma placed the basket of fruit on her counter and left the apartment. She locked the door, then rode the elevator into the lobby and didn't see her father anywhere. He must've left for Fairhaven already. She walked by herself for a while as the sky darkened, not wanting to waste money on another cab, then smiled when she saw Ian's bar.

If there was one thing Ian was good at, it was putting a smile on Gemma's face when she felt like the whole world was collapsing around her. As things progressed with him, she wondered—should she tell him about Fairhaven? Would he be upset she had kept such a huge secret from him?

Noah had come to accept Princess Esme's heritage. But they were two different men, and right now, Gemma was afraid of letting the one good thing in her life down. So she kept her mouth shut, entering the bar and swearing to tell Ian another time.

As she walked deeper inside, the bar was packed. Dozens of patrons were there to compete in the trivia contest. A small trophy with the words TRIVIA WINNER sat on a table, the prize for the evening. The tables were full, coated in beer stains and bar food. Gemma pushed through the crowd and headed to the bar where Ian served a man another beer.

When he saw Gemma, he looked up, grinning. "Ah, there she is—my fairytale princess. You're just in time for the trivia night."

He leaned over the bar, kissing her on the lips. Gemma smiled. "Perfect, I'm ready. Not sure how much I'll get right, but I'll try my best."

"Sounds good. Hey, are you okay?" Ian stepped back,

analyzing Gemma's face. "You just look ... I don't know. A bit upset."

He had been the second person to tell her that tonight. How could she possibly explain that she had found her mother and was worried she was up to no good? And that her father's betrayal stung like acid on her skin?

Gemma just faked a smile. "Yeah, I'm fine—It's just been a long day. Could I order a soda? A ginger ale?"

Ian nodded, reaching behind the bar. "For my favorite lady? Of course, coming right up."

She was relieved when he didn't ask about her low mood again. She sipped her soda at the bar, watching as Ian walked over to the microphone on the small stage. An employee Gemma assumed was Barney came out of the backroom and filled people's mugs as Ian began the trivia contest.

"Welcome, everyone, to the weekly trivia contest! Thank you for being here," Ian began, glancing around. "I'd like to introduce you all to my lovely girlfriend, Gemma. This is her first trivia night, so please give her a round of applause!"

As the patrons clapped for her, Gemma blushed, giving them all a little wave. Ian beamed at her from the stage.

"Thank you. I'm so glad she's here tonight," Ian said, then turned back to the audience. "All right, first trivia question. We'll start with something easy and work our way up. Who invented the telephone?"

Gemma had no idea, but judging by all the hands that went up, people seemed to know the answer. The name Alexander Graham Bell was shouted by a bunch of patrons.

"Correct! Alexander Graham Bell did indeed develop the telephone," Ian said. "And fun fact—he had the idea for it right here in our lovely province, in the city of Brantford. He would go on to make the telephone back in Boston."

The patrons cheered, holding up their mugs for Barney to

refill. As Gemma sipped her soda, hoping she'd at least get one answer right tonight, the door to the bar swung open. A man entered and pushed through the crowd who Gemma only saw out of the corner of her eye.

And he had a snake tattoo on his arm—one she had seen up close before.

CHAPTER 28

Gemma walked over to Ian, waiting until he'd finished awarding points for the latest trivia question. "Um, Ian, can we talk for a moment?"

"Just a second, folks," he said into the mic. He angled his back to the room and blocked her from most of the patrons. "Of course. Everything all right?"

She shook her head. "No, everything's not all right. Don't look now, but the guy who robbed the bookstore and murdered someone—with that strange magic around him—he's right over there. And I've seen him in here before."

Ian turned around, glancing at the man in the hoodie. He sat at a table and looked through the bar's small menu. Then he turned back to Gemma. "Are you sure? That guy's a regular in here—his name's Bobby Blevins, I think. I've chatted with him a few times. Never thought he was dangerous, though."

Gemma nodded. "Ian, I would stake my life on it. That's the guy. I'd recognize him anywhere."

Especially after he pointed a gun at Gemma and nearly killed Fairy Godmother Blanche. She hoped she had made it back to Fairhaven safely.

"Shit, okay." Ian set the pitcher down. "What should we do? Call the police?"

"I have Detective Crawford's number. Go talk to Bobby; keep him here. I'll tell the detective to get to the bar as soon as possible."

Ian walked toward the table, faking a smile as he chatted with Bobby. He seemed like a regular customer, but even from afar, Gemma could see little particles of magic floating around him. They were like leaves off a shedding tree.

She walked toward the phone sitting on the bar, then dialed Detective Crawford's number. The phone rang and rang and eventually went to voicemail. Gemma scowled, hanging up. She only trusted the detective to handle this—especially when he knew the truth about Fairhaven.

But with no other choice, Gemma dialed 9-1-1. The operator answered a moment later. "9-1-1, what is your emergency?"

"Yes, hello. The man who's been using magic to steal and kill is here," Gemma whispered, eyeing him at the table. "At the Horizon Bar downtown. Hurry—I'm not sure how long he'll stay for."

"Dispatching police to your location, ma'am. Stay safe. Try not to provoke him. And please remain on the line ..."

As the 9-1-1 operator continued talking, Gemma was barely listening. This was her chance to talk to the robber-turned-killer alone—to ask him how he got his magic. She might never have a chance like this again once they arrested him.

If he even came quietly—or maybe he had an escape plan ready to go.

Gemma quietly hung up the phone, then pushed her way through the bar. Ian had been stopped by a patron at another table and couldn't get back to her. As she approached the man in the hoodie, his snake tattoo gleaming under the dim light of the bar, he heard her coming and looked up.

And when their eyes met, Gemma knew he recognized her as much as she recognized him.

He quickly stood, then flung his chair at Gemma. She screamed and ducked as the chair crashed into the wall. The patrons looked over, murmuring at the commotion as the man sprinted toward the back door.

He was escaping—again. And Gemma wasn't having it.

She went running after him, catching Ian's attention. He sprinted to keep up with her, getting slowed down by the crowd as she ran through the back door, ending up in the small alley behind the bar. She saw the man in the hoodie only a few feet away, but the alley was a dead-end. A tall brick wall blocked him from getting away.

He spun around, snarling as he pulled a gun out of his pocket. Magic pulsated around him even harder as he lifted the pistol toward Gemma. He stood over a storm drain, anger written across his face. "You again. Can't a guy get a drink in this city?"

"Not when he's a thief and murderer, no," Gemma shot back, keeping her distance. "What are you doing here?"

"The hell does it look like? I came for a beer. I love this bar—always have."

"How did you even get magic? Where did it come from?"

His eyes twinkled. "Ah. You know about magic. Are you one of them?"

"Yes, I am. I come from Fairhaven. And I demand to know how you got this power."

The door opened behind her, then Ian stepped out into the street. He glanced between the man in the hoodie and Gemma before stepping in front of her to protect her from the pistol.

"Whoa, whoa, whoa. What's going on here?" Ian demanded. "Put down the gun, Bobby. Whatever's going on, let's talk it through."

"It's him, Ian," Gemma said. "He did all those evil things."

Bobby laughed. "Evil? Please. I'm an opportunist—I saw the power in front of me and I took it. Simple as that."

"What is he talking about?" Ian asked, turning to Gemma.

Gemma's mouth opened and then closed. She'd have to explain everything to Ian—about Fairhaven, about magic—in order for it to make sense. But then Bobby started laughing.

"Your little boyfriend doesn't know, does he? That you're not from this world?" Bobby asked, the gun still high in his hand. "Yeah, it was a shock to me, too. I was homeless and living in that abandoned warehouse the day that weird fairy godmother lady took control. I was down on my luck ... until that day."

Ian said nothing, his face scrunched in confusion. Gemma mentally promised she'd tell him everything later. Right now, stopping Bobby was more important.

"You were?" Gemma asked. "How did you escape?"

"I hid in the basement. I overheard the whole thing— learned the truth about Fairhaven right then and there. What-ever concoctions that fairy godmother had whipped up must've gotten into my bloodstream. I found myself with some strange magical powers after that. I think it's what saved me from the mind wipe you freaks used." Bobby reached into his pocket, pulling out a few vials. "I also took some potions for the road, whatever she left behind."

Gemma couldn't believe it. No one could cast magic except for the fairy godmothers. This human was an anomaly—a fluke. And a very dangerous one.

"Of course you did," Gemma muttered. "Why do this? Why use magic to steal and kill?"

"And why not? I think your senator had it right—the strong should rule the Earth. His capture was good for me," Bobby said. "Without him gone, I wouldn't have been able to put this magic to use. It gave me the edge I needed. My parents abused me, so the government took me away. Sent me to group homes where I was bullied. This world has never treated me kindly. So why should I be kind to it? The magic meant I could do whatever I wanted—and when I started experimenting with it, I didn't want to stop. The robberies were just the start until I worked up to what I really wanted. Murder. It was almost too easy. The magic gave me the courage I needed."

Bobby sounded so sure of himself, so dedicated to his plan. Gemma didn't think any amount of begging could change his mind.

"I finally have a chance to be powerful—to abuse people instead of getting abused for once—and I'm going to take it." Bobby cocked the gun, still aimed at Ian. "A shame I'll have to kill you, though. After all, thanks to your people, I have the power that I do. So, in a way, you made this possible. Thanks for that. And godspeed, lady."

With a flick of his wrist and some magical dust, Bobby flung Ian out of the way. He fell to the ground with a groan. As Bobby aimed his gun at Gemma, Ian flung himself in front of her.

Gemma screamed as Bobby prepared to shoot, but then the storm drain opened beneath him with a squeak. He stepped out of the way just in time but tripped and fell onto the ground, the gun flying out of his hands. Gemma ran over and grabbed the pistol off the ground before he could hurt anyone else with it. His magic, on the other hand, would not be so easy to contain.

Gemma heard a fight on the ladder that led up to the surface. Cal had opened the grate and popped his head up, but Bobby had attacked him, then started to beat him on the ground.

Panic tightened her chest, and her vision started to tunnel. *No!* She forced herself forward, using the butt of the gun as a weapon, she slammed it into the back of Bobby's skull. Then he fell to the ground, unconscious. Cal rose to his feet, clutching his swollen face before he kicked Bobby in the side to make sure he was still alive. The man didn't stir but he was still breathing.

She exhaled and stared down at Bobby's still form. She'd done it. Gemma had shown her anxiety who was boss.

"What a warm welcome," Cal muttered, turning to Gemma. Then his eyes widened. "Gemma, you're here! I'm so glad you decided to stay on the surface after all."

Ian cleared his throat. "Sorry to interrupt, but could someone explain what's going on here?"

Gemma turned around, nodding. "I think I should. But before I start ... Ian, you were prepared to take a bullet for me. Thank you. You would've saved my life."

"That's what you do for someone you love," Ian said, then he crossed his arms. "But what's going on? How did this man come out from the storm drain? What's all this about Fairhaven and magic?"

When police sirens wailed in the distance, Gemma turned back to Cal. "Hey, can you make sure the cops arrest this man? He's the one who was using our magic to steal and kill up here."

Cal nodded. "Sure can. I'm glad I took that sleep potion with me for protection. It'll wear off in a few hours."

"Good. Tell the cops they'll want to be careful with Bobby— that he has magic in his bloodstream. Restrain his hands so he can't use magic and be extra careful. But Cal, what are you doing here?"

"Just wanted to see Toronto, really. And make sure you're okay. Looks like I came up at the right time."

"I'll say. Very few people are allowed onto the surface, you know. The king made that clear."

Cal paused. "Yeah, I know we're not supposed to. But after you and Princess Esme came up here, I wanted to see what all the fuss was about. And without me, you never would've stopped that human."

"True. Just be careful up here, Cal." Gemma turned back to Ian who was still staring down at Bobby in disbelief. "Come on, follow me. We'll find some place to talk."

Ian nodded, following Gemma back through the bar. They welcomed the police when they arrived a minute later and led them outside. They arrested the unconscious Bobby, listening to Cal as he explained the story. The patrons left, too scared to stay as Gemma sat Ian down at an empty table.

"I ... haven't been honest with you about my background. I was worried what you'd say—and I was supposed to keep my people's existence a secret. You saw what happened when humans found out about our magic. They exploit it, which was always King Tedros' fear," Gemma said, gesturing at Bobby as the police officers carried him out of the back alley. The bar window had a clear view of it all. "But the time has come for me to tell you everything. I think you can handle it. Are you ready?"

Ian's adam's apple bobbed. "I think so. What's going on?"

Gemma started at the beginning, telling Ian the history of Fairhaven. How they had existed for centuries beneath Toronto and had their own magic and potions—even fairy godmothers. Ian couldn't believe he had met one when Blanche had come to visit, how Senator Remus had once tried to enslave humans, and that her own mother was a terrorist sympathizer. Ian's face went pale, looking like he was struggling to digest it all.

"And this is why I didn't want you to meet my family," Gemma said. "I overheard my dad saying some unkind things when I went back to Fairhaven. But I was also worried they would blow my cover—accidentally reveal Fairhaven. I've come close to it many times myself."

Ian shook his head, his eyes wide. "I just ... I can't believe it. But thinking back, it's starting to make sense. Your ignorance of this world, never having pancakes or spaghetti, not wanting to tell me where you were from. God, why didn't I see it?"

"It's not your fault, Ian. No one would believe this. It's pretty insane to think there's a magical kingdom beneath your city. It goes against everything you know as a human, so take your time."

"No, it's not that." Ian rose to his feet. "You just ... you lied to me. About everything. Was anything you told me true?"

"Of course, it was! About my parents, my love of romantasy books, my job as a librarian. I just left out the part about Fairhaven and its magic." Gemma rose to her feet, coming face-to-face with Ian. "I hope you can understand that I was scared to tell you—that Fairhaven is supposed to be kept a secret. That its magical power is too dangerous if it falls into the wrong hands, especially now that it's compatible on the surface. But I felt bad about it the whole time, I swear. Especially as we grew closer."

"Oh, that makes me feel so much better," Ian muttered sarcastically. "Gemma—If that even is your real name—I told you everything about me. I opened up in ways I never opened up to anyone before. And now I find out you're not even from this world? Are you kidding?"

"Ian—"

"Look, I understand why your world has to be kept a secret. But you should've told me anyway. I could've handled it—I would've kept your secret. To find out like this, right after I almost took a bullet for you ..." Ian shook his head. "Well, this hurts worse than any bullet would have. It feels like a betrayal."

Betrayal. Gemma hated that word. It was reserved for people like Senator Remus and her mother, not someone like her who was only trying to keep her kingdom—and the surface world—safe.

"Ian, please," Gemma said, on the verge of tears. "I didn't

mean to hurt you. I was just following the King's orders. And I planned to tell you one day, it's just—"

"When? At our wedding? My deathbed?" Ian shook his head. "Trust me, if you found out I was from some other world, you'd be hurt, too. There's just so much I don't know about you. And I'm not sure I can look the other way."

Gemma's stomach dropped. "Then … what does that mean? For us?"

"It means … I want to be alone. You should go." Ian turned away. "Please."

Gemma couldn't believe it. Was this really the end of her relationship with Ian? After everything they had been through? She knew the truth would be a shock, but she assumed he would accept her reasoning and get over it.

She thought wrong.

"I've been lied to by a lot of people, Gemma. My parents, my ex," Ian said. "I've been through a lot of abuse. But never in a million years did I think you would ever lie to me. And that's why it hurts so bad."

Gemma racked her brain for something to say, but the words wouldn't come. What *could* she say? It seemed like it was too late.

Gemma grabbed her things and left the bar. Ian locked the door behind her as soon as she had stepped out into the street. She sat on the curb, putting her head in her hands as the tears came.

She thought she had met her soulmate—even if he had been from another world. And now, it seemed like she had lost him forever.

Cal came around the corner, wincing when he saw her crying. "Hey, Gemma, the police just took that human away. They're taking statements as we speak. You okay?"

She looked up, sniffling. "No … I don't think I am. I think my boyfriend just broke up with me. Because I lied to him about Fairhaven."

"What, really? Come on; you had no choice." Cal shook his head, sitting next to Gemma and holding her hand. "I'm so sorry. Any guy who would leave you, especially over something so stupid, is an idiot."

She forced a smile. "Thanks, Cal. I'm glad I'm not going through this alone. But I really am surprised you'd come to the surface. Few people from Fairhaven do. You never have before, have you?"

He shook his head. "Never, though I read some things before coming here. And to be honest … I really missed you."

"Yeah, I missed you too. And Fairhaven. Then I met Ian and … I fell in love. I just can't believe it's over."

Cal patted her shoulder. "When one door closes, a window opens. Humans say that, I think. Or so I've heard."

As Gemma dried her eyes, nodding, she spotted another storm drain opening down the street. A few guards slipped out, then Gemma noticed Senator Remus, his wife, his daughter, and Duke Cullen following. They brushed off their clothes as they stood on the dark street and glanced around.

Gemma's eyes widened as she stood. "Oh my gosh … Senator Remus is free. He should still be in jail! Come on, we need to get back to Fairhaven and warn Princess Esme."

But Cal grabbed her hand, holding her in place. "You don't want to go back to Fairhaven, Gemma. Not now, not ever. Not if you want to live. There's a reason I told you to stay away. Why I tried so hard to convince you to leave your old life behind."

"What are you talking about?"

Cal said nothing, continuing to stare at Senator Remus and his allies. Gemma had no idea how he escaped, but he must've had inside help—yet more of her people that he had brainwashed. She noticed magical elixirs poking out of their pockets, making Gemma fear they'd destroy the surface world with them.

A van pulled down the street, then came to a halt. Her mother stepped out, then the other sympathizers from Fairhaven Gemma had seen in the townhouse followed her. They grabbed the barrels from the back of the van and headed toward the different storm drains down the street. They began unscrewing the caps, opening the grates in the street for all to see.

"What are they doing?" Gemma asked, staring over in disbelief. "Mom! What's going on? Why are you here?"

Her mother glanced over her shoulder, noticing Gemma. Senator Remus and the others did, too. "I'm sorry, Gemma—but this is the way it should be. Senator Remus was right."

The Senator grinned behind her, one that was evil and triumphant. And then Gemma's mother and the other sympathizers dropped the barrels of oil down the storm drain and a massive explosion went off under her feet.

CHAPTER 29

The loud boom hurt Gemma's ears, making her teeth rattle. Car alarms on the street went off as dogs barked in the distance. Some of the streets cracked, the pavement rupturing beneath her feet as the earth-shattering explosions finally stopped. She flung herself toward the nearest storm drain to investigate when Cal grabbed her arm and held her back.

"Don't!" he cried. "Fairhaven's gone, all of it. Our explosions made sure nothing survived."

Gemma pulled herself out of his grasp with a cry. Her father, her home, her beloved library. Obliterated within seconds by the explosive barrels that her own mother had set off. Gemma had only one question on her mind as she fell to her knees, the ground still swaying beneath her.

"Why?" she wailed.

"My motives were always clear," Senator Remus said, walking toward Gemma. "This world should be ours to rule—we've got this power for a reason. One of those pathetic humans thought the same, didn't he? I heard someone up here got their hands on magic and was using it to steal and kill."

Gemma nodded, tears pouring out of her eyes. "Because you made that possible. You forced magic to be compatible on Earth. This is all your fault!"

"I'll admit, that one is my fault. Whoever that human is, he must be found and stopped. No one but us should get to use magic—our birthright," Senator Remus said, bending down in front of her. "But don't look so sad, Gemma. You've got your mother back. And I hear you're enjoying your new life. This is for the best—you'll see."

"Go to hell," Gemma spat.

He laughed. "Oh, no—we're going to build heaven on this pathetic planet. We're going to rule over every human just as we should. All thanks to your friend, Cal. He crafted the potion that freed me and my family from our cells."

Gemma looked up at Cal. "How could you do this?"

"I'm sorry, Gemma. I got to talking with Senator Remus one day and realized he was right. I was delivering food to the prison cells. Remus invited me back, and after a while, I found myself really thinking about his words. About Fairhaven, about our existence, about all of it," Cal said softly. "He makes some good points. Why shouldn't we rule over Earth? The surface world is right here for the taking."

Gemma shook her head. "Remus is tricking you somehow. Don't you see you're falling for a conman?"

"No, Gemma. I'm not. But I didn't mean to hurt you. I even tricked you about your father—I used an illusion potion to make you think he hated you, so you'd never come back. I wanted you to be out of Fairhaven when the bombs went off. I needed you safe."

And there it was—finally, the truth. Her father had never said those awful words, something that was so out of character for him. But she had believed it, tricked by an old friend, and turned her father away.

And now, he was dead. She hadn't even gotten the chance to tell him how much she loved him.

"See? Happy ending for everyone," Senator Remus said, rising to his feet. "Except your father, but oh well. We're better off without him. And that awful royal family. I hope the poison you put into the king's food really hurt, Cal."

Cal nodded. "I made sure it did—and left no trace behind. He suffered right up until the explosion."

"And I helped steal these bombs from the local warehouse myself, then added some magical powder to it," Gemma's mother said. "Fairhaven is gone—there's no way it could've survived that. King Tedros and everyone else who opposed us will never stop us again. The human world will be ours."

"Just as it should be," Senator Remus said, bowing at Gemma's mother. "Thank you, Katherine. It's been a pleasure."

The Senator had lied—he *did* know Gemma's mother. And they were working together this whole time, along with Cal.

Gemma couldn't believe what she was hearing. Her own mother, not just a traitor but also a murderer. And her oldest friend—someone she thought she loved once. She couldn't just let this happen.

Gemma rose to her feet, her hands shaking. "If you think I'm going to let you do all this, you're wrong. Maybe it's too late for Fairhaven, but I won't let you rule over Earth!"

Senator Remus slapped Gemma across the face, making her fall to the ground. Her cheek stung from the assault. "Insolent girl! You have no say in this—the plan is already in motion. Cal, keep her in line. If she gets in the way of our progress, I'll kill her myself."

Cal nodded, reaching into his pocket. He pulled out a potion and flung it at Gemma. As the silver particles spread through the air, magical handcuffs tightened around her wrists, preventing her from using her arms.

"There, that'll hold her," Cal said, glancing down at Gemma. "Please, don't make this hard on yourself. Stay out of the way. I'm trying to keep you alive, Gem."

Now bound and helpless, Gemma didn't know what to do. She had no one to call for help now that Fairhaven was lost.

Humans on the street came out of their apartments and buildings, murmuring about the explosion. Everyone across the city must've heard it. Even Ian came outside, his gaze going to Gemma in handcuffs on the ground. His eyes widened as he ran toward her.

"Hey, let her go!" Ian cried. "Whatever's going on here, stop!"

Senator Remus laughed. "You're just a human—you know nothing, boy. Off with you."

Senator Remus waved his hand and muttered a spell under his breath, then Ian went flying backward into the wall of the bar. He hit his head with a groan and fell to the ground. Gemma looked over, miserable to see him hurt. It was all her fault.

"No, leave him alone!" Gemma cried. "Don't hurt him!"

"That must be the boyfriend I've heard about," her mother muttered. "He's handsome—if a little naïve to think he can stop us."

Ian groaned, reaching up to touch his head. He was bleeding and in no shape to stop anyone.

"He broke up with her, apparently. His loss," Cal said. "Leave him—he can't stop us. Let's move on with the plan."

"My thoughts exactly." Senator Remus gestured at the van on the street. "Off we go. City hall's awaiting."

City hall? What did they have planned there?

As they all clamored into the back of the van, Cal picked up Gemma, forcing her to come along. She tugged at her handcuffs, but they were too tight. As she was thrust into the back of the van, she noticed an old lady with white hair and wrinkled brown eyes tied up with tape over her mouth. Judging by the wand on her hip and wide gown of silver and gold, she looked like a fairy godmother.

"Wondering about our guest?" Remus asked. "This is Fairy Godmother Calinda. After breaking out, we kidnapped the first fairy godmother we found. We'll need someone to make more magical potions for us in the future. She protested at first, of course, but we showed her what happens to those who go against us. Calinda should just be grateful we're letting her live! Not everyone was so lucky."

The fairy godmother had bruises along her cheeks and jaw. Her eyes were wide in fear as they landed on Gemma. She said something, muffled by the tape around her mouth. Gemma felt so bad for everyone caught in Remus' web. As Cal plopped her next to him, her mother, and the other traitors, she focused on Ian on the street.

He had risen to his feet, staggering where he stood. She wanted nothing more than to help him. But then the van doors closed, and the vehicle took off, his face disappearing from view.

"He and all the other humans will be slaves soon enough. That's what our plan was in the first place before Princess Esme stopped us," Senator Remus said from the front seat. "I was wrong about one thing—I should've been the one to kill that meddling woman myself. A quick death was too good for her."

As the others nodded, Gemma scoffed, saying nothing. It was clear she couldn't convince them to stop. Senator Remus and his allies were too far gone to be saved—something Gemma had to accept.

Her mother turned to her, petting her hair. "I'm sorry you had to see all that, Gemma, but it's for the best. You'll believe it one day—trust me."

Cal nodded. "When all the humans have bowed to us."

"I'll never support you," Gemma said, moving out of her mother's grasp. "These humans are my friends. I've come to know them—to love them! Whether we're more powerful or not, we have no right to take this planet from them and turn them into slaves."

"Spoken like a true human lover. I see Princess Esme has rubbed off on you," Senator Remus said from the front seat. "No matter—the plan will fall into place whether you accept it or not. You *are* their superior, and you *will* support me. Or else."

Gemma said nothing, trying to figure out how she was going to escape. She was among the last survivors of Fairhaven —and the only one who didn't support this plan. What was she going to do?

"Now that we can speak candidly," her mother said, breaking the silence, "I need you to know something. Those nightmares you struggled with? Ones of me, begging you to find and save me? They went away when you came to the surface, didn't they?"

Gemma thought about it, then glared at her out of the corner of her eye. "Yeah, they did, actually. How did you know that?"

"I've been using magical potions to reach you in your dreams—to convince you to follow me to the surface. I wanted you out of there when our plan went into motion and Fairhaven blew up. And you listened." Her mother smiled, looking relieved. "We can finally be together again."

Gemma felt nauseous. Was it all manipulation, this whole time? She had no idea about any of it. Shaking her head, she hated how blind she had been.

"You're sick," Gemma finally said. "What about Papa? He's gone now. Don't you still love him?"

Her mother sighed. "I knew your father would never leave

—he was too stubborn. That fool loved Fairhaven far too much, and he was really angry with me for becoming a sympathizer. We both said some choice words and didn't part on good terms. But you? I knew I had a better shot of getting through to you, so I went after your dreams only. Yes, I still love him, but what's done is done. I couldn't abandon my child."

As Gemma tried to process everything—her home being gone and all her family and friends dead—the van came to a screeching halt a few minutes later outside Toronto's City Hall. More people were out on the street, including reporters with video cameras. A maintenance crew had arrived to check out the storm drains but Gemma knew it was too late.

Fairhaven was gone, blown to dust.

The side door to the van opened, then Senator Remus and his followers stepped out. Cal and Gemma's mother dragged her and the fairy godmother inside. The old woman struggled and screamed beneath the tape, but it was no use—she was trapped just like Gemma. When an employee at City Hall tried to stop them, Senator Remus would spray another elixir, sending them flying backward into a wall. The other employees screamed, rushing out of the building.

"Ah, good—the whole place to ourselves," Senator Remus said, approaching the mayor's office. "Someone set up these damn cameras. I want to broadcast my message to the whole city—and then eventually the planet."

Gemma's mother and Cal set her and Fairy Godmother Calinda down in the corner, then assembled live cameras for Senator Remus to give a speech. He chatted with his wife, daughter, and Duke Cullen before checking himself out in the mirror. When the cameras were rolling with red dots, signaling that they were live, Senator Remus forced a smile.

"Hello, people of Earth. For so long, you have been living in ignorance," he began. "A magical kingdom called Fairhaven has been beneath Toronto's storm drains, and now, it's time for us to rule over your petty city. Surrender and I'll allow you to live —as my slaves."

Gemma closed her eyes, praying this was all a bad dream. But it was very real when she opened them again.

"For my first act, I, Senator Remus, will take control of the entire planet. Anyone who tries to stop me will be killed. I have all the magical power at my disposal right here," Senator Remus said, holding up several elixirs. His followers had stolen even more from Fairhaven. "We even kidnapped a fairy godmother to make more for us. Now, you will submit to us, your overlords, and allow us to take your planet from you for our own pleasure ..."

As he droned on, Gemma looked around and spotted Princess Esme through the window. She gawked for a moment, wondering how the woman had lived. Was it some sort of trick? Or was she really alive?

"And a secret, dark, underground kingdom is no place for people as powerful as us," Remus continued. "We deserve to live out in the open, with magic for all to see. Then, we will raid your houses and enslave your children ..."

Whether they were alive or not, Gemma had to make a stand. The old Gemma would've sat there like a damsel in distress, helpless to what was going on. But this Gemma?

She was going to kick some ass.

Gemma lunged at Remus with her wrists still in handcuffs, tackling him to the floor. She began to bite at him, the only defense she had left, as he snarled and tried to push her off. With the crash of windows, several people stormed into the office. When Gemma looked over, it was Princess Esme, Noah, King Tedros, and their guards. They began to fight Senator Remus and his allies, using magic spells and potions on them.

Gemma figured she'd better move before she got caught in some awful potion meant for him.

As she rose to her feet and moved back, a massive battle broke out, taking Gemma's breath away. She gagged and coughed as potions clouded the room with pink and purple hues. They burned her eyes and throat, thrown by Princess Esme and her people as distractions. The fog was so thick that she couldn't see anything. When she felt a hand grab her and drag her out of the office into the hallway, she fought back.

"Let me go!" Gemma cried. "Get your hands off me!"

When the smoke cleared in the hallway, the battle continuing in the office, Gemma looked up and noticed it was Ian. Her eyes widened.

"Ian ... oh my gosh. You're here. And you're all right!" she cried. "I'm so glad to see you."

He pulled her to her feet, hugging her tight. "And I'm glad to see you. When I heard that guy say you were heading to city hall, I ran as fast as I could to get here. I had to protect you. Everything I said before ... I'm sorry. I was just angry. And scared you were like all the people in my past. But you're not—I see that now. All it took was a head injury to make me realize that."

He reached up, prodding a lump on his head that was still bleeding. Gemma wished she could reach out and touch him, but her hands were still magically cuffed together.

"No, you were right to get upset. I *did* lie to you. And I'm really sorry," Gemma said. "I promise to be more honest with you from now on."

"Thank you. But really, none of it matters now, Gemma. With all this going on, I'm just glad I found you. And I love you. So much."

Gemma smiled. "I love you too. Always."

They smiled at each other for a moment, then Ian reached

for her hands. "I'm no magic expert, but let me try to get these off you."

He turned her around, fiddling with the magical handcuffs. They still wouldn't come off after a minute of tugging. When Gemma saw Senator Remus coughing and walking through the smoke, trying to get away, she nudged Ian.

"He's here," she muttered. "Senator Remus. Get ready."

Senator Remus paused in the hallway, noticing the two. "Oh, there you are. I was wondering where you'd run off to after jumping on me like a barbarian."

"I had to try to stop you somehow. Taking over the surface world isn't as easy as you thought, was it?" Gemma taunted. "Just give it up, Remus. Let go of your plan for world domination. It's clear Princess Esme and her guards aren't going to stop fighting you. I'm glad they survived. And that King Tedros recovered."

"Yes, turns out they were already on the surface, investigating pockets of magical energy. That annoying fairy godmother of hers found a way to cure King Tedros just in time for the battle," Senator Remus muttered. "They've already apprehended my daughter, wife, and Duke Cullen. Again. Meddling bastards."

"And what about my mother? And Cal?"

"Arrested, too. Damn it all." Senator Remus reached into his pocket, then pulled out a magical dagger. The silver blade glittered with purple light. "But I'm still here—and with this new weapon I designed. And if I can't kill Princess Esme, I'll have to settle for you and your little human boy toy instead. Say bye-bye, Gemma. I never knew what Cal saw in you anyway to fight for your pathetic life. This is for interfering with my plans."

As Senator Remus came to Gemma and Ian, she knew what she had to do. It was her turn to sacrifice herself to save the one she loved.

She lunged in front of Ian, then lifted her wrists just as Senator Remus swung his dagger. It sliced through the handcuffs, cutting them clean off. They clanged to the floor with magical light as Gemma rubbed her wrists.

"Clever," Senator Remus spat. "But you still don't have a weapon. Are you really willing to die for this human?"

"I am," Gemma said. "Because that's love—it's beautiful and difficult and enchanting and worth dying for. And I'm sorry your heart is so cold and dead that you don't realize it's better to spend your life loving than fighting."

Senator Remus snarled, lifting his dagger again. Both Gemma and Ian reached for each other, trying to protect one another from the attack when Senator Remus gasped. He dropped his dagger, then a massive wound appeared in his chest.

Princess Esme came out of the smoky mayor's office, holding a magical staff in her hand that she had thrust into the Senator's chest. She removed it, causing him to fall to his death in a pool of blood. Finally, his reign of terror was over.

"Gemma, good to see you again," Princess Esme said. "I'm sorry I had to kill the former senator—that isn't our way in Fairhaven—but I had no choice. I had to save you. Now, are you all right?"

Gemma nodded. "We are now. Princess Esme, this is Ian, my boyfriend. Ian, this is Princess Esme, the daughter of Fairhaven's king."

"Uh, hello," Ian said awkwardly. "Never met a princess before. Nice to meet you."

"And it's nice to meet you—I've heard so many good things about you from Gemma. I'm just sorry our meeting had to be under these circumstances." Princess Esme lowered her staff. "Come, the office is safe. We've apprehended our enemies—including your mother. Noah and my father are extinguishing the magic from the room. Unfortunately, the fairy godmother they kidnapped didn't survive the battle. She was caught in a potion that caused her to disintegrate."

"Goodness. How awful."

"Very." Princess Esme looked down. "Perhaps Remus got what he deserved, then. Now, if you'll follow me."

Gemma nodded, stepping inside the mayor's office with Princess Esme and Ian. Gemma was relieved to see all of Senator Remus' allies in magical handcuffs on the floor. Cal, her mother, and Senator Remus' families were fuming as Princess Esme's guards held them in place.

"Well, I'm glad you stopped them. I just wish Fairhaven didn't have to blow up first," Gemma said sadly. "My father ... he's gone."

Guilt and sadness tugged at her heart. She had been so mean to him—sent him away and turned her back—and all because of Cal's lie. She sat on the ground, her gown splayed around her as tears slipped out of her eyes. The sorrow and emptiness were almost too much to handle. Ian fell to his knees and hugged her, though not even his comforting touch could erase the pain.

How would she ever sleep at night knowing her father had died? And on such bad terms?

Princess Esme sighed. "I know—I'm so very sorry. I can't believe my home is gone either. I'm just lucky my family is safe, but so many have lost their lives. And now, humans know about Fairhaven. I suppose it was only a matter of time until our presence became known."

"What are you going to do now?" Ian asked.

Princess Esme paused and tapped her chin. "Well, we'll need a new home since ours is gone. And we'll have to reveal ourselves to the humans properly and hope they'll accept us. I pray that will go well. First, we need to call the police and report these criminals. Father?"

King Tedros nodded, then they murmured about their plans in the corner. Gemma was just relieved to have Ian back as she turned to him. "God, I'm so glad you're okay."

"I'm glad you're okay too. But I'm so sorry about your dad and Fairhaven. To lose it all like that ... it's just devastating."

Gemma nodded, then leaned in and hugged Ian. She tried not to cry on his shoulder as she took in his scent. It felt safe and familiar, the only home she had now that Fairhaven was gone.

As she hugged him tighter, she glanced over his shoulder, looking through the window. She thought she saw a ghost before she realized it was her father and Fairy Godmother Blanche. Her eyes widened, then she ran to the window and climbed out. Ian followed in confusion.

"Papa! Blanche!" Gemma threw herself into their arms, hugging them tight. "You made it. You're alive! How?"

Fairy Godmother Blanche patted her shoulder. "I decided to stay on Earth and check out the sights once they let me out of the hospital. I healed up pretty quickly. I'm glad I did or I would've been dead like the others. It's a tragedy."

Her father nodded. "And I stayed to make sure you were okay. We didn't say goodbye on good terms."

"I know. I'm so sorry, Papa," Gemma said, pulling back. "Cal lied to me—he showed me an illusion of you saying cruel things about me. He wanted me to never go back to Fairhaven. To protect me when the bombs went off. Mother did, too. She even inspired my nightmares, using magic to manipulate me from afar."

"A devious plan, but it makes sense. And not to worry, kiddo —I'm not angry. Devastated we lost Fairhaven, though. And for the record, I would never say anything cruel about you. You're my daughter, and I love you."

Gemma smiled. "I love you too, Papa. And you, Blanche. I'm so glad you're all right."

"I am too," Ian said behind them softly. "So sorry about Fairhaven."

"Thanks, Ian. Papa, Blanche, this is Ian—the love of my life," Gemma introduced, gesturing at Ian. "I guess you got to meet them after all. I'm just sorry it was like this."

"I am too," Ian said, shaking their hands. "But nice to meet you."

"You must really love her if you're going to stay after all this drama," her father said. "I like you already, son."

As Ian smiled, the police arrived. They listened to Princess Esme and were extra careful with the prisoners. They took Senator Remus' body away, then her mother and Cal. Her mother was screaming and trying to get to Gemma, but she refused to speak with her.

Detective Crawford showed up, hugging Noah. He said he would find a way to get the people of Earth to accept them— but it would be a different world now. One that none of them would recognize.

"Also, I have bad news," Detective Crawford said. "That human with the magic, Bobby Blevins? He regained consciousness and escaped. Just another problem to add to the list."

Gemma sighed, grieving for Fairhaven and all the lives Senator Remus had taken. He might have been dead, but his evil was still felt, his influence spreading. And who knew how many other humans would experiment with magic in the days to come?

But Gemma clung to Ian, then he kissed her forehead through tears for Fairhaven. She had him—he was in her arms again. As painful as it was to lose her home, at least he was still there, her love, her safe harbor through all this chaos. And when she saw Barbara, Jacob, Carly, Abby, and other curious humans walking down the street to investigate, she was relieved they were all right. She just hoped they would accept her once she explained everything.

And they would get her through Fairhaven's destruction. They would move forward stronger—together. They had to for whatever came at them next.

ALSO BY DANA GRICKEN

The Maidens of Fairhaven

Modern Fairytale

Enchantingly Yours

Spellbound Heart

The Soulless War Trilogy

The Dark Queen

The Dark Evolution

The Dark Cage

The Dragonwitch Chronicles Trilogy

The Girl Who Walked Through Fire

The Girl with the Invincible Blood

The Girl and The Silver Mark

The Hearts Companion

Ten Years: A Poetry Collection

Reverie: A Poetry Collection

Short Stories and Novellas

Whispers in the Woods: A Short Story Collection

Little Things: A horror novella

Drifting Darkly: A sci-fi novella

ABOUT THE AUTHOR

 Dana Gricken is an author from Ottawa, Ontario, Canada. The Dragonwitch Chronicles was her first series. Since then, she's published THE DARK QUEEN, THE DARK EVOLUTION, and THE DARK CAGE—the full trilogy in the Soulless War series. You can find those books at online retailers in both e-book and paperback forms.

In January 2020, she signed with Jessica Reino of the Metamorphosis Literary Agency. Please stay tuned for announcements on new books! In the meantime, if you've read and enjoyed her work, please don't hesitate to reach out to Dana on Twitter and Instagram—both @DanaGricken.

In her spare time, she enjoys watching Star Trek with her cats, reading, and playing video games. She hopes her books bring joy to people and wants to write over a hundred novels in her lifetime.